Praise for
Santa Steps Out

"The only tw   ng
is sacred and   er
attain one-th⟨   's
least toenail ⟨......⟩. ⟨...⟩ ⟨...⟩ ⟨...⟩—despite its enticing/
cautionary subtitle—that this Santa story might be read to
children everywhere on Christmas Eve."
—Poppy Z. Brite

"There are scenes from this book that will haunt me forever.
I know I'll never innocently or absent-mindedly suck on
a candy cane again. Reading this book made me want to
bitch-slap Robert Devereaux. So icky, yet so magnificently
rendered."
—Elizabeth Engstrom

"The kind of fairy tale that could make Walt Disney burst
from his cryogenic ice cube and go on a mad killing spree."
—Ray Garton

"A delirious slice of Nabokovian porno whimsy. Wholesome,
savory, weird and blasphemous, all at the same time—just
like the best sex. I believe in Robert Devereaux."
—Tim Lucas

"In its violation of our sensibilities and our cherished
childhood icons, in its topping of its over-the-top scenarios,
Santa Steps Out manages to be at once fascinating, funny,
and enlightening. Devereaux's most outrageous achievement
is that as he destroys our childhood myths, he rebuilds them
in a twisted yet equally magical and compelling way."
—Jeanne Cavelos

"Exactly the kind of dangerous book that a small press should
publish: the kind that makes mainstream publishers sweat."
—Hank Wagner

"Robert Devereaux is a master of vivid scene-setting, especially gory scenes and sex scenes. There is a lot of sex in this book—mostly happy, lubricious sex that is sometimes downright amazing. Prepare for a strange and stimulating ride when you hop in the sleigh with Santa and witness all his adventures."
—Fiona Webster

"Never until now have so many sacred childhood deities been subjected to such vile reinvention, in what has to be one of the most perversely hilarious books ever written."
—Brian Hodge

"Santa Steps Out is breathtaking. It's almost life changing. A novel so refreshing and inspiring to read that it breaks down the walls of genres and sits comfortably outside of everything."
—Andy Fairclough

"A perfectly sincere, seriocomic exploration of myth and taboo, sexuality and relationships, and the evolution of the godhead. Yes, Virginia, there really is a Robert Devereaux."
—Edward Bryant

"By the time Mrs. Claus is exacting her revenge with the help of Santa's elves, and the Tooth Fairy and Easter Bunny are tearing each other apart in an act of sexual congress, any comfort we may find in these figures is way out the window."
—Thomas Deja

"Devereaux breaks every mold imaginable, and he does it with élan, and with an unabashed glee."
—Monica J. O'Rourke

So, grab a cup of hot cocoa, snuggle up in your warmest blankie, and settle back for a reading experience the likes of which you've never had. One warning should accompany this book, however: KEEP THIS and all other dangerous objects OUT OF THE REACH OF CHILDREN!"
—P. D. Cacek

Santa Claus Conquers the Homophobes

deadite
press

DEADITE PRESS
205 NE BRYANT
PORTLAND, OR 97211
www.DEADITEPRESS.com

AN ERASERHEAD PRESS COMPANY
www.ERASERHEADPRESS.com

ISBN: 978-1-62105-014-8

Copyright © 1998, 2000, 2011 by Robert Devereaux

Cover and Interior art copyright © 2011 Alan M. Clark
www.ALANMCLARK.com

Printed in the USA.

SANTA CLAUS
CONQUERS THE HOMOPHOBES

ROBERT DEVEREAUX

deadite
press

OTHER DEADITE PRESS BOOKS
BY ROBERT DEVEREAUX

Slaughterhouse High
Baby's First Book of Seriously Fucked-Up Shit
Walking Wounded
Santa Steps Out
Santa Claus Conquers the Homophobes

For Victoria of course.

PART 1
SAVING JAMIE STRATTON

1.

IMMORTALS OUT OF BALANCE

IT HAD BEEN the best Christmas ever.

Never had his deliveries gone with greater efficiency, in hovel and manse, by modest sprig or beneath towering Douglas fir. His reindeer, never flagging, sprang straight into the air, every takeoff smooth and belly-tickling, every landing soft and on point. And in each house, the living room air was infused with parental love—at times begrudgingly bestowed, grown-ups being what they were—for the children.

Headed home at last, Santa sat high in his sleigh and cracked his whip over the glistening backs of his reindeer. Form's sake only, those whipsmacks, for his team longed for home as much as he did, eager to be led to their stalls for a brisk rubdown, a well-deserved meal of aspen shoots, willow buds, and berries, and a long regenerative rest.

"Look lively there, Comet, Cupid," called Santa, casting a kind eye upon them. "Well lit, my lad, well lit," said he to his lead reindeer. Lucifer's tail flicked proudly, the branchwork of his antlers glowing lightning-white in all directions.

As they neared the North Pole, stepdaughter Wendy's sleigh emerged from a cloudbank on the right. Spirited Galatea of the milk-white fur and beacon-green nose pounded her hooves against the darkness, bringing Wendy even with Santa as they glided in swift tandem through the gathering dawn.

"Morning, sweetheart," said Santa, his loving words carrying effortlessly to her ears. "How did the visits go?"

Wendy hesitated.

Then her face brightened.

"They were wonderful," she said. "The kids woke, as always, a little disoriented and confused. But they quickly came around and hopped on board to join me in flight, asking question after question as Galatea drew us on. Each had at least one talent; several, scads of them. But all were delighted at what I showed them of their future triumphs. One little girl, Bethany Zander from North Spokane, clapped her hands and said, 'That's me all right, that's me all over.' She'll be a gifted physicist."

Santa's bold round laugh boomed out. "Bethany's pure gold. She's got extra stars beside her name on my niceness list."

Thus did Wendy unfold the highlights of her hundred visits to good little boys and girls, her words dancing over the crisp jingle of sleighbells.

Ahead, Santa spied the protective bubble that enclosed their community in the mildest of winters. "Thar she blows, darlin'. Home, sweet home. Magic time, off with you." Santa's gesture brought them out of the expandable time that allows millions of visits in a single night, a time used as well by the Tooth Fairy, the Easter Bunny, and the Sandman.

Fierce floods of snow flew scattershot against his team.

Galatea lowered her antlers into the storm, her nose's powerful gleam transforming the flurries into a mad scatter of emeralds.

When they pierced the protective bubble, the snow turned at once random and feathery. Wendy pointed ahead in wonder. "Look, Daddy. We're almost home!"

Their runners brushed the treetops, raising mist-clouds of snow dust behind them as they flew. A swirl of dark dots in the commons resolved into individual elves. Over the mica sheen of the skating pond Santa and Wendy passed, then over the elves' quarters, the periwinkle-blue stables, and the workshop's fire-engine red, swiftly eclipsed by the gingerbread house and the cottage where Santa and his family made their home.

Rachel and Anya waved excitedly from the porch.

Santa felt such love for them, Anya his mate since their mortal days in Myra, Rachel only newly come into their lives. Though he took much joy in his annual trip around the globe, to be parted so long from his beloved helpmates tempered that joy.

Santa yielded the lead to Wendy, coming in. One final sweep above his helpers, their shouts rising in fountains of elfin delight, and the runners swept down to kiss the snow and bring them to a smooth stop.

Swarming in, the elves lifted him and Wendy on a surge of hands. Thrice about they carried them, high above their heads, then wrestled them good-naturedly to the ground and at last brushed them off and delivered them to the fond embraces awaiting them on the porch. This, thought Santa, was surely heaven on earth.

Yet something nagged.

Something was out of place.

Try as he might, he could not fix upon what it might be. He reviewed his deliveries. Everything was in order there, no child overlooked, no gifts switched or omitted.

What was ever so slightly off?

Consternation bedeviled him.

Could Wendy have—?

But Santa suddenly found himself overwhelmed by visions of his darling children the world over, snug in their beds and being so perfectly behaved it sent wave after wave of giggles rippling through him. How blessed he was in his task of making them happy!

His momentary upset no more than the shadow of a memory, Santa surrendered to the sea of mirth that surrounded him.

The Tooth Fairy squatted near the twisted cedar at the northern tip of her island, pelted by raindrops the size of dimes. Water fell from her necklace of blood-flecked teeth, struck her belly, and trickled down her thighs.

Tonight, she had finished her visits early—the eating of teeth, the excreting of coins—and awaited now the return of her sons in their night-black Santa suits, their eyes brimming with lust, their throats disgorging tales of ruffian waifs chased down and gobbled up.

Taking in the gray horizon and the dull thud of waves, she raged against heaven's constraints. Try as she might, she could not again cross paths with the miscreant who called himself Santa Claus. Since their affair, broken off eight years before, such path crossings had been strictly forbidden. Nor, in punishment for her misbehavior, could she feel, once inside their bedrooms, the least menace toward the brats whose teeth she claimed. Done and de-coined, outside their bedroom doors, only then was her hatred given free rein. But vile thoughts went no further than the thresholds of those doors, leaving the gap-toothed rug rats untroubled in their sleep.

Bitter triumph that.

Zeus had disallowed wicked thoughts toward children on the day he blasted her womb with thunderbolts. A moment later her imps, from Gronk to Chuff, had blatted fat, bloody, and deformed from her charred sex. But the moment Zeus vanished from the sky, she labored to defy his injunction. It had taken years. She had started on the island and gradually pushed the geography outward. Seven years later, her hatred stretched to the outsides of house. Six months more and the boundary had advanced to the bedroom's exterior. Beyond that, her efforts had failed. It left her choked with fury.

Then there was the North Pole. Something was shifting up there. She could sense it. Stirring and perturbations in that inbred little community might give her ingress. If she could no longer have the once king of the satyrs sexually, then she would destroy him.

Pan had once been hers, seduced and ensnared when their paths crossed one Christmas Eve. With each secret tryst in home or hidden hut, he had regained the goatish desire of old and deceived the fir nymph Pitys, who had flesh-doughed into a withered kitchen wench of a wife. Then had come his denial of their lust, followed by his ardor for that Rachel mortal, a tantalizing taste disappearing down the Tooth Fairy's gullet. She had turned the woman into a giant coin and made her daughter suffer. Then the big blowhard in the sky, Zeus hidden behind white beard and robes, had pressed Pan back inside Santa, de-satyrized the elves, unsexed the Easter Bunny, and plagued *her* with thirteen stench-ridden brats.

She had always detested children. But atop the mountain of despised brats crawled the vicious brood Zeus had got upon her.

A dark blot appeared on the horizon, a faint buzz in her ears. Its pattern of flight belonged to her firstborn, the sleekest of a fat lot, the smartest of her witless bastards. As he took on form, three more blots stained the gray dropcloth of the heavens, then nine more.

Coming in, Gronk ripped off his blood-caked Santa suit and dropped to the beach. "Mother!" he exclaimed. So too Cagger and Clunch. So Quint and Bunner and Bay. So Prounce, Pum, Frash, Faddle, Zylo, and Zest. So likewise lackluster Chuff, her fattest, ugliest, and least engaged son, scorned by the others for his tepid embrace of evil. Each had brought her the leg bone of a child.

With their mommy they tumbled, suffering the pain she meted out and turning the sand red. When they had had their fill, they hunkered about her, dumb as posts.

"Boys," she said, "I'm hungry for tales of mayhem."

"Me first," said Pum, "me first."

Gronk socked Pum in the eye. "Firstborn first," he insisted. "I

14

bagged fifty urchins, Ma. I tackled the scurrying rats on the run and sucked terror from their skulls. In Bombay and Berlin, in Topeka and Tangiers, I grabbed them, tormenting and torturing and shoving them screaming down my gullet. The first was a big-boned beggar boy."

The Tooth Fairy savored the details, repelled by the teller but caught by the tale. Chuff sat on the sidelines as usual, waiting his turn as the last teller while his brothers roughhoused for position. Eyes were blacked, flesh flayed, arm bones snapped and mended. "Hurt him," she shouted as they tore into one another. "Hurt that scum bum." She didn't care who doled out or suffered injury. Violence trumped the niceties of identity.

At last the tales were told, including Chuff's meager three child killings, which drew jeers and beatings about the head from the others. "Splendid, boys. Pain and death are the just deserts of every child. Theirs from the womb are the seeds of nastiness. The so-called good ones are simply better at concealing the blackness of their hearts. We'll get to them, fear not.

"Does Mommy love you?"

"No!" they shouted.

"Do you love Mommy?"

"No!"

"Love is a fable," she said. "What force binds us?"

"Hatred!"

"Rightly do we fear and hate our differences. Sink your claws deep enough into them and you reach a common denominator of blood. Cling to mayhem. Adore the fist. Gullet and gore first, then sleep. Right, boys?"

Brutish concurrence befouled the air.

"Pan's got it good now. But we'll seek out cracks in his smarmy little community and shatter it. We'll goad his elves. We'll destroy Wendy's respect for him. Gone all harmony there. And gone all harmony on earth, what meager amount exists. Generosity of spirit? It shall scarce be remembered, let alone felt and acted upon. We'll continue humankind's well-advanced corruption. Do I want to avenge myself upon Pan, to goad his hidden nature into the open? Of course. But more than that, I would shatter the Sky God's complacency, undermining his faith in his own creation. Do these goals seem too ambitious? I tell you, they are within reach. The time is coming. I can feel it. The time when the earth turns, when we topple the big blowhard in the sky and take control. Gone all hope, gone charity, fragile myths of goodness and redemption exploded everywhere."

Dull though her boys were, at this their eyes glowed.

"So nurse your bile. Bicker and brawl. Stay in shape, my sons, stay attuned. This is thy nature, this the destiny of humankind."

At that, they rose up and retackled their mother. And mayhem most foul again stained the strand, as rain fell upon them in smacks and stabs from a gray-black bank of clouds.

One of Santa's helpers never frolicked on Christmas Day.

That one was Gregor, who sat slumped and glowering at his spotless desk. Engelbert and Josef were out there somewhere, compromising the dignity of their family. When they were gone from the stables, Gregor often sat here, his lantern casting its emerald glare across a clutter-free desktop and its foursquare, precisely positioned blotter. Sitting bolt upright in his office chair, he muttered and mulled.

"Something isn't right with us. We've changed, and I don't know why. It's connected with the arrival of Rachel and Wendy. That much I know." Gregor wrestled with eight years of memory loss, a loose tooth he was forever niggling at before turning to whatever currently vexed him. "Something very...untoward went on back then. *I* was okay. I kept my virtue. But aren't all the elves virtuous? Hah! We are not. *They* were not. God robbed us of our untoward memories. But I sense a nasty lurker, around a corner my mind cannot turn no matter how vigorously it tries. They were sinners, their cover of simpering innocence blown.

"Happy? Of course, we're happy. Servile, vapid, and bubble-headed happy. Why, if it weren't for good old Gregor, chaos would reign. I'm the linchpin. Old Saint Nick, he's just a big baby, fascinated by children and childhood. See how he looks at Wendy, a perfect age on the outside, but he's not so sure about her growing up in her mind. He'd rather she remain an ideal eternal little girl. Anya and Rachel? Blindworms who encourage their jolly old hubby's boyish nature. Well, if Santa won't lead, I will. Step into the vacuum of guidance, impose order, regiment the busy bees, marshal our forces to take back those stolen memories."

Gregor brooded.

An index finger moved toward his nose.

I will not, he thought.

16

But he did, a slave to habit.

Infuriating!

"We're *all* doing this. The fools think they're unobserved. But Gregor knows all. The nervous tic crept in about the time Rachel and Wendy showed up, after the untoward whatever-it-was. I watch them do it. Fingers that probe. Nose. Mouth. It's disgusting. But I do it too. Heaven help me, I'm doing it right now—Gregor, the moral compass for this wayward band of elves. No one has seen me sinning, of that I'm sure. I've admonished some of them. Stop doing that, I insist. Keep that finger away from your nose. For the love of God, pay attention to what you're about. Do they listen? Does it stick? It does not.

"Something more is needed to whip them into shape. But what?"

Gregor mulled in torment, rooting for a booger even as he berated himself.

Be strong, he thought.

Then the idea blossomed. Gregor thump-fisted his blotter. "I can do it. But wait, can I really? Or am I deceiving myself? This deserves careful cogitation."

His eyes narrowed. There in the harsh lantern light, he dug and indulged, both his tormented thoughts and his probing finger. From fresh-strewn stalls came the shifts and settlings of Santa's slumbering team. But Gregor, deeply ensconced in fierce brooding, noticed it hardly at all.

2.

THINGS EVER SO SLIGHTLY AWRY

THE NEXT MORNING Santa was in fine fettle. At each workbench he had placed a copy of the year's plans. They were ambitious, as always, but his helpers' ability to reach and exceed whatever goals he set had never come up short.

He spoke extempore at the lectern, his note cards before him in a neat untouched pile. "Welcome," he said, "welcome each one, you of skilled hands, gentle hearts, and great good humor. My multitudinous crew of cheerful companions, in this divine endeavor we are brothers all. There exists no greater joy than to be generous to children and so encourage generosity in them."

Santa had become adept at hiding fear and anger since the day the Father had suppressed his Pan side. Fear that the goat god would reemerge or that the Tooth Fairy would once more try his virtue. Anger at her past outrages against his loved ones. These emotions were at times great within him, but always under his control. Still, he played the jolly old elf now, and was jolly indeed, inspiring his helpers and getting off to a grand start the new year of toymaking.

"So rev up those engines," he concluded, "stoke the fires of your enthusiasm, and let us bring smiles to the faces of good little children everywhere next Christmas."

For months, Santa's life was bliss. Wendy helped keep his elves focused. His wives enriched his life, both in the bedroom and out of it. And he maintained a healthy balance between work and play. He especially cherished walks in the woods, by himself in the hours before dawn, and with Rachel, Wendy, Anya, or all three, at other times of the day. But his favorite pastime was reading to Wendy, snuggled against him on his lap or, more often, tucked in and listening enthralled.

The community, as always, dove joyously into the task of restocking their shelves, for it took precisely a year of diligent effort to prepare for the next Christmas delivery.

Still, undercurrents of unease flowed within him that winter, spring, and far into the summer. In all that time, Santa's feeling that something had gone awry never quite lifted. Lately it had returned in full force. Many were the nights he lay abed between Rachel and Anya, wide awake under moonlight, trying to seize by the arms the elusive problem and stare it full in the face.

One August night in his workshop office, with his helpers tucked snug in their beds and midnight long fled, Santa removed a Coke bottle from the squat red dispenser in the far corner of his office and sat down to focus on what had changed since Rachel and Wendy's arrival.

"Must take stock," he murmured.

To be sure, they had brought an abundance of grace and joy into his life. How splendid it had been to befriend and grow to love these mortals, how satisfying to overcome his Pan-inspired lust for the Tooth Fairy, to beat back her attack against them, and to see them resurrect, through miracle, from horrendous deaths unto immortality. How beyond the blessings one could wish, to be wedded by God Almighty himself to Rachel and Anya in the forest, as the elves marveled and sang and made merry.

Santa set these wonders aside. "If I'm to address the Problem That Resists Detection, I've got to focus on what must be accepted—here in this private sanctum—as my failings.

"First," he said, ticking the issues off on his fingers, "I've been drinking far too much Coke. It's become a mindless habit." He lifted the bottle to his lips, stared at it, and set it aside. One a day had become half a dozen. Sometimes he could not recall retrieving the bottle from the dispenser, so automatic had the habit grown. "I'll wean myself, go gradual into diminishment."

This simple resolve pleased him. "Second, I've been giving my helpers far less guidance than they're used to. Not that they're not completely competent without it. They simply need more engagement than I've afforded them lately. A wink, a nod. There's a childishness about me these days, a tendency to avoid the serious, even when it would be appropriate." Was that where the problem lay? He pondered in his heart, shook his head, and ticked off another finger.

"Third, Rachel and Anya." Santa smiled. Simply grand having two such loving helpmates. No problems there. "I've never been happier. And I know they're happy too, because they tell me so, often, in many ways." Was he tempted by the Tooth Fairy, once the fierce ash nymph Adrasteia, who had been willingly ravaged by Pan more frequently and with greater gusto than her sister nymphs? Not in the least. "She's monstrous." He wondered what he had ever seen in her. As far as he was concerned, their trysts were ancient history.

"Ah yes, fourth, Pan." He put a hand to his lips, dreading that having uttered the name might once more summon that side of him, might awaken that voice of savagery and disrespect for all civilized norms. "I fear him, a dark rumbling terror that never quite leaves me." Hmm, could that be it? He didn't think so, but it would reward revisiting. Though God had tucked his Pan self deep inside his psyche, Santa sensed the goat god lurking.

He shuddered and went on.

"Fifth, my own intolerance."

Ooh, warm indeed. He glanced at the thick book resting on its special podium in one corner of the office. Bound in black leather, it shifted and changed during his weekly survey of the globe, editing or deleting entries when naughtiness, adulthood, or death claimed a child. The niceness section of the book had grown noticeably slimmer, in number of pages yes, but also in commentary. "And the annotations on my naughty list have become more acerbic these past many years. Used to be simply a name and a phrase." Talks back to her mom. Cheats on tests. Thinks mean thoughts about his little sister. Torments the cat.

"Now I go on for paragraphs, berating them for falling away from the innocence of toddlerdom." Maybe that's why he had been overdoing the jolly old elf, to counterbalance his increased outrage at the sorry state of modern children. Still, that wasn't based on misperception. The world had indeed grown grimmer. Grown-ups and wicked kids hurtling tail-over-teakettle toward adulthood *deserved* his scorn. "Hmm," he said, stopping himself from getting worked up. "Perhaps Pan isn't so dead in me, after all."

Another issue to revisit.

He turned down his fifth finger and raised his other thumb.

"Sixth and last, there's Wendy." A high soft chime sounded in his brain. "My dear, darling girl. All seems to be well with her. But oh, that...hesitation as we flew in." In his mind's eye, he sat in his sleigh, looking over at her, asking about her visits.

Surely inconsequential in the grand scheme of things, that momentary pause. But he saw now, eight months after the fact, that it was anything *but* inconsequential. "There was a certain tonal shift when she mentioned—what was the boy's name?—Jamie Stratton."

He hunched forward in his chair. "That's it. I minimized the signs. Wendy hesitates to speak of uncomfortable things, not wanting to deflate my buoyancy. But if I can't—"

He choked up. If he couldn't get right with his own little girl, how could he hope to get right with all the world's children? That was the most pressing problem. The others would wait.

"Tomorrow, when I tuck the covers about her, I'll assure her I'm okay with whatever discomfort she throws at me. Like the caring dad I am. Not some silly jokester who holds off sorrows with a jest."

That was it.

He replayed the moments in the sleigh and kicked himself for not seeing it sooner. "But I see it now." And he would address it, give comfort to his child who looked nine but was seventeen inside. It was time to grow up, take the reins of parental responsibility firmly in hand, and offer his counsel or condolence for whatever was troubling her. For he saw now, replaying the months since Christmas, how many other signs there had been, looks, sighs, shrugs. How could he have missed them all?

"No need to berate or browbeat." He took a deep swig of Coke, the bittersweet bubbles gassy in his belly. "I recognize them now. Must lay my cards on the table and ask her to do the same. Yes, that's what I'll do."

Eight years had elapsed since Wendy's mom had passed horrendously through the guts of the Tooth Fairy into the likeness of a huge coin and, by God's grace, become Santa and Anya's immortal mate; eight years since Wendy herself had been blessed with immortality. She took delight in helping Anya cook and sew, in learning elfin crafts, in being read bedtime stories as her eyelids grew heavy and an invisible Sandman made his nightly visit to sprinkle sleepy dust into her eyes.

But she took special delight in choosing one hundred deserving boys and girls to visit on Christmas Eve. These she woke one by one, giving them world-revealing rides in her sleigh, projecting into their bedrooms highlights of their futures, and leaving them with a kiss on the forehead and memories which, though they faded into dream, helped keep their destinies focused ever after.

Earlier on the day Santa agonized in his study, Wendy took Fritz and Herbert aside and posed the question.

"Why are they so mean?" Fritz repeated between wee nibbles on a hollyberry croissant. "Maybe they convince themselves they know best; and so great are their convictions, that they force things, bad things that seem good to them, upon others. Ooh, this croissant is delicious. Take a bite. No a bigger bite! Truth to tell, I have no idea. Other than you and Rachel, I've never seen a mortal, up close in real life. And you two are as far from meanness as a smile is from a frown. What about you, Herbert? Any ideas?"

His companion looked blank, shrugged, and said nothing as usual, though his mouth moved in half-hearted guppy puckers and his wide eyes begged pardon for his ignorance.

"Herbert doesn't know either. Have you asked Santa? I'll bet he'd have an answer right off."

Wendy said she hadn't, but would definitely consider it. Then she thanked them. "Hey, Herbert," she said, "Don't look so glum. No one can know everything. And I think you make the bestest cameras in the whole wide world."

Herbert brightened at that, which cheered Wendy too.

Months before, she had posed the question to her mommies, tossing it off as casual as could be. "Don't you go fretting," Anya had said. "Mortals are just that way."

Which was no help at all.

Rachel had been a little better. "Some people," she said, "are drawn to be selfish or hurtful, to play power games that one-up themselves and one-down everybody else."

Wendy had asked *why* they were drawn that way and Rachel danced around the issue in a tone more suited to a nine-year-old.

Wendy thanked her and went her way.

On the very day they returned, as she brushed Galatea in the stables, she had asked Gregor. Harrumphing in the grand Gregor manner, he said, "By 'mean,' you're referring no doubt to the wars, the lies, the cheating, the posturing, the violence, the twisted warps of their minds down countless rat holes of rottenness, all that nonsense."

And when she said yes: "They're no damned good, that's why." He gave a sharp nod and a hmmph, as though he had solved the riddle of the Sphinx. "Your good little girls and boys? They're not all they're cracked up to be. Relax the whip hand and they stray. You've heard of gravity? As they bulk up, gravity drags them down into mischief. Babies are light as feathers, more angel than beast. Ah, but put on flesh, let hormones flow, and excess carnality moves them to crime and lies, backbiting and bad habits, just like certain elves I could name.

Tight rein must be kept on the lot of them!"

Gregor had amused but not enlightened.

Why *not* ask Santa Claus? When matters took on great urgency, one had to speak or explode. But her stepfather was such a wonderful grown-up little boy, beaming with mirth at good little children, but so disappointed with the bad ones that he never spoke of them. How could he possibly help with poor Jamie and the mean people in his life? How could she think to wound her father's spirit by bringing them up?

Wendy reached the gingerbread house where she often went to ponder weighty matters. It was quiet here, bright with gingham and bone china and flowered wallpaper and a gold-and-rosewood grandfather clock that gently knocked aside every other second.

She sat in the rocking chair by the picture window and gazed out at a peaceful blanket of snow upon the commons and fresh drifts on the roofs across the way. So peaceful up here, so needlessly stressful the world of mortals. It was the height of satisfaction to assist the elves when she was able, to track toys she had helped with into the homes of good little children, seeing their faces light up at their caregivers' generosity. Such was the true spirit of Christmas. Selfless giving. And Santa Claus, above all, epitomized that abundant spirit of generosity— toward her, his helpers, his wives, and all the world's youngsters.

He was a cornucopia of giving, an outpouring that never let up, not for one moment. How could she ask him for more? She grew aware of frown lines on her forehead. Her shoulders were tense. Her hands gripped the lacquered dragonheads at the ends of the rocker's arms as her pinkies slipped into their sharp-toothed mouths and dared them to bite down.

"I'll ask him, though," she said with conviction. He's *got* to help, even if he just listens and consoles and admits he's helpless to do anything. But maybe he isn't so helpless after all. Santa was always surprising her, even after eight years of growing in the generous soil of his nurturing. Perhaps there were surprises still, even ones that would surprise *him.*

Wendy pushed off with her feet and slid back into the big rocker's rollicking bucket. The snowscape suddenly climbed on board, cradled in the clumsy arms of a vast sea. "Hey, I can hope," she said. "And where there's hope, there's fire. That's what Santa says, and I intend to hold him to it!"

She giggled at that, then stopped and felt anew her frown lines, growing very solemn indeed and choking back tears at her memories of Jamie Stratton and what lay, not so very far ahead, in his future.

23

3.
CONFIDING IN SANTA CLAUS

THAT NIGHT, after reading Wendy a chapter of *Les Misérables,* Santa closed the book and set it on her nightstand. But instead of bending to kiss her cheek, he sat back and sighed and looked straight at her. "Sweetheart," he said, "Rachel and Anya and I have noticed that all is not right with you. Please don't deny it. Something's bothering you. Something big."

Relief appeared on her face. "Yes."

"I've minimized the signs," said Santa. "But I won't do that any longer. You're growing up inside, and your concerns, I'll wager, are growing up too."

Once he had begun, it felt good to be leveling, good to give up his absurd little-girl wish about her and let her be who she was. She seemed to blossom. Where he had seen only the innocence of the child, now he saw maturity informing the precious intelligence before him.

"The last boy I visited Christmas Eve?" she said, sitting up and tenting the blankets with her knees. "Jamie Stratton?" She threatened to choke up, but kept her emotions in check. Only the moistness of her eyes and a catch in her voice betrayed her. "I show the kids scenes from their futures, skipping over childhood cruelties, scrapes, shin barks, bee stings, all of that. And so I did with Jamie.

"But I looked deeper into his future, and what I left out was pretty disturbing. Since Christmas, I've gone back and looked again. I don't like what I see."

Santa guessed she had ventured into his teen years, or worse, his years as a grown-up. He wanted no part in these visions, but Wendy's well-being trumped his distaste. "Perhaps," he said, "you should show me."

"Yes," said Wendy, relieved. "I'd like that."

She nodded toward the far wall. Out sprang Jamie as he was, an eight-year-old on a banana bike, pumping through his neighborhood, the deafening scatter of dead leaves beneath his wheels. He was bright, wiry, and full of energy. It was clear why he had made Wendy's list. There followed short scenes that buttressed that view: Jamie playing a halting violin piece for his mother's birthday, astonishing his third-grade teacher with the wisdom of an answer, soothing a little girl with a scraped knee until her parents rushed to her aid.

"Okay, now watch."

Wendy gave a barely perceptible nod.

In the moments that followed, Wendy watched Santa lose his innocence. It was heart-wrenching. She berated herself, yet she went on, needing to share her terrible knowledge and to seek her stepfather's guidance.

First she showed him a schoolyard skirmish, more hurtful to Jamie emotionally than physically. "Sissy Jamie, Sissy Jamie," taunted the boys. A fifth grader, Freddy Maxon, held him down and pinched his ears.

"But I visited little Freddy's house," said Santa, the wind gone from his sails. "I visited all their houses."

"There were more such incidents," said Wendy. "Then this."

Dusk. An older taller Jamie, carrying a bag of groceries, walked past a vacant lot. "He's twelve." The lot wasn't so vacant after all. "These three kids hang out together. The one in front is Matt Beluzzo. Held back twice, a ninth grader here, sixteen."

Jamie looked up, startled. When he made to bolt, the two others grabbed him from behind and his bag spilled onto the sidewalk. Matt jabbed a finger at Jamie's face. "You're a queer boy," he said.

"I'm not," protested Jamie.

"Yeah, that's it, only a queer boy would brownnose the fuckin' teachers like you do. You got a queer boy's name. Not like me. Matt. A good, solid name, as solid as my fist. You like lessons. I hate 'em. But I got a lesson for you. Right here and now."

Then the beating began.

Wendy shut it off. "Daddy? Are you all right?"

"You see why I prefer the company of young children." He pulled out a handkerchief, blew his nose, and dried his eyes. "But I can take it. Show me more."

Wendy told him that Jamie's face was bloodied and bruised and he walked with difficulty for days, but no bones were broken. Beluzzo had threatened worse if he told, and Jamie hadn't told. Wendy brought up Jamie's father, red-faced, standing before his son, shouting at him, "You gotta stand up to bullies. They're cowards. They deserve reform school is what they deserve. You tell me their names and I'll sic the cops on them."

"Walter Stratton, all grown up," said Santa with scorn.

"He means well," said Wendy, "but he's...he's distant from Jamie. A sports fanatic. Closer to his other son."

"The older brother. Kurt's a great kid."

Wendy agreed. Then she said, "There are three critical factors that lead to...to what I'll show you at the end. The beating was one of them. The second was the cumulative effect of hearing this next man Sunday after Sunday."

Before them thundered a tall, thin, white-haired preacher, mute now, behind a podium. "Ty Taylor. Over there, seventh pew on the right, are the Strattons, Kurt on the aisle, then Dad, Mom, and Jamie."

"Ty was a nice little boy, very neat, happy, and obedient. I put a rocking horse, a cowboy hat, and a cap pistol under the tree when he was seven. What's he all worked up about?"

"This." Wendy turned up the gain.

"I see before me a vast multitude of families," said Ty Taylor, "the proud bulwark of the church and of what's left of virtue in this sad secular society. But the family is crumbling. And upon the sand of weakened families, the house known as the United States of America shall crumble and fall. Unless, my friends, unless righteous followers of Christ hold back the floodwaters and shore up the levees of this nation's moral might, unless we renovate and rebuild in God's image.

"Gays and lesbians, they call themselves. But call them what they are. Sodomites, sinners, sheep strayed into the wolfish wilds of homosexual misbehavior. They have the temerity to tout their ungodly ways, strutting and preening like peacocks, and setting up so-called churches of their own. But creatures of Satan can only worship Satan, no matter how hard they pretend otherwise. They prattle in vain, these deviants from the straight and narrow. Come Judgment Day, they shall be harshly judged. In the days of glory, they will not be with us in heaven. No, for they shall burn eternally in the bowels of hell, the all-consuming fires of their infinite suffering declaiming the glory of their creator and redeemer, whose words they heeded not, though they were given every chance to repent and reform."

Wendy muted the preacher. "There's lots more."

26

"They suffer this man to preach?" There was an ache in Santa's voice that touched Wendy's heart.

"They can't get enough of him," she said. "His is the best-attended evangelical church in their community. But look." Wendy gestured, and she and Santa and the bed glided down the center aisle. Jamie's family came closer and then his face. It spoke volumes.

"I'm guessing," said Santa softly, "the Strattons are faithful churchgoers."

"Every Sunday without fail. Tearing down homosexuals is Ty's favorite tactic. It fills the coffers twice as fast as his railings against abortion. Daddy, you're so pale. I have to show you two more scenes, but I can do it another time."

"No, go on. You see why I have no truck with grown-ups. How far they fall from childhood. It's an eternal mystery to me, why they fail to remain wrapped in divinity, turning away from creativity and kindness. Go on, Wendy. Show me the rest."

"All right." The church vanished. "Four years pass and Jamie's in the eleventh grade." The den where Wendy had watched him practice the violin appeared, an easy chair, a couch, a TV set, and a paint-by-number harbor scene on a wood-paneled wall. Jamie, a handsome sixteen, sat in shame on the couch, his hands clasped between his knees. His parents stood over him.

"You are *not* gay," his mother said, rigid and pasty-faced.

"Come to your senses, son," said his father. "Don't upset your mother with such talk."

"It's disgusting," she said. "*You're* disgusting. Who recruited you? Some older boy? I'll claw his eyes out. You are *not* this way. You're my son, you hear me? God will hurl you into hell and you'll burn forever. Do you want that? Answer me!"

"No, Mom."

"Walter, talk some sense into your son."

Wendy let the scene play on in pantomime.

Santa's voice was husky and soft. "Kathy's her name. Her last name was MacLaren when I visited her house, Christmas Eves long ago. She loved floppy dolls. She hugged her stuffed cat Jeffrey until he was lumpy and faded. Back then, Kathy wore pigtails and beamed with joy."

"In her own way, she loves her sons. But she loves God more."

Santa laughed. "Some God."

27

Wendy replaced the den scene with an overpass across a highway. The traffic below was busy and fast, the sound muted.

"They took him out of school and sent him to an intensive one-week cure-all in the Adirondacks. A stern-faced counselor berated him, threatened hellfire, and mocked his tears and protests." Jamie appeared along the sidewalk. When he reached the center of the overpass, he shrugged off his backpack, unzipped it, and removed two apples.

"The cure-all people starved him. Several times a night, they woke him with harsh lights and barked orders to get down and do fifty push-ups. They showed him photos of attractive boys and slapped him hard. They showed him prim-faced girls in their Sunday best and gave him ice cream. In the end he pretended conversion. They let him go."

Jamie stared intently along the interstate. He dropped an apple over the side, following its fall.

"What's he doing?" asked Santa.

"He's gauging when to drop the apple so it hits the roadway just in front of an oncoming big rig."

Jamie raised the second apple, that same intent stare. He held it over the parapet and let it go.

"You don't mean he's..."

Jamie hoisted himself to a sitting position facing traffic and watched the flow. Wendy floated herself and Santa over the parapet and down into traffic. They were peering into the cabin at a driver, whose body tensed as his eyes went wide. Then she wiped away the screech of brakes and the expletive coming from him and his muscular arms stiff on the steering wheel. "That's Ernie Strauss, barreling toward New Mexico with a cargo of washer-dryer combinations behind him. By some miracle, he didn't die. Nor did he cause a pile-up."

"I should have come to you sooner."

"I'm sorry, Daddy."

"No, it's okay. I—"

"I'm so sorry." Wendy could no longer keep from crying. Santa seemed broken, like her old neighbor Mrs. Fredericks' husband. She had done this. She had taken him from joviality to shock and despair.

He held her tight. "You mustn't blame yourself. Whatever is bothering you you've got to share with me or Anya or your mom. Always, always. That's all we want."

That freed something in her and she sobbed against Santa's chest until her throat hurt. "We've got to *do* something to rescue him. Can we, Daddy? Can we save his life?"

"Yes," said Santa, without hesitation. "We've got to. But I don't see how. We're up here. We deliver toys and wonder. What can we do? I don't yet know the answer, but we will do something. I'll discuss it with Anya and Rachel. We'll put our minds to it. We'll devise a plan."

Santa's resolve touched her. To him, every life was precious. In her heart of hearts, Wendy knew he could work wonders. She trusted him to find a way to alter Jamie Stratton's future. But she also steeled herself for disappointment. Though she and Santa touched the lives of children intimately in many ways, there seemed an unbridgeable gap between this world and the world of mortals.

Still, for a time, Wendy took comfort in the assured embrace of her father, and hoped for the best.

4.

PARENTAL DISCUSSIONS AND MULLINGS

RACHEL HAD NEVER SEEN SANTA so distraught, pacing before them in the bedroom. His red robe flapped impatiently against his ankles.

"Oh, Claus," said Anya, "you promised to do something?"

"That was foolish, wasn't it? Yet somehow I felt, beyond all reason, that a door will open, a path unfold. I haven't been shown such horrors for nothing."

Rachel wisely held her tongue until Anya was done. She was the reconciler. She patched things up in their threesome. Not that Santa and Anya had violent disagreements. But Santa's Pan side flared up, as did Anya's fir nymph, more frequently than either of them liked to admit.

"You'll disappoint her," said Anya, propped against a pillow in her flannel nightgown and wire-rimmed glasses. "Wendy trusts the great Santa Claus to figure out how to spare this little boy his fate. Well, forgive an old lady her frankness, but preventing the suffering of one child among millions is not what you're here for."

"Anya, please."

"You make and distribute toys. You're the scent of pine needles and the glitter of tinsel. You're anticipation, the jingle of bells and the brief sorrow at just missing your visit because they can't keep their eyelids open. But really, Claus, saving a teenager from suicide? How? Why?"

"Because Wendy pleaded. And because I knew right then that it's possible. If I had shrugged and said, 'I'm sorry, Wendy, I can't,' it would have been a lie."

Anya glanced at Rachel for support, then back at Santa. "It defies logic."

"Precisely," he said. "There's no logic to it at all. Might she be disappointed? She might. But I don't think so. I think, against all logic, that there's something Wendy and I can do to save this boy."

"Even supposing you can, where will it end? Do you think Wendy will stop at one? No, there will be scores, hundreds of little boys and girls whose futures need brightening. Perhaps you should promise to make everything rosy for all the people in the whole world, now and to come, in perpetuity. Perhaps *you're* the Savior after all; it isn't the Son of God at all. Forgive me, I'm being sarcastic. Sarcasm isn't much help."

"No," said Santa, "I understand."

The argument's sharp edges had started to dull, and Rachel saw her entree: "I'm concerned mostly, I guess, about Wendy. Then I remind myself that inside she's seventeen. And for all its heartache, seventeen's pretty resilient. I agree, Anya, that there's no way Santa can do anything." She looked at her husband. "But, I also agree with *you* that something must be done."

The hint of a smile played upon Santa's face, not in triumph over Anya but in appreciation for Rachel.

"It seems to me," she went on, "that you and Wendy are too close to the shock of what you've witnessed to arrive at an easy conclusion. These are future events. If indeed there *is* a way to avert them, you have time to figure out how."

Santa, considering her words, approached the bed. He sat on its edge and took his wives' hands. "You're right of course. And Anya, you're right too. Nothing either one of you has said hasn't already occurred to me. This question needs sleeping on. Maybe I'm deluding myself. But I'm going to bang my head against the heavens anyway. I'll either have a breakthrough or give up in defeat. But I'll be okay, and so will Wendy, if it comes to that."

"If it's any consolation," said Anya, "I hope I'm wrong."

"Thank you, sweetheart." He leaned in and gave his first wife a kiss. "And thank you, Rachel dear." She took Santa's generous lips onto hers, thrilled as always by his touch. "I do believe," he said, honey in his voice, "it's time to douse the lights, celebrate our holy union, and let Hypnos, the God of Sleep—what's he called these days, the Sandman?—and his sons lure us into the land of dreams."

"Why you old satyr," said Anya in mock scold. "You're always ready, aren't you?"

"For my darling nymph and my once-mortal lover, yes yes and yes again."

Anya smiled. Then, leaning to her nightstand, she blew out her lantern, as Rachel did hers. And for a time, naught but giggles and sighs, gasps and caresses, and the sweet intimacies of love held sway in the Clausean marriage bed.

31

5.

INNOCENCE AND SHAME

WHEN HE ISN'T DELIVERING BASKETS on his special night each year, the Easter Bunny has time to kill. The colored eggs his hens lay roll down long ramps to be stored away, never spoiling or cracking, but hardboiled as they emerge. Likewise his well-lubricated, maintenance-free machines turn out an abundance of jellybeans, marshmallow chicks, chocolate bunnies, and clear, thin shreds of shiny green plastic. Without intervention of any kind, ingredients appear and are processed, their end products stored in spotless bins or upon shelves, to be miraculously assembled at unfathomable depths into baskets as Easter approaches. Come the night of delivery, into magic time he vanishes, reaching a paw into the void and pulling out just the right basket for the mortal whose life, at that moment, he graces. Then a tumble across carpet and a quick dive through permeable windows brings him out into the night air where he speeds to his next destination.

So goes the Easter Bunny's divinely decreed routine. Content he is, and more than content, with this.

What then does he do after each morning's look-in at the hens? He roams the earth, searching for loving couples in their moments of intimacy. Now you are not to think his voyeurism unholy, as indeed it had been before the Father's neutering transformation of him. Though he recalled none of his past, he had been monstrous then, steeped in lust and envy and capable of monstrous deeds. He had sold his soul to the Tooth Fairy, tormented Wendy, attacked Anya, and violated Rachel. Then had God visited his burrow and reached back in time to the moment of his creation to eradicate his sex organs.

Nowadays, he sought the most loving couples instinct led him to, blessing, by observing them, their intimacies. At the moment, he was sitting on his haunches in a high-fenced backyard where, between two trees, a hammock was stretched. Within it lay an Australian man and woman, upon a temperate afternoon, wiling away the time in marital

32

bliss. As Ray gripped her inner thigh, Penelope pleasured herself. Her face went taut and Ray told her she was beautiful.

In the Easter Bunny's opinion, both of them were paragons of beauty—not simply in the skin or limbs or musculature, but in their hearts, which lay exposed to him. Penelope and Ray were recent newlyweds, second marriages both, childless their first, by design in her case, by low sperm count in his. They had spoken of adoption, though they much preferred spawning a child of their own. This, in fact, was the other criterion that influenced the Easter Bunny's choice of lovers to visit.

For he was able to observe the liquidity of their letting-go, to guide eggward the jet of sperm, and with a twitch of his nose and a bit of body English to propel one hearty spermatozoa into the great plunge, thereby setting into motion the wondrous process of incubation. Once he had accomplished that task for Penelope and Ray, he leaped for joy, splitting the sky with inaudible yips of delight.

Then he settled down to bask in the afterglow and listen in on their sweet conversation. Penelope said she felt as if some benevolent god had spread a canopy of divine approval over their coupling, and Ray agreed.

Even so, despite his chittering joy, the Easter Bunny felt a decided lack of something. This lack wasn't connected to the aforementioned lust or envy, for he no longer suffered under their spell.

Shame was what he felt, vague but ever present.

He knew not why. To his knowledge, he had done nothing to be ashamed of. Still, there the shame was. He felt a need to make restitution, to recover something that had been lost.

Now you are not to suppose that this recoverable something was his penis and testicles, for he missed them not at all. God's makeover had been thorough, and an envy of mortal organs in no way figured in his sense of loss.

If pressed to say what precisely he had lost, the Easter Bunny would have paused and pondered and said, "I guess it's the pastel goodness of Easter, the happiness of the hunt for eggs in tall grass, the contentment of sunny spring days with the air fresh and quiet, and the companionship loving, familial, and free." For his shame had in some small measure dulled for him the sensory delights of Easter. Scents were a tad muted, colors not quite so intense, textures less distinct.

The sheen upon the eggshell of life had dimmed.

He sighed. Even so, it contented him to observe the Rays and Penelopes of the world and to usher along the regeneration of life, womb-whole and poised to drop squalling and perfect into the world. Into the sky over Brisbane he bounded, shooting north and east toward a humble home outside of Santa Fe, a few miles along Artist Road yet not quite as far as Ten Thousand Waves.

The next day, Santa's distraught looks were bruited about from workbench to workbench. Something in him had changed, but no one dared ask what. They observed him sighing and pacing in his office, sitting jittery-legged on a tall stool downing Coke after Coke, worrying over a cuckoo clock with wee little screwdrivers beneath an intense pool of light. He seemed older, more frazzled, far less sure of himself than usual.

Why don't I just ask him, Fritz wondered. It isn't as if he isn't approachable. He's *very* approachable.

But Fritz knew nobody was about to ask him. If Santa had something to tell them, he would choose his own time to do so.

So far had the buzz spread that Gregor and his brothers, Josef and Engelbert, dropped by from the stables, ostensibly to pitch in where they were needed. But Gregor's fierce eyes, darting everywhere at once, told a different tale. It surprised no one when his brothers spread word of a meeting at the Chapel after lights out.

The day having fled, Fritz and Herbert trudged through moonlit snow, past the stables and up into the woods behind the workshop. In twos and threes traipsed Santa's helpers, threading past boulders and clusters of pine trees. They carried lanterns, held high or swinging from lax hands. The long line of elves snaked its way to the Chapel, a bowed configuration of trees where God had joined Santa and Anya and Rachel in holy matrimony eight years before.

As the final stragglers found their places, Gregor strode to the fore. The moonlight was most intense where the Almighty had stood, and into it stepped Gregor. He planted his feet firm, crossed his arms in a tight harrumph, and glared over the sea of elves, saying nothing. He nodded. Again. A third nod. Laughter rippled through the crowd. But Gregor did not crack a smile and the laughter died down as quickly as it had begun.

Fritz leaned to Herbert. "This must be about Santa, don't you think?"

Herbert shrugged and nodded, shook his head no, and shrugged again.

Gregor pointed sharply into the crowd. Stabs, as if to say, Caught you! Caught you! He would point, then withdraw his hand and tuck it decisively back into the crook of his opposite elbow.

"I see you," he said at last. "I see you all. You think Santa has changed? *We* have changed. We all saw Santa in his office, looking older. Some weight has been dropped on the big baby's toes. I have no idea what. Tomorrow, it may vanish. He'll be his same damned cheery old self. But you and I have changed in the years since Wendy and Rachel arrived, since Knecht Rupert played the organ for the wedding while Johann and Gustav worked the bellows. Our hands stayed at our sides, or busied themselves with making toys, or buried themselves in our pockets, or gesticulated to match our words, or little-boy'd behind our backs, or tossed our caps into the heavens at Santa's return on Christmas morning.

"But more and more our hands have begun acting shamefully. It has become habitual. I notice it. I marvel that no one else notices it."

Fritz wondered what Gregor was talking about. He thought himself fairly observant, yet he had seen nothing special. He stared at his hands and let them drop.

Gregor extended his index fingers as though making a point. His elbows were bent at perfect right angles. "Observe these fingers. They have never, not once, known sin." He stood erect and fierce. "Fingers find nostrils, do they not? They root about in them. They ferret out certain...prizes. Certain soft foul discolorations that gloop up into shameless droppings at a fingertip's end. Sometimes these prizes—"

(again he put a nasty spin on the word)

"—are smeared on sleeves or handkerchiefs or workbench surfaces, to dry and crust and be brushed away. But in the extreme, certain as yet unnamed miscreants *eat* what they find. I have seen it. In the workshop, I have seen it. In the commons, I have seen it. Tonight, at this very gathering, here in this hallowed place, I have seen it. Over and over and over. The practice squanders our energy. It vitiates us. The act is vile, disgusting, bestial, self-abusive, and downright unelflike."

Fritz looked at Herbert, who no longer smiled but stared at him from beneath a cloud of shame. In truth, Fritz felt shame of his own, though he was not sure why. Did Gregor have a point?

"The nose," continued Gregor, tapping his bulbous proboscis, "is a wondrous organ. Sensitive to mere hints of aroma, capacious and wide of nostril to welcome in fresh air, capable of issuing sharp sniffs of disapproval—and there is so much in this world to disapprove of. What a wondrous organ is the nose."

He paused to impale them on his glare and to set up, by silence, his next point, as a tennis player lofts his ball before serving it.

"Mucus. Properly respected and unfingered, mucus has been designed, by God and his angels, to capture and conglomerate germs and bodily grit. Its tasteful removal is the function of the handkerchief, not the finger. Pray observe. I take a folded red kerchief from my back pocket. I shake it out. It is clean, notice. I double-fold it—no thin fabric shall expose these fingers to the accidental taint of distasteful liquid—then I drape it over one hand. Now I bring it to my nose and close one nostril as I blow the other clear, back and forth, like this."

Gregor gave two pronounced goose honks, followed by three short, quick ones, then wiped vigorously back and forth. The now-crumpled handkerchief he held before him like an offense.

"Thus is it done. The soiled cloth now goes carefully back into the pocket and, once I reach home, into the hamper, to be replaced by a clean, freshly-folded one."

Master weaver Ludwig raised a hand. Gregor glared, refusing to acknowledge the questioner. Ludwig chimed in anyway: "But Gregor, where's the harm? What matter whether handkerchief or finger removes the stuff so long as it's removed? Did you really call us together for this?"

Gregor reddened. "You see?" he said, cutting off Ludwig's last word. "*That's* the attitude. Lax, lazy, insufficiently vigilant. Our master weaver picks his nose and eats what he has picked. Those same fingers, unwashed, take up the needle and handle bolts of cloth. Do you suffer under the illusion that Ludwig's filthy nose products do not slime their way into his weave? What befouled toys does Santa place beneath children's trees? Do you see? Do you see how pernicious and invasive an evil is spread by such acts? I tell you, my brother elves, we have devolved. This vile habit, which I have vowed to vanquish and to help all of you consign to the oblivion it deserves, cloaks some terrible truth about our past. Whatever its cause, this obscenity shall not stand. When I see it, I will call the offender on his folly. My brothers have vowed to do likewise." Truth be told, fat Josef and Engelbert looked dubious. "Moreover, these meetings, to shame us and steel our resolve, shall continue until this scourge has been routed."

Herbert's guilt hung like lead in his eyes. If only Gregor knew the *half* of it, thought Fritz, he would go apoplectic.

"You have been put on notice. I expect this ungodly practice to cease. Spy on one another. Spy on your unworthiest selves. Report offenders at once to Engelbert, Josef, or me. We shall shame them into surrender, I swear upon my sacred honor."

And Gregor strode off, gesturing them back toward the dormitory. Amidst much murmuring, the elves took up the march, self-conscious now about their bodies. Gone the casual arm swing, the lax sway of hands alongside easy-breathing chests.

Shame hung heavy about Fritz, and worse, he saw, about his friend Herbert. I should feel anger, he thought, anger at the grump-meister's bullying and at Herbert's dismay.

But all was shock and confusion within him.

Chuff, the Tooth Fairy's lackluster youngest, sat forlorn in his least unfavorite spot, peering at the moon through a thicket of blighted trees halfway up the mountain's west slope. The moon was cold and full and uncaring, its sheen the harsh, metallic glint in his brothers' eyes when they sailed into him with tooth and claw.

"If I could only have a sign," he said to the moon, so softly that only the odd syllable came out. Nonetheless, he lofted his eyes upward and said, "Please, the smallest sign. Something to assure me there's more to life than this." Chuff winced at memories of beatings and railings, of bad children running from him in terror as he obeyed his worst instincts. Lately, his self-loathing had increased. "I'm not like my brothers," he said. "They sense it. So does Mom."

At the thought of her, Chuff's throat narrowed. She preferred her sons vicious. But Chuff found viciousness harder to conjure up with each passing day. She rewarded mayhem in the telling. Even when one of his brothers lied, and everyone knew he was embellishing his nasty deeds, Mom praised the liar.

When the blood of vengeance rode high in her, a certain nostril flare and lip curl distorted her looks. Chuff's tales, contrive them though he might, never managed to please her. Hard and cold as her heart, she listened. If he escaped the telling without a scornful word or a command to the others to beat him senseless, he counted himself lucky. "She means well. No, that's wrong. She never means well. I don't want her approval or praise. But I do. It's the coin of the realm, and dear pale moon—who at least, in your indifference, spares me your sneers—I sit here impoverished. Enrich me, or at least grant me minimal sustenance. There must be a way out, some way to...to find my true family, not these awful changelings."

His brothers' scowls rose before him. He dismissed them, but they came again. Then he calmed and let them vanish into the chill air of the island.

"A sign. One small sign pointing the way out."

But the moon's glare held steady. No wink. No warmth. No wavering. Clouds came in to cover it, until it was but a gray smudge hidden inside a darker gray.

For the longest time, Chuff tried to coax the moon back into view. It refused to return.

6.
THE POWER OF PRAYER

THE ELVES WEREN'T THE ONLY creatures at the North Pole who had slipped into magic time that night.

Santa, having scrutinized the ceiling above his bed for hours, finally crawled from beneath his blankets and over the bottom lip of the bed, doing his best not to disturb his wives. He pulled on flannel underwear, shrugged into a suit and boots, and trudged across the commons to the workshop. There he sat for many an hour, summoning scenes past and present from the four mortals whose futures Wendy had shown him.

First he examined Ty Taylor, a proper lad who had adopted without question his parents' strictness. From his earliest days, he seemed destined for the ministry. Santa observed the young man at seminary, swallowing as gospel his denomination's lies. Evangelicals were a cockeyed fringe back then, as the seventies began and Ty turned twenty-two. Outside, authority was being questioned, defied, rebelled against. But inside, Ty and his classmates were admonished to obey absolutely and to buttress with rhetorical flourishes the beliefs of the buttoned-down.

Santa brought up scene after scene of Ty's indoctrination into institutional homophobia, into selective Bible parsing that slathered a false sheen of God-acceptance over the prejudices of the day. Though Santa longed to wrench these teachings from Ty's mind, he could only observe their inculcation.

In his teens, Ty passed two vagrants on a park bench in Chicago and burned at the suggestions they shouted after him. Santa felt his discomfort, as if he thought that heterosexuality ought to blare with trumpeted certainty from him, but did not.

Then came assignments to this or that church, sermons on sin, the gradual development of a beguiling preaching style that honed the fear, hatred, and self-righteousness that worked upon the sinful.

Despairing at what he saw, Santa let Ty Taylor go.

39

He next probed Jamie's parents, likewise tracing them from their childhoods, how they met, the dominance of Kathy MacLaren in their marriage. Here as well he noted the gender uncertainty in both of them, dropped references to manliness as their sons developed and diverged. Though Jamie was only eight, Santa observed his father's worried looks and felt the fears of both parents as they discussed the boys in the privacy of their bedroom.

But what most upset Santa was the life of Matt Beluzzo at his current sullen age of twelve.

His father, languishing in jail, despised his wife and son and had let them know it with curses, slaps, and belt-whippings. Matt's mother smoked and overate, covering her misery in excess makeup. She rarely looked Matt in the eye but stared past him, speaking, when she spoke at all, in insults.

For Santa, who had focused all his life on good little boys and girls, Matt's family repulsed him. And that repulsion distressed him no end. Worse, he knew that what he had seen played itself out repeatedly in homes throughout the world. Seeing *one* such family was unbearable. Imagining their misery multiplied drove Santa to his knees, his hands clasped in prayer, his eyes red and wet.

"Dear God," he began, "I thank you for my many blessings and above all for my loving friends and family here at the North Pole and for the children who hold my truth in their hearts. My life, save for that unfortunate interlude with the Tooth Fairy, is one of contentment. Even my struggles with my...my less savory side led eventually to Rachel and Wendy's welcome into our community and the enrichment and expansion of my marriage, for which I could praise you for all eternity and not begin to praise you enough. But tonight I must speak a prayer of pleading, a request to be granted the power to right a wrong, to extend my charter, and not to shrink from extended contact with grown-ups.

"I am Santa Claus. It has been my rare pleasure and duty to be childlike, though ancient, the better to resonate with mortal children. The naughty ones I gave not a thought to, so full of joy was I for the others, for the effervescence of desire that filled their hearts. This was my task, and I embraced it with all my heart.

"But now, at Wendy's urging, I have seen how mortals fall as they leave childhood, how even well-behaved children join the grown-up world and make its lies their own. I am the heart of generosity. Now I beg permission to extend my generosity to Wendy herself.

"She has asked the impossible. Children do that all the time, and I nod and smile, give what I can, and they forget their extravagant wishes and are content. But this time, there is no easy substitute. Wendy is on the cusp of adulthood, yet still she is my little girl. She is pushing me to grow, but I cannot see how. Teach me the way, o Lord. Show me how to save Jamie Stratton and his tormentors.

"Please, God, do not think that I question for one moment your ways with mortals. There must be some point to the suffering, the cruelty, the cosmic game they play of exalting goodness with their words while committing the most vicious assaults upon each other—all of it must be part of your divine plan, inscrutable as it is.

"And though the simplest of minds can easily conjure utopias—a wonder it is that not *one* of these alternate worlds, infinitely better, has been your gift to humankind—I do not question your ways. After all, I and Anya and my elves and, God knows, Rachel and Wendy, suffered much before the awful storm abated. But then, perhaps my second wife and my stepdaughter are more precious for having been won after such pain and suffering. Who am I to judge? So I do not question your ways, nor even expect that the gift I request you will bestow upon me.

"That gift, dear Lord, is the ability to save Jamie Stratton from his suicide and from the suffering fated to lead him to self-slaughter. If I cannot sway his tormentors to withhold their torment, let me at least somehow divert their negativity.

"But I dare not stray into particulars. I have made my request. You know best if and how that request will be granted. I leave it in your bounteous hands, assured by faith that you will give my plea your attention and, as always, make the wisest choice. The greatest good for all the universe, whatever it may be, is all I ask." Santa shut his eyes, sent his anguished plea heavenward, gave thanks for his blessings, and spoke a final "Amen."

As he doused the lights and trudged across the commons to the warmth of his marriage bed, his words like moonbeams in reverse traveled through the firmament, up up up through the cloud-covered floor of heaven to the ear of the Father, who glanced down, momentarily annoyed, from his interminable conversation with the Son, tugged at his earlobe, and asked, "Where were we?"

"Some disturbance, Father?"

"Just a whining suppliant. Go on."

And their never-ending debate continued.

41

***

The Son felt eternally betrayed all the time.

He had visited humankind to save them from damnation. And he'd done his damnedest. Some he had inspired. But far too many perverted his message, using it to justify cruelties of one kind or another. More critical than that betrayal, they betrayed, by denying, what was best in themselves. That squandering of their talents, well nigh unforgivable, made his burden heavier. Since his visit to earth, he always wore a doleful and downcast look, though it never overshadowed his essence as a being most loving, forgiving, and intercessive with the Father.

As for the suppliant God had mentioned, the Son had seen who that suppliant was and, there being no secrets in heaven, his father knew that he knew.

And so the Son, once Dionysus now Christ, kept close watch over Santa Claus, tracking his disturbed sleep and the content of his dreams. He watched him soap and shampoo his capacious body, mournful as he passed his open mouth beneath the shower spray. Through Santa's long days of industry the eye of Christ was upon him, upon his increased consumption of Coke, his scarcely concealed agitation, and his feverish toymaking, productive days driven by equal parts love of children and anguish over whether God would answer his prayer.

He saw Santa take Wendy aside to assure her he had not forgotten and was going all out to find a solution, though solution there might not be. And he felt Santa's anguish at the hint of disappointment that passed over her features.

In the midst of these observings, the Divine Mother asked whom he observed. This she did though she too knew all, what was occurring, what would occur, and what her role would be. Even now, her lactose, lachrymose mammaries were readying the milk of human kindness for...but we'll come to that in due time.

The Son told her anyway.

He comprehended the shape of what had been and what was to come, the great sacrifice he had made for humankind and Santa's impending sacrifice in the same vein...but we'll get to that, we'll get to that.

It's a challenge, describing the *über*-temporal in temporal terms, the *über*-spatial in terms of space. For the Divine Mother was near and far, inside him and he inside her at the same time. And all converse

42

between them was necessary and unnecessary, as it had always been and would always be, world without end.

As that day drew to a close, Santa trudged once more to his workshop, lit a thin candle, fell to his knees, and clasped his hands in prayer.

"Is he at it again?" asked the Father.

"He is," said the Son.

"That's right. Be compassionate. It's your way. And my way is to snap and snarl at him. How dare he ask for anything, he who has it made? He hasn't thought through his piety, his pretense at fervor. How dare he question my ways, even as he pretends not to? Where was *he* when the universe was created?"

"His concern is only for Wendy, and for the suffering boy. His heart—"

"Yes, yes," said the Father. "But he's out of his league. If I answer this prayer, where will it end? There would *be* no end. I'd have to fix the whole damned race. They're never satisfied. Not mortals, and not immortals either. Look at him. Two loving wives, to whom he was married by no less than me, a wonderful stepdaughter, adoring and adorable elves, millions of enthralled children, the perfect workplace, access to magic time, flying reindeer—the list goes on. But is he content? He is not content. There's always one more thing he needs. He slanders me in the asking. I have my reasons for allowing suffering. Don't ask me what they are. It's no one's goddamned business but mine. I refuse to be second-guessed. Oh, great. Just listen to him."

"Calm down, Father."

"He wants all four of them fixed. Jamie's tormentors, he calls them. It's clear of course that fixing the parents would save the child, that alone. But, no, he wants the preacher and the bully fixed too. If I do that, if I grant him any part of what he wants, the floodgates will burst wide. Fix their tormentors too, why don't you? Fix everyone's tormentors. You're God, for the love of Christ. You can do anything. Work those miracles, tote that barge, lift that bale, fix that world. Well I've got news for Santa. The world doesn't need fixing."

"You're getting worked up again."

"The temerity of the little elf. I ought to demote him is what I ought to do. One swaybacked reindeer I'll give him, half a helper (the lower half), and some hell hole to toil in, sweaty, stinky, and confining—with no reduction in workload!"

On and on the Father railed, so upset that hints of Zeus, hurler of thunderbolts, peered through his façade of white-robed grandeur, the fire in his eyes, the armor, the fists full of heavenly vengeance. But the Son kept up his soothing words until Santa's prayer ended. And as the unjolly old elf trudged back to his cottage and the Father checked his temper to ask, "Where were we?" the Son decided to be Santa's champion, to persuade God to grant him this one small concession, putting reasonable bounds upon it, if need be. He had already made changes for Santa's sake eight years before. And the ones Santa now requested would serve a good cause.

But, truth be told, the Son fretted over his father's health. He was surely eternal. Of that, there could be no doubt. But he ought to *enjoy* eternity more than he did.

The Son vowed to do what he could to make it so.

The following day, the Father looked down on his creation, of which the earth and its creatures were the centerpiece.

It pleased him that the Son existed. For it allowed him to be judgmental, even curmudgeonly, playing off a foil. Could he change things? In an instant, whenever the urge took hold. But he chose not to. "Creation is perfect," he said to no one in particular. A perfect mess, he thought. But perfection dwelt even in mess and sprawl. The world as it was was good enough.

Besides, he had sent the Christ child down there with a transparent and unambiguous message of love and forgiveness, of redemption and a firm refusal to embrace the cruelties of dumbed-down moral lemmings—yet they were, on the whole, worse than ever! He had bestowed upon them the greatest symbol, excepting of course the Buddha and other worthy avatars, of generosity of spirit they had ever beheld, a savior who had redeemed them through his suffering, resurrection, and rebirth. And still, they warred and hated and sat in judgment like tin pot gods, sniping at each other in the very *name* of that symbol.

So that night, when Santa Claus fell to his knees and renewed his mewling prayers, the Father swept into apoplexy. The Son soothed. The Divine Mother looked upon him with compassion. Angel choirs sang calming hymns as they soft-touched harp strings and fleecy clouds wisped along their wing tops.

But his anger soon passed. As Santa prayed and the Divine Mother observed him with compassion and the Son soothed, there came a shift. I'm God, he told himself. Not only can I *do* anything. I can *un*do anything. If I don't like how certain actions unfold, I can fold them up tight, as though they had never been unfolded at all.

The Father knew of course that the reversal of any action, once set in motion, was likely not only to be challenging but to bring on the unforeseen. Despite the exceptions of the Easter Bunny's priapic expunging and various resurrections, there were certain elaborate mosaics it were best not to rework, once the tiles were laid in.

But this day, the Father was in a giving mood. "If Santa really wants to complexify his life, so be it," he said.

The Son, surprised and unsurprised, said, "Good. That's as it should be."

"For me, nothing is impossible."

"True, Father."

"I'll throw him this one sop."

"He'll be grateful."

"As well he might." God gazed about in annoyance. "Where's our bumbler?"

"I appear." The archangel Michael bloomed full-blown before the throne, haloed and holy. His look bore, as always, a hint of contrition at having allowed Santa and the Tooth Fairy to cross paths while the Father vacationed nearly three decades before. His Hermes side had been tucked back inside, though not as deep as prudence might dictate.

They allowed Michael access to Santa's prayers, the one now unreeling and those that had previously flown to heaven.

"Here's your chance," said the Father, "to get back into my good graces. You have carte blanche. Devise a plan to attack this problem, then implement it. Maintain modesty of purpose, and don't overreach. Is that clear?"

Michael said it was. Then he bowed and forelocked and hosanna'd and hallelujah'd his gratitude until God waved that away.

"But..." said Michael.

"Go on."

"Isn't fixing all four of them more than is strictly necessary? Why not just the parents? Or *one* parent?"

"Do you dare question my will?" God's robes billowed and grew dark. His eyes flared with righteous fire.

"Calm yourself, Father. Michael, it's simply that Santa so loves these mortals, not the child alone, that he wants them all fixed."

Michael had gone white and cowering, not daring to speak another word. Had he a bladder, it would have been voided.

Then the Father gave over all threat. "My Son, in whom I am well pleased, speaks true. We are stopping with these few."

Fret fell from the archangel, who vowed every effort—carefully considered this time—to carry out the divine will. He bowed and rose on a wing and a prayer, then dropped intently earthward on his mission.

"Will he be all right?" wondered the Son.

God looked askance. "I think we *both* know the answer to *that!*"

7.
ANGELIC BUMBLER
MAKES GOOD

MICHAEL WAS BESIDE HIMSELF WITH JOY. The opportunity for any of them to annunciate came but rarely. Why, the number of angelic annunciations all told could be counted on two hands; the ones he had been involved in, on a couple of fingers.

Moreover, if memory served, this was the first time any of them had annunciated to immortals. The one made by Gabriel to the Divine Mother had occurred during her mortal years, so that didn't count.

The Father had simply said, without fanfare, "Go do it, Michael." Now here he was, hurtling earthward, his wings alternately buckling for a dive and catching astral currents to slow and direct his descent.

As he approached the earth, there came thundering into his soul mortality's great mumble and murmur, its hopes and fears, snips of envy and anger, each slothful tomorrow-is-time-enough, lustful I'll-seduce-her, and greedy that-object-will-surely-complete-me. Mortals were a confused bunch, a riot of weeds punctuated by random lilies and roses, their potential massively wasted except for the few and far between. Such inertia pulled them all in every wrong direction. And too many errant impulses moved makers of critical decisions. The planet's survival lay in the hands of madmen.

In one sense, then, naught but cacophony.

In another, the most complex interweaving of patterns possible.

The paths of righteousness in heaven were uncluttered by such diabolical chokeweed. Yet its denizens did not judge those who walked the earth. Judgment was the exclusive province of the all-knowing Father.

Beyond the riotous stew of emotions, Michael also took in the deeds, violent and benevolent alike—the raised fist, the forcings, the addictions, the words that hurt, the pen strokes that set money over people, knife plunges, gunshots, land mines that maimed or put paid to a life. He saw tender embraces as well, sacrifices for the common good, worthy churchmen who did what they could to battle backwardness

47

and ossification in ecclesiastical hierarchies. But Michael's task lay not in this hopelessly tangled writhe of spaghetti, but in one special place on earth, to which he now sped.

Below him, the enchanting community at the North Pole opened to reveal its wonders. Ah, yes. The simpler, more disciplined mental lives of elves. Of Anya and Rachel in workshop and cottage. Of Santa and Wendy taking their morning walk.

Michael shivered with delight.

He would be privileged to help Wendy, steeped now in anticipated disappointment; and Santa Claus, doleful in the certainty that he would shortly crush Wendy's faith in him.

Michael, though not incapable of excess pride, skirted far from temptation, doing instead the angelic thing, which was to feel just the right amount of childlike pride in helping another creature, for the glory of God and his creation, and only incidentally noting the glory that would redound upon himself.

As he floated above unseen, Santa and Wendy passed clusters of fir trees through fresh-fallen snow to the Chapel. Santa's anguish brought an ache to Michael's heart.

"I must confess my limits to Wendy," the elf was thinking. "She'll see how circumscribed I am. No longer will she think me a godlike parent who can fulfill every promise. She'll know my fallibility as I know it myself. I'll admit failure, she'll hold my hand and assure me she understands, and Jamie Stratton will choose death over the daily drumbeat of suffering. The moment of his death will torment me until it occurs, and ever afterwards."

Wendy broke Michael's heart. "My poor stepfather," she thought, "has been crestfallen since my request. He has failed, and he must suspect that I know it. He'll think he has fallen in my esteem. But the opposite is true. I don't expect him to be Superman, and I'll tell him so. Then we'll weep for Jamie's fate and agonize afterward, until we resign ourselves to accepting what we're powerless to change."

Michael felt utterly tickled, hovering in the treetops, knowing the joy he would shortly deliver. Oh, but how can I be sure, he wondered, my plan won't go awry? I've bumbled before. Badly. Then he realized that the very asking was all anyone, God included, could expect of him. That question, posed and reposed, would keep him on course and quell his Hermes impulses.

Michael took a breath and prepared to manifest.

***

Wendy's shiny red boots crunched fresh snow. The rich aroma of pine infused the air. Then they reached the Chapel, where Mommy had married Anya and Santa eight years before, and where she came often to feel vibrant and alive and thank God for her blessings. She knew what her stepfather was about to say, and she steeled herself, like a brave little girl, to hear it and *not* dissolve into tears but to accept, accept, accept and to love him even more for his attempts and for wanting to spare her disappointment.

Santa turned to her, his face somber. "Wendy," he managed. Then he stopped and stared upward.

Wendy felt it almost as quickly. The sunshine grew brighter and more vibrant. There was a bounce in the air, a lilt, a fulfillment of ancient promises. Flower petals, white and pink, floated before her. No, not petals but feathers, laid down one upon the other, curving soft over wide high angles. The folds of a snow-white robe fell to the tops of two boyish feet planted shoulder-high in the air above the snow. And a halo'd head, cheeks unblemished, eyes awash with dew, smiled down at them. The angel's hair was lustrous and shiny, its long auburn locks breaking over the shoulders just ahead of the prayerful arcs described by his wing tops.

"Behold," said he. Wendy thrilled from head to toe. "I bring tidings of great joy from God himself, from the Son, and from the Divine Mother."

Behind her, Santa held Wendy's shoulders in a soft grip, no fear or protection in the gesture, but rather the need to touch her as they shared this visitation.

"To what do we...?" He faltered in awe.

"You were afraid that God would not answer your prayer. Your fears were unfounded. Probe not for reasons. But accept this my annunciation."

The angel opened his hands and gazed upon Wendy with boundless love. "Wendy," he said, "type of the perfect child, and Santa Claus, thou ever-replenished fount of generosity, on behalf of heaven itself, I grant you this boon: On the night before Thanksgiving, you will be granted leave to visit three households, to persuade those you visit to choose a different path, and thereby save the boy you would save. You know which households I mean?"

49

Wendy nodded, naming those whose cumulative barbs would drive Jamie Stratton to suicide.

"We wish to visit their bedrooms," said Santa.

"It is God's will," said the angel, gesturing beyond them with a finger and the nod of his head. "Behind your workshop, where the hills slope into the forest, stand replicas of those bedrooms. However your helpers bedeck them, upon your appearing to the mortals, the same shall be overlaid upon the real bedroom as magic time envelops it. At the conclusion of each visit, sleep will claim those you have visited. For that one night shall they share a dreamscape, where their dreams will reinforce your message."

Wendy thrilled as the angel charged them. There was no guarantee that the mortals would mend their ways. But if persuasion could turn just one of them, even a little, Jamie's life might be spared.

"Thus has God decreed. Go forth. Bend your best efforts to the task." Turning to leave, he spoke a parting word. "If you need further aid in this effort, simply speak aloud the name Michael, that's me, and I will appear at once."

He raised his hands in benediction. "Blessed be, o favored ones of the Lord. Thou art beloved of him and of all the world."

Then his eyes lifted heavenward and he melded with the air. The scent of ozone and a lingering glow upon the landscape were the only hints he had been there.

"God be praised," said Santa.

"Is it possible?" asked Wendy. "Can we do it?" But her words held no doubt. "We can," she said, "and we will, to the limits of our power."

Santa hugged her, his huge palms confident along her back. Then he took her hands and gazed at her with fervor. "God has touched us yet again, this time through the archangel. Our way was lost, but now is found. Wendy, sweetheart, I love you so. If Jamie is to be saved, it shall be through our agency. To the limits of our power indeed! Let's go tell everyone at once. We have much planning to do before Thanksgiving."

"We do." Wendy had not seen her stepfather so excited in ages. Her spirits too were buoyed with expectation. "I have a few ideas."

Santa laughed. "Let's hear them," he said, as they struck out homeward at a brisk pace.

***

As Michael rose toward heaven, he opened himself to doubt. Had he bumbled or in any way overstepped? He didn't think so.

He knew from prior annunciations that angelic visits invariably raised hope in the visitants. As they were *meant* to do. Such hope guaranteed nothing. But in the worthiest, the knowledge that divinity supported a righteous course of action sparked resolve, determination, and the will to confront and defeat adversity.

How sweet Wendy had been, how grand and generous Santa, standing there in the snow, attuned to one another and enthralled at his every word.

Had he done well? He believed he had. Should he check with the Higher Ups? No. The Father had trusted him to redeem himself for past mistakes, and so he was determined to do.

The clouds thinned. Above the atmosphere he shot, rising through darkness and a sparkle of stars toward the Empyrean. If he entertained doubts, as indeed he did, they were divine, the emotional stuff which keeps one on course, filling in one's plans with intelligent detail.

I did well, he thought. It was a nice touch, opening the door to future contact. More chances to annunciate.

From on high, Michael heard angelic voices and the faint sweep and pluck of harp strings. Redoubling his intent, he rose more swiftly toward his proper place in heaven.

8.

PREPARING FOR ELVES

AT THE FIRST DULL POP, Santa's helpers looked up from their tinkering. Though muffled by the outer walls of the workshop, it sounded to Fritz like a pine knot exploding in a fireplace. Odd. But one couldn't stop making toys at every peculiar sound. Fritz returned his attention to the clay gnome in his hand and dipped his horsehair brush into a pot of crimson paint.

Then came a louder snap and then the loudest, a great *crrr-ack*, as though the heart of a great old oak had burst for sheer joy.

Workers near the back windows rose to peer outside. One by one, others joined them, pointing and talking among themselves until their excited jabbering brought Fritz off his stool to find out what all the palaver was about.

Playhouses? On platforms? Absurd.

But when he reached the picture window, what he glimpsed through a bobbing sea of heads in a fresh field of fallen snow, were indeed three perfect pinewood platforms, twenty feet square. And upon each was...well that was difficult to describe. Furnished bedrooms. Modern American, one smaller than the others, which were master bedrooms with built-in sink areas to one side.

The view into them seemed odd. Then Fritz saw why. Though the bedroom walls were transparent, suggestions of wallpaper, posters, or paintings, or the backs of dressers, partly blocked the eye's access to the interior.

"What's all the fuss?" Rachel, having heard the commotion from Santa's office, appeared behind them. "My goodness! Someone's been slipping into magic time, I think."

But no one had, and all were quick to say so.

"Let's take a look," she said.

The elves dutifully followed her outside and around the workshop. There they mounted the steps on all sides of the platforms and examined the bedrooms. Each ceiling had great steel hinges on one side. "Hey, look," said Friedrich the globe maker. "The walls are on tracks."

Indeed they were. At each corner stood a strong steel bar, twice as tall as the bedrooms themselves. The walls fit snug into well-oiled grooves in these bars. With the touch of a finger and slight pressure upward anywhere on the surface, each wall rose soundlessly along its runners and stayed upraised until similarly directed to descend. In the bright sunlight, twelve walls slid up and down, up and down, the elves standing on one another's shoulders and stretching tippytoe to maneuver them.

Speculation ran rampant. Had Santa slipped into magic time and built them? He had, after all, built the cozy hut in the woods far off behind the elves' quarters for reasons none of them could quite recall, though later it had served as a honeymoon retreat for Santa and his wives.

Who else could have done this? Rachel had no idea, and Anya, joining them from the cottage, came up blank as well.

Then Ernst, a thin-fingered button sewer with needle eyes and a nimble wit, raised a piping shout: "Here come Wendy and Santa, back from their walk. I bet they'll know."

And they swarmed off to accost the returning pair.

Santa and Wendy had chattered nonstop on their way home, bright with ideas as to how best to nudge those steeped in bigotry back onto long-abandoned paths of righteousness.

Through a copse of trees, they caught glimpses of the bedroom replicas and the buzzing multitude poking and probing at them. And when the elves saw them approaching and ran to meet them, Santa's excitement redoubled.

Raising his hands as though to ward off an attack, he said with a laugh, "All in good time, lads. Talk to Wendy, why don't you? It's her doing." Then he slipped through the crowd to kiss Anya and Rachel, encircle their waists, and draw them aside. Wendy began, "You're not going to believe this," at which the elves burst into babble.

Santa tuned them out. "Oh my darlings," he confided, "we were visited by an angel, the archangel Michael, to be precise."

Rachel put a hand to her face.

"Land sakes, Claus," said Anya, "is it about your prayers?"

"It is indeed." He repeated Michael's every word, relating what stance he took, what expressions passed over his face, how unbearably beautiful he had been, how utterly sad and joyful they grew as the archangel left them. "But now I'd better address the troops."

They returned to the buzzing throng about Wendy, who was laughing and clapping her hands and conveying, by mimicked word and gesture, the task the archangel had charged them with.

Santa bounded onto the central platform, where the sunlight struck bright and bold. "Friends, colleagues, brothers," said he. "We have been blessed yet again by the Holiest of Holies. There are no guarantees in this business of salvation. But we will do our utmost to save the life of Jamie Stratton, a wonderful nine-year-old, gifted, thoughtful, as gentle and generous as one could wish. We shall bend all of our persuasive powers toward convincing four mortals to awaken, in an area where they wander blinded, bewildered, and astray, to the divine generosity that once burned bright at the hearth-center of their souls. They slumber, but shall be roused. They hurt the sinned against, but shall themselves be healed. They dare to denigrate God's rich and varied creation, but soon they shall exalt it, they shall revel in it, they shall burst the bonds of wretched habit and form new behaviors, boldly challenging the waywardness of similarly straying mortals."

Though the elves cheered often as he spoke, Santa sensed a kind of disquiet, or discomfort, perhaps even disunity among them. Not of course about sexual orientation. There wasn't a prejudicial bone in their bodies. But something was in the air. Should he probe? Best not. Whatever it was, they would sort it out on their own. They always did. It always proved to be something trivial, blown out of proportion and quickly faded. Barging in might only fan the flames.

"What I have stated," he went on, "is our grand goal, mine and Wendy's. Aim high and your arrow hits a target far more distant than if your bow arm declines at a more modest angle. Or as Holy Scripture says, whatever your hand finds to do, do it with all your might.

"The bedroom behind me belongs to Matt Beluzzo, a twelve-year-old whose life is a war zone and who bullies children who have it better than he. Him shall we first visit. On my right is Jamie's parents' bedroom, on my left that of Ty Taylor, a preacher whose prejudicial lenses distort and discolor the truths at the heart of the gospel he pretends to preach.

"Fritz, you and your bunkmates are to head up a workforce to decorate and make magical these replicas, so that our visits carry more weight than our poor words can. Wendy and I will confer with you, in the days ahead, as to how we'd like them bedecked at each visit."

Fritz, red-haired, gap-toothed, and ageless, beamed.

"But be inventive. Trust your creative instincts. Remember, all of you: We dedicate ourselves to saving the life of a good little boy. The delivery of Christmas cheer has always been our primary concern. This one small task, granted us by God himself, is a natural extension of that concern. Never forgetting to honor those we seek to persuade, we shall nonetheless not dilute our efforts to render more Christlike their view of their fellow man."

Santa sawed the air as he spoke, so firm were his convictions. But truth to tell, this venture into grown-up territory frightened him, and now he brought his rhetoric down a notch. "Dear friends, let me confide in you. I much prefer making good little boys and girls happy. Adults, particularly the most egregiously fallen ones, so sophisticated and subtle in the mental prisons they construct for themselves, have ever been beyond the pale. I don't like observing them. I don't like thinking about them. I would much prefer a world without them.

"But for Jamie Stratton, I will venture outside my comfort zone. With gusto shall I confront his tormentors. And, God willing, Wendy and I will change a few minds, remove blinders from their eyes, and restore our visitants' childlike grace this Thanksgiving Eve."

Seeing the smile on his daughter's face, Santa fell in love with her all over again.

"We must never forget that these grown-ups and the bully boy were once innocent babes not yet tangled in the prejudices of their elders. As I meet them, the image of their prelapsarian selves I shall strive to keep before me always.

"For we are not about simply saving Jamie Stratton. We are about saving these four as well. Be with me in this, my brothers. Set aside all petty bickering, embracing the warm glow of magic time and crafting the perfect environments for persuasion. This I ask of you, as you love me, as you love Wendy, as you honor your own generous natures."

Santa ending on a resounding note, the elves rushed him and heaved him heavenward, passing him along, wrestling him to the snow, and tickling him without mercy, as they did each Christmas morning. And he threw off gales of laughter and pleaded for them to stop, while flocks of green caps jingled skyward in the crisp morning air.

But speeches punch up one's resolve in the ringingest tones of which one is capable, setting aside for the moment whatever doubts might weaken that resolve.

Could he do it? Could he truly encounter grown-ups, those abundantly judgmental souls whose words were empty, whose hearts had shriveled into black fists, whose minds were blighted with canker and cant? These were creatures that lived in a hell of their own making. Could he really harrow the hell of even *one* such being, bringing him or her out of those blasted circles into the divine light of heaven on earth?

He had no idea.

But he would try.

If he failed, he would fail grandly.

This he vowed as his jelly-bowl belly bounced, and his cherry cheeks shook from his helpers' good-humored roughhouse, and the day shone grand and glorious all about them.

9.
A BULLY SHAKEN TO THE CORE

MATT BELUZZO FELL exhausted into bed.

Turkeys on classroom walls. Cartoon pilgrims with toothless grins and blunderbusses. And a steaming pile of crap, couched in cautiously non-denominational terms, about being thankful for one's lot in life. Fat chance of that. His old man in the slammer, Mom boozing it up, stoking her lungs with cancer, stern-faced teachers cramping his style, holding him back for a second try at sixth grade with eleven-year-old pipsqueaks. Yeah, he had plenty to be thankful for.

Dirty clothes were strewn everywhere. Tomorrow he would yell at Mom to get her act together, haul her bones out of bed, and wash them. Damned if *he'd* do it. Women's work. Shirts had three good days in 'em tops, bring his sweat smell into homeroom, stink up Whittier Elementary something fierce. But his underwear was starting to itch.

He'd deal with that tomorrow.

Day off. Small favors.

He slept fitfully, in and out of dreams, dead to the world, then waking to the moonlit bedroom with its slump-ugly dresser, a squeaky-hinged closet, a grimy window stuck an inch open, winter or summer, then back to sleep.

Somewhere in there, something changed.

There was a scent of...of baby oil, or ocean air. Or was it Mom before she'd gone blowsy and doused herself with cheap perfume? Whatever it was made Matt calm and sad and glad all at the same time. When he opened his eyes, someone had lit a candle. Several, actually, poking up everywhere he looked. Matt sat up, gawked at his surroundings, and released a breath he hadn't realized he was holding.

His bedroom, bathed in candle flame and some peculiar light, soft and coppery, was still the same room, yet it wasn't at all. The stuck window had been flung wide, but the air was toasty warm, not the late November chill outside. The battleship gray walls had been painted a light rose color, girly stuff but Matt didn't mind. His strewn clothing had been replaced by a plush, rich-bitch carpet, white like poodles, that looked as if, were he to leap off the bed, he'd sink in up to his waist. The mattress had misplaced its lumps and poking springs, the blankets were fresh, unpilled, and abundant with stuffing. I must be dreaming, he thought. Yet no dream had ever felt so real.

Then Santa Claus, tall and chubby, a wide grin blooming out of his beard, materialized at the foot of the bed. Beside him stood a little girl in a green dress, her face wise and kind, her eyes twinkling. And Matt *knew* he was dreaming.

"Huh," he said, a gut punch of awe and wonder.

"Hello, Matt," said Santa.

Matt sobbed at the beauty of his name.

"That's right. Adjust. Take your time. You're not dreaming, by the way. This is my stepdaughter Wendy."

"I didn't know you had one," he managed, sounding as if he'd had the stuffing punched out of him.

"Hi, Matt," said the girl. Her voice, high-pitched and loving, made his throat choke up anew.

"Hi," he said.

Santa came around the side of the bed, sat close by, and pulled Wendy onto his lap. "Matt," he said, "can you guess why we've come?"

In his heart, he knew. But he pushed the answer away. He played dumb so often, he believed he *was* dumb. That tactic had worked in the past to protect him, to keep away the pain of feeling anything. He shook his head, wanting these fantastically lovely creatures to go away, even as he wished they would stay forever.

Santa laughed. "Let's see if you can figure it out. I'll give you a hint. You're a naughty boy. And if you don't straighten up, you'll only get naughtier. But your future's for our second visit."

They would be coming back. Two visits.

With the sweep of Santa's hand, the bed lurched forward without moving an inch. Matt's view of the room vanished, or more precisely, his surroundings receded and his old man, pacing his jail cell, came into view.

"It's him," said Matt, not concealing his distaste. As he said it, the sounds and smells of the prison arose. Harsh light gleamed on the bars and the stainless-steel toilet and sink. But what astonished Matt was that he could hear his father's thoughts. He touched the old man's mind, a rambling blither of resentments and dumb, dull rounds of pain and rage and sorrow, and a steel-plated resistance to regret.

"It's him all right," said Santa. "Pete Beluzzo, grown up and gone bad. His smile at three months was just like yours at the same age. But his parents didn't want him and they let him know that, by looks first, then by word and deed. Pete wasn't about to deprive his son, when he had one, of that gift. Take a look at him, Matt. Tell me what you think of him."

Matt's first impulse was to blast the grizzly old bastard with curses. You could heap blame on him all day long and barely cover the bases: smacking his mom around, backhanding Matt across the face and taking him down a whole lot of pegs, the whiskey, the dead-eyed buddies he brought home for beer and football, his open carousing with barfly bitches, and finally his botched attempt at armed robbery.

But having Santa Claus there, and the little girl, changed all that. "He's connected to me, isn't he?"

"Yes, and you to him."

"I think...he's sad. His mind runs in such tiny circles. He could have been, I don't know, magnificent. But he's small. A bunch of choices, one day at a time, brought him down. He let every else's view of him tell him who he was." From bed to toilet to bed his dad paced, muttering at the guards, at the lowlifes around him, sucking death into his lungs from a Marlboro, running his hand over stubble.

At Santa's gesture, the bedroom loomed back up to shut out the prison cell. "Remember him. Remember how you felt about him. Now, Matt, before I show you a certain child, let me tell you something."

Santa whispered into his daughter's ear, and she said, "Yes, of course it's okay, Daddy."

Then he said, "I've got to confess, I dreaded visiting you, Matt. I thought to myself, Matt Beluzzo is a bad boy on his way to becoming a worse grown-up. But now that we're here, I see, under the rottenness you've walled yourself behind, a far better Matt languishing. He pines for life. I hope you'll give it to him."

Santa's words made Matt feel empty but not put down at all.

Again Santa gestured. A kid was riding his bike in the sunlight. "Now *this* is the sort of boy you could be. But I'm not showing you him for that reason."

Matt had never seen this kid before, but the neighborhood seemed familiar.

"Another part of Colorado Springs. The boy's name is Terry Samuelson. He's ten." Matt's bed felt as if it were on wheels, tracking the boy's bike. As his tires crunched crisp leaves on the streets and sidewalks, the kid grinned ear to ear. He would pedal, stand tall, then crouch and pedal some more. Matt thought he must be some goody-twoshoes, a smart little face on him, well treated, and Matt began to resent him. Then night fell, the bed stopped moving, and the bedroom rose again before him. "What's with the runt?"

"You'll see him again in other visits."

More than two visits, thought Matt. He glanced at the clock. The hands hadn't moved. "Some kids have all the luck," he muttered.

"Matt," said Santa, "some kids make their own luck."

That choked Matt up. But Santa raised a finger. "No self-pity." He wasn't blaming Matt. He was only observing, cutting through the crap. That same finger swept beyond the bed. "Yesterday at school."

Before them clustered bunches of kids in the playground, shouting at something. For a moment, Matt was disoriented. Then he recognized them and the sequence of taunts. "Lunchtime." He caught a glimpse of the two boys tussling on the ground. "Hey, that's me." Seeing himself was freak city, like when you passed a store window and caught your reflection and it didn't look like you at all. "I'm pounding the crap out of that sissy boy. He's nothing but a loser wimp." As he watched himself smack the kid, he felt ashamed before Santa, even as he thrilled to the relived surge of power. "I've got him on the ropes."

"He's no match for you," said Wendy.

"Right," he said. Then softer: "Right."

Matt felt the kid's fear as if it were his own. A second shove, harder, and the fear billowed. The kid's mewling protests gave way to calls of "Sissy!" and "Way to go, Matt! Beat him to a pulp!"

Then a teacher barged in, as Matt scrambled to pin the kid to the ground. An army buzz-cut grown-up, Mr. Harvey, grabbed Matt's arm, shook him, hustled him out of the circle, you kids break it up, the fight's over; Beluzzo, you're coming to the principal's office. Stupid teacher's face barked, I'm better than you. Matt wanted to kick him in the nuts.

"Meddling bastard," he said.

Santa flared, which made Matt feel terrible. "He's protecting a powerless kid who never did you any harm." Wendy touched Santa's arm and he backed off. "This is very hard for me," he said, not looking at Matt. "Look, and learn."

Now Matt saw himself sitting in front of Principal Longsworth, who was drilling those pastry-punched beady eyes into him, making the back of Matt's neck burn. "You called him a sissy? Well, *you're* the sissy, you little brat, picking on safe targets. You bullied that boy. You will not—you hear me?—you will not bully anyone as long as I'm principal of this school. You try this crap one more time and you're history. You got me? Do you? Answer me."

The heat at the back of Matt's neck raged fierce again. But now he could hear Mr. Longsworth's thoughts. He understood what the glint in his eyes meant. "Damned sissies," the principal was thinking. "Closeted faggots bring it on themselves."

"Hey, Santa, he's just like me, only he's pretending not to be." Then, noting Santa's alarm: "He's got problems too, hasn't he?"

"That's right, Matt. Sometimes grown-ups do the right thing for the wrong reasons." Santa lifted Wendy to the floor and stood up. "Sleep now. We'll be back."

"But wait, I—"

Santa put a finger to the side of his nose, gave a tortured wink, and was gone. Gone too the improvements in the bedroom, the paint job, the restored dresser which slumped there as ugly as ever with its stuck drawers and missing knobs. Gone the inviting aromas and the warmth and the candles and the coppery light.

But drowsiness drew Matt away from disappointment, down into the strangest dreamscape he had ever known.

10.
DOGMA ERODES A FAMILY

PART WAY INTO HER ROUNDS that same Thanksgiving Eve, the Tooth Fairy stopped to sniff the air. She had just harvested a molar from beneath Missy Wenner's pillow in Boise and left a smattering of dimes. Benign in the bedroom she was, but furious as soon as she left. Zeus's suppression of her anger made it flair with greater ferocity when she was free of his restraint.

But as she flew from the Wenner home to the Carters across town, she paused, sniffed, and sensed at once that Pan and his whiny little girl were out of their domain. They had dropped in on a mortal child off-season, some older boy, a bully with a prominent place on Pan's naughty list.

"Gronk," she called.

On her island, Gronk raised his head in mid-snore, instantly awake. His brothers slept on. Waves lapped at their bodies, draping ribbons of seaweed over hairless heads, over shoulders and buttocks, then drawing back into the sea. Apart from them, bruised black and blue from his latest beating, Chuff whimpered in his sleep.

Into magic time and up through cloud cover, Gronk bumblebee'd, homing in on his mother's scent. Tens of thousands of miles flew by in an instant and there she was, hovering above stuck traffic. Moonlight bathed her nakedness, painting blood-flecked highlights on her necklace of teeth.

"The goat god," she said, "has left his lair and roams the earth, his brat in tow."

"But he...but Christmas is—"

"That's why I summoned you, dolt. They dropped in on a twelve-year-old in Colorado Springs. Now they're headed for another home there. Sniff them out. Observe them. Find out what's up and report back at once, no matter where I am."

"Are you still upset about Santa's having jilted—?"

The Tooth Fairy shot over to him in fury and smacked his face so hard she drew blood. "Always. The fat fuck threw me over for his bag of a wife and that McGinnis whore. Thanks to Zeus's meddling, he's denying the best part of himself. I won't have it. What's the randy old satyr doing away from the North Pole? Whatever it is, we're going to put a stop to it. We'll crush the goatish giftgiver. We'll smash to smithereens his happy little community. Now get moving."

"But I—"

"Go!" She grabbed a shoulder and buttock and spun him high and far away in the direction of Colorado. Gronk zoomed off, his nostrils flaring to catch Santa's mistletoe and candy cane scent.

Gronk and his brothers worked their Christmas mayhem beneath a cloak of invisibility. This cloak Gronk now donned as Santa's sleigh touched down before a home not three miles from the Garden of the Gods. He had never seen Santa and Wendy and the sleigh and the entire team of reindeer before. They took his breath away.

When the pair alighted, Gronk shook off his awe and sped after them through the locked door and up the stairs.

They're on a mission, thought Gronk. Mom'll disrupt it. She calls him Pan and I guess that's who he is, but I sure don't see it.

Through a closed door they passed, all three. As they crossed the threshold, the bedroom shed its darkness to take on glow and wonder. At once there appeared strews of ivy, a host of ancient lanterns casting parchment light into every corner, and a magnificent diamond-studded bedspread surging up along the bed to the chins of the slumbering couple, who stirred and blinked and sat up in astonished disbelief.

Gronk hunkered down on the dresser, intently watching, awaiting his chance to whisper nasty notions in their ears.

Kathy Stratton instantly awoke. She was always a little anxious about burglars, but the warmth and wonder that infused the bedroom disarmed her. Her husband blinked beside her, sitting up and wiping away sleepy dirt with a couple of fingers. "What's—?"

"Look, Walter," she said, "it's Santa Claus." She knew at once that this was no dressed-up man but the real thing. "And a delightful little girl."

"Hello, Kathy," said Santa. "Meet my daughter Wendy."

Santa's voice thrilled her in ways that seemed a teeny bit, well, sinful.

"Hello," said Wendy. "I've met your son."

"Kurt?" asked Walter, wild-haired in his pajamas.

"Nope, Jamie."

Kathy panicked. "There's nothing wrong with him?"

Santa laughed. "Not at all." Then: "Not for a long time."

Her alarm increased. "But eventually?"

"We'll come to that. Jamie's well-being depends in large part on the two of you. Adjustments must be made." She sensed that Santa was less than comfortable around them and it made her feel slightly out of sorts. "But first, let me show you scenes from the day just past."

The bedroom fell away.

"Jeepers," said Walter. As well he might, for they were sitting up with a magnificent bedspread draped over their laps, watching Walter at the sports bar he and his colleagues frequented after work. "That's me and Joe Flynn, belting down a few beers. Joe's our support guy."

Their mouths moved soundlessly.

"Wait," said Kathy. "Isn't he...?" Kathy could see deeper than normal. Her husband there at the bar, all sorts of thoughts and impulses flitting through his mind, lay open to her. And his co-worker, a nice young man. But what was that beneath the façade?

"You're telling a joke. Do you remember it?"

"I joke a lot," said Walter. "It could have been anything."

"I think you know which one it was."

"Sure," he confessed. "The one about the two...the two gay guys walking into a bar and ordering a couple of screwdrivers."

Walter laughed silently and slapped Joe on the back.

Joe laughed too.

"Listen to what you said next," said Santa, flicking a finger to turn up the gain.

"Good old Walter can spot 'em a mile away," said the Walter at the bar, tapping his temple twice. "Queers're different from us regular guys. You know, I don't get it. They're pervs and proud of it, no shame at all. They used to hang their heads. Nowadays, the media laps it up and shoves it down our throats. It's enough to make you gag."

Santa muted the conversation.

"I must be blind," said Walter.

"We're seeing deeper, I think," Kathy said.

"Joe's a homo, and I'm a chump. But they say alcoholics hide it too, even from their friends. And smokers use breath mints."

The bedroom rushed up around them. Kathy patted Walter on the back. "Calm down, honey." Then to Santa: "Is this proper for your little girl? Why show us this anyway?"

In reply, Santa gestured and Kathy's workplace came into view. The dyke from down the hall had dropped by for feedback on an article she had written, Jane Miller, her hair that shocking short crop of red that alerted other lezzies to her propensities. Jane was bold and shameless. She pressed every wrong button.

Kathy stiffened. "Are you suggesting, you are, aren't you, that I should accept this creature—who does unspeakable things with others of her ilk—as normal?" She was having a hard time. Here stood this miraculous elf, the epitome of goodness, long associated with the season of her Savior's birth, confronting her with one of the most distasteful elements of the secular world.

"Take a closer look," said Santa.

She did. And Jane Miller's thoughts and impulses too were open to her. Anticipation of being with the boyfriend she lived with. Her complete lack of religious feeling, yet a fundamental decency at her core. A view of life Kathy could not parse.

"Why," said Kathy, "she isn't a lesbian at all. She's one of us. But then why does she make herself look so...so spartan? I've been narrow, haven't I? I shouldn't be so quick to judge or assume."

"Don't judge," said Santa. "Don't assume at all." The frown marks about her mouth were the last things Kathy saw as the work scene faded. "Simply love. It's what Christ commanded."

"You know, Santa," said Walter, "I'm starting to notice a thread in what you're showing us. All this homo stuff. Listen, we're just a normal family living day by day. I'm a good provider. We're active in our church. We have two great kids. Kurt's a killer athlete. And Jamie...well, Jamie excels at school. You're trying to make us change, aren't you? But why should we? These people have no right to special privileges. They ought to crawl back inside the closet, cover themselves in shame, and rein in their ungodly tendencies. But whatever they do, it has nothing to do with us. We're upstanding Christians, we pick our friends carefully, and we've chosen to lead a life of righteousness. What more can be asked of us?"

As Walter spoke, Kathy saw that Santa was fighting to keep from interrupting. Then he calmed himself, came over to Walter, put a hand on his shoulder, and said softly, "Behold your sons."

Once more the bedroom dissolved, and before them arose her boys' bedroom. There lay Kurt, a soccer star at thirteen, his father's pride and joy. Near him slept his more fragile, more studious brother Jamie, only eight.

But Kathy saw more deeply into them than ever before.

She had always marveled at the differences between them. Kurt was wild and unbounded, good but not great in his studies, a prankish humor about him, always looking years older than his age, a cut-up at Bible camp, starting to show an interest in girls but respectful toward them. She and Walter had been at pains to keep him away from the filth in movie theaters and the jungle noise that blared from car radios.

Then she peered into Jamie, her mild boy, clinging to her much longer than Kurt as a toddler. Jamie was more intent, more serious, disliking physical activity. He had gravitated toward music, the good kind, classical and uplifting musicals from the past that taught moral lessons. She was struck by his determined devotion to the violin, a driving impulse in him even more than she had realized. But something else shocked her to the heart. "He's eight years old," she said, "how can he be...no, he can't be."

"Who touched him?" asked Walter. "Tell me who it was. I'll kill the son of a bitch."

"No one touched him," said Santa.

How can Santa be so persuasive, thought Kathy, so impatient, so unlike the Santa Claus I imagined as a child, yet so much like him? "My body could not have produced...it's monstrous...that's my child. Jamie will not dishonor God with...." She went light in the head. "He *can't* be that way. I refuse to believe it."

"No son of mine," said her husband, "goes in for that kind of stuff. He's a red-blooded American boy. We've brought him up right. You're deceiving us with sick fantasies."

But Kathy knew it wasn't so. The hint of pleading in her husband's voice told her he didn't believe it himself. "He can resist the call of this addiction," she said. "The Good Lord will make him strong. You're here as a gift from God to alert us, to make us vigilant. Jamie needs a little tough love is all. We'll keep him from temptation. Kurt's safe, but Jamie requires a firm hand."

The little girl looked distraught. "But that's not—"

"Can't you see?" said Santa. "It's inborn. It's natural."

"It's perverse," said Walter.

66

"We're all sinners in the eyes of God," said Kathy, feeling more assured. "But we can keep ourselves from the opportunity for sin. I always thought it was recruitment. I still do, when it comes to *acting* sinful. Sinners support each other in the illusion that what they do is no sin. This weakness, this being drawn to temptation, is part of Jamie. I thank you both. And I thank the Lord for sending you. We'll be vigilant from now on. We won't let the gay agenda seduce him."

"Music is out," said Walter.

"Yes. No more violin. We'll monitor his listening. There are questionable composers. Tchaikovsky, Bernstein, I'll read up."

"Enough!" said Santa. His upset brought terror to Kathy's heart. "You don't see."

"We don't?" said Walter.

"No, I—"

Wendy touched Santa's arm. "Maybe we should let them—"

"Yes, you're right. Rest. We'll be back. The sharing of dreams may achieve what we cannot."

Before Kathy could probe further, Santa waved a hand and he and Wendy were gone, the room stripped of greenery and lamplight in an instant.

"What the heck just happened?" asked Walter, his voice weakening into sleep as he reached the last word.

Kathy barely managed to parse what he said before she too fell asleep.

11.
A SPELLBINDER'S SPELL UNRAVELS

GRONK FOLLOWED THEM OUT OF MAGIC TIME and down the stairs. Santa tore through the house in high dudgeon, out the front door, and off the porch, Wendy hurrying to keep up. Bounding into his sleigh and taking up the reins, he paused an instant for Wendy to leap in before leather smacked his team's idle haunches and he shouted, "Away!"

Were it not for that pause, Gronk would have missed the rising runners. As it was, he clung now, his grip precarious, to the black lacquered curve of the sleigh-back as they jostled and rose.

"I've never seen such strayward adults in my life."

"It's habit," said Wendy. "Deeply engrained modes of thought. Undoing them won't be easy."

Santa again slapped rein to haunch and cracked his whip. "By God, they'll shut that boy down before they'll honor who he is! Alcoholism indeed. I tell you, Wendy girl, I'm out of my league. You see why I like children? They sparkle with natural humility and purity and wide-eyed wonder. The good ones anyway, and that's who I'm best with. Their minds flex. They can lay aside one set of goggles and try on another, quick as a wink. Why, even that bully, with his wretched parents and naughty friends, shows more flexibility than these damned Strattons."

Though Gronk was devilishly pleased at Santa's difficulties and knew his mother would take great delight in them too, he marveled at how upset Santa was. Wendy did as well, judging from the way she let his tempest blow over her.

"If I could only tear their eyes out and shove in a fresh pair," he continued. "Cultural brainwashing, Wendy, that's what we're seeing. They're doomed, all of them. There simply aren't enough meditators, and Buddhists, and window washers among them. How can we possibly persuade such people that what they're seeing is not only normal but blessed by God? And, oh my heavens, the preacher's bound to be worse, accepting the lies dunned into his noggin at seminary, then blithering on and on about them from the pulpit for thirty years."

"Not to mention his flock!

"You saw the Strattons. They're mostly good people, polite and kind. But they hold these warped views on certain issues, views that compromise their integrity-based lives. They do their best to act out of righteousness, but their lockstep allegiance to institutionalized nonsense damns them to their own hell! How does one even *begin* to change that?"

"Lead with the heart," said the little girl calmly, "and the mind will follow."

Santa seemed not to hear her. "I can't play the power card. I can't say, I'm from God, he's right, you're wrong. They've got to see the big picture and embrace it freely, or it won't stick. How does one undo years of habit? Let mortals sneak past nine years old and they're lost!"

"I'm seventeen, Daddy."

"Yes, but you're nine at heart. You've kept your connection to childhood. They've strayed a ba-zillion miles from it. How do we get them back? It's hopeless."

"Daddy," said Wendy, "we've still got a bunch more visits. And there's the dreamscape, don't forget that."

Gronk watched Santa loft his great head to renew his rant. Then he calmed. A smile peeked out of his whiskers. "You're right. Our visitants will be sharing a dreamscape. They'll gather together over the lessons we've taught them." Then he grew agitated again. "Some lessons! What guarantee is there that they won't go further off the rails? That they won't sink deeper into prejudice and make things worse, years earlier, for Jamie?"

"We've got to have faith," insisted Wendy. "You know what I love most about you, Daddy? You overflow with generosity. It's your stock in trade. When you get so angry, you frighten me. It means you've given up before you even try. Be more generous toward yourself, that's my advice. You can do it. We can both do it. Michael wouldn't have appeared to us if that weren't so. We haven't even seen the preacher yet. Maybe our visit will be, I don't know, this huge miracle for him, the blinding light on his road to Damascus. Our mission has the backing of God himself. That's going to count for much with Ty Taylor. And if we can persuade *him,* why he'll go into the dreamscape with all sorts of truly righteous ammunition to turn Jamie's parents around. He's their pastor. Please don't give up hope, Daddy. It's too early in the game for that."

The girl's eyes glistened. Gronk could have leaned forward and licked the tears off her cheeks. But he dared not do that. No, he would observe their third visit, getting as close as he could to the next mortal, as he had with the other three. Again would he offer subliminal suggestions to magnify the mortals' unspoken fears and stoke their naughtiest impulses.

The sleigh shifted abruptly downward. Gronk's grip failed and he fell off behind it. Down toward a house on the south side arrowed the sleigh, Gronk following in hot pursuit.

Earlier that day, having polished the text of his Thanksgiving Day sermon, Ty Taylor washed and ironed his pajamas, the monogrammed ones Alison had given him the Christmas before she died, and folded them neatly into his dresser drawer. He prided himself on keeping the house spotless. *Men sana in corpore sano;* indeed, a clean house *encouraged* a cleanliness of body, mind, and spirit which truly went hand-in-hand with godliness. A thorough cleansing would correct so many of society's ills. The minds of sinners, even the faithful, were so cluttered with secular trash, it was difficult to reach them. He needed a God-sized broom and a divine mandate to sweep their lives clean. The chore was Herculean. For not only were the faithful fallen, but those in Satan's iron grip were *deeply* fallen. The worst were defiant in their hellish ways, lambs bleating from the satanic sheepcote as though they roared like lions ramping free and proud.

Keeping his house immaculate allowed Ty to focus on these things, to gird his loins against the foe, keeping himself holy, then banding together with other worthy believers to beat back on all fronts the rising tides of secularism. The Almighty had his ways, which were mysterious indeed. Even so, the righteous were not to question them, but be God's soldiers with every breath granted them. This special season brought much to be thankful for. Topping Ty's list were the strength and stamina to hold Christ's banner high and press boldly into the moral fray.

He showered and toweled himself dry. Those same pajamas he took from the well-oiled drawer to cover himself. Placing his slippers just so by his bedside, he set his glasses neatly on his night stand, slid beneath the crisp sheets and comforter, closed his eyelids to ask

God's forgiveness and to bless Alison and a list of recently deceased, grieving, or ailing parishioners, and fell asleep.

Only to find himself, moments later, fumbling awake.

"Hello, Ty," said a male voice he had never heard, but knew at once. "Hi, Mister Taylor," echoed a girlish voice in equally astounding tones.

"Marauders," said Ty, slurry with dream. He groped for his glasses. "I should be afraid. But I feel such joy in your presence. Let me look at you. Dear God in heaven, I'm insane out of my head. And oh my, the scent of pine is overwhelming."

"Ty," said one who could not be, but was indeed, Santa Claus, "this is Wendy, my stepdaughter. We're here for the first of three visits tonight, to open up new vistas for you."

"I must be dreaming." He put a hand to his face. His heart pounded. "This can't be good for me. But it's marvelous! You're a godsend. Literally. Am I right?"

Santa said yes to that. But Ty saw that he had no interest in dwelling on his connection with God. The girl chimed in, "To be more exact, the archangel Michael sent us."

"Did he, dear?" said Ty, delighted.

"Whether Michael or God himself," said Santa, sweeping a hand past the baseboard of Ty's bed, "we're here to show you some of your flock."

The bedroom walls fell away, and there before him sat the Stupplebeens at their breakfast table, egg-encrusted plates set aside, newspaper sections snapped open over coffee.

"My heavens, it's George and Vera. They're very righteous, very generous, double tithers, and always deeply engaged by my sermons."

"Listen," said Santa.

And the old couple's words came bell-clear to Ty's ears. George smacked the newspaper. "The queer boys and cross-dressers are pushing their agenda again. Another bleeding heart corporation's added benefits for so-called domestic partners."

"They'll roast in hell," said Vera. "Which company is it this time?" George told her.

"All right, we won't spend a penny on their products ever again. Find out who the CEO is. I'll singe his cowardly ears with a few choice words."

"Money's all they understand," said George. "Homo's are rich.

No kids, no responsibilities. But us Christians are richer. We'll throw enough money at this to drive them back into the closet where they belong."

"In hell paying for the sins of the flesh is where they belong."

Santa cut the sound off.

"Their faces are so...ugly," said Ty in astonishment. "Dripping with hatred. That's not the way they are with me."

The Stupplebeens faded and Santa brought up Bill and Susie Franklin, trading anti-gay barbs as they window-shopped in Manitou Springs. Then Freddie Collins sitting on a park bench sharing vicious jibes with his cairn terrier about a lesbian couple passing by. Ty was astonished. "But Freddie's eyes glow with such joy as he shakes my hand at the church door. The Franklins too. Their words hold nothing but praise to the Lord."

"People are different in their private lives," said Santa. "But let's observe them in a more public setting."

Before Ty's bed arose a view of himself preaching. In the near pews sat Freddie Collins and the Franklins and Stupplebeens. But Ty saw silken ribbons of connection between his heart and theirs, ribbons that shimmered at his words. "Woe unto the sodomites," he thundered. Last Sunday's sermon. "For in hellfire more intense than any fireball, eternally refueled by the ferocity of their sins on earth, shall the sodomites burn. They must turn from their wicked ways, my friends. This bound guidebook from God himself, this Holy Scripture whose text is eternally fixed, condemns them for what they do. The Bible verses are incontrovertible. Oh, they do their damnedest to minimize them, do they not? Or pervert their meanings, just as they pervert and pollute and befoul and besmirch the bodies the good Lord has given them to sing his praises with. They even have the temerity—dear God, are there no limits—to found so-called Christian churches of their own. How hooded are their eyes? How deaf their ears? As deaf as demons. As hooded as hawks."

Ty thrilled at his delivery. Yet what he saw moving along the connecting ribbons, and the overheard thoughts of those hanging on his every word, gave him pause. They were filled with pride at not being among those who would burn in hell. They hated the sodomites, or rather the image he himself had painted. And for all his golden words, for all his carefully wrought phrases, the one message he saw snaking along those ribbons into their hearts was, "Hate queers."

72

"But I don't understand," he said. "What I'm telling them is the gospel truth."

The little girl said, "No it isn't, Mister Taylor."

"Child," he said, "Leviticus tells us—"

"You shall not," said Santa, blushing with anger, "befoul my daughter's ears with your fixation on questionable passages from the Old Testament, draping your own prejudice in sanctimony, exalting a man-made collection of writings over the self-evident truth of God's love for all he has created."

"But I—"

"Look at yourself, flailing your arms and contorting your face. You're no better than a showman, and worse than many, because you hawk poison to the soul. Of all the sects you could have embraced, this is the one you chose. Behold the young."

And Ty saw thin ribbons to the children, some very young indeed, most of them half listening or sighing in boredom. But even these his ribbons of judgment entered. Here sat Cully Harmon and his anorexic mother; there the Pine twins, Gayle and Tara, between their parents.

"We'll see them again on our next visit, older."

Wendy touched his sleeve. "Now show Mister Taylor...you know."

With a flick of Santa's finger, Ty's entire congregation came into view. But it seemed as if two bright lights shone in varying mixes upon them, a red light indicating attraction to their own gender; a blue, attraction to the opposite. While most of his flock were bathed in varying shades of blue, many were tinged pink or red, and some were completely red, though they expended much mental activity in denying it. Hank Febinger, sitting beside his wife of sixty years, was a bright cherry-red. A babe in arms, as well; a third-grader named Jamie Stratton; and Bessie Pullman, a middle-aged spinster who had joined the church last week.

But what most startled Ty was the color of his own body as he stood at the pulpit, bright blue broken up by intense patches of red, perhaps twenty percent of the whole. It would explain his youthful uncertainties, at seminary especially, about such matters.

"So that old devil Kinsey had it right after all."

"Yes," said Santa. "A scale of attraction."

"But that doesn't abrogate God's word."

The elf took umbrage at that.

"Daddy!" Wendy grabbed her father's upraised arm.

73

"In fact it confirms it," said Ty. "Are you threatening me? God's true emissary would not threaten."

Blood pounded in Ty's temples as the enraged creature hovered over him, his eyes ablaze with intolerance. That this immortal elf could, at any instant, strike him dead he had no doubt. Jacob had wrestled with an angel. Perhaps such a death would be his fate.

Santa contained his rage. "I'm all right. I'm fine."

"The alcoholic is born so, yet he learns—"

"Enough!" said Santa. "I ought to smite you on the spot. But I'll not do that. I won't. Wendy, come. You, sleep, little Ty all grown up. You haven't seen the last of us."

"God has sent you as a trial, to test my resolve to uphold his word, no matter what."

"Ah," said Santa, taking a swipe at Ty's face. And he was gone, him and the girl and the pine boughs and their marvelous scent. The bedroom plunged abruptly into darkness, Ty's tight blinds shutting out the least hint of moonlight.

Ty marveled then, but somnolence drained the life from him and he slipped at once into the land of dreams.

12.

FRIENDS REFORM,
FOES REGROUP

AT THE NORTH POLE, FRITZ, HERBERT, and two dozen others worked on the Beluzzo replica, adding ornate carvings to the oak drawers of a replacement dresser and four thick turned bedposts where Matt's actual bed had none. They arced back the roof on its hinges so that snowdrifts could be strategically built up in scatterings about the bedroom, enough to make an impact without hindering their work.

Ordinarily, they would have been a happy crew, trading quips and pitching in wherever extra hands were needed. Not so now. For Gregor had kept up the pressure. His rants at the Chapel continued and grew more condemnatory. He had gone so far as to have a centrally situated bed, with a thin mattress and no posts to obscure his view, built in the dormitory, abandoning on nights unpredictable his bed in the stables to sleep among them.

Some time during the night he would appear. You could never tell when, but you could always be sure he would be gone in the morning, and no one had ever seen him shut his eyes or put on a nightshirt. Always the eagle eye. If you dared glance toward his bed, Gregor would be staring back at you, his fierce glower accusing you of looking his way because you were about to sneak a fingertip up your nostril.

And sometimes that was so.

It was most unsettling.

What had been a harmless, unconscious habit became for many an obsession. Their thoughts turned continually to the nose and the finger, to observing the noses and fingers of their brothers, wondering if they had come into satisfying contact when Gregor or his spies let their guard down.

That was the worst of it. Gregor had split their once harmonious community in half. There were those who joined him wholeheartedly in his police efforts. Fritz knew, and Herbert confirmed with a nod, that the most public of these were in fact deeply closeted nosepickers, who,

75

when they weren't busy snitching or scolding, slipped off in solitude to extract bodily manufacture from a nostril, licking and sucking in the throes of guilt, savoring and swallowing, enjoying the added zing of doing something completely sinful and getting away with it.

Hypocrisy tasted sweet.

So did mucus.

The other elves had no strong opinion one way or the other. Some picked their noses, some did not. But all of them marveled at their community's down-drooping devolution and felt helpless to halt or reverse it. At first they murmured about it in hushed tones. But soon that felt like a waste of time and dangerous to boot. For having no strong opinion was tantamount to subversion. And being seen murmuring in hushed tones about anything at all, well, that was regarded in some circles as well-nigh treasonous.

Fritz had seen their work suffer. The very work they were now engaged upon, these replicas, suffered. Santa had put him in charge of them. He had remonstrated with his colleagues. To an elf, they had nodded eagerly. But nothing had changed.

Their toymaking suffered as well. Morale had plummeted. Yet Santa seemed not to notice. Or if he did, he minimized the problem. Why didn't anyone tell him what was going on? Fritz had asked Herbert this very question.

The flaxen-haired elf, wordless as always, simply shrugged.

But Fritz knew why. To tell was to be too much like a spy, an informer, a snitch. Too much like Gregor. Besides, Santa was a little boy at heart. He hated having to deal with discord. He expected things to run smoothly, as they always had.

Fritz applied cherrywood stain to the dresser. There rose from the replicas a righteous racket of planing and sawing and hammering. Herbert and three co-workers were busy painting the walls of the Beluzzo replica a lemon-peel yellow. On occasion, Herbert glanced over at Fritz and they exchanged significant looks. They had grown more careful, their stolen moments of intimacy far more discreet. It had once been easy to slip away. But in the poisoned atmosphere that now surrounded them, they had grown stealthier.

Fritz disliked that, and so did Herbert.

They could have cut it off entirely. But Fritz would be damned if he'd give up the pleasure of their trysts to feed the ego of a self-righteous prig like Gregor. Yet as soon as he thought that, he berated himself for thinking ill of a fellow elf.

Then his anger took wing, anger over Herbert's unmerited dismay, the communal chaos, Saint Nicholas' willful blindness, everyone's ingrained inability to confront Gregor's egregious behavior, and his own impotence in the face of tyranny, a state he had once believed could never take hold at the North Pole.

Fritz sighed. How far they had fallen.

But what could he do? Then he brightened. I know, he thought. I'll have a few words with Gregor. In private. Surely he mustn't understand the impact of his actions. Maybe a talk, maybe the gentlest nudge, would persuade him to call off this nonsense.

I'll do it. I will.

But when he imagined himself crossing the commons, when he pictured flinty-eyed Gregor staring at him as he approached, his limbs grew cold, his resolve flagged, and everything seemed more hopeless than ever.

A dreamscape shared by four dreamers tends to be far more stable than your typical solitary one, especially when it has been designed by the angels to reinforce righteous behavior.

Kathy and Walter Stratton found themselves holding hands as they floated into this particular dreamscape. They had on long white flannel nightgowns, not at all what they usually wore to bed. On either side, in similar attire, lazily drifted the Reverend Taylor and a wide-eyed teen whose name Kathy somehow knew was Matt. He slipped his hand into Walter's as the preacher took Kathy's hand. Her mood was jubilant, the air balmy and rich with oxygen, the clouds surrounding them full and wispy by turns.

"There they are!" exclaimed Matt.

Kathy looked, and Santa Claus, Wendy beside him in the sleigh, passed below the dreamers waving. Behind them, a full-to-bursting sack of toys, suede leather stretched and poked out at odd angles, threatened to spill its abundance over the sides of the sleigh. The four of them fell toward that sack, whose puckered top unthonged and peeled open. But instead of sleds and stuffed stockings and gaily wrapped and beribboned gifts, the glorious green and blue earth revealed itself.

Over it they sailed, marveling. For the sights and sounds and smells came to them as if for the first time, sharp, full, and vivid. Here was the white of a heron in full flight, there the slap and retreat of surf on a briny beach, the scent of a pear as it ripens and falls to a squirrel's prodding, the red-brown fur of that squirrel as it stares and nibbles and tenses and darts treeward from the ground. Below them, the earth yielded and gushed, vegetation spreading forth in joyous riot, birds flying out of it in formation, the seas replete with crab and mussel, with dolphin, minnow, and whale.

"Such abundance," marveled the preacher, to which Kathy said, "Yes."

They came to light on a high hill. As their feet touched ground, there sprouted from the burgeoning earth the entire race of humanity, busily buzzing about. But what was odd in Kathy's eyes was the contrast between the abundant earth and humanity's self-imposed restraints. For she could see deep into every living soul. And that same abundance lay at their foundation. Generosity flowed in their veins. It infused the marrow of their bones. Yet a certain gloomy ugliness clamped down upon them by common consent, by conspiratorial fiat. A rich confusion of words swarmed about them and enwrapped their skulls in a stew of divine babble. Some who dove into it resurfaced with delightful concoctions, with dances upon the tongue and music. But others, hobbled by fear or laziness, wrenched ill-formed dicta from it, ground imperfect lenses in haste, and clamped filters on their unfiltered senses. Into tribes they clustered.

"They shouldn't do that," scolded Walter.

But the moment he said it, the dreamers picked themselves out of that same roil of humanity and saw that they were acting with just as much foolishness as any of the others. "Wow, there I am," said Matt, "shuffling through fog." And so he was, his potential for limitless goodness quashed by his own dim vision and by signals coming from his family, his peers, and the surrounding herd. "Wake up!" he screamed. But for all the notice his observed self took, he might have been a ghost.

Below them unfolded all of human history. Brutality held sway. In painful clarity, each brutal act rasped and unrolled—rapes, wars, words unkind diminishing their intended victims, the barbs and insults which throttled vitality and encouraged resignation and despair. Feints at goodness threaded tentative through the inertia, pockets of creativity and kindness too often discouraged and crushed. "It's human nature," came the phrase. "What are you going to do?" But it wasn't human nature at all, not the underlying nature evident in babes-in-arms and in those rare souls who reveled in creativity, not in Michelangelo, Mozart, or Shakespeare. Works of art, even those that depicted strife, celebrated life in all its abundance and variety. From the simplest elements emerged a complex of delightful patterning, an acceptance and embrace of what was falsely perceived as alien.

But the thunder of destruction, wanton blasts that shattered the work of centuries beneath a moment's fist—these made a mockery of human nature. And they were so pervasive, it was an easy temptation to mistake them for the embodiment of natural humanity.

Then things froze and began to roll backward.

"It's reversing," said Kathy, "the whole sorry mess."

Indeed it was, landmines unplanted and disassembled in factories, soldiers taking back death and undeploying home, grown men and women youthening through childhood and babyhood into the fetal clutch, then deflating and splitting to sperm and egg, which likewise disappeared into the organs of degeneration. Bombed towns were unbombed, reconstructed in an instant as corpses rose to life and walked backward out of their upraised looks of terror into indifference, benignity, or the dry dead mull of judgmentalism. Advancing fashions reversed. Michelangelo's brushes sucked up and repotted the paint that moistened on the Sistine Chapel ceiling. Beethoven lifted stroke by stroke his Ninth Symphony from depopulated staves, tucking the glory of one masterwork after another back inside his cranium, which burgeoned enriched with anticipation a-dying. And on it went.

"We're headed for Golgotha," said Ty. "They'll spare him, it'll be the turning point, he'll live forever, growing in power. The course of history will change." And as soon as Ty said that, the dreamers shifted into myth. For dream logic tends to oblige. Golgotha it was. And indeed, instead of condemning Yeshua to crucifixion, Pilate recognized the avatar of God and yielded all power to him. And time began moving forward again. But with what a difference!

For his gentle love infused all it touched, so that they lived up to humankind's highest ideals. And Christ laughed to see men and women utterly transformed in an instant. And that laugh rolled on as a soft steady underpinning for future events, so that the dreamers witnessed divine acceptance and embrace, a celebration of the magnificent diversity of humanity sweeping through the generations to the present moment. In this revised history passing before them, there were no wars, no weapons, no spite, but only creativity and cooperation, the banding together of people without mad grasps at power, without lording it over anyone—all of that fell away, and generosity flourished in every soul.

With that, the urge to awaken took them. Feeling light, they rose from the hilltop. And back into the burgeoning sack the earth slipped. Its puckering top thonged shut.

"Wait," said Kathy.

Wendy waved and Santa winked. "We'll see you shortly," he sang out, as reindeer hoofs pounded divots from the sky and antlers bobbed to and fro like thickets of branched lightning.

Leaving Kathy and Walter, the boy and the preacher drifted upward. And all four sleepers eased into their slumbering bodies and a state of wakeful anticipation.

When Gronk bumbled home, the Tooth Fairy was sitting at the mouth of her cave, her bedroom visits concluded, glaring seaward and munching on a bowl of molars gathered from a midnight round of grave robbing.

While freshly drawn teeth from young jaws always resulted in spit-shiny, spanking-new coins, these teeth, depending how long the corpses had lain aground, produced coins that showed degrees of wear and tarnish, the serrations tire-tread thin, the edges crimped or jagged, the sort of coin that mortals withdrew from circulation and melted down. After eons of such molar munching, there fell away from the cliff upon which her great chair perched a perilous slope of metallic offal.

Ordinarily this was his mother's private domain, a place Gronk avoided as off-limits. But she had insisted he find her wherever she was. With great trepidation he alighted, graceful as a rubber boot flung upon a wharf, at her side.

She continued munching and ruminating, acknowledging not in the least his presence. Gronk waited, listening to the crunch of bone upon bone, watching her swallow, wanting and not wanting her to punish him for his trespass, to deliver the hurt that reassured him he was alive.

At last, still staring into a troubled sky, the Tooth Fairy said, "Your report?"

"He's out there all right, him and his little girl," said Gronk, "by the authority of God Almighty, through the agency of the archangel Michael."

"Zeus the skirt-chasing thunderbolt-hurler, and Hermes his fleet-footed trickster and psychopomp, you mean. Go on."

Gronk told her that Pan and his daughter had visited a preacher, a bully, and the parents of an eight-year-old boy. They intended three visits, he said, the first just finished in which the mortals had been shown scenes from recent days.

"To what end?" she asked.

Laying a hand on one of her armrests, Gronk told her they wanted to deflect, soften, or eliminate the mortals' homophobia, so that the boy would not kill himself eight years hence. Moreover, he said, after each visit, these mortals would share a dreamscape designed to further Pan and Wendy's ends.

Gronk's report so increased the Tooth Fairy's indignation, she threatened to explode into random violence. But when he mentioned the dreamscape, his mother calmed considerably. "Reinforcing Zeus's message in the land of dreams."

"Yes, Mother."

"This holds promise." Gronk held fire as she mulled. "Go back. Continue your mission. If we're lucky, I see an opening."

"What opening?"

She turned her fury on him. "I give orders. You obey. Get that stinking hand off my chair! In good time, if there's anything to tell, you and your miserable brothers will be told. Now go."

She grabbed him and Gronk was hurled skyward, grateful for her touch and sailing off, but not before he watched her stride into her cave, buff, muscular, and hatching some scheme to exact revenge on Santa Claus and his brood of do-gooders at the North Pole.

13.

A BULLY FURTHER SOFTENED

FROM TY TAYLOR'S HOME, Santa and Wendy circled the globe, gazing through magic time's soft glow upon cityscapes caught beneath moonlight or all abustle with daylight pedestrians frozen in mid-step. Over shantytowns and mansions, over the homeless and the homed, the desperate and the contented they flew, remarking to one another about the sights below.

Santa thought it grand to be sharing this special mission with Wendy. He so adored sharing his sleigh with her, letting her take the reins at times. She was in so many ways a lovely nine-year-old, feisty, innocent, and utterly childlike; yet she was also in full command, as one venturing over the dawn line of womanhood tends to be. That was good to see, though truth to tell it raised a teensy bit of anxiety in him. Children far distant from adulthood were so much easier to love.

They spoke of the special aura that had surrounded the archangel Michael and how wonderful it was to be doing something to save Jamie Stratton, whether they succeeded or no.

"Are you happy?" asked Wendy.

A curious question. It meant she had sensed his distress at touching the lives of grown-ups.

"Very," he said, and that was in part true. No cause to raise alarms in her. Perhaps, thought Santa, they wouldn't need to continue these visits at all. Maybe the dreamscape would finish the job and Michael would materialize and tell them to go home, there was no need to suffer proximity to the fallen any more. Ah, but that was his anxiety talking.

"Our dreamers are doing okay," she said. "Have a look."

Giving Lucifer his head, Santa observed them dozing, their spirits deep in dream. They seemed to be softening nicely. It was appalling how hardened mortals grew, with how much eagerness they embraced calcification after the freedom of childhood. But their shared dreamscape seemed to be reversing that process. As a chicken bone in vinegar softens and bends, so the perspectives of the dreamers expanded beyond the rigid, blinkered, rulebound views they had cobbled together out of communal prejudice and doctrinal lies. Even the bitter child, Matt Beluzzo, had begun to see beyond his broken family and the traps that hobbled his mind.

Though the first visits had proven a trial, Santa had high hopes for the remaining ones. One misstep did not determine an outcome. He still had time, if he could only keep his Pan side suppressed, to approach persuasion persuasively. He would make Wendy proud. He would deliver on the task the Father had given them. More important, he would save, nay enrich if he could, the life of this good little boy. Gifts of toys and Christmas cheer were worthy indeed, but far worthier the lifting of sorrows unto death.

It would most certainly transform his annual giftgiving. As much as he gloried in his Christmas deliveries, so much more joy would he derive, having explored in detail one boy's life and yes even the lives of his principal tormentors. Every grown-up had once been a child. Go back as far as babes-in-arms to find unspoiled innocence if you must, but there it was. At their very core, there it was. And it could be tapped and brought forth. It might infuse their lives, breaking the cold hard grip of habit and letting the Christ inside emerge into open air.

It was possible, he thought. I know it is. I can do it. My Pan side can be damped down.

And through the night sky, headed for Matt Beluzzo's bedroom once more, sailed Santa Claus, laughing to beat the band, cracking his whip, and hugging Wendy, as the sleigh left a wide swath of radiant joy in its wake.

With the Beluzzo replica near completion and the Strattons' well under way, Fritz trudged through the alpenglow of magic time toward the stables, his slippers ovaling ice-blue pits in the new-fallen snow.

He pictured himself knocking and being grudgingly ushered in for intense conversation with a fellow elf who would quickly come to see the error of his ways. Instead, Gregor stood at the half-door, arms folded, glowering out on the commons with utter grump and scowl. An eyebrow rose on his deeply etched face, his eyes flaring outrage that anyone dared approach unbidden. It gave Fritz pause.

"Hi there, Gregor," he said, with half a heart.

The eyebrow arched higher.

"May I come in?"

"Hmph."

"Ah, I see. You want to be contrary. All to the good. Well, I guess we can talk right here. Nice door, by the way. I've got to hand it to you, the stable's always spotless. So, listen, you know, your lectures at the Chapel, they...they're well intended, it's clear. But honey attracts the cheerful flies of compliance far better than vinegar, I think that's how the saying goes. Your fellow elves are for the most part simple folk. They need encouragement. Praise. Now you take shame and fear. They don't motivate at all. They feel bad too. They end up having a contrary effect. See what I mean? Ah, there's that glower again. It's off-putting, I must say. Right now, standing here, I'm starting to sweat. It feels as if you're, I don't know, as if you're judging me. It's like that with the others too. How can we concentrate on doing superb work if we have half an eye toward you and whether you're staring at us with scorn, and judging us, and finding us coming up short?"

"You *do* come up short."

"Ah, words. That's good. You're a man of few of them, I know. Now maybe you think that's a position of strength. But after a while, to speak frankly, it wears thin. You know, sometimes I think, for all of our camaraderie up here, we don't communicate enough. Amongst ourselves, I mean. We're too nice. We'd rather not rock the boat. If we're upset, we just swallow it. Or form little whispering cliques. And things get worse. If we could just air our upsets freely, without fear of being put down, with mutual respect—"

"I respect the hell out of everybody."

"I'm sure you do—"

"But they lack respect for themselves. *You* lack self-respect. Would any self-respecting elf pick his nose? He would not. That's the long and the short of it."

The back of Fritz's neck grew hot.

Gregor wagged a finger three times sharp, as if he were shaking out a thermometer. "Get right with your nostrils, little elf, before you come marching over here blowing smoke up mine. You speak to me of scorn? You deserve it in spades. Santa's little favorite, huh? You know how long that would last if he caught wind of this foul practice? Gone in a trice. Now, you just march your meddling little slippers right back across the commons and tend to your own garden. I'll tend to mine, with no unsought advice from the likes of you!"

With that, Gregor slammed the upper door in Fritz's face. Fritz stood there, in shock, forgetting to breathe. Then his breath returned over the pounding of his heart.

Well, he thought. How about that?

With a huff and a sigh, Fritz shook his head, and trudged back toward the replicas, doing his best to shake off Gregor's belittling and feeling very bad indeed about the deteriorating state of affairs.

The aroma of hot chocolate lured Matt from sleep. When he opened his eyes, there stood Santa with a steaming mug redolent with the beguiling scent of cocoa and mint and marshmallow. At his side, Wendy held a piping hot plate of shortbread.

"Courtesy of my wives," said Santa.

Matt sat up, accepted the food and drink, and glanced about his bedroom. "Wives," he said. "Whatever. Man, how'd you get snow in here?" Drifts glistened beyond the bedposts. Bedposts? Where had *they* come from?

"A gift from my helpers," said Santa. "But we have more serious matters to speak of."

Matt stiffened. There was that tone. Some grown-up was about to tell him what to do. What to think. How to behave. Refuse, and that grown-up would beat him until he cried uncle. That's how his father had been before they put his ass in stir. That's how his boozy bitch of a mom was, with her smoker's breath and her jowly made-up face and her red-lipped, hate-spewing pie hole.

He wouldn't be shoved around. Not by anyone.

"Okay, Wendy," said Santa. "Bring on the future."

With a gesture, the lemon-yellow walls of the bedroom sparkled and fell away. There before them slumped three slit-lidded punks against the wall of an alley, dragging on cheap cigarettes.

"Hey, it's me!" said Matt, though the kid he pointed at was pimply, tightlipped, and needed a haircut. "And there's Robbie Stover. But the other guy...who the heck is he?"

"You'll meet him next year in junior high. Jack Pangborn's his name, a good little boy until he turned four."

Robbie Stover had put on bulk and was stooped over, one shoulder higher than the other as he listened to Matt and glared at the bricks under his boots. The other kid was more compact and stared intently from under a wild shock of hair. Matt could tell this Pangborn dude wanted to topple him as leader but didn't have the guts to take him on.

The scene switched. Now the three of them were pistoning slow and sullen along a sidewalk, watching the approach of an alarmed kid in white band pants. When he tried to cross the street, they cut him off. "Hey, queer boy, no problem," Matt said, giving him a shove, "there's room on the sidewalk for everybody. We'll just brush past you. You'd like that, I bet, huh?"

"Please, I'm only trying to—"

"Yeah. I know. In your ice cream pants. You got any ice cream for us, queer boy?"

Matt smacked the kid's head and he took off terrified, Stover and Pangborn hurling taunts after him. Stover hooted through megaphone hands, while the other kid looked fierce and yelled and threw his fists into the air.

"That's you at fourteen, two years from now."

"The kid's a fruit, a gutless wonder. He deserves...." Matt stopped, ashamed. "Okay, maybe not. But I got the power. You can taste it, can't you? So I get to slam rich queers. I get to screw up their smug little world."

Santa started to say something, then stopped himself. Matt could tell he was pissed. "Let's add two more years, Wendy."

The same three, Matt's gang, emerged from a bar carrying beer bottles. Matt held the neck of his between two fingers, the bottle swinging easy as he walked. He looked one way, the other, found his target. "Let's head the cocksucker off," he said. They fleetfooted it over one street and parallel to the one the bar was on, then back just in time to run into the guy at an intersection. Matt stopped him with a hand to the chest. "Hey, faggot, you looked at me funny in there. What's with that? You find me good-looking or sumpin'?"

"I didn't—"

Matt slammed his beer bottle into the guy's head and they dragged him into the bushes and kicked him and punched out his lights. There'd be no chance he would raise a cry. Stover pummeled the kid's face with his fists, but Pangborn gave him the worst of it.

The scene went blank and the bedroom came back. "Jeepers," said Matt. "That's me?"

Santa smoldered, a terrifying sight indeed. Matt's throat went dry. "If you don't wise up. You and your naughty friends get into this quite a lot." In quick succession, Matt saw terrified young victims being taunted and trounced by his gang. He felt stunned and exhilarated and ashamed and light-headed all at once.

"This next episode," said Santa, "sends you to prison." Wendy froze on a kid, the same one he had seen on the bike, Terry something, but halfway through his teens, a sweet face, the kind that made you think weird thoughts. And that face—because no way in hell did he dare show Robbie and this Jack dude what he really felt—he struck over and over, gut-punching the kid with his left fist and breaking his jaw with his right. At last the kid lay there unconscious, his body jerking with the beating they gave him.

The scene abruptly wiped away.

Santa was in tears, and that tore at Matt's heart. But a great rage, barely contained, boiled beneath the surface too. Finally, he stormed off toward the dresser. "Wendy, show him the rest!"

The girl touched Matt's arm and said softly, "You can change. I know you can. We wouldn't be here if you couldn't." Then she laid open before him his life behind bars. How he would bully weaker prisoners into rape, while always watching his back for this bull-headed, dead-eyed farm boy, in jail for taking an axe to his father. Wendy shut it off as the farm boy's assault began. But Matt remained shaken at his helplessness in the face of terror.

Santa stormed back. For an instant, Matt feared the great elf's massive fists would beat him bloody. Instead, Santa once more summoned up Terry Samuelson's death by beating. Close-up, in freeze-frame, stood the members of his gang. Matt felt their desperate need for family, for male bonding, all of it masked by anger and fear.

"We're shackled," said Matt. "We're uptight and stupid, closed off and full of fake bravado."

"Yes," said Santa.

Matt broke down and wept then, cradled in Santa's arms. He cried so hard he felt light in the head. Somewhere in there, Santa eased him down, covered him, and kissed his forehead, and Matt felt the bedroom lose its charm and slip back into squalor, as sleep carried him far far away.

14.

AWAKENINGS

BY TORCHLIGHT ANGLED across dripping rock, the Tooth Fairy drew from an ancient stash of treasures a jewel-encrusted box. Carrying it with care to her stone altar, she blew away centuries of dust and raised the lid, which was stopped at an obtuse angle by thin gold bands. The air above the altar turned a harsh red from the glow cast by its contents. Inside, gripped by a worn velvet extrusion, sat a glass vial stoppered and sealed with lead.

In that vial was a single drop of blood caught when Kronos swung his sickle of ox teeth to castrate his father Ouranos, overthrowing him and thereby separating heaven from earth. His blood had drenched the soil, and from that soil sprang the Giants, the Furies, and the ash nymphs, of which she, the Tooth Fairy, had been the firstborn and most fierce, Adrasteia by name.

She flung wide her arms, the necklace of teeth slapping against her breasts at the abruptness of her movements. "By the blood of Ouranos," she intoned, the cave depths sending up a sorrowful echo, "given me by Alecto, winged fury of the snaky hair at the instant of my birth, as I and my sisters fled from the battle that raged about us, I summon from the outer circle of Tartarus black-winged Nyx, goddess of night, daughter of Chaos, granddaughter of Kronos, and the mother of Hypnos and Thanatos.

"Arise, o mighty Nyx, I command it." The drop of god-blood gleamed with a deepening ferocity as she spoke, the cavern dancing with crimson fires. So close grew the air, so red and glistening the moisture that trickled down the walls, it seemed like the chamber of some vast dead heart, new beating.

"By the blood of the great god Ouranos, I command it!"

Then, without noise or shattering, the vial's contents seemed to burst from its confinement, flooding the cavern. There before her rose a black-winged creature, dark her brow, dreadful her face. Her breasts were spent and withered, her nipples in-turned conical pits.

It had been eons since the Tooth Fairy had known fear. It wasn't that Nyx towered over her, for she didn't. Indeed, her dimensions were impossible to fix, seeming one moment to be as small as the blue flame of a cook's torch, the next glaring down from impossible heights.

When she spoke, she did not boom, yet her words bruised eardrums and hurt the heart. "Who dares summon Nyx from the Underworld?" She fixed her eyes on the summoner. "The blood of Ouranos may have the power to force immortals to its presence, but if your reasons for disturbing my rest prove inadequate, I'll crush you into oblivion, Adrasteia, boldest of the ash nymphs."

"Hear me, goddess of night," said the Tooth Fairy, falling to her knees. "Zeus, who turned me into a wretched childhood icon and saddled me with thirteen brats, he who, upon making himself into the Christian god, slaughtered my sisters, broke into kindling the sky chariot with which you drew the mists of darkness across the sky, consigned you to the oblivion of your palace in Tartarus, and trivialized your son Hypnos, god of sleep, and his three sons by collapsing them into the Sandman—this Zeus has overstepped his self-imposed limits once more. He is allowing Pan and his stepdaughter to dissuade four mortals from their predestined course, by nocturnal visit, by dazzling them with magic and miracle, and worse, by thrusting them into a dreamscape designed to propagandize on behalf of this violation of the natural order." She bowed her head and raised her palms in supplication. "I beg this boon: Allow me and my imps access to that dreamscape. We will foil the plans of the insufferable sky god and his minions. Nay, we vow to coarsen these mortals, increasing the woes Zeus and Pan would ease, avenging myself, you, and all who have suffered or lost their lives at the hand of Zeus-turned-Jehovah."

The echo of the Tooth Fairy's words died away. Silence fell, a silence full of foreboding. She dared not raise her eyes, but the fine hairs rose on the back of her neck.

"Am I to understand," began Nyx, "that you have summoned me from the rim of Tartarus, through rock and earth—"

As the contempt in her voice deepened, the Tooth Fairy's body was lifted off the cavern floor and pressed slowly and relentlessly against a jagged wall of rock.

"—which tattered my flesh and tore my limbs, wreaking havoc upon my entire physical being—"

The wall was cold and wet against her buttocks and shoulders. An invisible hand pushed her hard into the stone jags. She winced as one rib, then another, cracked under the pressure.

"—merely to avenge yourself on Pan?"

Her necklace of teeth pressed pits into her chest, broke skin, and drew blood, the teeth against the nape of her neck doing likewise.

"Not Pan," she managed. "Zeus."

"We're not stupid down below. We hear things. Santa Claus had his way with you. Twenty years, wasn't it? Then he dumped you for a mortal woman. You and the Easter Bunny caused quite a stir. You devoured your rival with one great gulp and turned her into a coin, as I hear. Zeus restored her life, degenitalized the Easter Bunny, and made you quick with imps, nasty little creatures that blight Christmas for bad urchins. They're a bother, no doubt. But it's Pan, isn't it? A woman scorned. Pan, in whom I take not the slightest interest."

"It is," admitted the Tooth Fairy, regretting her summoning. "I would topple them both."

"Well," said Nyx, softening. She gave a dark chuckle. "That is indeed a worthy goal. You flatter me, Adrasteia, with appeals to my wounded pride. That irks me. But everything irks me these days. You are a flea. Pan is a flea. Zeus? A vile little flea of a god. He fears me, you know. He always has."

The pressure eased. The necklace, its thong cut by a stray bite, fell with a clatter to the floor. The Tooth Fairy's ribs healed and her breath came easier.

"Look at me."

Against her will, her eyes met the dread glare of Night. Into whirlpools of negation she peered, grasping for one positive thing on which to anchor her sanity.

"Your brats." Nyx gestured. The Tooth Fairy heard distant shouts as they were seized, followed by bellows of pain as the dread goddess drew them through solid rock to this cavern. Bloody pools of bone and brain and flesh appeared in blotches on the floor, each one reconstituting into a son, Chuff here, Frash there, Gronk nearest her, groaning in agony.

"Silence!"

With a resounding clack, their jaws slammed shut.

Nyx pointed her finger at the Tooth Fairy and drew it down. As she descended, her back tore to ribbons against the jags and blood ran in rivulets down her thighs.

"I will consider granting your wish." At these words the Tooth Fairy thrilled. "But not here." Nyx's voice dripped venom. "You were kind enough to force me through untold miles of painful obstruction, now I shall return the favor. All of you!" Her voice towered into majesty. "At once to Tartarus!"

The imps rose protesting into the air, then plunged with a cry through the cavern floor. The Tooth Fairy too was dragged inexorably downward, subject to massive trauma as she was pressed through stone, struggling to stay together, her body's integrity violated, nor no mercy shown as her consciousness remained sharp and pained and acutely fixed upon the journey Nyx forced her to take.

Moments before, en route to the Stratton house, Wendy had asked Santa if he was all right. She knew his damped-down anger at Matt Beluzzo had upset him. He had steamed and mumbled all the way to the sleigh, trying in vain for jolly.

Santa looked away. "It's the elves," he said in a transparent attempt to spare her. "Their work on the bedrooms is getting sloppy. Matt didn't notice, but I did. The paint was streaked in places and thinly applied. The heads of wood screws weren't always countersunk. If you had brushed past the dresser, your tunic would have snagged on one of them. It's unlike my helpers to overlook such things. Something's up."

"I must have missed that," said Wendy. "Everything looked pretty impressive to me."

Santa slapped a lax rein against Blitzen's flank.

"What else, Daddy? You can tell me. I'm a big girl now."

"It's just that...," he began. Then he fell silent, the bright lights of the Broadmoor Hotel passing beneath them. "I became angry at that boy, murderously angry. He goaded me. I've told you I was Pan in an earlier life. When God brought you back from death, I thought he had shoved that old revived self down sufficiently far, I'd never have to worry about him again. But as much as my generous nature predominates, vile impulses lurk just below the surface. I'm out of my league with these closed-minded grown-ups and rotten bullies. I almost struck that child back there. He deserved a solid smack in the teeth and I would have enjoyed delivering it, for an instant. But if I had done that, Santa Claus as we know him would have died." He shook his great locks and lowered his head. "I'm not sure I can see this through."

"You can," Wendy insisted, encircling his great arm and resting her head on his biceps. "I know you can. You're Santa Claus, and my father. You can do anything."

Santa smiled bitterly. "For your sake, I won't argue the point. Though failure may await us, I'll make the attempt. No, wait, that's the wrong attitude. I *will* succeed. *We* will succeed. With God's help, we will right these listing mortals. At the very least, we'll shift their course just enough that they walk right past the critical moments fated to sap Jamie's will to live. We'll do our best to save these four, but we shall most certainly save the child."

Wendy hugged him tight. "That's my daddy," she said. Though seventeen in years, she allowed the nine-year-old to come out in her embrace. She and Santa were embarked on a grand adventure, and they would infuse it with as much risk-taking and daring-do and sheer unfettered zest as they possibly could.

At that moment, Wendy heard a noise so faint she wasn't sure she had heard it; so faint that Santa took no notice, or at least made no mention, of it. Finally, she dismissed it and set her sights on the Stratton house spiraling up from below.

But it hadn't been imagined. Gronk had let out a gasp as Nyx's summons yanked him from the sleigh and slammed him downward through the earth toward his mother's island.

The sleigh descended, stars twinkling merrily above, a soft breeze in their ears, and the jingle of bells on the team's traces beating out a gleeful *tzing-tzing-tzing* as they flew.

The instant its runners touched down, Santa leaped out. Gripping Wendy by the waist, he lifted her to the late autumn lawn. "Let's have at them!" he said, and up the porch steps they bounded, passing through the locked front door. It was strange entering homes with nary a Christmas trapping laid out. A coffee table strewn with magazines stood in the space the Strattons' tree usually occupied, where Santa would set out presents and stockings for Kurt and Jamie, their names embroidered on flat red felt stockings, which Santa filled with trinkets and gold-wrapped chocolate coins and other oddments until they plumped up like overstuffed peapods.

If the glow of magic time hadn't lit their way to the upstairs landing, luminescent green nightlights in a series of outlets would have. On their left lay the boys' bedrooms. Though Santa was tempted to look in on them, he followed Wendy toward the master bedroom.

"Ready?" she asked, a twinkle in her eye.

"Yes," he said, and over the threshold they stepped, passing through the door as if it weren't there.

Cherrywood furniture gleamed momentarily in moonlight. Then magic time cast its soft glow all about and a moment later, the replica, without hitch or jolt, slipped in around them. Walter and Kathy Stratton lay a-slumbering, unbreathing, still locked in normal time.

"Shall I wake them?" asked Wendy.

"Soon. Look there. You see?" An ornate Japanese screen stood by the door where none had stood before. Snowdrifts rose against either side of it. A dragon, rampant with a huge head and unsheathed claws had been painted on the screen in opalescent greens, reds, and blacks. "The dragon's proportions are all wrong. The hinges are cut-rate. The lacquer is moist, the angles out of true. And that's just one item." Santa moved around the room, pointing out flaws in the furniture, in the swirls of stucco on the ceiling, in the curlicues carved into the bedroom door. "And look at this." He knelt, scooped up a pile of wood shavings, and let them fall through his fingers.

"Jeepers," said Wendy.

"Something's amiss. This isn't like them. I expect perfection because that's what they always deliver. They'll get a talking to, I'll tell you that. But I refuse to let this throw me. Actors know that how the flats are hung matters little to their performance. These trappings set off the pearl of our persuasion. But it's the pearl, not its setting, which must be of great price. If it fails to impress, no amount of window dressing will do the trick. So yes, Wendy. Please bring these good people into magic time. It's time we showed them the effect of their actions on their son."

Wendy said okay and gestured toward the couple, seeming to bring them to life. Santa took a calming breath, steeled his resolve, and prepared for the encounter ahead. Pan, he thought, I will keep under wraps at all times. And I will not despise these grown-ups, no matter how deserving of spite they prove.

When Kathy awoke this time, the aromatic snap of sizzling pine logs greeted her, though there was neither fireplace nor logs in their bedroom. Walter was already sitting up, staring about in wonder. She found herself feeling...more compliant. It had something to do with her dream, though she recalled none of it. Then she remembered what she was expected to become compliant about, and her resolve stiffened.

"Hello again, Kathy," said Santa.

"Before you start, let me just say that I refuse to believe my son is that way. And now that you've alerted us, he *definitely* won't be that way."

"You can count on it," said Walter.

Santa said, "All right, Wendy."

And the little girl, looking a bit shy, pointed into the space before their bed. At once, they were at Grandview Memorial Gardens, peering past images of themselves at a small crowd gathered around a coffin. Reverend Taylor, his prayer book open, intoned in pantomime. From the way he held himself, Kathy could tell something about the deceased troubled him. She had seen him at other funerals, where he would often weep and carry on over the dearly departed. Not so now.

"Whose funeral is this?" asked Walter.

Kathy recognized members of their congregation, the Graysons, the Stupplebeens, crab-faced Hanna Bach, shaking with palsy. Everyone seemed a bit off, as though they were attending out of obligation or morbid curiosity.

"We're older," Walter noted. Kathy saw that that was so. Grief, the evidence of which shown on her cheeks, aged one; but there were new lines in her face and an apparent decision to let the gray show, which signaled the passage of time.

"This is eight years on," said Santa. "The young man beside you is Kurt at twenty-one. He's back from college."

Kathy gave a start. Of course that's who it was. How handsome he had become. Though he stood beside her, he neither touched nor held her. His eyes had difficulty settling anywhere.

"Where's Jamie?" she asked.

And the scene faded, to be replaced by a series of vignettes in and around the house. Jamie, of junior high age, coming home with books in hand. Walter asking, "Met any new girls today?" "No, Dad." Jamie, somewhat older now, at the dinner table. "So you taking the Pavlovich girl? She seems the studious type." "I haven't decided yet, Dad. I may not go at all. It's only a stupid dance." "Hey, come on, Jamie, it's what healthy boys do," said Walter.

Kathy stiffened. "I don't like where this is going."

There was Jamie's bedroom, a Coronado High pennant on his

wall, his father solemn-faced and clasp-handed beside him on the bed. "That book will clue you in. Your brother's got himself a nice girl, cute and smart. You should too. But you need to be careful. In control. It's too easy to let your hormones carry you away. Best not go there at all."

"Go where, Dad?"

"Where you shouldn't. Where your natural tendencies will try to take you. Just read the book. They're described in gory detail. You gotta squelch 'em is all. Girls are tender. They need to be treated with kid gloves, like I treated your mother. Remember that, son." He put a hand on Jamie's knee. "Will you remember that?"

"Sure, Dad."

Kathy said, "You're showing us a future that's changeable, right? It isn't hard and fast. Jamie's much too soft. We'll harden him."

"It's all right, Missus Stratton," said Wendy. "That's the way he is. There's nothing you have to change about Jamie. You only have to love him."

"Don't lecture me, little girl," said Kathy sharply. "This whole subject is making me ill."

Looking cowed, Wendy gestured. Now Jamie was slumped on a couch in the den, his parents standing over him.

"Walter," said Kathy, "talk sense into your son."

Jamie's features were pained, his face red. "I can't help it. I'm just that way. I need you to accept that."

"No son of mine is gay," said Walter. "And that includes you. You're mixed up in the head is all."

Kathy said, "It's disgusting. Who's been at you? You haven't actually...this is all theory, tell me it's all theory. The Devil's got you. Do you really want to let Satan have his way with you? This is ridiculous. I ought to pray with you, but I want to strike you, I want you out of this house. You did not come from this body. You couldn't have."

Walter said, "You're upsetting your mother. You see that?"

"Please, Dad, Mom, it's not about you, it's about me."

Wendy faded the scene and brought the bedroom back.

"I won't let this happen," said Kathy, shaken now. "We'll send him to Bible camp. We'll get him counseling."

Walter said, "Military school will drum this out of him."

"No more TV," said Kathy. "No more movies."

Santa interrupted. "Now wait. Jamie was born this way and he can't be changed. For the love of God, you're his mom and dad. Your job is to accept and embrace and celebrate *all* of him, even and especially his homosexuality."

"Never," said Kathy.

"To do less than that is to dishonor the abundant variety of God's creation. I tell you this as his emissary. Your preacher and your whole misguided sect have got this issue dead wrong, just as they had the slavery question wrong two hundred years ago, and interracial marriage fifty years ago. Now, you can't change things for the mass of people needlessly suffering. But you can and you must change yourselves to spare your son an otherwise crushing burden of pain."

"I don't care if you *are* Santa Claus," said Walter, "and frankly I have my doubts about that. You're no emissary from any God *I* care to worship. Our God condemns this practice in clear and certain terms. Queers are hellbound. The Good Book says so. No son of mine is hellbound. I think you've concocted this whole display is what I think. Now why don't you just haul your fat red ass out of my house pronto, mister?"

In response to which, Wendy gestured and traffic noise filled the room. The bedroom setting dropped away. There was Jamie trudging despondently along an overpass, his backpack slung over one shoulder.

"What's this?" asked Kathy.

"Watch," said Santa, his voice thin and harsh.

Trucks barreled by below in swift smears of color. Jamie took two apples from his backpack. He dropped one over the side.

"Oh God, he's not...."

Jamie dropped the other apple.

Cars going eighty pierced the soundscape and vanished in a sigh. A semi shoved massive amounts of air aside.

Jamie hauled himself up onto the parapet and sat there, transfixed by the traffic.

Walter said, "He can't be serious. What the hell could drive him to this?"

Jamie's arms stiffened with resolve where his hands clenched the concrete's rough edge. Then, mouth grim-set, eyes resolute and teary, he slipped off and Wendy wiped the scene away.

Stunned silence from the bed. Kathy came nearly unglued but stubbornly held back her tears. Walter drew her to his chest. "All of this is a lie," he said.

But Kathy knew it wasn't.

"We've got to look into this, Walter," she said. "What if we do everything to fight it, and we're wrong, and Jamie ends up there, doing that? What if Reverend Taylor's wrong too? Maybe he's right. But do you want to gamble Jamie's life on that? I don't."

Walter looked defeated. "What happens then?"

At Wendy's gesture, a series of muted scenes passed before them. "You argue more frequently," said Santa. "You spend less time together. Walter starts having affairs, a short-term fling or two, looking for a shoulder to cry on. He leaves the church and reverts to Catholicism of an activist sort. Kathy, you cling to your Bible more fiercely, blaming yourself and Walter and the whole world. The church becomes your all-consuming passion. You continue living in the same house, but Walter sleeps in Kurt's old room, makes his own meals, and you barely exchange a word."

Santa nodded and Wendy stopped the scenes.

Kathy began, "But how can we—?"

"Sleep," said Santa. "We'll be back one last time. All will become clear then."

A great weariness seeped into her bones. "All right," she said, but it came out a mumble. Just before her eyelids closed, the flicker and smell and crackle of pine logs vanished. Recalling the dreamscape, Kathy slid eagerly down toward its comforts once more.

15.

DARKNESS AND LIGHT

OVER AND OVER, the Tooth Fairy and her imps lost skin and bone as they hurtled toward the earth's center. Reconstituted in air pockets, their immortal flesh shattered anew when they smashed through rock. At last they broke free of that torment and emerged into the underworld, speeding toward the pit of Tartarus. A sphere of brass surrounded it, three layers of night around that. Upon the edge of the outer layer stood a great palace, dark and spiked and sparse-windowed.

In at a stone casement they tumbled, breaking their bones again on the marble floor. They lay in a heap before an ornate throne, upon which sat the goddess of night. Torchlight bathed the room in intensities of black, an absence of color that stole detail from, and thereby delineated, all it touched.

"Hear me," said Nyx, stabbing a finger at the Tooth Fairy. "I will grant you your wish on two conditions. First, you must sacrifice one of your teeth."

"But, I—"

"This one." Some foul hand gripped the right incisor in her lower jaw and wrenched it out by the roots. Blood flowed bitter and salt, the empty canal a sharp needle-thrust. But this tooth, unlike other teeth immortals lose, did not grow back. She cursed Nyx under her breath.

"Same to you, tenfold. Second condition: You must speak the absolute truth, no guile, no mewling, and no grandstanding in your request."

The Tooth Fairy drew herself up. If she were to be blasted, it would be for insolence, never mewling. "Pan threw me aside for a mortal woman, this after two decades of incredible sex. I had him by the stalk. I was this close to tossing the fir nymph out on her ear. I would have whipped his former satyrs into shape. Toys slapped together under my reign would have hurt and saddened brats worldwide, delivering misery, rage, and fear deep to the heart. But enough of Pan. Know this only: I would make any sacrifice to avenge myself on the goat god turned goody-twoshoes.

"As for Zeus, in the Great Transformation, he slaughtered my sister ash nymphs. With thirteen thunderbolts he violated me, saddling me with these malformed imps, who offend my every sense. Worse, each time I enter some rug rat's bedroom, Zeus's strictures reach into the private place of loathing from which I despise the little shits and turn me toward...indifference. Not until I've left their bedrooms do my true feelings return—for the brats, for their foul progenitors, for the whole sorry race of mortals.

"Give us access to this dreamscape, o Goddess of Night, and we will whip into a frenzy the inhumanity Zeus, Pan, and their henchmen would destroy."

Nyx's smile cast a pall upon the proceedings. She raised a hand into the darkness and spoke a phrase in an ancient tongue. At once, on the opposite side of the throne, appeared a gaunt, hairless creature, everywhere a dull gray, his skin crusted, diseased, and dandruffy. He opened his palms in supplication, and flecks of skin, so fine they might have been dust, drifted to the floor. "But I mustn't stop," he said in a panic, "I'll never catch up, I...." His voice sifted and sighed. "Who are you to—?"

Nyx's fingers twitched. A swirl of skin dust wafted up and fell into the creature's eyes. "This ruined child," said Nyx, "is my reason for helping you fight the Father God. My son never rests. He moves at random upon the earth. His mind is so addled, he has lost all memory of his mother." The creature collapsed in slumber, curling up beneath a gentle snore. "Unfold, for a time, into your former selves." From the sleeper, four majestic figures fountained up.

"You summoned us, Mother?" asked the tallest.

"Dolt," she said. "Why else would you be here?"

The Tooth Fairy looked askance at him, for staring directly at Hypnos induced instant drowsiness. Several of her imps, Chuff, Faddle, Frash, and Prounce among them, sat down heavy-lidded and fell into a deep sleep.

Behind Hypnos loomed the gods of dream, Morpheus for human images, Phobetor and Phantasos for images of animals and objects. Nyx addressed them. "Zeus is up to new tricks. Tonight, he has granted four mortals a single dreamscape."

The god of sleep peered upward, scanning the earth. "I see it," he said. "An odd construct. But Zeus must have his reasons."

"To hell with Zeus's reasons. You will allow Adrasteia and her imps free access to this dreamscape. At her whim shall she be free to alter and populate it as she desires. You, Hypnos, will grant her access, and your sons will bend before the winds of her fancy. Of this dreamscape and for this night alone shall she and her brood have free rein."

"But mother, what of Zeus's waked wrath?"

Nyx laughed. "For all his bluster, the Father God fears me."

"Then we obey."

"Of course you do," said Nyx in anger. "Stupid boy." She waved a dismissive hand and the creatures funneled back into the sleeping Sandman. He blinked, rose unsteadily to his feet, and protested with a somnolent stare, "I'll never catch up."

"So a million mortals suffer sleeplessness for a few minutes. Better get moving, boy. More interminable leapfrogging about the globe for you. No rest for the weary. Go!"

And he was gone.

"Given the state he's in," said the Tooth Fairy, "he's bound to make mistakes."

"He'll stumble and overlook a few eyes, put a shoulder or leg to sleep instead. But routine will catch up with him. The poor boy never rests. He hasn't rested since his creation, a renewer never renewed."

The Tooth Fairy watched her imps awaken and gaze in fresh horror about the throne room.

"I believe your trespass on my time and property is coming to a close." Nyx grinned. "Anything else?"

Before she could request a painless return to her island, Nyx lofted her head and said, "I didn't think so. Off with you."

At once the Tooth Fairy and her brood began the bone-shattering journey backward, agony driving out all but the will to survive and keep surviving.

When Ty Taylor woke to magic time, he found himself saddened to the heart. Some maddeningly elusive dream had loosed his hold on his beliefs. Dreams processed waking events, trying to unknot them or cut through the knots. So scientists claimed. Whatever he had dreamed, he knew it had something to do with vast improvements in humankind, with a shift in mindset.

The room was once more magically transformed, but Santa and Wendy hadn't yet arrived, giving perhaps a contemplative fellow time to contemplate. From beyond the walls, a faint jingle of bells sounded. Mist-fine pings of snow fell against Ty's cheeks and eyelashes, melting to pinpoints of moisture as they landed, then at once evaporating.

Were he not so becalmed by doubt, he would have laughed. But doubts there were. Deep ones. Despite Ty's dig at Santa's rage, the elf showed every sign of being God's emissary indeed. Had not Christ himself turned righteously rageful against the moneychangers? And here, for decades it seemed, he, Ty, had been dealing in counterfeit coin. He recalled witnessing the effect of his words on his parishioners. And his own not quite clear-cut sexual orientation. Yet he felt pure and natural in his bones, a sinner surely, but not in that realm. No, nor would he be, were he to act upon those long-suppressed urges.

The latter feeling astounded him with its certainty. Was not the Holy Bible the final arbiter? And didn't the Word of God unequivocally condemn homosexual acts as sinful? Something in the soft miraculous light surrounding him made him deeply secure, so secure that ferocious advocacy for the Bible seemed utterly beside the point.

In this silent sadness, he grew acutely aware of his unyielding stance toward so many issues. He had always wanted things clear-cut. Yet here he was, ready to embrace the obverse view and champion it just as vehemently and with just as fiery a voice. Could he not entertain doubt even for a little while? What a relief from tired old habit that would be.

Just then, Wendy passed through the bedroom door, which ought to have startled him but did not. "Hello," she said like an old acquaintance. Santa Claus strode in after her wearing a forced smile. "Good," said he. "You're a little softer. So am I. Wonderful, isn't it, what a cooling-off period can do?"

Santa's less-than-complete acceptance of him brought back Ty's stubbornness. Holier than thou. Besides, Santa looked, how to put it, like one given over to carnal delights, a lover of the flesh, generous to children yes, but generous in his appetites as well, a Henry the Eighth, a Falstaff, a walking advertisement for hedonism. And yet, a little boy. It was absurd to let such a creature influence him so profoundly. "Appetites," said Ty, raising a finger to make the point. "Addiction to things carnal. I'll grant you it's inborn and not a choice. But the same could be said for alcoholism."

Santa turned to Wendy. "You're a genius, sweetheart." Then to Ty, "It's a question of instinct. I'll tell you the truth, little Ty all grown up, my heart isn't fully engaged in this task, because I'm afraid you adults are hopeless, stuck in habit, trapped in judgment—and your kind, you preachers, are the worst! But I must be generous, mustn't I? Wendy believes in the possibility of change. And I believe in Wendy. So I too will strive to be open to change. Okay, darling, show Ty the scenes you showed me."

Wendy smiled and nodded, then brought the church interior into view. "Mister Taylor, sir, see these two people sitting one right behind the other in your pews?"

"Of course," said Ty. "That's Bret Dornan and behind him Sarah Brand. He sells insurance. She works in a bakery, as I recall."

"Now look closer." Ty looked and saw how they were constituted, the deep desires in them. "They'll both leave your church."

"They won't."

"Watch." Snatches of their lives passed before him. He saw Sarah Brand bolt down a snifter of whiskey, again, again, freshening her breath to cover how much, how early, and how often she drank. She fought her addiction, sought help, buddied up with a fellow alcoholic, kicked the habit, fell again, rose again, this time succeeded, admitted to herself she had to manage this thing lifelong, and did so. All the while, Ty was privy to the weakness in her will, places in brain and body where urges lurked and desires beckoned, especially when stress or anxiety were at their height.

Interwoven with those moments, Ty watched Bret Dornan age as well. But while Sarah's urges ate away at her health, Bret's had a different cast. He longed, as all human beings do, to be touched. But the touch he longed for happened to be male. Ty felt Bret's guilt and shame, approved of them, then felt his own shame for judging him so. For he saw that Bret's urges were as natural as Sarah's were perverse. "He acts out of desperation at first," said Wendy, as they watched Bret visit bars, hang out in parks, pick up and be picked up. "He tries to change." Brett at a counseling center, subjecting himself to aversion therapy. "Then he finds a support group, they help him see how natural his impulses are, his desire to love and be loved. He learns to live alone, to love himself, see there, he finds a church which accepts and embraces him just as he is, he confides in the minister that a smile, a nod, and a kind word from him have helped Bret become whole." Bret was now older, in his early thirties. Ty observed, as Wendy provided her narration, Bret's pursuit of other interests, climbing in the Rockies, horseback riding, acting classes, attending the screening of classic films at the university and art theaters and, an hour north in Denver, at the Mayan, the Esquire. Ty saw him meet someone his age, pursue love, be loved. He delighted as love bloomed in his former parishioner. A moment later, it occurred to him that Bret's love interest was male, but it no longer seemed to make a bit of difference. No, that wasn't so. His own prejudices, drummed into him as a youth and adopted and promulgated thereafter, cast a warped light over the private moments Wendy showed him. But what this light illumined was not perverse at all.

"It's love, isn't it?" said Ty.

Santa replied, "The very thing that Christ urged. It's just that mortals are polymorphous in how they express that love."

"I'm sorry I caused Bret so much pain. But people tend to be pretty resilient, do they not?"

"Unfortunately, Mister Taylor," said Wendy, "not all of them do." Santa's voice grew harsh. "Especially the very young."

Wendy gestured and there stood Ty at the pulpit. But beyond him, picked out by special light, were the children touched by the beguiling ribbons of his words, as before. But now, the boys and girls grew in time lapse, shifting pews—and always the ribbons pierced their hearts. He saw bored toddlers and older kids, Gayle and Tara Pine among them, absorb his lessons as they grew, devolve into haters, echo imperfectly in their minds his words against sodomites, not knowing precisely what a sodomite was, but learning soon enough to focus the misplaced fears that Ty had nurtured in them. There were three or four children, likewise putting on mass and stature under his gaze, who donned heavy cloaks of shame and guilt, who slumped as they grew, who knew—even as they denied it—that they were different, that it was *them* that Reverend Taylor railed against so often, or rather, that in their hidden hearts, Satan had established a stronghold.

The child whose inward slump was most pronounced was the younger Stratton boy. Ty watched him curl inward in worry and fret, then dare a little defiance. Jamie became an adolescent, and a spark of tentative pride grew. Ty found himself rooting for the child, even though it was against his sermons that Jamie struggled. Abruptly, Jamie vanished from the pews. A spotlight held on his empty place. Then the church dimmed and faded.

In its stead arose Grandview Memorial Gardens and a burial plot.

Ty stood in a small circle of mourners. "Whose funeral is this?" he asked. Then he noticed that the Strattons held center stage, Walter, his wife Kathy, and their older son grown beyond his current age. "It's Jamie's, isn't it?"

"He took his own life," said Santa.

A chill rode up Ty's back and scruffed him by the neck. "But it couldn't have been my words that drove him to it. We just saw his spirit resisting them."

Then Wendy showed Ty thundering at the pulpit. Phrases fell from his lips. Juxtaposed, Walter and Kathy Stratton berated their son in near-identical phrases, in biblical passages he had cited continually across the years. Ty watched Jamie's spirit wither before the onslaught of his parents' condemnation, of Ty's condemnation, of the crushing drumbeat of societal condemnation—pounding into him the lie that not they but *he* was perverse, so that living grew gradually impossible.

There returned at last the funeral party and Ty's face, mock-pious and filled with scorn, hating the child even in his grave. It made him nauseous to see himself this way. The bedroom with its enchanted snow and its distant jingle of bells replaced the graveyard scene, but Ty wept. "My God," he said. "I had no idea. I'm so sorry."

Wendy patted his hand. "It'll be all right, Mister Taylor."

Her kindness made him weep the harder.

"I can change, I swear it."

"You can," said Santa, "and you will. I believe it with all my heart. It's already begun. Now sleep. We'll come by once more before morning. Pleasant dreams, little one."

Ty wiped his eyes and said, "Thank you."

But Santa and Wendy were already halfway to the door, and a deep sleep cradled Ty gently in its arms.

16.

PERVERSIONS AND REVERSALS

FRITZ HAD ENTERED the workshop to retrieve a custom-made drill bit for work on the third replica of the Strattons' bedroom when he heard Santa's sleigh jingle in. Indeed, he saw it sweep by a picture window and come to an abrupt stop in the snow. So he wasn't surprised when Santa strode in. What surprised him, to the point of shock, was Santa's mood.

He looked stern and acted—how could it be?—grumpy. From workbench to workbench he went, snatching toys from the hands of one elf or another. As he reached the door, he looked back and said, "All of you, out by the replicas, now!"

The door slammed after him. At once, Fritz and the others hopped to. "I wonder what we did wrong," he said to Herbert as they hurried outside. Herbert merely shrugged in puzzlement and followed him.

In the distance, Wendy was sitting in the sleigh stroking Snowball and Nightwind, who had picked their haughty way through deep snow from the cottage to greet her.

Santa surveyed the replicas, his eyes flashing here and there. When he came to the Strattons' replica, he bounded onto the platform and set all but one of the toys down. "Don't dawdle. Santa's helpers do not dawdle. Can everyone hear me? Good."

Fritz felt uneasy. He could not recall seeing Santa so agitated. Was that true? In the year of Rachel and Wendy's coming, during that lapse of elfin memory, perhaps he had acted so then.

"Look at this doll. Shoddy construction, a half-hearted paint job. Brother elves, we have always prided ourselves on superior work. Craftsmen who don't care or are distracted let defects go by, do they not? Take this dump truck. The action is less than smooth, the tires do not spin free, the tailgate sometimes sticks, not opening at all, you see? For all our age and experience, you and I are children at heart. It's essential that our work be infused with such joy, the recipient feels it in his or her bones.

"These replicas are no less important than our toys. They may be more important. But you are falling down. You're failing me. Every last one of you. Fritz, Karlheinz, Max, I entrusted this task to you, and it has been mismanaged. I will not allow such stumbling, do you hear me?"

The elves nodded and hung their heads, their doffed caps like limp leaves in their hands.

Fritz stood there in shock. Saint Nicholas had shamed him and his bunkmates before the community. Not that they didn't deserve it, but this was most unlike their master. What was preventing him from seeing the damage Gregor was causing? Why didn't he step in and set things right?

"You had *better* hear. And heed! Now Wendy and I are going to head out for one last visit to our mortals. I want every inch of these rooms spotless, perfectly jointed, flawlessly painted, done to a turn. These final replicas are intended to evoke childhood memories. A child's sensory recall is vivid and well-nigh impeccable. Every detail must be exact. I want nothing that spoils the effect, no wood shavings scattered about, no loose screws, none of that. Do you understand?"

"We do, Santa," said Fritz and the others. Herbert, wide-eyed, beside him, nodded vigorously.

"Now, I have no idea what sort of bug has burrowed its way up inside you. If I need to, I'll handhold you through it. But you're responsible elves. You can work out whatever problems are percolating through this community. Do it. Resolve them. Gather your scattered wits, bend every effort to producing work that is nothing less than superb. Start with these replicas. Then bring your renewed resolve back into the workshop. You are not mortal grown-ups; you are not slackers on the job. So stop pretending you are. Now clear the way. Wendy and I have mortals to visit."

And he strode through the crowd, pressing toys into their makers' hands and setting his course for the sleigh. Snowball and Nightwind hopped down from Wendy's lap as Gregor and his brothers stepped away from the reindeer. A vicious whipsmack asterisked the air above their antlers, and up they rose. Though Santa did not wave farewell, Wendy gave a tiny finger-twiddle when he wasn't looking. Then they headed back the way they had come, until the sleigh was a smudge and a speck and then nothing at all.

Fritz felt numb. In the moments just endured, something seemed to have died. He had the feeling Gregor was gloating.

"Let's go, Herbert," he said.

But it quickly became clear that no one was going anywhere.

***

"All right," said Gregor, bounding onto the platform Santa had vacated, "gather 'round, all of you." They had been shamed, and Gregor wasn't about to lose a chance to hammer home his message.

His brothers emerged from the workshop carrying Santa's lectern. They brought it to the platform and set it up before him, then stood at his left and right with folded arms.

"Now," said Gregor, rapping the lectern sharply with his fist. "You heard what Santa said. Time and again, I have railed against a vile habit, a habit that has run rampart through our community and at last degraded our work. Our esteem in the eyes of the good saint who relies upon our labor has eroded. Barring a miracle, it will soon be washed away entirely. Is that what you want? Is it?"

"No, Gregor," they mumbled.

"Nor do I. But you, unlike me, lack self-control. Do you think Gregor is never tempted to sneak a finger up his nose? I am not so impervious to temptation as that. What I am is ever vigilant, vigilant to a fault."

This of course was nonsense, and he knew it. But getting away with it thrilled him. And perhaps claiming so in public would make it true. If nothing else, it established his moral supremacy and brought Fritz into further disrepute.

"At the merest hint of temptation, my brothers, I squelch it, I pulverize it, I toss its ashes into the dustbin of never! Never shall Gregor sully his fingers with the vile snail-stuff of mucus, never shall that germ-riddled gloop pass the sacred portal of my lips, never profane my tongue, never outrage my taste buds, never slither down my throat. For I, and you, and all of us are meant for nobler things."

Inwardly he preened. I'm a far better speaker than Santa Claus, he thought. Perhaps toppling Fritz and imposing stricter order on his helpers will sufficiently elevate me, that taking Santa's place enters the realm of possibility.

"To some of you, Gregor may seem obsessed, a johnny-one-note, ever harping on this single problem. Do you know why I do it? Anyone."

The watchmaker raised his hand. "To make us better elves?"

"That's right, Franz. Perfectly expressed. To make us better elves. You've been worse elves lately. You have been horrendous elves. By

God, a lesser guardian of your moral well-being would have thrown in the towel long ago. Shame on you. Shame on you all. I point out one shortcoming and what do you do? You come even shorter! You *increase* the frequency of your misbehavior. In the back there, you know who you are, keep your hands away from your face! Our skilled watchmaker says, to make you better elves. And he is right.

"But what does that mean? It means being less like grown-up mortals, those post-childhood slaves to habit. A wise fellow named Sam Beckett once said, habit is a great deadener. And so it is. Habits deaden. But practices freely elected enliven. Let one habit in, open the door a hairline crack, and its brother habits swiftly follow. They buzz about, they distract, they eat up time and energy, focus and intent, championing sloth where diligence and industry once reigned. We cannot allow it, my brothers. For the sake of the children, we must not allow it. Henceforth I shall redouble my efforts on your behalf. My eagle eye, beaming restraints as sturdy as leather, shall help rein you in. If such be obsession, why then Gregor is obsessed. He freely admits it." Gregor opened his hands in appeal. "But to be obsessed in so worthy a cause is nobly to be obsessed. It is to be touched, dare I say it, by the hand of God Almighty himself. The tip of God's gargantuan finger has found his servant Gregor and conveyed him to his mouth; down through God's digestive tract travels Gregor, transformed, brought forth as divine waste and returned to you with renewed purpose. I shall be your harness, dear friends, I your traces, I the whip that keeps your attention focused in the proper direction. Under my guidance shall your hooves beat with confidence against the wind, your antlers loft high in proud purpose. Together, as one, nostrils flaring and unprobed, shall we traverse eternal night, our ever-replenished sleigh gliding through unimpeded atmosphere. Together we will beat this obsession, together trample habit in the dust, reviving once more our finest selves. Do it, said Santa. Do it, say I. We can, my brothers, and we will!" He finished with a flurry, his audience entranced.

Good, he thought, but I won't allow them to raise me up, as they do Santa. No telling where those hands of theirs have been. The elves kept a respectable distance as he and his brothers cut a swath through them and made for the stables. No, he thought, they shall not raise me up, though the idea had in fact occurred to none of them.

***

Kathy awoke on a sunny mountain trail standing beside the other dreamers. It was a warm fall afternoon, the trees riotous with yellow and orange, among russet hawthorn and defiantly blue-green spruce.

Robed in white as before, they held hands in a circle. A smiling Ty Taylor said, "Let us give thanks for God's blessings. He has given us the opportunity for radical change, in the place where prejudice and ill will take root. He has shown us one of our sins, its consequences, and how we might abandon it and move toward true righteousness."

"I've changed," said Matt. "That's for sure."

A nearby stand of aspens rustled its thin gold coins. "I think we've changed as well," said Kathy, and Walter agreed.

They seemed to be somewhere in the Rockies. Down the mountain, vistas opened into people's lives. "Marvelous," said the preacher, and Kathy knew that, as before, their vision was shared. The conversations that came to their ears, though they overlapped a hundredfold, were in all cases clear and easy to comprehend. The words were mundane, full of jokes and topical references—yet they connected people, and those connections were buoyed by undercurrents of love. Love was something Kathy prized in her life, and here it was, man to woman, man to man, woman to woman. This was no ordinary dream. It would not fade into forgetfulness, or if it did, the essence would burn in her, day by day. It was a blessing, one she marveled she had been chosen to receive.

Then Kathy gasped.

An arctic breeze rose to chill them to the bone. Fire seared their hands, which they at once drew in. The sky grew dark and split open. Down dropped a leering crew of man-sized toad-like creatures, bald, naked, three-fingered, blunt-browed, and stinking of gutted fish. These slumped hunched things herded Kathy and the others further apart, and into their midst appeared a hard-eyed nymph wearing nothing but a blood-flecked necklace of teeth. Woman-shaped she was, but no woman at all. Still, her breasts were firm and tipped tight and pointed, her legs long, her thighs muscled, her hips and buttocks perfectly curved, her sex smooth-haired and wide with invitation. The creatures, Kathy had no doubt, belonged to the nymph. Leering at her, they stood hard between the legs.

Her serenity yielded to panic. "Foolish mortals," the nymph said in a voice that made Kathy's throat seize up. The nymph's cold beauty,

109

her beguiling scent, had opened forbidden places in Kathy's soul. This was not the gentle persuasion of Santa, but an invasive wrenching into dark and shameful realms.

"You really think the creatures who have invaded your bedrooms are what they claim to be?" As much as Kathy had resisted Santa Claus, she wished him truly to be an emissary from God. "Wish away." The nymph could read minds. "But he is not that." Kathy concentrated on the twenty-third Psalm, valley of death, fear no evil. "Nor the girl. Behold them."

And the nymph brought up Santa and Wendy as Kathy had last seen them, the soul of generosity, innocence, and caring. Then Kathy's eye was drawn deep beneath the façade to a place foul and brackish.

"Heaven protect us," said Reverend Taylor.

Kathy was alarmed at Walter, whose eyes flitted between the demon wearing the Santa mask and the nymph's naked allure. When he saw her watching him, he lowered his eyes in shame.

"Hear them," commanded the nymph.

"We're almost home," the Santa demon was saying.

"A little further," said the other. "One more visit, and their souls will drop like fruit into the Master's hand."

"How easy it is to fool them. A smile, the scent of fresh pine, the jolly old elf and his darling whelp—their perceptions are paper thin. The devil wears a pleasing face."

Kathy trembled at the menace their voices concealed. She began again to recite the psalm.

"They'll return," said the nymph. "But now you're armed against them. You have heard the lies behind their feigned generosity. They have thrown your own good sense into doubt. Hold fast to your beliefs and their satanic mission will fail."

The conversations from the plains below returned. But now, the love they had heard turned sour. In some cases, the words changed; in others, Kathy tasted bile beneath the treacle. She caught Walter's covert leer at the nymph and knew, as she had always known, that his professed love for her was calculated and opportunistic. Save for God's mercy, they were damned. The preacher, the bully, her husband, herself.

And down the mountainside, all were damned. But damned beyond redemption were the unrepentant sodomites. Their skin was poxed and pustulant, their organs of generation disgusting. Their minds rioted in the urge to perform revolting bedroom acts. They were unknowable, unfathomable, beyond the grace of the Lord, who was all-forgiving but for these willful servants of Satan.

Kathy had no doubt that the nymph and her offspring were demons as well. But just as angels were mutually supportive, so demons tore at one another in envy and hatred. It took a thief to catch a thief, one Judas to betray another. But Kathy resolved to cling to the old rugged cross. Her Savior's unwavering truth would be her bulwark in time of trouble.

The ground shook. Fissures appeared. The sky grew dark and troubled. And in her mind, balance went awry. Unable to stand, she fell to her knees on the path, which split wide and tumbled her down into hellfire, her companions close behind screaming.

Kathy could hardly hear Walter's screams for her own.

17.
A RECRUIT LEAPS
INTO THE FRAY

"SCOLD THEM, WENDY? I read them the riot act," replied Santa. "This time, the bedrooms will be perfect." He cracked his whip above the heads of his team, who pretended to pick up speed but really simply maintained the swift pace Lucifer had already established.

"Maybe I should ask Fritz what's going on," said Wendy.

"They'll work it out. They always do. A wise master sets his workers loose on a task and leaves them be. Mine are highly skilled, good-natured, and industrious. But what a dull world it would be if everyone was perfect."

"I suppose so," said Wendy. Then, with a sigh, "It's such a lovely night!"

"It is indeed," said Santa, gazing at the canopy of stars and the slumbering planet below. He really ought to fret less about things, he thought. Coming into contact with grown-ups and bad kids only stirred up the Pan in him, and dwelling on their faults made matters worse.

"They're dreaming together, the Strattons, Ty Taylor, and Matt Beluzzo," she continued. "In a little while, we'll visit them one last time. This will be the bestest night ever!"

Santa had an idea. "Let's look in on them, shall we? It'll give us a bead on their progress."

Wendy clapped her hands. "All right," she said. But when she scanned the foursome, her face went white. "Jeepers."

"What is it?" he asked.

"Just look at them."

He quickly surveyed the dreamers one by one. Their souls were of course misshapen in many ways. But in generosity toward homosexuals, he fully expected leaps and bounds. Not so. Something had envenomed them there. Even as he watched, their souls fell into ever-increasing fear and hatred.

"It's gone awry," he said anxiously. "Why did we ever start this?"

"Calm down, Daddy. There's got to be an explanation."

Rising in his seat, Santa sent great urgency along the length of his whip. "Take us down without delay!" he commanded, calling Lucifer and the others by name. And down they went, so fast that Wendy said, "Whee!" and Santa said, "Whoa!" Through a ferocious snowstorm they plunged, protected as always by a bubble of calm and warmth. When they touched down in the barren wastes of the Yukon, Santa threw wide the mantle of magic time and shouted, "Michael!"

The storm went instantly still. Arrested flurries speckled the air with white feathers. At once the archangel appeared in all his glory, streaming light, his wings white and magnificent behind him.

"To what do I—?"

"Look at them," said Santa. "Just look at the state of our visitants' souls. They're getting worse. I knew I was out of my league with fallen grown-ups and a compromised twelve-year-old. My rage has backfired. Or they're too ensconced in their old ways to change. Erase our visits. Reverse them. Can you do that? Back out our clumsy interventions. Or mine, rather. Wendy was the soul of patience with them."

"I'm sorry," said Michael, "I can't reverse or erase or back out anything. Only the Father can do that."

"Well then ask him!"

"Let me examine them. Ah! It's the Tooth Fairy. Her and her imps. They've somehow managed to penetrate the dreamscape and counter its effects. The mortals have retreated in panic to the safe haven of prejudice."

Santa didn't like the look on the archangel's face. "You can fix them, can't you?"

"Please say you can," pleaded Wendy.

Michael shook his head sadly. "Your final visit has got to do the trick. Everything depends on appealing to their childhoods. Once you've persuaded them one hundred percent, she'll be powerless against them. Oh but, good Lord, she's convinced them you're demons who only *seem* nice. Boy, you two have your work cut out for you."

"Now wait a minute," said Santa, his brain on fire. "Isn't there anything you can do?"

"Hold on," said Michael. His effulgent brow momentarily darkened with thought. "She's trumped us. How can we trump her? I don't want to bring in God if I don't have to. He's pretty busy. And he would probably say no. Besides, he wouldn't have entrusted me with this task if he didn't think....Wait! That's it! I'll enlist a recruit."

"A recruit?"

"Of course." Michael grew suddenly animated. "You were planning to appeal to the innocence of childhood anyway. Who better? And the Tooth Fairy hasn't yet tainted his image. Stay right here. I have to make sure he's willing."

"Make sure *who's* willing?"

"Back in a flash." The archangel vanished.

Santa huffed. "Wonderful," he said. "Here we are, stuck in a blizzard, our mortals compromised, our task derailed, and he tells us to wait. I'm beginning to think we've been bamboozled by an incompetent."

"He'll be back, Father, I know he will," said Wendy, giving him a hug. "Don't give up hope. That's not like you. He's bringing reinforcements. He's an archangel. I'm sure he knows what he's doing."

"Reinforcements," said Santa, distraught. "We'll wait. For your sake, we'll wait." But despair and dread and a distinct lack of *ho-ho-ho* were all he felt.

That evening, the Easter Bunny retired early to his burrow.

On the anniversary and at the very spot of God's visit here eight years before, he always spent a quiet evening counting his blessings. This he followed with a full day of giving thanks, loudly and joyously before his hens and his perpetual and mercifully noiseless machines, making great leaps about the burrow, in his quarters, in the exercise area, and in the clearing near the burrow's mouth. Every year, without fail, the forest floor brimmed with crisp noisy leaves, red, yellow, and brown, among which the Easter Bunny would kick up raucous shufflings of jocundity and thanksgiving.

He truly had much to be thankful for. Uncountable years—well, all right, coming on to two thousand—of delivering Easter baskets. A maintenance-free environment. Zero commute. And a central role in the celebration of Christ's resurrection and of course (though this was mostly hush-hush) of the pagan fecundity rites Christianity had absorbed. But surely the thing he had most to be thankful for was the Father's visit to his burrow.

He knew his memory of that event had been severely altered. But that didn't matter. Yea, though the visit had lasted an hour—dare he hope it had?—were he to recall but one second, nay the thousandth part of a second, such special attention from the Almighty would have made his life a supreme satisfaction entire. But he remembered far more than a second. Indeed he did. He had nestled in the divine palm, and God had praised the efficiency and appropriateness of his deliveries, the early spring happiness he brought to little boys and girls.

To be sure, there was a gap in his memory, something which, were it known, he ought to spend eternity repenting for, a terrible misdeed whose specifics escaped him. But whatever that elusive ugliness was, it paled before the privilege of having been created by the Father and walked through these quarters so many centuries ago, and then of having him drop in again so recently. Though eight years had passed, the sweet scent of divinity still infused the burrow's every chamber and expanse. The hens had begun to lay more vigorously, their eggs more precisely ovoid than ever, the designs upon the shells ever more impressive as they rolled down the ramps into vast unfillable bins.

So here he sat in the always-crisp straw of the exercise area, wide-eyed, dagger-eared, wet-nosed, his front paws in parallel before him, his back ones flat beneath the tense curve of haunch and thigh. In the distance, the machines hummed and the eggs knocked along like non-spherical billiard balls, rolling end over end down the switchbacks of perfectly maintained ramps. This was the sound of divinity, the sound of childish glee not quite unleashed but soon, soon. To its rump and roll, the Easter Bunny contentedly counted his blessings.

Think then with what wonder it was that a change in the light, a fresh waft of divine perfumes, the hint of wings, of shoulders, of an angelic eye and face and form, quite enraptured our meditative if high-strung rabbit. His eyes grew wide. His nose twitched. His tail dust-mopped furiously in the air. A back leg stirred, a foot began to thump.

And when the form clarified itself—a boyish figure berobed in white, wide-winged, wanton-locked, a beatific smile upon its face, its golden halo nearly brushing the dirt-curves of ceiling, the soles of its feet suspended inches above the floor—why, the Easter Bunny simply had to burst free, to racetrack madly about his exercise area, stopping for a quick roll in the dirt and a vigorous gnaw upon scraps of bark, only to leap up and resume his frenzied career once more.

"Blessed art thou, best of bunnies," said the angel. That froze him where he was. "For thou hast been chosen to serve the Lord in yet another way."

"You mean," he asked, "other than my Easter chores?"

"I do. For I am Michael, of archangels the highest, who stayed the hand of Abraham when his sacrificial knife touched the throat of his son Isaac, who routed the army of Sennacherib, who leads the souls of the dead to the afterlife. From my tears are the cherubim formed. From my breath do autumn leaves take their dying, drifting downward to scatter and scoot below."

"Do tell."

"There is a task," he continued. "A task begun by Santa Claus and his stepdaughter Wendy. You must, if you will, help them see this task to completion."

At the names the archangel spoke, panic seized the Easter Bunny. His mouth went dry. Unfocused shame welled up in him. What was it? What had he done? And how had this girl and her stepfather figured into it? He was heartsick. How could he possibly accept the angel's charge if it meant having to collude with Santa Claus and Wendy? She had a cat, two cats, this girl. How did he know that?

"No, really, it's impossible. I couldn't possibly join those good souls in a task of *any* kind. We operate in such different spheres, in the service of completely different holiday traditions, don't you see?"

The angel simply gazed upon him with love.

"On the other hand...I would be honored to accept, and I do."

Who had said that? Yet how could he say otherwise?

Michael beamed. The Easter Bunny, filled to the brim with panic, was also flooded with relief. He warred and worried, the joy within him leaping as great as the dread that weighed him down.

Then the angel, in florid phrases, filled in the outlines of what lay ahead. His task involved visits to mortals, bringing them in touch with the purity of their childhoods, all for the sake of one boy, Jamie Stratton, eight years old, happy now, but headed, as he aged, for shipwreck on the shoals of societal mishap.

The Easter Bunny nodded and said he was most effervescently eager to be enlisted in God's army of the righteous. And so he was. But it was also true that he inwardly cowered and flinched and trembled at the thought of working with Santa and the child. What dread memories would be dredged up at the sight of them? Would they shun or denounce him? Would they expose and shame him, casting him forever into disfavor with the Almighty? Ah but the Almighty, who knew all, had not taken away the demi-paradise in which the Easter

Bunny lived and worked and had his being.

Be calm, he thought.

He nodded, and listened, and watched the archangel vanish, waiting in dread and longing for the red-suited, black-booted, white-bearded benefactor of children to sweep down before the burrow and gather him up.

18.

INNOCENCE TRIUMPANT

"WHAT DID MICHAEL MEAN, the Easter Bunny has changed?" asked Wendy.

Santa's lip line was tight as he overlooked his galloping reindeer and Lucifer's glowing antlers. "More docile, I hear. Not as nasty as he once was. More worthy of delivering baskets to decent homes."

"When was he ever *not* worthy?"

"I'd rather not say."

"Why doesn't he visit the North Pole?"

"He used to. Now it's forbidden."

"But why?"

Santa looked at her, then forward again. "It would upset your mother. It would upset Anya and me. Someday I'll tell you why, but not now."

Santa's tone gave Wendy the creeps. But she knew enough to press the point no further. Maybe she would ask Mommy when she got the chance. She tried to recover the thrill she had felt when Michael told them he had enlisted the Easter Bunny's aid. She had clapped her hands at that and squealed with delight, only to see Santa grow pale and his eyes widen in disbelief.

"Why him?" he had asked the archangel.

That's when Michael told them the Easter Bunny had been utterly transformed, in the twinkling of an eye.

An assurance. But of what?

"We have to assume," said Santa, "that the archangel knows what he's doing. That he's not an incompetent bumbler making an absolute hash of things. We'll try to have faith in that at least. Ah, there's the place."

"Where?" Wendy saw only a dark sea of unbroken treetops. Then suddenly there appeared a clearing and the entrance to an underground burrow. They swooped down and came smoothly to a stop near the entrance.

"Bunny!" shouted Santa. "Look lively. We haven't got all night."
Nothing.

Santa hauled back to shout again when a furry head with long pink ears popped out of the entranceway. He blinked once, then bounded into the clearing to stand an impressive eight feet tall, ten if you counted the ears.

"Good evening," he began, "and may I say what a great—"

"Get in," said Santa.

Wendy was stunned by her father's rudeness.

"I'm Wendy," she said, thrusting out a hand. One of them, at least, would show some manners.

When the Easter Bunny raised his paw, Santa said, "Don't touch her! I told you to get in. There in the back."

"Father, where are your...?" She gritted back her anger and her upset. "Shake, Mister Rabbit." Wendy seized his paw and shook it, thrilled to be meeting this warm and generous creature at last. Many were the Easter baskets he had left at her home in Sacramento. Though monstrous in size, he was the soul of gentleness. "With your help, we will save little Jamie's life. It's a privilege to be working with you, kind sir."

"Likewise, I'm sure," said the Easter Bunny.

He nearly tipped the sleigh over getting in. He squeezed himself into the back seat where Santa's bulging pack rode on Christmas Eve. "It's a tight fit," he said.

Santa cracked his whip and shouted, "Up with you, my four-footed beasties!" The team shot skyward with such abruptness that Wendy's head angled up and her back pressed against the lacquered seat.

"Whee!" said the Easter Bunny.

"It's fun, isn't it?" said Wendy, looking over her shoulder.

"Goodness, yes." Silence. "May I say again how grateful I am to be on this mission. I've seen plenty of mortals of course, sleeping in their beds and...and so forth. But I've never spoken to them, and I must say little ants of anticipatory joy are crawling up and down my spine at the prospect." Silence. "If I may be so bold, I sense a wee bit of discomfort emanating from the driver of this magnificent vehicle. If I have done aught to offend, and I have the vaguest feeling that I have, I humbly and profusely apologize. We are none of us perfect—"

"What you did is beyond apology."

The hairs rose on the back of Wendy's neck.

"So don't even try."

"I...I surely wish I knew what I've—"

"Your memories have been erased," said Santa. "Mine have not. And no, I will not go into it. You will drop this now. I'm doing my best to focus on Jamie Stratton. Were it the Devil himself, though that's a creature that doesn't exist, I would work with him to reverse this boy's fate. Let's just say, you'd better deliver, Mister Rabbit. This had better be worth the grief caused by being in your presence. No, wait, I mustn't be so harsh. You're here. You'll serve whatever purpose you're meant to serve. I don't have to like it, but I will do my best to be charitable while we're together. Two rules." He turned and glared at the Easter Bunny in a way that Wendy had never seen him glare at anyone. "You will get no closer to me or Wendy than you are now. And you will not bring up my discomfort again. This I demand, and these demands are subject neither to negotiation nor to further discussion. In a moment, I'm going to ask you if I have made myself clear. Your answer had better be yes sir, or I will throw you out of this magnificent sleigh.

"Now.

"Have I made myself clear?"

The Easter Bunny stared in wide-eyed amazement. Then his brow wrinkled, and he slumped into a mumbled "Yes, sir."

"Good." He faced forward again. "Sorry, Wendy, but he...." Then he lapsed into silence, shoulders tense, avoiding her.

Wendy looked back and gave a tiny shrug of encouragement. She was all at sea with Santa's strange behavior, shocked and upset even as she was thrilled with their mission and their new recruit.

The Easter Bunny raised a paw as if to say, no matter. Still, the gesture could not hide his discomfort, and Wendy was determined to be as kind to him as possible and to confront her stepfather—on a walk in the woods, perhaps—when this was over.

Wendy stole a glance at Santa's grim-set face, then did what she could to dismiss it, gazing with anticipation into the night sky.

The nightmare had shattered Matt Beluzzo.

Its torment went deep indeed, increasing where increase seemed impossible. Moreover, that torment had been meted out by the same immortals who appeared before him now. Their cheery demeanor struck him as obscene. Their presence so frightened him, he hardly noticed how changed the room was. Though he lay in his own bed, the walls, floor, and ceiling were those of his tiny room in the trailer, where they had lived until he turned eight. Dozens of candles bathed the bedroom in warm light.

He shivered uncontrollably. "Stay away from me, man. Just keep your distance, okay?"

"You've been dreaming," said the Santa thing. "Whatever you've been told or shown or made to suffer, it's all a lie." But the creature's drawn face did not inspire trust.

Then the Easter Bunny leaped into the room, a great surge of fur and soft brown eyes shiny in the flicker of candle flame. Though Matt ought to have been terrified, he felt instantly at ease.

The new visitor hopped past the other two and placed a paw on the blankets closest to him. "Greetings, Matt," he said in a voice that melted his remaining defenses. "May I say what an honor it is to meet you. I want to apologize for the meager baskets I've left in the past. But you were, and still are, a naughty little fellow, you know, to be scrupulously honest about it. Still, I'm quite sure this visit will turn you into one of the nice ones, and then I'll feel far more generous toward you on Easter Eve. Now, that isn't *why* you should change. A craving for chocolate and jellybeans would be insufficient to justify or sustain such an abrupt readjustment in your life. No, simple love of all humans everywhere, conspicuously lacking in you thus far, ought to be your guide, Matt." He glanced at Santa and Wendy, who had lost all taint of the demonic. "But I blather. Pray, forgive me, you're the first mortal I've ever addressed."

"That's all right," said Matt. It was strange to see and hear a giant bunny rabbit form intelligible words and phrases.

"You spoke to me," said a delighted Easter Bunny. "He did. He spoke to me."

"Let's get to the business at hand, shall we?" said Santa, with a gesture beyond the bed that dissolved the walls.

"Yes, of course," said the Easter Bunny.

"Here you are at four months," said Wendy, "almost able to roll over and crawl." There he lay upon a thin blanket on a threadbare carpet in the trailer's living room, Mom and Pop shouting at each other across a table littered with grease-stained bags of fried chicken. Matt tried to hate them, but found it impossible with the Easter Bunny beside him. His father fumed cigarette smoke from his nostrils. "Yeah well, I'm steamed cuz some punk faggot cut me off coming home. I came this close to flooring it and ramming the sucker's bumper sideways up his candy ass."

The Easter Bunny raised a paw to his cheek. "Oh dear me, your father's definitely not a nice man, is he? But the point of this, of course, Matt, is that while your wide-eyed infant self understood not a word of what he just said, your whole being was shaped by everything around you, and this instance of bigotry, so casually spewed by your paterfamilias, has right now nestled snug and secure at the base of your brain's linguistic center. Okay, Santa, bring up the next scene, please."

His parents were replaced by a schoolyard in the brilliance of the noonday sun. "Hey, look, there I am." And so he was, his hair tousled, running in the playground, not looking where he was going.

"Oops-a-daisy, down goes Matt!" said the Easter Bunny with a sympathetic chuckle. Then he grew somber. "Now this is the really sad part, because you see those older boys? You're crying. You're bawling your eyes out, the unreliable ground has ripped itself out from under you and dealt you a skinned knee, a real ouch-a-roonie, and it smarts. But instead of helping you, these naughty boys taunt you." And there they were, a memory rushing vividly back, three ugly brat-faces pie-holing open around the word sissy and a singsong "Matty is a gur-ull, Matty is a gur-ull." Even now, at twelve and tough as nails, Matt felt his throat catch and his gut seize up with hurt. "There, there, Matt," said the Easter Bunny, "it feels really bad, doesn't it?"

"Uh huh."

"Now see what happens next." The schoolyard shifted. Matt was a few years older, shoving a little kid down, holding his shoulders, and getting in his face with, "Sissy, sissy, Joey's a sissy."

"You didn't cry very much after those kids called you bad names, except sometimes in your room at home, into your pillow so your mommy and daddy wouldn't hear."

It was odd.

As scene after scene sprang to life, it wasn't so much their content that turned him as the presence of the Easter Bunny. He was so warm and loving, so funny and quirky, and so gentle with the truth, yet not afraid to offend, not really, around his apologies. He showed him Terry at eight, the boy Matt had once been—but seemed no longer—fated to kill. How sweet he was, running into a candy store, methodically setting down two quarters and a dime and pointing excitedly into a glass case to claim his prize. Matt was shown other boys too, and himself at many ages. And always in this, though the Easter Bunny never called attention to it, Matt saw that he himself was in fact attracted far more to males than females, and that his entire life had become an elaborate denial of it.

The Easter Bunny nodded. "You see how things are. That's nice. It's the first step in straightening out your crooked walk. You can be kind, though nasty folks call you names. Some people will tromp and trounce you. If they do, answer them with kindness, not as if you're better than they, though indeed you are; but because it's the right thing to do, and you, Matt, from this moment on, are a right-thing-doer."

"I am?" asked Matt. Then upon reflection: "I am. I can do that. And I will. I have Santa Claus and the Easter Bunny on my side. That's got to count for something. Oh, and you too, Wendy. I didn't mean to leave you out."

"That's okay." Wendy beamed.

"Santa, bring back that first scene, would you?" asked the Easter Bunny. Considerably more at ease now, Santa gestured. Matt's parents once more sat before them, gnawing chicken bones. "He's the true test of your resolve, isn't he?"

"My dad." Matt's hatred was visceral.

"Go further. Stare right straight into him." Matt gazed deep down into the world of sorrows his father carried. As he watched, the old man's life unraveled in time through all the nastiness done to him and by him to others, until the adolescent appeared and rolled backward into a childhood state of innocence. Then forward again they flew, to the kitchen table and the smoke fuming from his nostrils. But when Matt arrived there, he found he could no longer hate his father.

"Now, your mom." And so with her, yet another timestream backward unrolled, a lifetime unlived and relived. My God, thought Matt, the misery. The paths closed off. The restraints placed on her so early, so often, and in so many ways, that she gave into them and defined herself by them, embraced a loser, sought solace in drink, and let herself go to seed.

"What a sad sight," said Matt with compassion.

Then his bedroom returned.

"Sad indeed. And how magical are your tears. I take joy in what now springs to life in you. Goodbye, dear boy," said the Easter Bunny, the warm leather of his paw touching Matt's face for the first time. Matt hugged the gentle creature, then exchanged hugs with Wendy and Santa.

"Don't go," he said.

His visitors told him they wished they could stay longer. But they all, Matt included, understood. They had served their purpose. The grime had been wiped from Matt's vision, which now sparkled vivid and clear.

Will I backslide? came the idle worry.

Then sleep took him, and assurance burned in his soul, an assurance that could not be gainsaid.

19.

PARENTHOOD UNSHACKLED

"YES, OF COURSE," SAID SANTA, TIGHTENING HIS HOLD on the reins. "Our furry friend did a fine job. We all did, Wendy. Not just him. The three of us did. But it's too early to pat ourselves on the back. Children, even nasty ones, can be pretty malleable. Grown-ups are the challenge. Their prejudices have had years to calcify. Even the best ones tend to turn into smug little know-it-alls. And let's not forget, these particular grown-ups have been misled by a certain fairy and her brood."

From behind: "If I may say so, sir—"

My God, thought Santa. Yet another assault of brutal honesty was in the offing. The creature may have been, according to the archangel, utterly transformed, but his frankness could use some toning down.

"—I sense envy toward me. You are less than secure perhaps in your stance toward Wendy here. You worry, as I do not, that she will admire me for having succeeded with little Matt where you (though, if I may assure you, Santa, I do not share your self-condemnation) have faltered, or failed, or fallen down utterly in your parental responsibilities."

"Nonsense." But Santa knew that the insufferable rabbit was spot on. He had lost himself, condemning these mortals when he ought to have been the soul of patience, intolerant in the face of intolerance. And toward the Easter Bunny? Dear Lord, how could he forgive or forget the outrages this creature had perpetrated upon his wives during the days in which the furry bearer of baskets had bartered his soul for the Tooth Fairy's favors? Yet here he was, doing good and making Santa look bad in Wendy's eyes.

Be generous, thought Santa, generous. The way Matt was fixed shows me a possible way past my Pan self.

"We're a team, Daddy, us three," said Wendy. "With Jamie's parents and the preacher, we'll just need to pitch in and try harder. The Easter Bunny has shown us how. By appealing to their childhood

125

innocence and making a heartfelt assault against their wobbly and wrong grown-up stances, we have a chance, in this one area, to restore their inborn divinity."

"Maybe you're right, dear."

"I'm sure she is."

"I didn't ask you," snapped Santa. "Did I ask you?"

In the sleigh, dead silence.

"All right," said Santa, "I apologize."

"Oh there's no need for—"

"But there is, and I do. Wendy's right, we're a team. We need to bend all our efforts toward Jamie's parents and the Reverend Taylor. The Tooth Fairy has thrown a terrifying veil over their eyes. We've got to rip it to shreds and bring them home to godliness. Truth is the way. Truth is our best weapon. I am content to have you spearhead the attack, bunny. We have our differences, that you know—"

"But whatever might they—?"

"They exist. That's all I'll say. But if we don't set them aside and join in common cause, the Tooth Fairy will have been right to call us demons and the boy will be lost."

"All for one," said Wendy, "and one for all!"

From behind Santa: "One for all!"

"Yes of course," agreed Santa. "I'll go along with that. We have the resolve. My helpers' handiwork has reverted to topnotch—"

"You know, sir," the Easter Bunny ventured, "I have an idea what might be bothering them."

"I don't want to hear it," said Santa. "Concentrate your efforts on Kathy and Walter Stratton. Scour their childhoods. We must come to them armed to the teeth." And so they did, furrowing their brows in an intense effort to comb the past, as the reindeer drew them across the skies over Colorado Springs.

Half a hand-span from the Easter Bunny's back, Gronk held on, drinking in every word. In the boy's bedroom, he had been pressed against wall and ceiling, unable to draw nearer and feeling queasy to be as near as he was. He debated fiercely with himself. Should he break away and report now, or hang on for the next visit? He and Mommy and his brothers had driven the grown-ups into a desperate embrace of prejudice. If Santa and his cohorts failed to pry their fingers loose from that prejudice, they would lose the game. Far better, Gronk thought, to report that triumph than the melting of some turncoat brat's will when faced with a big fuzzy bunny.

He decided he would wait, enduring the nausea of one more bedroom before making his report. When the sleigh banked, he clung fiercely to its back.

The Stratton house, for the third time, loomed from below.

Kathy awoke with the shakes, her skin still burning from eternal hellfire. Inviting warmth filled the bedroom and the odd glow that had *seemed* inviting but was...no, it again embraced her, and the sizzle and burst of pine knots upon an invisible hearth greeted her once more. How real the nightmare had felt. And how real the fantastical scene before her, the jolly old elf and his green-clad girl, and, oh my God, a brown-eyed bunny rabbit whose ear-tips nearly touched the ceiling and whose size and demeanor instantly identified him.

"You're demons." Walter's voice trembled. "We're on to you. I command you to leave this house."

Kathy noticed folds and shadows on their visitors' faces. Seemingly pure innocence glinted, in the candle glow, with hints of menace. How could she be sure? Then she set her jaw. Why struggle for certainty when she could simply surrender her will to God? The Bible could not be gainsaid. Right was right, and only the Devil would try to argue against it. It frightened her how pleasing a shape he could assume. "Get thee behind me," she commanded, blinking back tears.

"Oh good heavens," said Santa, "trust your eyes, will you? Trust your heart. We're who we say we are, and Almighty God has sent us to save your son."

"Salvation comes only through Christ."

"It's okay, Missus Stratton," said Santa's stepdaughter in that heartbreaking voice of hers. "We're in the same camp as Christ. Somehow the Tooth Fairy got into your dreams and tried to trick you. She isn't very nice at all. Daddy says she once did mean things to me and my parents, but God took away my memory of exactly what."

"I always believed," said Kathy, "that Satan's minions would be ugly with dark brows and hard eyes. But now I see that they can appear however they like, and still be wicked inside." The hurt on the girl's face gave Kathy pause, but she steeled herself. "I refuse to be swayed by your pretend sweetness, young lady. You're nothing but a little devil."

"That's quite enough," said the Santa demon.

The Easter Bunny raised a paw. "If I may, please." His loving

127

assurance instantly melted Kathy's resolve. "You don't know which camp to trust. I understand that. How can we prove to you that we are not demons? We cannot. Even the gentlest of mortals can harbor terrible monsters inside. But we are not like them. Our hearts are pure. All we can do is proclaim the truth and ask you to open yourselves to our words, to test them in the purest place in your hearts, in the place where God waits beyond fear and doubt."

Kathy let out a sniff and wiped her tears on her pajama sleeve. "Walter," she said. "I trust them."

He looked surprised at himself. "So do I."

"Good," said the Easter Bunny. "Santa, if you would be so kind."

Only then did Kathy notice the surroundings. On the right side rose up half the bedroom she had slept in as a girl in Cedar Rapids, the closet, the dresser, the flowered wallpaper. The left side was decked out, she guessed, like Walter's boyhood bedroom in Santa Fe. On one wall hung a plastic crucifix he had won at a sideshow.

Those bedrooms dimmed, but the scenes that surged up to replace them maintained the split. "Here you both are, taking your first steps."

Kathy, captivated by the toddlers before them, delighted to see Walter not in faded black and white photos, but as he had been in life. There sat his parents and hers, young and spry, without a trace of gray hair or wrinkles.

"That's my dad," said Walter, a catch in his throat.

"Yes," said the Easter Bunny, "and see how pure your hearts were then."

Kathy looked. The toddlers shown with divine innocence and only a trace of the parental failings they had begun to absorb. Even their parents were far more free in spirit, observing those triumphant first steps, than she remembered from recent visits.

"Observe your first days at school."

Kathy and her mom walked up the steps of Harrison Elementary, a buried memory at once brilliantly revived. In her frilly dress, she looked pouty-lipped and doleful as Mommy hugged her and spoke tearful assurances. On the other side stood Walter in a blue jumper and bright yellow shirt, bawling his heart out. Uncanny how every bit of him, as she knew him now, showed itself fully formed right there.

"One more glimpse from early childhood," said the Easter Bunny, "and my favorite." As well it might be: Easter egg hunts, hers in a park near her home, Walter's in a schoolyard. Boys and girls scurried past,

128

swift but deliberate, careful not to overlook any clump of grass that might conceal a splash of pastel.

Walter's chubby legs carried him proudly to Ellie Stratton. "Mommy, look what *I* found," he said in a voice that made Kathy fall in love with him all over again. He held up a bright blue egg capped by a canted oval of purple. "That's great, Walter. Here, I'll keep it with the others. Go find another, okay?"

Kathy's younger self merely screamed in delight, half looking but mostly just dancing about, overjoyed to be inside a sunlit explosion of boys and girl yelling and running and going mad with glee.

"Now watch this." He swept his paw. The children changed color, not just their faces and hands and legs but their clothing as well. A few were pure blue or pure yellow, but most were shades of green, from yellow green to olive, from hunter green to emerald, from olive green to chartreuse to teal. "My Easter egg children," laughed the Easter Bunny. "The blue ones were born with the impulse to be completely enraptured by the opposite sex, the yellow ones by the same. Observe the engaging mix and mingle in most children at that age. Of course, the off-blue ones will shortly learn to suppress any hint of yellow. And many of the bright yellow ones will hotly insist they are nothing but blue, blue as a clear blue sky, and that they never have been, nor could be, anything else."

"It looks," said Walter, "as if I'm mostly blue."

The Easter Bunny laughed. "Bluish-green as a deep dark sea. But you'll accept the culture's tinged lenses soon enough. You'll convince yourself you're a true blue American heterosexual boy from your cowlick right on down to your boots."

Then Kathy saw that her child self was a solid lawn-green. "Look at *me*," she said. "Are you sure that's me?"

"Yes indeed, Kathy. The Almighty formed you to be attracted to males and females in just about equal measure."

"But if that's true, why don't I feel it now?"

"If you allowed yourself, and if the messages you've heard all your life hadn't been so powerful and pervasive, you would."

Kathy felt robbed. The little girl gleefully giggling in all of her unabashed greenness seemed so much more fully dimensional than she felt herself now, a flat woman sitting in a flat bed, her mind sculpted to fit the grown-up world, her heart penned in by strictures, baffles on her eyes and filters on her thoughts. As if in response to what she was feeling, the Easter Bunny said, "Look at this."

129

Gone were the Easter egg hunts, and in their place scenes of themselves growing up. Signals from parents and preachers and older peers and TV and songs, sights on the street, who got to hold hands and who did not, lumberjack women and sylphlike men shunned and made fun off—all of it impinged upon them. This was the process by which her heart had been darkened, her judgment warped, and the bright light of generous embrace had been extinguished from her soul.

Walter too Kathy watched turn from a smiling child to a confused preteen to a glum high-schooler, caught up in sports, clamping down on any exuberance save for team spirit, crazy yocks with his friends, and leering jokes at the expense of big-bosomed girls.

Then their childhood bedrooms returned.

"Let's look in on your boys," said Wendy. There slept Kurt and Jamie in their beds. The Easter Bunny swept his paw, and Kurt turned the same hue as his father. But Jamie lay there as yellow as could be, compromised by the merest tinge of green.

In that moment, Kathy loved her sons with all her heart and soul. "They're perfect, aren't they?"

"Indeed they are," said the Easter Bunny. "And you must tell them so every day of their lives."

"I like your boys very much, Missus Stratton," said Wendy.

"They're good lads," chimed in Santa. "They, and all children, deserve unconditional acceptance from their parents in every stage of life, including their passage through puberty. I'll tell you honestly, Kathy and Walter, I don't have much truck with mortals once they turn nine or ten. You see why. That they stop believing in me isn't so bothersome, really, except that it's a warning signal that misguided judgmentalism is beginning to creep in. Young boys and girls resonate with me. But then, tricked into believing that grown-ups must surely be far wiser than they, they adopt their foolish manner of carving up the world. Precious few are brave enough to hang on to the fantastic realities they enjoy at seven or eight. You see what happens. Don't let it happen to Jamie."

"I won't," said Kathy, surprised at her vehemence.

"Me neither," said Walter.

"Stay a little," she went on. "Show us more." But her limbs grew heavy and her eyelids ached to close. She felt Santa's embrace and his comforting kiss on her forehead. "Goodnight, dear one," he said as sleep claimed her. "Be good always."

"I will," she murmured. "I promise."

130

20.
INNOCENCE RESCUES
A PREACHER

"IT FEELS GREAT, HELPING these good people," said Wendy.

"Yes, it does," replied Santa.

"It looks as if it's really going to happen."

"Oh, but Wendy," said the Easter Bunny, "you shouldn't bite into the marshmallow chick before it's reached your lips."

Wendy laughed at that.

But Santa steamed, and cursed himself for steaming. What had gotten into him? Here they were, on the final leg of their journey, his team galloping triumphantly through the night sky, and he felt a large measure of discontent.

"Things are going well," he said to fill the silence, then bit his lip and wished he hadn't spoken at all. His voice was tight, and he knew that Wendy and the accursed creature in back could hear it.

His discontent stemmed in part of course from an inability to forgive the Easter Bunny his transgressions. Santa didn't care how transformed he might be. It didn't erase his past, and his apparent obliviousness to that past was downright infuriating. He ought to be humble, riddled with guilt, unable to make eye contact, eternally penitent. Instead, he charmed their visitants. He charmed Wendy. He even charmed Saint Nick himself, which ticked off the jolly old elf all the more.

But mostly, it was envy. I'm out of my league, thought Santa. The rabbit's right at home. He takes, in complete innocence, these fallen mortals as they are, accepting and loving them no matter what. He's the soul of patience, while I lose all patience. That's not how I was before Pan flared up. Oh, I would've been awkward in the presence of adults, but not angry to the point of giving in to the desire to smash their smug little faces. I can't *stand* their moral blindness, their belligerence, their damned holier-than-thou attitude. Yet in my intolerance toward them, I fall into the same trap!

No matter. "On to the Reverend Taylor," he continued.

"He'll be a challenge," laughed the Easter Bunny. "But I look forward to melting even *his* hard heart. Eh, Wendy girl?"

"We've simply got to win him over," she said earnestly. "There's no other way."

"We will," said Santa. But at precisely that moment, with even greater resolve, the Easter Bunny said, "We will," and Santa let his words trail off.

One more visit, he thought. Just one more. Then it's goodbye, Easter Bunny. Goodbye, grown-ups. And I'll be in charge again. Things will settle down.

But alas, that was not to be.

When Ty Taylor awoke to the enticing aroma of roasting chestnuts, the crackle of Yule logs, and the warm flicker of a roomful of candle flames, he swiftly marshaled his mental faculties. All I have, he thought, is my resolve as a man and a Christian. Once more, I'm in my bedroom, at the argumentative mercy of a persuasive and plausible Santa Claus and child.

Indeed, when he sat up, there appeared before him not just the demons he had met previously but a new one. "And you, let me guess," he said, surprised that the creature's size did not terrify him, "are the Easter Bunny."

"Why yes, I am," said the creature in a voice that brought Ty's boyhood, in all its richness, back to him.

"Oh you're good," said Ty. "Very good indeed."

"Thank you."

"But you'll not sway me. I was close to falling, so guileful the show these two demons put on. But whatever you're poised to do, you can tell your Master that Ty Taylor remains fixed upon his Lord and Savior. Homosexuality is a sin. The Bible says so, and that's more than good enough for me. That you would think to convince a preacher of the Lord that such perversity is not only acceptable but to be embraced is, frankly, laughable."

The Easter Bunny was taken aback. "Really, Reverend Taylor, sir, if I may be so bold, the truly demonic is what was forced upon you in your nightmare. The Tooth Fairy is a creature of chaos. We understand she has appealed to your prejudices, has indeed shored them up. All we have come for is to show you scenes from the past and let you draw your own conclusions." His voice was simple and reassuring.

His limpid eyes touched Ty's heart.

"I will not fall," Ty insisted. "I will be strong."

"Be as strong as you like," said the Easter Bunny.

"Don't be upset, Mister Taylor," said the little girl.

Santa Claus stood to one side. There was something off about him. Why wasn't he more jolly? More spirited? He had certainly been so in prior visits. Was this bunny demon stealing his thunder? That was what Ty guessed was going on.

"Do you see where you are?"

Ty followed his raised paw to the closet with the sliding doors from his childhood, out of which he had been terrified a bear would emerge. There stood the dark-oak bookcase containing *Treasure Island* and *Uncle Remus* and other books. In one corner of the floor, his Bozo doll dozed against a Howdy Doody dummy.

Ty bristled. "I put away childish things long ago."

"Well," said the bunny demon, "if I might venture an opinion, maybe you put away too many of them. Observe yourself when you were rich in childish things. Perhaps you'll decide to pick and choose differently tonight."

The room exploded with overhead fluorescents from a ceiling as high as a three-story extension ladder. Below fidgeted rows of boys and girls in squat wooden chairs. "Calm down," said the severe woman standing in front of them. "I know it's Easter and your mothers and fathers are communing with God, and all you can think about are Easter baskets. Right?" A mumble of yeah's rose up. "I know, I know. But we're going to make a nice present for Mommy." She brought out a large tray of alphabet letters, made out of pasta dyed red and blue and green.

Ty said, "'Whatever your hand finds to do—"

"—do it with all your might,'" completed the Easter Bunny. "Time passes, and here you are, prim little Ty, sitting dutifully at a table pasting on the last letter."

His memory, even fifty years on, remained sharp. The plate, floral designs around the edges, the Bible verse in the center. But his eyes went again and again to the small diligent boy he had been, tonguetip pressed against the corner of his mouth. No demon could fake the profound impact this vision had on him. "He's so...open." On his left sat a Negro boy. As an adult, Ty had a well-nigh automatic judgmental response to him; but his eight-year-old self was completely at ease. He saw past the boy's skin color, or rather, his acceptance embraced that skin, unquestioned, as part of his glory. To his right, another boy was going on and on about an Easter basket. "I got two gigantic bunnies, and nine big huge eggs with real bright colors, and jellybeans spilling over the sides and out into the streets so that people slipped and fell, and green grass that reaches clear on up to the sky!" Ty felt the innocent envy of his boyhood heart. But even that was engaging, not sinful, a simple wish for more than the boy on the right had received. Later, adults would teach him to censor that feeling, to name it and bury it deep in his soul.

"That's right," said Easter Bunny. "That's how it happens. If we may show you..."

Ty watched in awe and horror, as the boy he was then, a look of pride in his eyes, appeared in brief scenes, some of them mute, some with telling comments from adults. Some scenes involved the boy he had been, others the adolescent, the young man, the mature man, the man getting on in years. From the first, he heard the intelligence in his voice, the power to string words together, to catch the rhythm of each phrase, to coat with gold the dross of spoon-fed conviction. But even spoon-fed conviction latched onto his spirit and that benighted spirit shaped his developing mind. Seeing the process sped up did nothing to reaffirm the correctness of his views; rather, it showed him how a fresh, open-minded boy let himself be shaped and sliced and penned in by narrow grown-ups who seemed to know what they were talking about but did not. They hid behind God. They claimed that God believed this or that, and that the Bible, here, here, and here, proved it. He saw what utter nonsense that was and how his elders' predispositions had shaped his view of scripture.

He was stunned. "I was ready to quote chapter and verse."

"Boy, were you ever!" said the Easter Bunny. "But you see now, don't you, good sir, how utterly beside the point such an exercise would have been? Santa and Wendy have told me how, on their prior visits, you saw into the hearts of many fine people and understood that their sexual nature is cause for rejoicing and embrace. It isn't a sin at all, but part of God's plan."

"I see now that that's so. But my God, the Tooth Fairy and her imps were so persuasive. Won't they invade my dreams again? And how am I to behave tomorrow morning? What sermon can I possibly deliver? I feel utterly changed, as if centuries of grime had been wiped away."

Santa seemed relieved. "Regarding your dream," he said, "the archangel assures me that the pure in spirit cannot, without willing it, be touched by evil. You will not forget the light. The Tooth Fairy will be powerless against you, no matter how much she rages, nor how much you are made to suffer. As for your frets about tomorrow's sermon—"

"You'll be okay, Mister Taylor."

"As Wendy says, you'll be okay. Trust to instinct. Trust to your rhetorical skill. Tell the truth. Be *forceful* in telling the truth. Will it be easy? It will not. But there is no alternative. Once your eyes are open, it is impossible to close them again." Santa pointed and there sat Ty once more in Bible school, holding up the plate, running his fingertip lightly over the letters, mouthing the words in wonder: "Whatever your hand finds to do, do it with all your might."

Then Ty's childhood bedroom reappeared and there stood his three visitors, clustered around his bed like the wise men. He sobbed with joy. "What did an old sinner like me do to deserve this?"

Santa said, "Had we but world enough and time, we would visit all of humankind in this way. But our mission has been to save one little boy from suicide. If by saving you, we have saved him, why, that's all to the good. Now, sleep. When you wake, you won't recall our visit, but its effects will stay with you forever."

"Goodnight, Mister Taylor." Wendy blew him a kiss.

"Thank you for indulging us, kind sir." The Easter Bunny's eyes twinkled. "We have merely reintroduced you to your worthiest self. He has long been buried, but thanks to the grace you have allowed to bloom within, he has risen and breathes free once more."

"God's blessings on you all," said Ty. Stifling a yawn, he slid beneath the covers, gave a weary wave to his departing guests, and surrendered to sleep.

As soon as Gronk witnessed the preacher's fascination with his boyhood self, he knew the game was lost. He knew as well, pressed to the ceiling with his ribs strained to the cracking point, that he should have raced back to the island right after the immortals' visit to the Strattons.

A tactical error.

But he hadn't wanted to report failure if he could report even partial success. And the evangelical pontificator had seemed so firmly in their camp. Why, he might have been so incensed at the attempt to turn him, as to corral Walter and Kathy Stratton after his Thanksgiving sermon and sway them with even greater ferocity into obedience to his unChristlike Savior, even though it meant the death of their son.

Mommy will tear me to pieces, thought Gronk.

The miles flew by. Over and through cloudbanks he passed on his way home. At the last minute, he cursed himself for not bringing with him, in propitiation, the bones of a hapless child.

He spied his brothers sprawled idly on the shore, Chuff moping alone near the dunes. Further on, there was his mother, scanning the skies in a squat, palms upturned in supplication to an unholy god.

He touched down badly, tumbling in a heap before her.

"Well?"

"Pan and his brat had quite a time of it."

"And they failed."

"One might ever wish for such failure."

Her lids tightened. "I don't like the way you said that."

"What I mean is, one who attempts to reverse the effect of nightmares might ever wish for such failure, for it looks and feels and tastes, in every respect, like success."

"To the point."

"They enlisted the Easter Bunny. He appealed to the mortals' childhood innocence. Our dreamscape invasion had no lasting effect. They've been turned. Please don't shoot the messenger."

But she leaped upon him, flaying his cheeks, gripping his great gray testicles and squeezing until he cried and beat the sand with his fists. "Their visits are over? You stupid little shit, you should have reported back at once. I might have tainted the still-to-be-visited mortals' image of the Easter Bunny, whose seeming innocence masks a history of unspeakable acts in past service to me and to his own unworthiness."

Thus did she rant and thus did Gronk suffer, broken and healed and broken anew, until the Tooth Fairy's wrath was spent and she left him there in great pain, plotting afresh as she paced the sand.

"Oh, don't bother, I'll find my own way home," he had told them, hopping close to the sleigh's right runner and setting one paw on the black lacquer of its scrollwork.

"You're sure?" said Santa.

Wendy looked disappointed, but said, "We did good, didn't we?"

136

stroking his paw and planting a kiss on his cheek. "Your whiskers are super-soft, my good friend bunny."

At which he blushed, averted his eyes, and aw-shucks'd his way toward again begging off a ride home. "I'm too excited to sit still," he insisted.

Which, though true, was not the whole story.

Santa offered a hesitant but hearty, "Thank you," meaning it but still with that undercurrent of bad blood between them. Then Lucifer's antlers lit up and the reindeer lofted the sleigh skyward, thundering soundlessly into the night. Wendy waved and Santa too, smears of green and red against black. The Easter Bunny raised a paw in farewell, but they were already too far distant to see it.

Being on his own gave him the chance to drop in on little Jamie. He gazed in fondness at the sleeping boy whose death they had postponed. Jamie lay fast asleep, his tousled hair careless on the pillow. The Easter Bunny blessed him and leaped through the window, flying swiftly away from Colorado Springs toward his far-flung burrow. Lights twinkled below, then abruptly yielded to expanses of darkness and seascape and wooded lands.

But his thoughts dwelt upon joy and vexation. Joy at having spoken with mortals, at having seen them touched by glimpses of their childhood and then transformed. Thrilled to the heart, he chittered with delight as he sped along, ears pressed back against his scalp. Yet he remained vexed at Santa's demeanor and his own hesitancy and shame. Santa had softened as they triumphed, but only a little. At Wendy's kiss, the Easter Bunny tensed for Santa's roar of objection. But it hadn't come.

Delayed perhaps?

Would Santa drop Wendy off and return to chastise him, or worse? He hoped not. But perhaps having it out was necessary.

Sighing, he sped on, eager to regain his living quarters and bask in memories of mortal contact.

Finished her pacing, the Tooth Fairy grabbed her imps and rushed them into the dreamscape. The mortals were seated at a tea party. Delicate bone china graced a damask tablecloth on a balmy beachfront, a lazy sway of palm leaves overhead.

Their souls had been washed clean. Their garments were colorful now, comfortable, and reflective of spiritual renewal.

She and her brood dropped down about them. With a sweep of her hand, the crockery shattered and the table collapsed. Scalding liquid splashed everywhere. The sudden attack, the burns they suffered, the lurch from paradise—these infuriating dreamers took it all in stride.

"Idiots," she said. "Have you forgotten our last meeting? The satanic nature of this Santa and Wendy? Their mission to turn you from God's truth?"

The boy leaped to his feet. "You're a liar!"

"Pay her no mind, Matt," said Kathy Stratton.

Her husband said, "She has no power over us."

"Go," commanded the preacher, standing behind the seated couple, his hands on their shoulders. "Leave us in peace."

"Foolish man," said the Tooth Fairy, "you've been duped as well, I see." She rose into the air and dissolved the broken table with a glance. A pool of steam-hung water took its place. "Gronk tells me they brought in the so-called Easter Bunny. Let me show you what this dark spirit did." The steam swirled aside to reveal glimpses of the creature's past. "He stared in at bedroom windows. With jets of invisible seed, he befouled siding. Here you see him tricking a coed, spaced out on drugs, into coupling with him before she realizes that her boyfriend is pounding on the door and now the saintly Easter Bunny loses hold of his invisibility. Look at the creature's mad red eyes." Mist swept in and swirled the scene away. "This is the innocent bunny whose guileful ways have lured you into the satanic camp of those who embrace sin."

Kathy Stratton said, "You're lying to us. We've seen the Easter Bunny. To his soul we have seen him. He's nothing like that."

"What you've shown," said Ty Taylor, "are the perversions of your own sick mind. We'll have none of it."

"Get lost," said the bully. "You don't belong in our dreams."

The Tooth Fairy swirled up in fury. "Doltish mortals. I show you the truth, and you reject it. Boys, have at them!"

Then her imps, Chuff lagging more than usual, swept in to attack the dreamers. Limbs were lost, only to regrow. Wounds bled and healed, blood unspilling back inside them as torn skin restitched and smoothed. But the dreamers in their unruffled defiance transcended the pain, or felt it not at all.

Though she raised a volcano and made it spill rivers of lava, caused the sea to roar and waves to fall heavy upon them, fissured the ground, then fissured those fissures, blasted their bodies apart—yet those bodies unblasted, the ground regained firmness beneath their feet, the ocean receded and relaxed into placidity, molten rock upflowed back inside the volcano, which eased into gentle hills rich with greenery.

"Retreat," she screamed, feeling foolish and defeated and tenfold defiant.

When they regained the island, she thrashed her boys, casting her impotence upon them. "Leave me," she shouted, and they scattered, but, "Not you, Gronk."

The others hustled Chuff along the beach until Gronk and their mother were two distant dots. There, to the slap of waves, they sailed into him.

Clunch gouged his eyes with the fat stubby knuckles of both hands. Bunner pistoned his fists into Chuff's back, bruising the skin and battering the spine until it broke, healed, and broke again. Zylo and Faddle wrenched his arms, violating with torque and torment the integrity of muscle and bone. Quint, Zest, and Cagger razored their claws along every inch of skin, ribboning the flesh and drawing blood. "Too good to hurt a mortal, eh? Leave us all the work? Mommy oughta toss you off this island. You're a freak. There ain't enough hate in you. Whatsa matter, boy? You prefer receiving pain to giving it? No problem."

Beneath their torment, Chuff kept up his spirits. For he held in his heart a small secret pride in being unlike them. Only Mommy could shame him for being different, not them. He was better than they were. It didn't swell his noggin, but it kept him from tumbling into despair. Despite this pride, Mommy could make him feel awful with just a look.

His brothers had thrashed him before. But this time they were more vicious than ever. They weren't used to defeat. They bullied bad boys and girls at Christmas, played foul pranks on hapless mortals, instantly gratified mean desires. Chuff could tell through his agony that his brothers disliked being bested by Santa, Wendy, and the Easter Bunny.

He, oddly enough, liked it a lot. Though he had never met them, they sounded appealing. And through the meting out of pain, the idea occurred to him—and at once took wing—to pray no longer to the indifferent moon, but to this immortal triumvirate.

They would rescue him from this hell, as surely as they had rescued the little boy.

To that hope, Chuff clung.

The Tooth Fairy's eldest imp cowered in the sand. "You're stuck with me," he said. "I made bad choices, but I did my best. The rest is hindsight. They've got greater powers on their side, is all."

She clamped a hand over his nose and mouth. "Never say that." He tore at it without effect. "Pan will overstep. It's the nature of triumph. It comes with the territory." Gronk's eyes filled with panic. His claws dug into his mother's arms, shredded skin, bloodied muscle. "You're radiant in triumph, your head swells, you want to win again but more decisively, you crave more toys, greater jolts of adrenaline coursing in your veins."

Abruptly, she turned from him. He gulped air. "The proud Pan will try to impress little Wendy further. He'll overstep. Change a tiny patch of the world, you want to change the whole damned thing." She wheeled. "Gronk!"

He scuttled away.

"You want to redeem yourself? Spy on that bastard at the North Pole. Can you do that for Mommy? Of course you can. We'll catch them this time. We'll skewer the fat little fuck. Report every day, without fail. Listen in on the daughter. On the polar creep. On his wives and helpers. Be all ears. Can you do that, boy?"

He brightened. "Yes, Mother," he said. Behind him, the waves slapped at the shore and receded.

"We'll probe for his weaknesses. Pan won't be content with saving one small boy. His suppressed appetites are far grander than that. By sanctioning these visits, Zeus has overstepped. Pan shall, in turn, overstep. Then we'll sweep in and shatter their plans, undo their kindnesses, and visit misery unending upon the earth. Watch and wait. That's all we need to do. By their power grab shall they be brought down."

The Tooth Fairy felt elated, sure of her purpose now.

"Be gone," she said. When he held back from leaving, she hurled him northward off the island.

Away flew her eldest, a rude blot upon the sky, shrinking until he was a smudge, a pinprick of gray distaste, and then nothing at all.

140

21.
BEING GRATEFUL, BEING SCORNED

THANKSGIVING DAY DAWNED LIKE THE FIRST DAY of creation, tremulous with anticipation, the air clear and crisp. All mortals that woke that morning, indeed all living beings poking their heads up out of slumber, felt at once vibrant with possibility.

For one wondrous instant, the scent of celebration hung upon the air—the steam of mashed potatoes, the aroma of sliced turkey, the tang of fresh cranberry. And this was true the world over, even in cultures for which Thanksgiving Day held no particular significance.

Such moments occur whenever the immortal world touches ours with benign intent. A boy's life had been saved, four other lives changed, and ripples were about to move out from those lives into the world as a whole. But the simple presence of Santa, Wendy, and the Easter Bunny thrice in those three bedrooms in one modest-sized city, so intensely benevolent, touched for an instant every soul on earth. The goodness in everyone shown more brightly, a tremolo of generosity, before reverting to its modest glow or dim-bulb obscurity.

Santa felt it as a jubilant shout. In spite of his feelings of inadequacy in confronting mortal grown-ups, he remained grateful for having had the chance to save a child. The Easter Bunny, leaping and chittering in absolute delight, experienced it as a caress and a smile. To the Tooth Fairy and her imps, it seemed more a goad, a pinch, a poke, a sharp jab to the bowels, heart, lungs, to the innards entire, a pain that left them uneasy and humiliated.

As for the visitants, who had lived through a night of extremes and forgotten every particular, they woke to a world of radical change. Its balm spread everywhere in them, even as they understood with sober clarity that their lives had uplifted onto a new plane entirely. For they recalled yesterday's sorry tint upon their souls, how it had developed and deepened to color every thought, word, and deed; and they felt the contrast between that tint and their new acceptance and embrace of the homosexual impulse in themselves and others. They knew, as sure as they knew the gentle necessity of breathing, that they must act in accord with this unbesmirched vision. That old friends would drop away, or be dropped, because of this small significant shift. That new friends would take their place. That a sea change, long overdue, would transform their lives.

Take Matt Beluzzo for instance, twelve and tough, hardened by a life of parental neglect, gravitation toward nasty peers, and grudges sufficient to spark riots. That morning, he woke in wide-eyed wonder. His pained squint was gone. Feeling more adult than ever, he surveyed his lop-drawered dresser, the faded wallpaper, a never-cleaned window hiding its streaks behind bent blinds. His bedroom bore the marks of neglect, the funds not spent on upkeep because Mom supplied herself with beer and cigarettes first, and there was never enough for what came second. To Matt's astonishment, all of that was okay with him. He tried to hate his mother; he invited the old resentments in, but they would not come. Like spirits before an exorcist, they had fled forever.

Matt showered and dressed. The ever unreliable thermometer outside the kitchen window read thirty-eight, so he knew it was around freezing and dressed accordingly. He had no goal in mind, other than to survey a changed world. As it happened, he walked a wide circle around the neighborhood, which still slept but for grown-up walkers in ones and twos. Whereas before, he would have thought nasty thoughts and avoided their eyes, today he acknowledged each one with a nod and a "Morning, ma'am," or "Morning, sir." And they, sensing his new maturity, his directness and generosity of spirit, responded in kind.

He tried to hate his father languishing in jail, his fists far from Matt and his mother. But again he failed. I'm turning into a softy, he thought.

A sissy.

How odd the word, how ridiculous the concept. Name-calling was childish, particularly when you directed it at yourself.

Maybe he should knock on Robbie Stover's window.

No. There'd be time enough to test himself against these sad little boys he had called friends once upon a time, yesterday, long ago.

Ty Taylor's first emotion upon waking was a twinge of unease and panic. He had finished his Thanksgiving Day sermon the day before, but it was a sermon he could no longer deliver.

Then he relaxed into a laugh. The generosity now coursing through his veins was strong and articulate. He had been spontaneous before. He would be spontaneous this morning. "A Thankful Heart in a Thankless World" had been his announced sermon topic. It would remain so. But certain sections, certain thunderous ridings of his usual hobbyhorses, would be excised.

Something miraculous had occurred during the night. What it was it was impossible to say. Still, he bowed his head. "Thank you, Father," he said, "for...well, I'm not sure what. I suppose for *everything!*"

He prayed for strength, and courage, and God's healing hand upon an ailing world. Then he tossed off the covers, made his ablutions, prepared and ate a bowl of oatmeal, and marveled at the freshness of the world and the freshness of his spirit this fine morning.

When he arrived at the church parking lot, he greeted Nora Blue, his choir director and organist, on the way to the rectory. There he robed himself and prayed again, this time for humility, forgiveness, and charity toward everyone. But unlike all such previous prayers, this time he did not secretly believe his plea for humility was, at heart, unnecessary. For once, his contrition was genuine.

The pews overflowed with worshipers. Three rows back, in their usual place, sat George and Vera Stupplebeen, proud, upright, and ready to be fortified. Over yonder, the Pyne family; and beside them, Becky Harmon and seven-year-old Cully. Halfway down the aisle, Ty spotted the Stratton clan, Walter, Kathy, Kurt, and Jamie. His gaze lingered upon them, as Nora Blue played a majestic organ prelude. A sudden sob of joy caught in Ty's throat. What was it? Some precious bond existed between him and them. Odd.

The community of believers had turned out in full force, dressed in their Sunday best. But today, his love for them felt a hundredfold more intense than ever. They were his flock, he their shepherd. They had honored him with the role of leading them into the paths of righteousness.

And he had failed them.

But no guilt tinged that recognition. However unworthy, he had done his best. Today, by God's grace, he would do better. He would strive to live up to his calling, to step out of the way of the still small voice inside.

He gave the invocation and intoned the opening verses ("Give thanks unto the Lord, all ye lands..."), then led the congregation in the singing of the first hymn. Brief announcements followed: the ladies' auxiliary's silent auction, preparations and a need for volunteers for the upcoming Christmas pageant. Then the choir mounted a spirited assault upon "Oh bounteous is Thy loving hand," the second hymn rolled out, and Ty made his way to the pulpit without his usual leather-bound folder, arms swinging free, growing a touch nervous (one never really overcame stage fright). There, Ty set his kind gaze upon on one parishioner after another as Nora Blue brought the hymn's soaring melody to its tonic and the final chord rolled up into an echo of itself. The usual round of coughing and shuffling of bulletins ensued as Nora slid off her bench into a folding chair beside the choir.

"Let us pray," said Ty, bowing his head. "Dear Lord, on this day of Thanksgiving, grant thy servant the wisdom to speak truth in humility, compassion, and generosity of spirit, the agility to sidestep for these precious moments our universal failings of pride and envy, of fear and hatred, of judgmentalism and condemnation in the service of self-exaltation. May we, in shared worship, exalt you alone and the mysteries of your truth, the Son who dwells in our midst, ever present and within easy reach, would we but hearken to his words. Amen."

From the assembled multitudes rose a mumbled amen.

More rustling and coughing.

Then quiet anticipation.

"Oh give thanks unto the Lord, all ye lands," he began, surprised at the assurance in his voice. "So commandeth today's text. And all of us gathered here, even those who suffer in body and heart and mind, have much to be thankful for, have we not? This building, with its stained glass and inspiring arches; this glorious morn, giddy with sunlight; this blessed land of freedom and justice and liberty; our friendships; our families; the crown of health; every precious breath the good lord grants us. The list is endless. To be honest, our list of sorrows, when we choose to dwell upon them, is equally endless. But today we dwell upon our blessings. We linger over the miracle of their abundance, over the rich wonder of loved ones gathered about splendid tables in fellowship and thanksgiving, and we rejoice in God's bounty, praising him and hoping in our heart of hearts that such praise will move the Almighty to continue bestowing those blessings, and more, much more, upon our unworthy souls."

He had them. He saw it in their eyes. Their mouths were open, seeking sustenance from the holy breast.

"You have perhaps noticed that I come before you with no sermon in hand. No, I haven't left it in the breakfast nook in my haste to join you, though I read such suspicions in a raised eyebrow or two." Chuckles from the pews. "What I thought last evening I wanted to say is no longer what I have to say. Call it yesterday's news. Today, I choose to trust my heart. A heart, dearly beloved, that is full to bursting. It is open to love as never before, and your poor pastor stands here naked and exposed, a bare forked animal, to tell you so."

Ty suffered an instant of anxiety.

He knew well the comfortable worldview in which these good people had invested years of their lives. In many cases, he had helped mold it. They would not take kindly, many of them, to what he was about to say. But that could not, nor would he allow it to, stop him from speaking his mind. Was this a momentary aberration? A decision he would regret and wish too late to rescind? Not in the least. As confident as he had been yesterday about his condemnation of homosexual behavior, so confident was he now of a conviction quite the opposite. And this conviction, he discovered to his surprise, had put down deep roots in him.

"Saul of Tarsus, on the road to Damascus, had his blindness lifted, and he became Paul, Saint Paul, the great apostle. Your pastor has had, though he knows not how, a similar revelation. The scales have fallen from my eyes. For years, I have railed against the sodomites, as I called them, as our church calls them. Dearly beloved, received wisdom is often unwise, and no wisdom at all. What is belief when it is based on such wisdom? With the best of intent, and for all my adult life, I have railed again homosexuality. I truly believed its practice was a sin, as much as addiction to alcohol or an indulgence in lust, adultery, thievery, or murder. I stand before you now, humbled by my past pride, to tell you I was wrong. The church is wrong. The dominant culture is wrong." Whispers began to circulate. Faces hardened. "I am intimately acquainted with all the usual verses we trot out and with every argument against homosexuality. I have made these arguments myself, over and over, from this very pulpit. They are as the dust beneath our feet. God is Love. Jesus is Love. There abideth these three, faith, hope, and love; but the greatest of these is love. From that same passage in 1st Corinthians 13 comes this marvelous truth: Though I speak with the tongues of men and of angels but have not love, I am nothing. I am resounding brass, a clanging cymbal."

145

The whispers grew to grumbling, the glares more fierce.

"We have done grievous wrong to our brothers and sisters and to ourselves. Through condemnation, we have attempted to circumscribe responsible expressions of adult love. We have dared to inform God which parts of his creation are acceptable and which are not."

A deacon in back bent to another in intense talk. George Stuppelbeen, red-faced and goggle-eyed, gripped the back of the pew in front of him. Compassion filled Ty's heart for these good people. But he also knew that some in his congregation were receiving his words as an unexpected balm to their souls. And they too belonged to his flock.

"Churches are not infallible. One hundred fifty years ago, our sect pressed the biblical justification for slavery. Passages were lifted onto pedestals, their meanings tortured to support racial inequality. Eventually, far too late, we yielded. That is an unspoken and little-known part of our history. All of this happened long before any of us were born. But history does not lie, and history attests to this shameful blot on the Christian faith. Today, homophobia similarly stains our religious practice."

"Blasphemer!" came a shout from the back. The cry was picked up, caroming at random from pew to pew.

"Hear me out," Ty pleaded. "This world is a brilliant jewel, a pearl of great price. Our prejudice, our holier-than-thou, our there-but-for-the-grace-of-God, diminishes the world's luster and spits in the face of our Almighty Benefactor. Denial of our gay brothers and lesbian sisters drives another spike into the palms of the crucified Christ. We nail Love to the holy rood and leave it there to languish and die, while centurions mock and Mary weeps. Shame on us. Shame on us all."

George Stupplebeen struggled to his feet. "Ty Taylor, you're no preacher of mine!"

"Nor mine," yelled Joe Pyne, his wife defiant and tightlipped by his side.

Pandemonium broke out. There was great liberation in Ty's heart, and dread and compassion and sorrow beyond telling.

A few brave parishioners rose to voice their support. Some members of the choir bore tense witness to their hidden hearts, standing amongst outraged companions in robes, looking on grimly in silent admiration. The Strattons, though teenaged Kurt looked a little embarrassed and go-along, stood foursquare behind him.

146

Though Ty tried to say more, he was shouted down, excoriated and pilloried, until at last he bowed his head in silent prayer. Then he recessed down the center aisle, scorn flung upon him, beast faces fleering from the once serene. This it was to disappoint expectation, to turn on a dime and pull the rug out. Though fists and voices were raised, the only congregant who touched him was Walter Stratton, who confided, "We're with you, Ty."

Indeed, the Strattons followed behind him, hardy souls, past the deacons in their starched demeanor, and out the church's tall doors into a sun-filled Thanksgiving morning.

22.
A JOYOUS THANKSGIVING

THIS YEAR, GREGOR AND HIS BROTHERS HAD BEEN CHOSEN as honored guests at Santa's Thanksgiving feast. Though they slept in the stables, Santa insisted they endure the traditional, good-natured preparation and hazing in the elves' dormitory. Gregor cast a gimlet eye on that insistence, which had no doubt been meant to bring him down a few pegs.

He would let his siblings get gussied up, let them suffer the mockery of the simpleminded. As for himself, he made no special preparations, no ribbons in his beard, no after-shave stink, none of that folderol. He was who he was, and Santa and his brood could accept him or go hang.

That morning, the usual jeering gauntlet was muted. The elves seemed only half-committed to the ritual. Gregor knew it was because he cowed them, and that was all to the good. But Engelbert and Josef, this one day, had let down their guard, and it disgusted him. Hands flailing, he batted away the nonsense about him in the dormitory and strode to the entrance, while behind him his brothers laughed and made pained being-wounded gestures as jeers and catcalls hit them from all sides.

Heading across the commons, his doltish sibs tried to get him to link arms. "Away with that noise," he scolded Engelbert. "Grow up, why don't you?" he scoffed at Josef, whose fat face instantly drained of mirth. "We have positions of authority to uphold."

The cottage door opened and out onto the porch spilled Snowball and Nightwind followed by Wendy and Rachel and Anya and Santa himself, looking portly and beaming ear to ear. "Weh-heh-hell," said Santa, glad-handing his guests. It made Gregor feel small and subservient, so exuberant was Santa's welcome. "Come in, come in, dear friends. Stamp the snow from your slippers and make yourselves at home. Josef, young and roly-poly, a brilliant burst of energy, welcome to you. Engelbert, who keeps my team in good feed, you too I welcome most heartily. And big brother Gregor, always scowling, forever sitting on a cactus, but I find that endearing, indeed I do, come in, come in, let me embrace you all." At that, Gregor melted beneath Santa's rapt attention; or more accurately, the icy surface of his personality gleamed for an instant with a thin sheen of water before it froze solid once again.

More ravings, more hugs from Rachel and Anya. Wendy's high-pitched squeals. Thank God the cats weren't that way. Snowball glared in shocked scandal at the goings-on, while Nightwind took the occasion to lick a less-than-private portion of his anatomy.

Then into the living room they went. "Take seats," said Santa. He settled into an easy chair and hefted a Coke bottle sitting beside him on a small table. "You good fellows want some? Wendy, get the lads Cokes, would you?"

"None for me, Santa," said Gregor.

"Nor me."

"Nor me."

"Plays havoc with the innards," added Gregor, raising a finger and an eyebrow of condemnation.

"Of course, of course," said Santa, letting it go. "We'll share a pipe after dinner instead. Camaraderie. Conspiratorial winks. Man talk."

Josef and Engelbert positively glowed. Gregor, appalled, said nothing. The gush had risen knee-deep already, and he had no wish to wade further into it.

Dinner went well. Sumptuous aromas swirled out of the kitchen to the dining room, held proud and entrayed beneath beaming faces. Wendy brought out a huge boat of gravy flavored with generous handfuls of porcini mushrooms, followed by cranberry sauce. Rachel swept in with heaping bowls of whipped potatoes mixed with fresh fennel, candied sweet potatoes with a pecan garnish, and buttered green beans slivered with almonds. Finally, Anya, her grandmotherly bosom broad and all-giving, with a grin that brightened the dining room, brought in a twenty-pound turkey on a cutting board, skin brown and shiny and ready to flake off, the steam rising from it as Santa carved and plates piled high with sliced meat moved about the table. Gregor's brothers praised the feast to the heavens, ooh'ing and aah'ing like appreciative lovers. Gregor clucked his tongue at them to no avail. Just as well. Their undignified behavior saved him the bother of pretending to wax orgasmic himself, which was simply not his style; he could lord it over them all the more later.

The table groaned from the weight of the food, until at last the diners took over that cheery task themselves. The talk, when their mouths were empty enough to fill with words, consisted of banter, compliments to the chefs, this or that expression of thanks for that or this blessing. Then, Wendy told the tale of saving Jamie Stratton. Gregor noted with interest her glancing references to the Easter Bunny, who had clearly played a major role in this salvation, a role Wendy downplayed to spare her mother discomfort. Why Rachel should feel discomfort was a puzzle and a conundrum. It swam in the general stew of suppressed memories, a stew whose ingredients Gregor vowed one day to tease out.

In his study after dinner, through a cheery haze of pipe smoke, Santa held up one hand. "Reason me no reasons. Gregor, there will be no badmouthing of Fritz, or anyone else, in this house. I simply want my old helpers back, the ones whose skilled hands are incapable of shoddy work."

Gregor gripped his cold dead clay pipe, not puffed on but held tight in his fist. "And you shall have them. Things are well in hand. Are they not, boys?"

Josef puffed and murmured, "Umm-hmm."

Engelbert, similarly cocooned in an aromatic haze of smoke, held the bowl of his pipe and nodded with as much sagacity as his simple mind could muster.

"Without getting into particulars," continued Gregor, "let's just say they've developed an odious personal habit. I and my brothers are breaking them of it."

Santa pondered, keeping Gregor in the rich purview of his canny stare. "Is my intervention required? Would it help, do you think?"

"None needed, Santa. This firm hand grips the teller."

Santa swatted his thigh. "By God, I believe I'll talk to them in the morning. It can't hurt."

"No call for that, Santa. Me and the boys, we're on the job."

Santa brushed it aside. "I'll give them thanks, then obliquely broach the subject. Be assured, there'll be no mention of our little talk. Just a small boost to your efforts. Oh and speaking of efforts, has my gratitude to you come up to the mark? Have my thanks for your superb care of my reindeer been sufficiently profuse?"

"Indeed they have," said Engelbert.

150

"More than profuse," managed Josef, choking on a puff of smoke, which Gregor whacked out of him with a smack between the shoulder blades.

Gregor peered at Santa. "More praise would be welcome, I think. It makes us...more equal, if you catch my drift."

Santa roared with laughter. "Gregor, you are a stitch," he said. "And yes indeed, I praise you from the bottom of my heart. Without a top-notch stable, Wendy's Galatea and my nine chargers would quickly grow indolent and discontent; not the crack team they are, powerful from hoof to antler. Diet. Exercise. Care. Ah, but not just care. You give each of them individual love and attention. I can tell. Fresh straw. Fresh water. Rubdowns, rest, and regular canters and gallops about the commons. When I need them, when Wendy needs Galatea, there they are, stamping and snorting and eager to take to the heavens. And the sleigh, oh my, you three do me proud in that department. It's a pleasure to ease my posterior down into that nice wide cushioned seat, the runners gliding stiletto-smooth across the snow. Bravo, say I. Bravo to you three fine fellows. Ah, Gregor, what a winning scowl you wear; I can tell my praise is hitting home. Josef, your wide jowly face is lit up like a thousand Christmas trees, a delight to behold. And dear sweet Engelbert, your pupils dance so with candy canes and tinsel that your cherry cheeks glisten and glow. Life is grand indeed, lads. I thank you for doing your part in making it so!"

"Aw, shucks," said Josef.

"'Tweren't nothin'," said Engelbert.

"Is that all?" said Gregor, casting an eye about the study and imagining it as his own, once he convinced Santa to retire. "Can you not praise us more than that? You've praised us to the sky. But not to the stars. How about to the stars, and beyond?"

And Santa laughed to shake the foundations of his cottage and said, all right, he would do his best to comply. At which he launched into a stem-winder of an encomium that lasted well into the night, that made the brothers' heads swell with pride, and went the teensiest, tiniest way toward assuaging Gregor's essentially unassuageable hunger for strokes.

But all was well with them. Even Gregor suffered the women's hugs as they were at last dispatched out the door and floated across the commons—more precisely, his brothers floated; Gregor tromped—to the stables for a good night's rest.

***

"Kurt, you look a little bewildered," said Ty, happy to be among friends but still shell-shocked at his flock's reaction to his sermon. To see such seemingly gentle souls turn nasty, to lose his job...ah, but he hadn't lost his vocation. A job was nothing compared to acting with integrity, and Ty knew deep down that he had made the right decision.

"I don't know," said Kurt as he spooned up another helping of peas. "You're all...so different."

Kathy laughed. "We are."

"As Reverend Taylor put it when he said grace, we've all been changed in an instant, in the twinkling of an eye."

"Your father's right," said the pastor. "We seem suddenly aware of so much to be grateful for. But this year, we're not simply going through the motions of Thanksgiving. Kathy, this cranberry recipe is divine!"

"Jamie seems to agree with you."

"Aw, Mom," said Jamie. "It's yummy. I like it. And I also like... how everything feels at the table."

"Me too," said Kathy. "We have been given so many blessings. Our health. Our love for one another. Abundant food. A warm lovely home. A kind-hearted pastor and friend to share our food with. And this year, the miraculous change that came over us last night. It's almost as if—now you're going to laugh at me—as if Santa Claus came early this year and left a little more generosity in our hearts."

"Come on, Mom. Even Jamie knows there's no Santa Claus."

Kathy smiled. "I wonder if that's really so."

"Son, don't wolf your food."

"Sorry, Dad," said Jamie.

"I think I believe in him all over again." She faltered. "If only everyone in our church did the same."

Ty squeezed her hand. "It's all right, Kathy. They that have ears to hear, as they say. Until last night, I shared their moral deafness. Heck, I spurred it on. But this morning I had no choice. No, that's not true. Willingly and with all my heart, I spoke the truth to these good people. It delivered a shock to their systems, even as it served as a refreshing balm to mine, to yours, and, I have no doubt, to others in the congregation. I've walked away from the pulpit. But even the hard of heart are going to find a lesson, perhaps over weeks or months, in having witnessed their pastor repudiate, in no uncertain terms, a central tenet of their church's teaching. Religious institutions change, despite the posturing of some that the Bible—or rather the passages they choose to highlight and distort—is inerrant, unchanging, a rock upon which to build one's faith. Perhaps my leaving will hasten a long overdue change of heart. Oh, but things have grown somber around this festive table. Listen to the poor preacher drone on, while the potatoes grow cold. Eat, everyone. Eat, drink, and be merry, for tomorrow we die. But today we live. And while we live, let us give thanks for God's bounty. Kathy? More white meat, if you please."

"With pleasure," she said, looking at him with fondness and admiration. "Hold out your plate."

"Take some more," insisted Matt.

His mother looked at him. "Are you feeling okay, honey?"

"Sure am. Come on, Mom, it'll get cold."

She stared at her plate. Her eyes grew watery, but she blinked away her tears. "It tastes good. It was thoughtful of you to get it."

Matt smiled. "Albertson's best. Turkey slices, dressing, yams, pumpkin pie. The whole nine yards."

A cigarette smoldered in the ashtray at his mother's elbow. She took a drag, set it down, and picked up her fork. The tines toyed with the dressing. She lifted some to her mouth.

Matt watched her. She seemed worn, drawn, her lipstick less than perfectly applied. Whatever had happened in dreamland, it was staying with him in spades. He was capable of change. He *had* changed. And he could bring Mom along with him. Of that, he had no doubt.

"I'm going to be okay from now on, Mom."

"Hm?"

"I've found my moral compass."

"Right. Now I *know* you're off your feed."

"No, really. You'll see. I'm going to apply myself. I'll find better friends. We'll get back on track, you and me both. And I'll go visit Dad."

She snorted. "That worthless son of a bitch."

"Don't. Please. He treated us lousy. But we're going to be different. No more meanness. Even if we think mean, we don't have to speak mean."

His mom's eyes teared up. "Matty? Is that my boy? I let you go

153

straight to hell, didn't I? But you're climbing out again, all on your own. It's enough to sober a poor woman up."

"You can do that if you want. I want you to. You can sober up."

"Uh huh, and pigs can fly."

"Don't say that. I'll help you."

"You will?"

"Yep."

She broke down. It scared Matt, and it thrilled him, to see her fall apart. "What did I do to deserve this?"

"Nothing, Mom. You were yourself, is all. You're my mom and we're together, and we're going to make the best of things. Day by day, we're going to make the really swell best of things."

Matt had never felt so sure of anything in his life. He got up and hugged his mom in her tired old dress and doused perfume. And she hugged him back, seizing him like the life preserver he was.

The oil lamp on Wendy's nightstand bathed her parents in wondrous light. Snowball and Nightwind hunched at the foot of the bed, waiting for her tucking-in and for the lamp to be blown out so they could circle into cozy nests on her left and right.

Wendy sighed. "It's been a good day, hasn't it?"

"Thanks to you and Santa," said her mother.

"Indeed," said Anya.

Santa looked boyishly modest. Wendy felt closer to him than ever before. He was much more like his old self than she could remember.

"Do you guys want a glimpse into Jamie's future?"

Her suggestion met with immediate approval.

"Okay." Wendy sat up and brought to life moments with Jamie and his parents, Jamie triumphant on the violin, amusing episodes from high school and beyond. He studied at the Oberlin Conservatory of Music, where he found and lost his first love. "But he'll be all right later, when he meets Tom." Wendy skipped ahead to that, their chance encounter at a mutual friend's birthday gathering in Manhattan.

"It's good to see him grown up," said Santa, his voice cracking a little.

Anya said, "I'm proud of you both."

"Me too," said Rachel, giving Wendy an extra fierce hug. "Now it's bedtime for all of us, don't you think?"

Wendy said, "Uh huh," and let the scenes fade away. She

exchanged hugs and kisses with soft-whiskered Santa, Anya in her knit cap and flannel nightgown, and Mommy wearing a red silk nightshirt that fell to mid-thigh and rode up a little as they embraced.

Santa blew out the lamp. "Good night, fellow savior," he said with a hearty chuckle. Then they stole from the bedroom and shut the door and at once two cozy cat bodies curved about to box Wendy in with their purrs.

She was too excited to fall asleep. She waited a bit, then brought up more of Jamie's future, muting the volume so much she could barely hear the mortals who passed before her.

Jamie's life wasn't perfect. But Wendy found herself transfixed by the imperfections, the meannesses visited upon this good little boy by bigoted people as he grew. They weren't as ugly as the ones she and Santa and the Easter Bunny had averted. Still, they troubled her.

I wonder, she thought. Would I have become just as mean if I had stayed mortal? Nope, definitely not!

But she wasn't all that different from those she observed, not in any fundamental way. So what stopped mortals from being more pleasant to one another? They spoke a whole bunch, in kindergarten and in their churches, mosques, and synagogues, about being good and kind. Why, even atheists, agnostics, and anarchists hewed to high moral standards. Everyone touted "acting nice" to their children. But when those children outgrew childhood, they followed the example of the generation before them, deeds, as always, trumping words. With rare exceptions, their heads of state turned into bloodsuckers and warmongers, embracing outright moral perversity while parroting religious platitudes about the sanctity of life and political tall tales that trumpeted their nation's unstained virtues.

It was completely insane, when you thought about it.

Wendy furrowed her brow and thought about it a lot.

But eventually, fatigue caught up with her. Snowball and Nightwind settled into sleep, and Wendy's eyes closed on the end of a very special Thanksgiving Day.

In the dead of night, Gronk crept into the elves' quarters. He had been here before, of course, eavesdropping on the odd early-morning conversation or on post-lights-out bull sessions, bunk to bunk.

But never had he stolen in betwixt snort and snore, observing the sleep of the innocent, this mostly harmonious band of brothers who took incomprehensible delight in nonstop toy making. What was missing in the rough and tumble of his brothers, these elves had. And Gronk stewed in envy of them. Their motives remained a mystery, yet he craved their perfect life even as he knew he would never, failing divine miracle, attain it.

His unclipped toenails clicked on the heated tile floor, sharp to his ears, soundless to theirs. The high oak ceiling offered an artful patterning of skylights, through which a sky filled with stars bathed the dozing elves in silver hues. Here lay the mute Herbert, even his night sighs silent. Nearby, the triple bunk bed with Fritz atop Karlheinz atop Max. And yonder, Heinrich, the dollmaking sextuplets who went by one name, their long black beards lying upon their blankets like half a dozen martens, sleek and well-brushed.

Gronk reviewed the roster of helpers, seeking those with the least penchant for judgmentalism. It mattered not upon what subject their judgments dwelt. If he had any chance of sowing dissension among the ranks, these elves would be the ones to whisper to as they slept. What had Mommy told him to stir up? Ah yes, holier-than-thou-ism.

His best chance, he thought, surely lay with the elves most in awe of Gregor. So dropping to all fours, he brought his lips to the ears of the score of sleepers who stood foursquare behind the grump-meister of the stables.

"Thou art special," whispered Gronk. "Because they are too dull to appreciate the merits of Gregor's cause (or worse, resist it), thy brothers are far more dense in the *pia mater* than thou, that shineth in intelligence and perception. If only all elves could be like thee. What harmony would be restored to the North Pole then."

It was exasperating work, this whispering at bedsides. The elves' natural goodness beat back Gronk's blandishments, even in the vulnerable and unguarded state of sleep.

But patience. Tonight was the first of many nights. What though he burrowed but the tenth part of a hair into their simple noggins this night, he would make steady progress, building on past inveiglings, seeking in his daily spying the slightest sign of success—an eyebrow raised, a mumbled demurral, a look askance at a fellow elf.

By these would his whisperings be guided and encouraged.

Those who opposed Gregor? They too he visited, tickling their ears with foul suggestion. Many were utterly impervious, Fritz, Herbert, Franz, and Gustav among them, stalwart souls even in slumber. But others offered ingress. Johann carried signs of weakness in his face, and Knecht Rupert wore the hint of a frown as Gronk disturbed his dreams. To them, he muttered, "Gregor sins. He is a lonely scamp whose job gives him too much free time to plot mayhem and lord it over the rest of you. He puts on the mantle of power to cloak inadequacies. Why, he himself is a ferocious nosepicker, a rank hypocrite. How much better an elf art thou, that sees through his antics? Better than Gregor, better than his thuggish brothers, better than your simpleminded brethren, who are utterly confused by Gregor's rants, or worse, embrace and promulgate them, heart and soul."

All night long, Gronk slipped from bunk to bunk.

Doltish all, thought he. Pan's compliant slaves, who had quite forgotten their lives as satyrs. They seemed like lost brothers to himself and his siblings. Creeping so close brought a further benefit: It gave the impression of camaraderie; it held off loneliness for the nonce. Gronk toyed in fancy. What if his words one day brought them full awake? What if they rose up and destroyed this balsawood world of perfection, the candles, the candy canes, the hot cider, the carols, the shine of tinsel, the rustle of wrapping paper, and the intricate craftsmanship of their creations—gone to hell in one frenzied hour, after which they turned their mayhem upon Santa Claus and his family, and at last, in the depravity of their madness, upon themselves, lost in a sea of hatred and blood?

Gronk chuckled at the vision. Dancing about in a silent night of envy, he continued making imperceptible gains at the receptive ears of these sweet-smelling sleepers.

PART 2
MICHAEL DOES GOOD

23.

THIS PLUM IS TOO RIPE

THE FOLLOWING DAY, AS HIS WORKSHOP buzzed with activity, Santa summoned master weaver Ludwig to the office. Ludwig was wise in the ways of elfdom, his conversation as richly textured, colorful, and appealing as the bolts of fabric that sprang to life when his fingers touched them.

"I was a bit harsh, flying in like that, wasn't I, speaking to all of you that way?"

"Well, Santa," said Ludwig with a squint and a thoughtful tug at his beard, "I can appreciate why. Shoddy is unacceptable. And we *were* off our feed. Still are, to a degree. Harsh? I'd say so. But you were on a divine mission, were you not? You can't have the troops not pulling their weight when you're on a divine mission. It reflects ill on the entire operation. Kinder in berating us you might have been. It isn't like you, this impatience. Only a saint could suffer shoddy with equanimity; yet you are, or were, and continue to be a saint."

"True."

"One might be excused for wondering, if I may be so bold, what possible perturbations churn in your *own* soul."

Santa bristled. "Master weaver, my good fellow, we are talking about my helpers—"

"I understand."

"—not about me. I want to know if there's anything more I can do to restore harmony."

Ludwig pursed his lips and pondered. "Well, now," he said with a sigh, putting a hand to the back of his neck. "I tell you, Santa, that's a hard 'un to answer. Thanks to certain unnamed elves who've got their eye on the ball, things are turning around. So they assure us, at any rate. Is there anxiety? A tad. About what, it were best not to say."

"Why not? Why conceal it from me?"

"There's a certain...embarrassment that would ensue. We are an ingrown group. Peculiarities develop, for reasons that defy knowing. But we have a handle on them. All will be well, and shortly, unless I much mistake."

A smile came to Santa's face. "Ah, Ludwig, you're as elusive as a fistful of air."

Ludwig maneuvered himself into a smile. "Elusive, am I? Well I don't mean to be. But things work out the way they're supposed to. We all have our tasks, our frets and joys and moments of idleness. But if our weaves get tangled, if the centipede tries to stop each leg from realizing its own nature in its own good time, there comes a stumbling, an unraveling, chaos heaped upon chaos. Best leave it alone. There's a sorting out it were better not to force. Or so a craftsman's instincts tell him."

Thoughtful silence wrapped them about.

"I see," said Santa. "All right, Ludwig. You may return to your weaving." He leaned forward. "But if your craftsman's instincts ever tell you something different, my door is always open."

Ludwig nodded. "Thank you, sir. It's a comfort."

Santa watched the master weaver bow and take his leave, not at all pleased with what had been said, what left unsaid. His and Wendy's recent triumph, as noble as it was, could not counter the disturbances that festered inside the community and Santa's heart.

He had a sudden urge to unload upon the Easter Bunny. A visit to that unworthy was due, though not yet. Keep your mind on your helpers, he thought. And on the issue. The one Ludwig so coyly sidestepped. Yet the vexatious rabbit lingered in his thoughts.

Santa raised his head, recalling a tang upon the tongue, a fizz in the nostrils. It was time for a Coke. His thirst was in desperate need of quenching.

Off he went to the squat red rectangular dispenser in one corner of his office. Harrigan Dispensing, Inc. was punched in raised metal letters painted in white script across its front.

A nagging itch, he thought, demands a good scratch.

Later that afternoon, the Easter Bunny sat hunched like a nervous pod in his exercise area. His nose twitched. His tail twitched. His ears caught the least disturbance: the distant hum of machinery, the brood and ruffle of innumerable hens, the romp and roll of pastel eggs down long smooth rosewood troughs toward storage bins deep underground.

At first he thought he was only imagining the sound of sleigh bells. He assured himself this auditory chimera merely reflected his guilt over...what? Something that refused all recollection. Though his life brimmed with joy and contentment, there was a leaden underlay of sorrow, of not-right-ness, to it.

What could be the cause?

Then the high jingle of bells, silver ones rounded into spheres and punched with an open cross, grew more distinct. Panic filled his heart. Santa Claus was coming and, as before, he would not be pleased. As before? The Easter Bunny could not recall a previous visit of any sort, yet his tummy hurt where a stab of hooves had once raised blood. His cheeks, across which the tip of an antler had seared a line of fire, likewise gave an involuntary twitch.

The ground trembled, a ring of light flared open, and through it dashed Lucifer carrying the somber old elf on his back.

Santa dismounted. "No need to panic," he said upon seeing the Easter Bunny's fright. "I'm not angry this time. You have a chair? No matter. Straw will suffice." He made to sit on the ground.

"Outside, perhaps?"

"Good. After you, sir."

The Easter Bunny hopped toward the entrance and found open ground among the trees in warm sunlight. An outcropping of rock afforded his visitor a seat. Nearby, Lucifer grazed among the mosses.

"Now sir, to my agenda."

It felt odd to be called sir, but he said nothing.

"First, my thanks for your part in saving the child. Do I envy you your skill with insufferably dense and wayward mortals? Of course. I admit it. But each of us has talents uniquely ours, and no one can be all things to all people. So thank you. Wendy's pleased, I'm pleased, and I'll wager the Father's pleased too. It's always good to be on the side of the angels.

"That said, something about last night's collaboration troubled me. I sensed your hurt and confusion at my mood. And you, no doubt, were aware of my upset over you. Well, I think you deserve to know why I harbor such a deep—oh, call it what it is—distaste and loathing for you."

The Easter Bunny choked up. "You loathe me?"

Santa nodded and went straight to the point. "You want to know why. I'll tell you. You once had genitals."

"I did?"

"But God erased them, along with all recollection of your misdeeds. Once not so long ago, you were lonely and lustful, you envied me my wives, my community of helpers, and my association with a cheerier time of the year than Easter; though in the end, of course, the underlying message of Easter is far cheerier and of greater import than Christmas's." He raised a hand. "No point in arguing that. I was told that you had been transformed, your crotch gone smooth beneath the fur, your hormones no longer raging, your memories of that time expunged. I was not told I could not stir up those memories. Therefore, open your eyes and see."

Santa, an intensity to his look, gestured at the clearing. There the Easter Bunny saw himself stare hungrily into bedroom windows; engage in his burrow with a wire-mesh doll-bunny named Petunia; attempt to seduce Mrs. Claus by showing her the woodland hut Santa had built for his trysts with the Tooth Fairy, and then showing her the self-same lovers going at it. There then arose the Tooth Fairy's island, where he heard himself snitch on Santa, who had jilted her for Rachel McGinnis, and witnessed the Tooth Fairy's savage rape of him to enlist his services as her henchmen and spy.

But the ultimate horror came in what he saw next. While Santa made his rounds the following Christmas Eve, he had hopped to the door of Santa's cottage, knocked, and tried to seduce his wives with the quincunxial egg which was to have remained in place until the final trump. When that attempt failed—God forgive him—he had attacked them, doing harsh but immediately healed damage to the immortal Anya, then forcing his way into the mortal wife Rachel and wounding her nearly to the point of death, before Anya groin-kicked him gone and applied her healing tongue to the dying woman's body.

The Easter Bunny froze at the magnitude of his misdeeds. For an eternity, he could not breathe.

Then, at last, the clearing returned, sunny but sinister now, his innocence gone. Santa's goads had been sufficient to unlock his memory of those times, kidnapping Snowball, wiring her down in the burrow, and Santa's rescue of her when Lucifer's hooves and antlers had drawn his blood. He even recalled God's visit to the burrow, his revelation of the Easter Bunny's origins, and being neutered in his soft, vast, all-forgiving palm.

"I did that?" he said, choked with revulsion.

80000

"Yes," said Santa.

"So that's why—"

"Yes, why you're not welcome at the North Pole. And why I will never forgive you; nor should you ever ask to be forgiven. Truth be told," admitted Santa, "it's all I can do to keep from attacking you right now. But I must remind myself, I am the soul of generosity, you have been altered, and if we do not make at least half-hearted attempts at reconciliation, our hatred for past wrongs is bound to eat us up."

When Santa got to his feet, the Easter Bunny flinched. "No, I won't attack you, though a good bloodletting would probably benefit us both. You needed to know what prompted my behavior. I needed to tell you. May that knowledge fester in you. May the guilt of having committed the ultimate sin against a mortal eat at your soul. No, that's not mine to say, though I've just said it. It's the punisher in me that wants you to suffer."

The Easter Bunny felt numb.

Lucifer came at Santa's whistle. His sturdy back took the elf's weight. "Sit with it. Let it sting. Think on what you have done. Think on it for all eternity." He gripped the reins. Lucifer's hooves tore at the turf. "There's no call for us to meet again. You will not attempt it, nor shall I." With that, Santa dug his heels lightly into Lucifer's sides. Instantly they bounded into the air, dashed up over the treetops, and vanished from sight.

In the clearing, all was calm. But inside the Easter Bunny's heart, nothing lived for a time but agitation and shame, shock and sorrow, misery and memory intermixed in a tale of unending woe. Yet even as he replayed those memories, they began to fade. For that was the way God had reshaped him, knowing that he could not long function with the knowledge of his great shame.

Did Santa just visit me? he wondered. Why yes. And we had the most pleasant time together. Or did we?

One night not long after, Santa and his wives were sitting up in bed reading.

"Did you hear something?" asked Rachel.

Santa closed his book about one finger and raised his head. The soft weeping that came to his ears withered his heart.

"Is that Wendy?" asked Anya, dumbfounded.

"It is," said Rachel, throwing off the covers.

Santa and Anya shrugged into terrycloth robes over their flannel nightwear as Rachel drew her blue silk robe from the closet and cinched it tight about her nakedness. When she opened their bedroom door, her daughter's sobs sounded with greater clarity.

Rachel rushed down the hall, Santa and Anya close behind. Her knock was light and quick and perfunctory. She turned the knob and they went inside.

Wendy sat trembling in bed. Overlapping scenes filled the room, scenes of violence and rejection, of parental love refused in God's name, of taunting and baiting, of making boys and girls feel small, inconsequential, less than human. Santa witnessed men and women executed for homosexual acts in the savage nations of Iran, Cuba, and Saudi Arabia. A Jewish mother and father sat Shiva for their lesbian daughter, proclaiming in public that she was dead to them. From the walls babbled many tongues, but the universal tongue was intolerance.

Before Wendy spoke, Santa recalled Anya's comment that she was so good-hearted, she wouldn't be content with saving just one gay child.

"Oh, Daddy," she said, choking back her tears, "we've got to *do* something about this."

Santa stood appalled in the midst of a vast outpouring of human misery. How could he have any truck with these distasteful grown-ups? His rage tugged so fiercely at the Pan inside him that he feared its revival, even as he determined to ease Wendy's sorrow. "How can once-innocent children," he said, "grow so monstrous? Is there no justice in heaven? No, I will not blaspheme, no matter how strong the temptation. And I will not give vent to my anger, I swear I won't."

Rachel touched his arm. Santa turned and hugged her, then drew Anya into their embrace. He sobbed as scene after scene assaulted them, the misguided who put words into the Father's mouth; confused kids trying to understand themselves; adults who denied even the slightest hint that they might harbor one iota of attraction to anybody of the same gender, even those who, with regular zest, masturbated and made no connection between touching their own divine organs and those similarly constituted on the body of another.

"But Wendy, what can I—?" said Santa in a panic. "How can I possibly do anything to..."

Wendy simply repeated softly, "We've got to *do* something about this." But her meaning was clear. This was a plea to her stepfather, who stood helpless in the face of it all.

"Sweetheart," said Rachel, "please remove these horrors."

The glut of snide voices, the outpouring of fear and hatred and moral superiority in communities large and small, in cultures backward and advanced, in schools, churches, and families—all of it ceased, the bedroom thrown abruptly into moonlight and silence.

Rachel swept Wendy up in her arms. "You mustn't expect the impossible of your stepfather. He can only do so much. What we all must do," she said, as Wendy sniffed back her tears, "is to bear witness, be kind, and speak out when the chance arises."

Santa could tell Rachel was just being the comforting parent, helpless, seeming wise, but feeling far from comforted inside, the situation beyond her control.

Then he and Anya joined them, and oh dear God, he found himself saying, out of innocent desperation, "I'll think of something. I will, Wendy. Your daddy will think of something. You'll see."

He wanted to stop talking, but he kept babbling away. His wives sat on the bed stunned. Wendy gazed at him with renewed hope in her eyes. And panic rose in his heart and joy too, and on he babbled like the perfect fool he was.

24.
MIGHT THE WORLD BE UTTERLY TRANSFORMED

AS TIME WENT ON, GREGOR FELT THINGS start to bend to his control. He and his brothers had observed fewer incidents of nosepicking. He suspected, of course, that the practice had gone underground, that the perpetrators of this outrage against respectability had become far more savvy about who might be watching. Eliminating the filthy habit must remain his goal. But dampening that peculiar pleasure by fear of exposure, keeping his fellow elves on tenterhooks, was a beginning.

Imagine, then, Gregor's shock and dismay when the fates gave him the chance to observe Fritz and Herbert engaged together.

Thuswise did it happen.

Across the commons from the stables, past the skating pond, lies a stretch of woods especially thick with trees. Gregor had taken to making his circuitous way there, not beelining, for he did not want his prints in the snow to reveal his destination. So he proceeded roundabout. If the curious cared at all, they most likely suspected he headed toward the Chapel.

Thus it was that, perched upon his favorite boulder and concealed by generous pine boughs thick with needles, Gregor cogitated over power, how it could be extended, how he might claim still more of Santa's unexercised authority—all the while picking his nose and meticulously cleaning his fingers with tongue and teeth. It was an utterly private exercise. No one need ever know. Besides, his mucus tasted good. And though he would never confess it to a soul, transgressing in secret was a thrill and a half.

Far off, a branch snapped underfoot.

Gregor froze. His busy hand shot to his lap. The sounds grew closer, softer sounds coming into his hearing as well, a voice, a throat being cleared. Then moving patches of green, exposed, hidden, exposed. There were two of them, not yet near enough to identify. He vowed not to move a muscle, lest he compromise his concealment. The approaching elves, after all, had sharp eyes too. And Gregor had no desire to be discovered.

"Nearer," he mouthed. A face glimpsed, a turn of the head, and Gregor recognized Fritz and Herbert. Fritz, Santa's favorite, who for no reason at all enjoyed the respect a leader deserves. They're here to badmouth me, he thought. That's what happens to the powerful. The envious tear us down. They rant and rave against us in the safety of backbiting isolation. What else would bring these two out here?

A snowball's throw away, they stopped. Fritz glanced about nervously. Gregor could only discern part of him, so thick was the foliage. "It's all right, Herbert," he said. "No one can see us. Relax, okay? Good. You go first." Then Herbert moved smack into his line of sight.

What Gregor observed next disgusted him.

Was there no end to the debauchery of these creatures? His gaze riveted on activities Fritz and Herbert had meant to hide from condemnatory eyes. As well they might. He was appalled and elated. God had set him here to sit in judgment on these elves. And judge them he would, Santa's favorite and his mute companion in sin. Right here and now, unbeknownst to them, would he judge them; and then publicly, shaming them before their brethren.

Scarcely did Gregor breathe, so intently did he observe the unholy acts in which they engaged. Not a day would pass before he exposed them to public ridicule. He had always suspected Fritz of sowing dissension, of undercutting his efforts. Now the dissenter's voice would be stilled, Fritz shamed into the silence his friend had been steeped in from birth.

When at last the two miscreants straightened their clothing and headed home, Gregory dared lift a finger to one nostril and cogitate with brutish ferocity, picking and tasting and cobbling together the withering remarks he would make on the morrow.

Upon the destruction of Fritz's reputation would he build his own. Santa's favorite would fall, and he, Gregor, would rise.

All that day, Santa felt miserable. He covered it convincingly, his workers too caught up in toy making to notice how many Cokes he downed, how ever-so-slightly-off his rhythms were.

Wendy had given plenty of help to Heinrich, the identical sextuplets who specialized in porcelain dolls. Since the night before, she and

Santa had confined themselves to the most trivial of interactions. He sensed her discomfort with everyone's jollity. He knew also that she wasn't fooled by his festive mood.

Now he sat, late at night, in his unlit office in the workshop. Unable to sleep, he had crept out of bed and strode across the commons past the elves' quarters and the stables to the workshop. The place was vast and idle, though shortly before dawn his helpers would throw the light switch and dive with glee into their tasks. He had retired to his office, shut the door, and church-keyed the cap off one more Coke bottle, smoking with mist as he raised it to his lips.

Perched on the stool at his workbench, he stared past a clutter of folders and papers and ran his fingers through his hair. "What can I do?" he murmured. Chills of helplessness bristled along his spine. "The great and benevolent Saint Nick, stymied."

Why was it, he wondered, that one could accomplish so much, yet feel a failure? There was never enough time to do all the good you were capable of. And sometimes, you couldn't even see your way clear to righting a wrong, not though it sat up on its filthy haunches and stared you down in defiance. Why ever had he told Wendy he would do something? The problem was too vast. He couldn't *begin* to think how he might tackle this, even were his annual Christmas tasks lifted from his shoulders. How could he possibly visit and divest of prejudice every last bigoted mortal on earth? Given how judgmentally inept he had been with four mortals, the prospect of transforming millions of them made him blanch. He was sure to bring misery upon himself and his little girl, raise defensive barriers in the homophobic masses, and fail miserably.

Santa took another swig of Coke.

He mocked himself. Oh, what a poor sad bloke am I!

Anxiously stroking his beard, he propped his head upon his fist, his elbow planted on his workbench's hard, scored oak. Michael. What had the archangel said as he ascended? If you need my aid and comfort, you have merely to summon me. "I do then," he murmured. "I summon you."

"Indeed you do."

Santa ought to have been startled at the voice, at the being who hovered there, the redemptive light of heaven emanating from him. But it seemed as though he had been ever-present. His manifestation to eye and ear merely extended the power of those organs to detect one who had never left.

"Oh, Michael," said Santa, wondering if he ought to fall to his knees, "I would not dare ask for what I desire. My daughter has shown me overwhelming instances of the misery non-heterosexual human beings suffer from childhood on. She has pleaded with me to do something to stop it. And I have assured her, with too much haste, that I would somehow set it right. But sometimes one makes promises in the heat of the moment and lives to regret them later. We have saved a good little boy from suicide. But even he is fated to suffer ridicule and rejection. And there are vast multitudes of boys and girls out there who are doomed to stagger beneath the yoke of bigotry as they mature, living every day in a world that belittles them and rejects their expressions of love. And all of it carried out in God's name, a profanation the prejudiced regard as the duty of the righteous."

Santa clasped his hands in prayer. "Help me, I beg you. Teach me how to ease Wendy's disappointment, to let her down gently and keep her from despising her stepfather too much. Or if there is indeed a way to ease the heartache of the world entire, show me that way. I do not presume to ask the impossible. Yet I fear I have already presumed in my heart."

Michael's face was unreadable.

Was he stunned? Bemused? On the verge of tears? Angered at the jolly old elf's temerity? All Santa knew for sure was that the archangel was utterly present, listening with every fiber of his being to Santa's plea.

At last he spoke: "Dearly beloved, be not dismayed. The world is as it is, joyous and sorrowful, broken and whole, an imperfect yet perfectible perfection. You have asked the impossible." His brow furrowed. "Indeed you have." Again, he lapsed into a silence whose import could not be known. "But to God," he continued, "all things are possible. I shall return on the morrow. Meantime, take heart, apply yourself diligently to your tasks, say neither yea nor nay to Wendy, and do this only: Embrace the comfort that surrounds you."

A smile of compassion lit his boyish face, though it was tinged with a hint of exasperation. Then he was gone. As before, Santa was heartstruck at his departure, even as he basked in a golden afterglow.

He sat for the longest time, buoyant, bubbly, blessed.

"How *about* that?" he said, laughing uproariously.

At length, he poured the flat Coke down the sink, recycled the bottle, and traipsed across the commons to bed, marveling as he went.

***

As Michael began his ascent, he was surprised to find himself yanked back to the North Pole, this time to Wendy's bedroom. She had lit a candle on her nightstand and sat, propped up against her pillow, in a flannel nightgown decorated pink and lavender with a small pale-green bow at the neck.

"Oh, goody," said Wendy, unclasping her hands and clapping them with glee. "You've come."

"I have indeed," said Michael, feeling peeved with himself for giving these two carte blanche. "Angels do not make promises lightly."

"Okay, so listen up, please. That's not a command, of course, only a request, I'm excited is all. I mean, I'm in *awe,* that's for sure, but I won't let it bowl me over or tie my tongue. If anything, it loosens it. But to the point. Santa's fretting. I know he is, and it's all on account of me and my stupid wish to prevent all these boys and girls from suffering over some dumb prejudice. Take a look. Oh but never mind, I'm sure you can read minds and see everything that ever was or will be on earth, so you already know all of that. Well anyway, I showed my parents and blurted out to Santa that we needed to save every last one of them somehow. I could tell he was distraught, but his heart's so pure, he said he'd think of something. But there's really nothing he can do, is there? It's out of his hands, the sheer vastness of human suffering. He already acts from a place of such overwhelming generosity. Even if it *were* possible, how could he take on more?

"So what I'm asking, and this is in the strictest confidence, is for you to ease his heart. I wish I hadn't brought it up. If I could take it back, I would. He's upset. It's my fault. And I wanted you to remove his upset, or help me figure out how to reverse what I said and restore him to his cheery self. Can you? Could you? It seems like you can do *anything* you set your mind to. I mean, aren't angels all powerful, as long as it fits into God's plan?"

She gazed at Michael with a wide-eyed look of anticipation that barely masked a grown-up sensibility inside. Her love for Santa filled him with delight. And her appeal to his pride, it must be admitted, struck a chord. Might he do something grand? Something that would please the Almighty greatly, and erase all the embarrassment his Hermes side had caused a while back? This called for serious thought.

"Dear heart," he said, "on the morrow, I will come again. I will devise a way to ease his suffering and yours. Fret not and know that you are loved. Be gentle with your father. Accept the child in him, though he sometimes misspeaks. The blessings of heaven be upon you."

He raised his right hand and brushed his fingertips—though no contact was made—against Wendy's brow. She gasped in wonder. Then, drawing a veil of invisibility over himself, he watched her blow out the candle and settle her head on the pillow with a contented sigh.

Heavenward Michael sped, mulling the pair of requests he had received from these most precious immortal souls.

25.
BOLD INITIATIVES

WHAT FIRST NUDGED FRITZ TOWARD WAKING was the soft glow of magic time. He drifted up from dream far enough to recognize its embrace, though not far enough to question why magic time should be embracing anyone tonight.

Then the throwing of a huge switch somewhere shattered the night's peace. Floodlights exploded against his eyelids. "What the dickens?" grumbled someone. Someone else gave an exaggerated yawn. Max, one of Fritz's bunkmates, shouted, "Turn that darned thing off!"

Fritz hardly had time to consider what a violation of the natural order this was. Only Santa and his wives were allowed to bathe the community in magic time. It was one thing to enter magic time of one's own volition; they all did that, as the need arose. It was quite another to...

Then Engelbert and Josef scattered his thoughts, striding among beds and bunks, shaking elves awake and barking at them to rise and shine and give God their glory glory. Gregor stood with folded arms at Santa's lectern, an eyebrow arched in the garish light, waiting impatiently for his brothers to bring the troops to their feet.

The floor was cold but Fritz managed, in the melee, to find his bedroom slippers. "Enough," yelled Gregor, slamming his fist against the lectern. "You will come to order."

Which, pretty much, they did.

Knecht Rupert, bleary-eyed and only half awake, said, "Aw, geez, Gregor, what's the point o' this? We need our sleep."

"Silence! You've slept enough, and far too deeply, in my estimation. Perversity slithers amongst you, but your eyes are shut. Sin smacks its lips and gobbles its nasty provender, but your snoring drowns out the vile sounds. A stench of misdeeds most foul swirls about your nostrils, but you are aware only of the fantastical aromas of dreamland."

173

He paced and punctuated, did Gregor. Fritz had never seen him so animated, never heard his words bite so sharp.

"Often have I lectured you on the picking of noses. I have excoriated you for it, you have deserved it, and it has done some little good. My words have penetrated one poor micron into your skulls, and many of you have abandoned your sin-sick ways. From diligence in personal hygiene come toys that are second to none. But even now, there are those who turn a deaf ear to my message. Blithely do their fingers find their docking place, from whence they extract those noisome nuggets, blaspheme their mouths with satanic bonbons, and head back for more.

"But my fellow elves, it isn't that which leads me to rouse you from sleep. Greater perversities are afoot. And I mean to bring them to light."

Fritz began to sweat. Could he possibly have...but no, they had been careful.

"Come forth, o unworthy ones," commanded Gregor, his eyes aglow. Do not force me to expose you. Confess your misdeeds, and the shame will fall lighter on your shoulders." He scanned the crowd, his gaze skipping past Fritz. "No response? Why am I not surprised?"

Friedrich the globemaker raised a tentative hand. "Forgive me, Gregor, for I have sinned."

"What the devil are you babbling about?"

"At times, getting dressed in the morning, I've skipped a button on my jerkin. Fumble fingers, you might call me. For this sin of omission, I am heartily sorry." Hearing the worthy Friedrich humble himself before Gregor's bullying made Fritz's blood boil.

"Idiot!" said Gregor, beet-red with scorn. "I don't give a tinker's dam *how* you button your jerkin. Now button your lip, and do that right at least. You and you, put your hands down. I know who the sinners in our midst are. They're too cowardly to admit their perversion, thinking perhaps that Gregor is merely bluffing in hopes of ferreting out minor infractions."

Herbert's face went white, to which Fritz shook his head ever so slightly in assurance.

"Oh, my friends, how the mighty have fallen. I hereby call to account...our once-beloved Fritz and his sin mate Herbert."

Fritz's heart sank.

"In the woods this afternoon did I see them, though from their slinking and the way they glanced nervously about, it was clear they did not wish to be seen. But God brings all misdeeds to light. Not content with the perverse thrill of violating nature's way with simple nosepicking, I have caught them picking each other's noses, feasting on the contents, and heading back for more in obvious enjoyment of this unspeakable practice." He jabbed a finger at Fritz. "Deny it if you will. You *cannot* deny it."

His mouth moved, but nothing came out. Herbert buried his face in his arms and wept.

Fritz's rage at Gregor for hurting his friend flared. But his mind was in such turmoil, he could do naught but stand there paralyzed, head bowed, brow burning, unable to look his fellow elves in the face.

"This comes of spiritual neglect. Let one vile tendril of sin slither in and the whole stinking mess, root, branch, and bitter fruit, surges eagerly after it. Who among us would *dare* indulge in such an abomination?"

Standing at the midpoint of the assembly, Knecht Rupert eased an uncertain hand into the air, and Gustav as well. More boldly, flaxen-haired Franz the watchmaker raised a hand. Beside him, Johann tepidly wiggled three fingers at the lectern.

Fritz took heart.

"Do you mean to say there are others?" Gregor spat the words, contempt dripping from his lips. "This shall not endure. O Sin, I Gregor vow to chase you from our midst, to restore once more the purity of our toymaking endeavors, to keep clean our fingers so that the dolls and fire engines and board games we fashion shall never carry the foul taint of misdeed. *All* of you, raise your right hands. Higher. Repeat after me. I solemnly vow...in the presence of my brothers...never to pick my nose...and never, for the love of Christ, to pick another's nose...so help me God. Good! We three are going to hold you to this vow. And you must hold one another to this vow. I shall personally administer a beating to any elf caught breaking it."

Beating? Fritz could scarcely believe his ears. Someone should speak up, he thought. I should speak up. But he was still stunned and could barely gasp, let alone protest.

"But I and Josef and Engelbert are but three pairs of eyes. We need more. If any of you witness these vile practices, though they be indulged in by your dearest friend, you are to tell us, so that we can properly punish the miscreant and guide him back onto the paths of righteousness. Indeed, if you catch yourself in the act, you are honor-bound to turn yourself in.

"Do not make me go to Santa with this. He's busy enough as it is. But if this behavior persists, I *will* go to him. And his wrath, when he learns what lies beneath the creeping shoddiness of our work, will put mine to shame. Go now. Get to bed. Be good. Be vigilant. Think worthy thoughts. And praise God for the efforts of Gregor and his brothers in policing our noble community."

With that, the floodlights snapped off.

Fritz took a moment, as they milled about, to go over to Herbert. But Herbert turned away in shame. And that stung far worse than any public humiliation.

Though his bunkmates were polite, they pointedly avoided looking at him as he climbed to the top bunk and buried himself beneath the covers.

When Michael reached his heavenly abode, he agonized all that night and into the morning about the best course of action. Should he go to God with the problem? No, God had trusted him to rectify his past bumblings on his own. And the smashing success of Santa, Wendy, and the Easter Bunny's Thanksgiving Eve visits bolstered Michael's courage. One might say, and be right in so saying, that it bolstered his courage a bit more than was strictly proper.

For there sprang into his mind, full blown, plans for a grand annunciation, not just to one or two souls, but the sort that was sometimes performed before a multitude. Yes indeed! He would take great risks, impress the Almighty, succeed on a far grander scale, and thereby expunge all memory of his earlier mistakes. 'Midst choirs and trumpets would he descend to the North Pole, where he would draw from Santa's recent mortal visitants, unawares, the essence of their transformations, shaping from them...in a flash, Michael saw how it would go and knew without doubt that his contemplated course of action would repair, nay burnish, his reputation in heaven.

He tore off earthward.

And in the sunlight of a cerulean morn upon the snowy commons, the archangel descended with great fanfare, divine radiance lighting his way. Out of the workshop poured Santa's helpers, followed by an astonished Santa Claus and Wendy. The elves who tended to the reindeer likewise left the stables, and Santa's wives their cottage, to greet him.

Hovering shoulder high above them, Michael lifted his hands to the assembled multitude. "Dearly beloved," he said, "Santa Claus

176

and Wendy have, with your help and support, done wondrous things for one small boy. Now they have requested my aid in extending that support. Heaven blesses their request, made from joyful hearts overflowing with love and generosity."

Santa took Wendy's hand. "Good archangel," he said, "we welcome you to our community and receive with gratitude heaven's blessing."

"Your desires are attainable," said Michael, "but attaining them means a great deal of extra work on Christmas Eve and intimate contact with the hearts of grown-ups, a contact not much to your liking, as I know. But the rewards, if you succeed, are great indeed."

He gestured to an open patch of commons and a hillock silently rose, the snow upon it melting, the grasses green and lush. Upon the hillock appeared a vision of the four mortals, going about their daily lives.

"These good people," said the angel, "were by Santa and Wendy's visits changed. Examine their souls." At his gesture, their bodies opened to reveal a mortal mixture of squalor and splendor. "Observe the places recently wiped clean of warped doctrine, self-righteousness, fantasies about a great war with a non-existent Satan, and the demonization of those who disagreed with them. It's one small part, I grant you. But that part is pristine, is it not?"

The archangel's hands sculpted the air. "From these new virtues in them, I shape a concentrated seed of goodness." Above the hillock, extractions from the four souls rose and coalesced into an ovoid, no bigger than a child's fist, the shape and size of an avocado pit, its little end up, its bright-green surface as smooth and transparent as glass. Into Michael's palm it floated. He raised it to his lips and kissed it, then sent it bobbing in the air toward Santa, who received it into his hands with grace and awe.

"This egg-seed, Santa, you are to carry to each mortal with even a hint of homophobia, even those whose homes you normally do not visit. At your wish shall this egg-seed be cloned. Then you must become one with the heart before you, contemplating without judgment its failings and wonders. Doing so will calibrate each clone to its recipient. You must then insert it, oriented precisely as you are holding it now, into the heart, and move on to the next. In the months that follow, these egg-seeds shall quietly germinate, to burst forth on Easter morn in all their glory. Be sure never to insert it little end down, for doing so, rather than removing their phobias, shall make them far worse. Will you do it, Santa? Will you embrace this task?"

In the instant's hesitation that followed, Michael read Santa's uncertainty. But the choice was his, and he made it.

"Wondrous angel," said Santa, "how can I refuse? To make such a change in humankind would be the ultimate act of generosity. For this shall I gladly extend my stay in magic time, praising God all my days for giving me this opportunity. Fritz, I charge you with the supervision of the workshop in the coming days. Gregor, you and your brothers are to prepare the team for a far grander journey than they are used to. Are you with me, lads?"

At this, the elves raised a shout and lofted their caps, which jingled as they left their hands and again when they were caught.

"How wondrous!" cried an unfamiliar voice. Herbert, the elf who had never spoken in his long life, spoke now. He clapped a hand to his mouth, his wide eyes shifting left, right, and left again.

An astonished Santa said, "Go ahead, Herbert."

And Herbert smiled to outshine the sun. "Bless you, Santa, and bless us all this day." Then with a laugh, "I'm thrilled to my toes at the prospects before us, and...merciful heavens, everybody, I can talk!"

"So you can, Herbert," exclaimed Max, "and quite well at that." Then all the elves swarmed about to congratulate and back-pat and glad-hand and lift him to their shoulders.

"With my newfound voice," Herbert shouted from his lofty perch, "I praise this day. We are all blessed, as we have been from the day we were created here to make toys and help Santa. But thrice blessed are we today, for this new task. May God speed Santa on his way, and may his success delight and astonish the world!"

Everyone cheered.

Herbert managed to look bashful and elated all at once.

"May it indeed be so," said Michael. With a gesture, the mortals vanished and the hillock went flat and reflocculated with snow.

The archangel noted, of course, the Tooth Fairy's invisible imp on the periphery listening in. But he gave scant thought to Gronk, the general jubilation claiming the lion's share of his attention. He pronounced a final benediction and rose smiling into the sky, basking in the sweet frenzy of rollick and glee that filled the commons.

This will set things right with the Father, he thought. Soon shall break a glorious Easter morn, and certain triumph.

***

Gregor watched openmouthed and dumbstruck. He too joined in the general marvel at the archangel's sudden appearance in the commons, the bright air atremble with grace, the soothing borne on the wings of each angelic word. How could he not be moved?

At the egg-seed's creation, he had wept with joy. He rejoiced as well at that rare glimpse of mortals and the inner map of their hearts, the newly purified areas, to be sure, but the rest as well—the giddy joys, the unrealized potential for goodness, and the foul and pestilent stew of unworthy thought and deed. It was humbling, how much of it, *all* of it really, resonated with his elfin heart.

But to hear Herbert burst into words after centuries of muteness! And such glorious words they were. Glorious too the feelings that inspired them and the voice that spoke them, honeyed like sunlight and maple syrup and liquid gold and an infant's tears rolled into one. Who would have imagined the mute elf's soul to be so pure, this unassuming creator of cameras who was always toddling after Fritz and had been so recently exposed as an enthusiastic cross-nosepicker. For a time, Gregor found it impossible to reconcile these warring images.

But soon the wonder began to wear off. Gregor hated being one of the boys, the gaggle clustered about Herbert, begging him to say more, and delighting at the gems of benevolence bubbling from his lips. The others, he thought (observing random glances his way), must wonder why the imperious Gregor was suddenly not so stern. Had he forgiven Herbert's misdeeds? He could not have them think that, lest he lose all advantage. Besides, the mute's newfound stature cast reflected glory upon his friend Fritz, and Fritz must not be allowed to re-ascend the few pegs down which Gregor had taken him.

And so, at length, after Santa had disappeared with Wendy and his wives into the cottage to marvel at the egg-seed in private, Gregor yanked his brothers from the sycophantic gush and hustled them toward the stables for a powwow and regrouping. In short order, he pressed them back into shape. But all day, his world felt out of kilter.

It made one question one's entire direction, this dropping in of archangels, this witnessing of miracles. Thank God for the resumption of habit, the hand that, losing control over one's resolve for a spell, grasps it again with renewed strength.

Gregor stood at the half-door and gazed out in judgment upon his fellow elves as they straggled back to work. Were it not for the glare of his beacon of righteousness upon them, they would devolve into moral chaos. Of that he was certain. His mask of rectitude had, to be sure, momentarily slipped. But that it had so swiftly clambered back onto his face and moored itself there again, reaffirmed its propriety and rightness.

Harrumph, he thought.

"Harrumph," he said.

It felt good to harrumph with such clarity into the fading chords of false harmony echoing even now upon the commons.

26.

A MIGHTY WIND SOWN

IN THE WEEK REMAINING BEFORE CHRISTMAS, all the elves hopped to. Even Gregor's hold on them slipped, they were so single-mindedly focused on the flawless execution of the final round of toymaking, stocking the shelves from which Santa's pack would be replenished en route and ensuring that the deliveries would go off without a hitch.

Gregor and his brothers put the reindeer through their paces, taking them out for twice as many test runs as usual, with greater speed and around more obstacles, swooping a brick-loaded sleigh up and down and sideways at perilous angles. As usual, Gregor let Josef and Engelbert do that, as he preferred his feet planted firm on the ground; he saw to their sleep and diet, serene and deep the former, fat-poor and protein-rich the latter.

Rachel pitched in everywhere around the workshop and Anya kept coffee pots full and spirits bright with light banter and encouraging pats upon the head. Both women gave Santa deep massages every night, assuaging his doubts as they thumbed stress from his muscles. They hugged him and told him how very much they loved him, keeping their bouts of marital intimacy at just the right length and ardor to avoid sapping his strength.

Everyone had been fired up by the angel's visit and the task ahead, functioning as one well-oiled engine set to deliver more than the usual payload of presents this Christmas Eve. If they paused for anything, it was to appreciate yet again Herbert's newfound voice, which spoke nothing but blessings—brief ones throughout the day and a far more elaborate one, extempore, from his bedside before lights out at night.

As for Wendy, she glowed all week, helping at one workbench or another. And each day just before Anya rang the dinner bell, Wendy slipped into her stepfather's office and enjoyed quiet conversation with him. In the cozy warmth of that inner sanctum, by lantern light, they spoke in wondrous tones about the gift that had fallen into their laps.

"You can do it, Father, I know you can," she said, gripping his anxious hands.

"To pause before them one by one, to stare into their depths," he said with a shake of his great head. "I don't know. I'm so judgmental these days. And they're all so tainted, far too many of them anyway; if not with homophobia, in other ways. Yet I must observe in minute detail every fallen soul, to insure the egg-seed's proper fit. One at a time, I've got to do it, ignoring wounds to my own sensibilities, or rather acknowledging them and letting them go. I fear it will break my spirit. But if that were true, why would God's emissary come with such assurance to grant us this gift? And yet, how can it not change me?"

Wendy gazed at him with adoration. "If you change, it can only be for the better. You're already so wise and kind and generous, those qualities can only grow in you. And I'll be there most of the night to give moral support." She told him how proud she was of him, no matter the outcome. "Even if, by some quirk of fate, your efforts come to naught, I will love you all the more for having tried."

Santa broke down and wept.

Making a finger ghost with a tissue, Wendy dried his cheeks.

"I have to remind myself that they were all once children, free of prejudice and open as the sky. I always feel so small, right about now. Yet, when we return home, I recall in wonder the vast terrain we have crisscrossed, me and my team, and our great dispensation...of goods, yes, but of generosity above all. What, I wonder, will I recall after this trip?"

Wendy laughed. "We won't know until it's over, will we? But we'll share every moment of it, except when I break away to visit my hundred children—and I promise I'll keep that brief." She threw her arms around his neck. "Daddy, I wouldn't miss this night for the whole wide world." Then she kissed his forehead, and he crushed her in a giant bear hug in return.

Thus did Wendy buoy Santa's spirits, and thus the busy week went by, animated by anticipation, the slightest edge of anxiety, and plenty of love and exertion. When the day before Christmas arrived, they were prepared.

Gronk had never known magic time could stretch so thin. He knew of course that it allowed his mother to visit as many homes each night as there were teeth under pillows. And that it could extend further to encompass the far more ambitious annual night-journeys of Santa

Claus and the Easter Bunny.

But that Christmas Eve, as Santa's rounds grew by three and four orders of magnitude, as he visited not only slumbering homes he had never visited before, but homeless people, and bustling time-frozen souls in day-lit agoras on the far side of the globe, and the ailing elderly, and all manner of naughty boys and girls of every age, and disease-wracked sufferers on their deathbeds, Gronk's marvel grew with his dismay at the nearly interminable list of places he had to commit to memory. Magic time must truly approach *stopped* time, he thought, where immortals could spend, if they chose, an eternity wandering through halted humanity.

Gronk watched Santa and Wendy closely as they worked with great efficiency. The girl held up the egg-seed, Santa brushed its tip with his index finger, and its clone popped into his other hand. Then came a touch upon the mortal's chest, a moment of intense concentration, a shift infinitesimal in the clone, and its insertion with a deft twist of the wrist. Santa withdrew his hand. Then he sighed, nodded to his daughter, and they were off to the next abode, Gronk scurrying to keep up.

Halfway through their itinerary, the imp feared his skull would burst from the list of visited places. Then he realized they were *far* from halfway, and that the mind-map his mother had insisted he create had plenty of white space yet to be inked in. "Leave no address out," she had commanded, "none, or I shall torment you unending through all eternity, every speck of you aching for surcease, and suffering tenfold with each fruitless plea." Fear was a great motivator, especially if one's energies were vast and one's life unending.

Then Gronk wised up. If he closed his eyes, he could grasp the golden cord of Santa's travels—from the instant his sleigh swept up into the polar air to its ever-moving endpoint—as one visual whole. And once he trusted that image, he dared to stop memorizing street names and house numbers, every zig and zag of the sleigh, every venture up stairs and down midnight corridors. Moreover, from this golden cord he found it easy to untwist and toss aside all threads having to do with traditional Christmas activities in the homes of "good" mortals, the placing of gifts inside stockings and beneath trees, the consumption of milk and cookies, the scribbled "Thank you" notes placed beside unconsumed carrot remnants. All of that he gratefully elided.

Even so, Gronk would be relieved when this night was over. He wished his mother weren't quite so demanding a taskmaster, for she was capable of inflicting great pain and quick to do so. He hated pain at the moment it was delivered, even though in recall it was exciting and it assured him he was alive.

What capped his dismay, though, was missing out on the Christmas Eve mayhem. But his brothers had vowed to bring back the bones of a few hapless brats, so that he could feed on cold remnants as they shrugged off their black Santa suits and regaled him and his mother with nasty tales.

So Gronk held on, settling in beside Santa's pack in the back of the sleigh, racing after him into each house, and adding yet another inch to the umpteen million miles that made up the length of Santa's serpentine journey across the globe.

Heading into his great adventure, Santa harbored one fear which he had shared with no one. He wondered if his helpers' shoddiness might have been caused by his first-ever proximity to the four mortals on Thanksgiving Eve. And having so wondered, he feared that tonight's intimacy with so many, planetwide, could prompt a breakdown in their work entire. Might his cozy little community crumble? No more toys, no more deliveries, his purpose gone, naught but thumb-twiddling and idle sighs for all eternity?

This unsettling thought had come to him in the process of saving Jamie Stratton. He had considered, for an instant, abandoning that effort rather than jeopardize his larger mission. But he had rejected the idea at once. If he could not, given the opportunity by God's archangel, save one small boy from suicide, if he had caved in to fear and walked away from that challenge, it would have rendered meaningless all else he achieved for the rest of his life. For that same reason, Santa was determined to overcome his distaste for grown-ups and embrace with gusto the task of implanting each perfectly calibrated egg-seed.

That task could not be done on autopilot. He had to be completely present to each mortal's failings. To keep the host from rejecting its implant, the witness he bore must be intense, precise as clockwork, and full of a compassion which, while not overlooking the slightest flaw, sees all and judges naught.

Indeed, the divine surgeon in him did its work dispassionately. Behind that, where emotion could not skew his deeds, Santa began the evening appalled at the depth and blackness of the tincts he found on once-innocent babes devolved into adulthood: murderous urges barely suppressed if suppressed at all; easy acquiescence to addictions; ethnic hatreds; envy of more fortunate gatherers and hoarders; self-denigrations without cause, learned in school or from scornful parents; emptying reservoirs of empathy in the stony hearts of politicians as they scrambled up the ladders of power; all the general and specific unhappinesses of a lost race of beings. These shocked Santa for a time. But shock yielded eventually to empathy and the complete dissolution of his fear of emotional intimacy. He even developed some small tolerance of Pan, fearing not quite so much the goat god's possible reemergence.

How mortals devolved continued to vex him. But it wasn't his mission to unravel that mystery. Nor was it his mission, even if he knew how it might be done, to fix them in every particular. He had simply to calibrate the egg-seed clone, insert it into the heart before him, and move on to the next.

Santa felt neither rushed nor overwhelmed. He found his rhythm and moved to it, growing in compassion, changing, even as Wendy—who watched each transplanted clone take root—changed and grew in compassion before his eyes.

When she summoned Galatea and her sleigh from the North Pole and broke away to pay night visits to her hundred handpicked children, Santa felt a twinge of misgiving. But by then, they were very much of one mind, and he felt Wendy's spirit with him as she carried on with her task and, millions of abodes into his deliveries, returned to his side.

Thus did they cover the world, person by person, house by house, until the last clone had been implanted, the last mortal touched, the last imperfect heart made a bit less imperfect, *in potentia*.

The original egg-seed glowed suddenly warm and brilliant in Wendy's hand, spinning with a thin high hum and vanishing in a whirr and swirl of benediction. "I think we're finished," she said simply.

"We are indeed," said Santa. "Let's go home, darling."

"All right, Daddy." She wiped a tear from his cheek.

Arm in arm, they left the final house, found the reindeer waiting patiently on the lawn, hugged and thanked each of them, and took their seats in the sleigh, which swept up—at Santa's whipsmack and joyful shout—into the night sky, setting a bead straight north through early hints of dawn.

***

On the ride home, Wendy's spirits soared. Between herself and the sleigh's front scroll, she began to project the future in miniature scenes.

"Do it against the snowflakes," suggested Santa, gesturing past Lucifer's glowing antlers to the flurries into which they flew. "Make it big."

"All right," said Wendy, loving his boyish enthusiasm.

Off to one side, where the blindered team wouldn't be distracted, Wendy projected revised futures for those her past projections had brought before them. The change was still too recent to allow for more than a few months' prescience. But she was able to observe the growth of the implants, the deepening of their roots, the spreading of righteousness into mortal psyches, into the locus of limbic emotion, the seat of reason, and the place where civility and thoughtfulness judge which impulses are appropriate to act upon.

Santa pointed. "Stay with that one. Meg Weddle. I turned her in your absence. She was the most wonderfully accepting girl-child. It was heartbreaking to find her, at twenty-six, on our list. Someday, I'll have to peer into her past and try to figure out what brought her to judge other people with such a breathtaking lack of shame."

Wendy never tired of hearing how much her stepfather cared for these mortals, even when they had disappointed him in their growing up. Could ever anyone love so well as him?

"How good it will be to watch her change," he continued. "When the change has taken root, let's pull Meg up again and watch her shrug off the heavy cloak of prejudice."

Thus did they beguile the time on their journey northward, Lucifer needing no guidance, after centuries of honed instinct, to point him toward home and a well-earned rest.

27.

UNNOTICED REPLANTINGS

DAWN, AS IT BREAKS UPON THE TOOTH FAIRY'S island, merely replaces a charcoal sky with an ashen one. No hint of sunlight has ever touched mountain or shore, nor have the roiling clouds and the battering storm ceased for one moment their battering and roiling, though odd catch-breaths of rhythmic variance occur to keep them from becoming background noise.

As Gronk came in, he saw Mommy squatting beside the blasted cedar tree, a long-dead starfish impaled on its top. Soon her sons would return from their Christmas mischief. But not before she forced Gronk to retrace Santa's journey. Keeping up with jolly old Saint Nick for decades of magic time had exhausted him, but that counted for nothing with her.

"Report," she barked as he landed.

And he launched into it.

"Cut the dross. There's no time."

He began again and she cuffed him.

"Bare essence, boy, or you'll squeal."

Terrified, Gronk skimmed the cream only: the number of stops, the way it was done, the pride expressed, the concluding gestures. Then he closed his mouth.

"Let's be off." She swept them into magic time. "Begin at his first stop, and don't dawdle."

"Yes'm." Up he rose, piercing the cloud cover, his harrying mom close behind, heading for a squalid street in Anchorage, where Santa Claus and Wendy had begun their impossibly long journey, a journey *he* would take twice, no rest between. I'll be able to forget each place we visit, he assured himself. Each time, the burden will grow lighter by one mortal. I'll survive.

"Faster," she said, "faster." It was a word Gronk soon grew to hate, now and for the rest of his life.

187

***

The elves' traditional snowball fight, as they awaited Santa's return, was far more spirited than usual, and that was saying a lot. Big bulky spheres, loose-packed, flew from mittened hands and landed smack on buttocks and backs, leaving huge white splats on pants and jerkins and knocking caps to the ground. Volleys from this or that contingent, hastily formed behind trees and as hastily disbanded, were launched without mercy, 'midst spirited shouts of "Look out, Fritz!" and "Obliterate the bastards, boys!"

Two things filled them with excess energy. One was the special nature of Santa and Wendy's journey this year. They had all seen the archangel, heard his words, and witnessed the making of the egg-seed. There was no doubt in anyone's mind that Santa would succeed, and the anticipated celebration fired each elfin heart.

But also contributing mightily to their zeal was their day off. For a day off meant that, for the moment, they had wriggled out from under Gregor's thumb. A work-free Christmas Day had ever been their abbreviated version of Saturnalia, when all authority, even Santa's benevolent sort, was utterly defied, toppled, and trampled underfoot. Not a few elves remarked on the prudent absence of Gregor, Engelbert, and Josef from the snowball fight and the avalanche that would surely have buried them more than once, had they dared show their faces.

Rachel's shouts cut through the elves' more rambunctious cries. She was bundled up in snow gear, a knit hat and the finest Gore-Tex-lined coat and boots. Anya stood at the cottage window alternately enjoying the mayhem and lifting her eyes to the heavens. Though the picture window muted voices, she heard them perfectly: Knecht Rupert leading a charge down snow-covered hills into the commons, Rachel's mock-panicked warning to Herbert (a special target this year), and Herbert's blither of blessings upon everybody, even as he vanished beneath a volley of snowballs only to reappear from the obliterating mound, shake snow from his ears, and bless them yet again through his ear-to-ear grin. The converging elves screamed their thanks, then buried him once more beneath a punishing barrage.

But Anya's immortal ears, despite overlapping waves of sound washing in from the commons, had no trouble picking out the first, thin, high, barely-discernible harness-shake of bells out beyond the protective dome that kept their winters mild. That sound she heard now, savoring her private knowledge a moment longer.

At last, she went out onto the porch in her bright red and green dress and her blue-gray woolen shawl. Brushing past her skirts, Snowball and Nightwind leaped onto the railings.

Several helpers raised a shout at her appearance. Anya pointed toward an empty quadrant of sky as the elves swarmed into the commons. Some collided, then picked themselves up to resume the swirl.

The sleigh and its team grew from nothing to a vibrating smudge, to a brown-black blot with hints of antler and pronounced dots of red and white, to a miniature conveyance whose parts became recognizable, the nine pulling Santa and Wendy behind. Santa made his traditional spiral over their heads and around and back again, Wendy waving wildly despite her weariness, and Santa waving in more stately arcs.

When at last they landed, the community swamped the sleigh until there bobbed to the surface of that roiling sea Santa and his daughter. Passed from hand to hand they went, wrestled at last to the snow and reemerging to hug and be hugged in a frenzy of joy.

Shoulder high to the porch were they carried. Then Anya and Rachel ushered the travelers inside, while the elves stood in awe and clapped and shouted with glee in the commons, as high and happy as anyone could remember.

The Tooth Fairy, driven by revenge along Santa's itinerary, never flagged. In her fury, she whipped Gronk like a whining guide dog. She called him names, laggard, mewler—worse names, some of them, than she shamed Chuff with. "There next," he would say. "Everyone in that house, eldest to youngest." And down she sped, not waiting for him to catch up.

Cowering over each mortal while Gronk squatted nearby, the Tooth Fairy reached in and gave the egg-seed a vicious twist so that the little end pointed down. Were the mortals not stuck in normal time, she knew a twinge of pain would wince across their faces. Indeed, she vowed, when they were back on the island and ready to leave magic time, to summon up views of a host of them and witness it.

Heartburn. That's what they would chalk it up to.

Despite her underlying anxiety at being found out, she indulged often in the momentary luxury of sticking a finger into a sleeper's mouth to touch the exposed bone of their surviving teeth.

Take Andrew Jonathan Campbell, in mid-snore beside his wife of fifty years. Though his hair was sparse, he was a hearty seventy-six, hiking and exercising and eating right to live out his remaining days in fine fettle. Foolish old coot, she mused. Little Andy ought to have indulged his lusts, made an art out of the pursuit of pleasure. These womb-dropped mortals toddled up into youth, then swiftly aged, drooped, and died, their lives but a finger snap.

She recalled Andrew Jonathan Campbell as a wee tyke. He had believed in her. He had tucked delicious baby teeth beneath his pillow. Even then, as he innocently slept, she probed his lollipop mouth, detesting him, longing to yank out his whole set of choppers and grinders, to devour them in that moonlit bedroom and shove fresh-minted coins under his head, so that he would awaken, a rich little boy, to bloody horror. Now, running her fingers across molar and bicuspid, his crowns gold and porcelain in corncrib alternation, she felt that same impulse. Zeus, eight years before, had shut off her ability to despise children in their bedrooms. But most of her visitants tonight were *former* children, and she reveled in her continuity of rage against every last one of them.

Zeus and Pan had overstepped. This might be her only chance to snuff out all generosity of spirit in humankind, set Pan's harmonious community to crumbling, and undermine Zeus's faith in his creation. She anticipated the taste of triumph.

Yet she could not afford to linger. To be sure, magic time would stretch to accommodate that indulgence. But she wanted to be in and out without discovery, without a chance at reversal, and that meant speed. Secrecy, and the critical months of germination ahead, were on her side.

So she whipped Gronk along Santa's route, flew down, and wrenched each egg-seed about in every mortal who had received a divine implant, replacing each instance of potential generosity with the dark flame of festering pinchedness—all of it done so swiftly and with such stealth that not a spirit in heaven or anywhere else noticed, though of course God, who knows all, knew all—but that's another tale entirely.

Later that day at the North Pole, the giftgiving was finished. Finished too the drinking of eggnog and hot cider and mulled wine, as also the feasting on ham and turkey, peas and mashed potatoes, pies pumpkin, apple, rhubarb, cherry, and pecan. The elves had with great vitality taken to the skating pond, whipping Santa off at the end of a long chain of skaters into the snow, then doing the same thing to Wendy, to her mom, and even to grandmotherly old Anya. Great merriment abounded, their celebrations extensive and fervent, raucous with laughter and at times solemn with bowed heads, doffed caps, and hands clasped in prayer and thanksgiving for the special blessings of this Christmas Day.

But night fell at last. Time for lights to be extinguished in the elves' quarters; for the reindeer, brushed and well-fed, to lay down their heads in sleep; for Santa and his loving wives to share marital intimacies in a magnificent four-poster bed, ivy everywhere entwined; even as Snowball and Nightwind snuggled against a blissfully exhausted Wendy in *her* bed.

Santa in his red flannel nightshirt had paused long enough, prior to joining Rachel and Anya, to tuck Wendy in and bestow an especially loving kiss upon her cheek, his beard cotton-candying her face with the inviting aroma of roasting chestnuts. When he pulled back, his smile filled her field of vision.

"You're so beautiful, Daddy."

"Not half so beautiful as you."

"I think we did a good thing tonight."

"We did a very good thing," he agreed.

"Are you feeling okay with everything?"

"Oh you mean, getting close to grown-ups in such great numbers?"

"Uh huh."

"Well, yes. I have to admit it was sobering, touching all that fallenness. Little wonder they invented Satan to blame it on."

"I was thinking," she said, "maybe we should monitor the implants on a regular basis, you know, to make sure nothing's gone wrong?"

"Now, now, young lady. No need for that. We should trust to the archangel. Don't try pushing the river, a watched pot never boils, and all that. I'll tell you what. I'll check in on occasion, just a few mortals. If anything's amiss, I'll let you know."

"Okay," she said. "So why is it, Daddy? How come they're so mean to each other?"

"What it boils down to, I suppose, is that they get in the way of their own goodness. Some of them do it so often that the goodness goes into hibernation. And parts of their waywardness pretend to a loftier virtue, though they are as far from virtue as can be."

"What really puzzles me," said Wendy, "are the rich people and

191

the ones in power, mortals with the wherewithal to magnify their goodness, if they would make half an effort."

"Intolerance spares no one," said Santa. He lowered his eyes and looked pained. "The powerful are some of the most troubled souls we dropped in on tonight. In their heart of hearts, they believe the religious platitudes about love and charity. Then they beat the drums of war. Riches that could ease suffering are squandered on weapons." He paused and brightened. "But let's not dwell on their shortcomings, not tonight. What we were given to do we have done. Let us rejoice in that."

Wendy felt the pain in his smile. "I'm afraid you've changed," she said, touching his arm.

His face fisted up tight, but he refused to cry.

"It's okay," she said. "It's okay."

"Once upon a time, they were such good little boys and girls, and they...." He waved it off. "No matter," he said. "Ah, but how selfish of me. What of my darling daughter? You've been witness to the same sleepers as I. Surely you've changed too. You seem all right, but are you?"

She smiled. "I'm stronger than I look, Daddy, in my heart and in my determination to do the right thing. Who filled this bedroom with the horrors of their sins? Besides, I put all my focus on supporting you, a nurse to your doctoring."

"You give me such comfort," he said. Then he kissed her once more and wished her goodnight.

"Goodnight, Daddy."

"Sleep tight, you hear? We're going to have the best year yet. I'll be all right. I just need a good night's rest."

Wendy yawned and nodded.

Concerned though she was, she was fast asleep before Santa eased the doorknob about to soften its click.

PART 3
DISASTER AVERTED

28.
GERMINATIONS IN THE DARK

THE DAY AFTER CHRISTMAS, THE ELVES PLUNGED BACK into work, eager, as always, to make the coming year better than the last. Herbert remained the talk of the workshop. On breaks, his workbench was always swarmed with eager listeners. For he spoke nothing but blessings, a skill at which he soon became adept. All the elves, but for Gregor and his brothers, clamored to be the recipient of those blessings.

Wendy split her time between workshop and cottage, helping whatever elf she was drawn to, not planning which that would be but trusting to instinct and spontaneity. At home, Anya taught her new domestic skills or tutored her further in those she had begun to master. And though she appeared to be a little girl, she grew in maturity and responsibility as befitted her true age.

She and Anya were seated now at the kitchen table, pouring over recipes for whole grain dishes. Soon they would tackle quinoa salad, but Anya conveyed first the underlying science, why using all of the grain was far more nutritionally beneficial than just the germ.

"But Anya," protested Wendy, "I can see why mortals ought to know this. But why us? We'll live forever, won't we? And even when we eat badly, we always have more than enough energy for the most arduous of tasks."

Anya smiled. "Santa has always had a huge appetite, not just for food but for all the good things life affords. He overeats. He binges on sweets, on fatty foods, on fried crullers and on chips and cookies without number. And he drinks far too much Coke, enough to induce diabetes ten times over in a mortal. In this arena at least, he's *not* a good role model for children. But for me, as chief cook and bottle washer, it's a question of knowing more about foods, how they play together and what effect various combinations have on the body."

"But that's on mortal bodies, right?"

195

"Land sakes, child," laughed Anya, "you are the stubborn one. We eat the same food as mortals, but its good effects are magnified in us. So it's part of the art of cooking in this community to optimize healthy foods, because they increase our energy many thousandfold what a mortal needs. Fortunately for us, and especially for Santa, the effect of *bad* eating habits is not likewise multiplied. He indulges, it's true. He overindulges. But seeing him so happy at the table, I ask you, how can I say nay to my great big lovable glutton?"

That was sufficient for Wendy, who threw herself heart and soul into the history of quinoa (which she at first pronounced kwa-NO-ah, but which Anya corrected as kee-NWAH), the divine grain of the Incas. She watched it bulk up and soften in boiling water, white mini-tapioca with beguiling little tails. Into the bowl went peanuts and scallions, walnut oil and golden raisins and mandarin oranges. Its taste on the mixing spoon was just short of heaven.

Everything she did, in cottage or workshop, was enhanced by memories of Christmas Eve's extended delivery and of Santa's sacrifice in becoming intimate with the failings of grown-ups. They had succeeded. She just knew they had. Once the egg-seeds took hold, the world would be at least a tiny bit transformed. And she placed absolute trust, as Santa had advised, in the archangel.

Outwardly, she cultivated patience.

But inside, she jumped up and down like a child basking in the glow of Christmas giftgiving. For her stepfather had given her the greatest gift of all as she grew beneath his tutelage: generosity of spirit, self-sacrifice, and the best role model one could wish for. Over and above the spiritual good that would come from the implantings, he had shown her the spirit in which she ought to carry out any assigned task.

Already she had begun to rethink her annual Christmas Eve visits. Perhaps among the hundred boys and girls she chose should be one or two who, though not strictly good by Santa's definition, had the *potential* to be good, and might, by virtue of her visit, realize that potential.

She vowed that next autumn, when came time to assemble her list, she would scan the world's children with a new eye.

"All right," said Anya, "now we cover it with clear wrap and into the fridge it goes. Rachel and Santa will bubble over with oohs and aahs at the dinner table tonight, see if they don't. Tomorrow, we'll tackle a kasha casserole."

"Kasha? What's that?"

And Anya launched into a disquisition about kasha, also known as buckwheat, while Wendy happily nodded, only half listening, and thanked God all over again for resurrecting her out of the death she had endured into such a delightful state of immortality among such delightful immortals.

A few days later, Santa suffered a bout of anxiety. What if the egg-seeds were duds? From a distance, he had scrutinized several of them germinating in various mortal chests—though, alas, he had failed to notice their change in orientation. And observing these same mortals day by day, he had seen only the infuriating persistence of their prejudice toward those whose sexuality differed from their own.

So restless was he that he summoned the archangel on a solitary walk the afternoon of New Year's Day. He stood on the precise spot in the Chapel where the Father had joined him to Anya and Rachel in holy wedlock. Before he could voice his concern, Michael said with a hint of exasperation, "These things take time. Fret not, worthy servant. Neither fidget nor be unduly concerned. Only the most dramatic of miracles, instigated directly by God Almighty, result in immediate change."

"When then, o great archangel?" Try as he might to keep impatience out of his voice, there it lurked, glaringly obvious to elf and angel alike.

Michael's laughter filled the Chapel with heavenly light. "By Good Friday, the change that is to spring forth Easter morning should be evident. Until then, banish all concern. Focus on toymaking. In the fallen world, it often happens that seeds of goodness, once they are pressed into the soil, take time to germinate and come to fruition. Things may even worsen, or appear to worsen, before the delicious uptick of permanent improvement takes hold. Ease thy mind and be comforted."

Santa felt the angel's palm upon his brow and released a gentle cry at his touch.

"You have done well," assured Michael, "and such doings cannot but result in a worthy outcome. Leave off staring at the ice on the river, or at tilled and planted soil. For in due time, the one shall melt, the other yield to a thrust of sprouts surging joyous sunward."

"So I shall, good Michael."

Then the angel rose and vanished, the comfort of his touch lingering all that day and far into the next.

197

***

"What are you whining about?" The Tooth Fairy gave Gronk a vicious smack. He tumbled backward upon the sand, grains flying. "Come here!" Gronk scurried back to cower before her. "Of *course* we have a prayer," she said.

"But you didn't see the archangel."

"Zeus's minions put on a good show. Don't be spooked. It's nothing but smoke and mirrors. Tell me more about the do-gooders dropping their guard."

"Well yeah, as far as I can tell—and I've been listening in on whole heaps of conversations—they think they've won. They've resumed making toys and being one big happy family. My midnight whisperings have helped upset Santa's elves, so things are well launched on that front. My job there, I'd say, is pretty much done."

"Like hell it is." She glared with such scorn, he was forced to look away. "Easter morning, you say?"

The Tooth Fairy picked an implant victim at random, some slumbering loser named Sadie Morgan, a Cincinnati slut with a luscious mouth, a penchant for tribalism both religious and political, and a wicked heart soon to grow wickeder. Into her capacious chest the Tooth Fairy peered. There sat the egg-seed inverted, the tendrils of its roots pushing deep inside her. Thin and pink they were, pulsing with evil intent. Impossible that Santa would not eventually notice. But at the rate the egg-seeds were germinating, a few weeks might be all that was needed. By then, extracting them would be impossible.

"The implants are coming along," she said. "It won't be long before..."

Then impatience bubbled up inside her and spilled over into rage. Gronk scuttled away, though not before she landed a savage kick to his belly and flew up frenzied into the air. "They ought to work at once! That fat little bastard is sure to catch on. He'll squeal to Hermes, go straight to Zeus, or twist the eggs back about and send his elves to stand guard. I like my mayhem swift. None of this germination crap!"

She pointed an imperious finger at Gronk. "You will keep spying on the whole namby-pamby crew until the mortals wake unto wickedness. Continue the whisperings. Make them more invasive. I don't just want the little shits to feel bad. I want them to do vile things to one another. We will not be trumped, you hear me? If you notice any alarm raised in anyone up there, rush to inform me. Will I beat you for bad news? You bet I will. But delays in reporting will go far worse."

She swooped down and seized his arms in a vise grip. A grin knifed across her face. "Succeed, and Mommy will give you a special treat, one your brothers will never enjoy." The grin vanished. "Fail, and you'll fall to the bottom of the heap in my estimation, even below mewling Chuff. I'll set your sibs on you, withhold my charms for all eternity, give you nothing but scorn, and make your life a living hell. Now go!"

Hurling him into the air, the Tooth Fairy watched him spin and flounder, then catch himself and arrow away like a smear of grayish light. She despised Gronk, as she despised all of the bastards Zeus had got upon her. But they had their use. Through them might she topple Pan, or eventually Zeus himself, dealing a deathblow to his cherished creation.

Her stomach growled. She craved teeth. In her mountain cave, a bowl of molars, ever replenished, waited. Munching them, she would sit brooding in her bone chair, converting calcium to coins, and watching the details fall into place on the devious playing field of her mind.

There she sped upon the instant, preoccupied with mayhem.

29.
INTOLERANCE AMONG THE ELVES

WEEKS PASSED. GREGOR REGAINED THE UPPER HAND at the North Pole, instigating a weekly series of harangues, during which he heaped scorn and ridicule on the act of nosepicking and excoriated the practitioners of same. Especially did he scapegoat the six previously exposed cross-nosepickers, and Fritz above all. Even Herbert's star, which had risen to astounding heights when he found his voice, Gregor tarnished anew, and a subtle shunning took hold.

One night late in February, Fritz had had enough. "After lights out," he confided to the persecuted, "wait half an hour, then make your way to Santa's hut in the woods." Gustav and Knecht Rupert nodded at this, as did Franz and Johann. Herbert began, "May the Good Lord be with us in—" but Fritz stopped his mouth, lest his enthusiasm alert the forces of repression that something was afoot.

The hut lay far off in a secluded part of the forest behind the elves' quarters. It had once been used by Santa for...well, they weren't quite sure for what. But his helpers had remodeled it as a honeymoon cottage and it now provided an occasional getaway for Santa and his wives. A raging fireplace, a huge bed, and absolute stillness nestled amongst the trees—no better refuge from the workaday world existed at the North Pole. The summoned elves flumphed down on the bed to sprawl and listen. Herbert wore about his neck a new camera he had created that very day.

Fritz paced. "I'll get right to the point. I'm fed up," he said. "We're all fed up with the judgmental bent of our confreres, are we not?"

This was greeted with a general murmur of agreement.

"The question is, what are we going to do about it? We have been driven to feel shame over something that isn't shameful in the least. Nosepicking feels good." Saying that out loud was very affirming, so he repeated it, bolder still. "And mutual nosepicking, far from being deviant, is an expression of love. How dare Gregor hold himself up so high and mighty? Who gave him the right to judge us?"

"It wasn't me," said Gustav.

"Me neither," said Franz the watchmaker.

"We ought to shout him down," said Knecht Rupert.

"If I may," objected Johann, "that seems a wee bit harsh."

"You have a better idea?"

Johann looked blankly at Rupert and slowly shook his head.

"Any other thoughts?" asked Fritz.

Herbert snapped his picture, there where Fritz stood before a crackling fire. He rested the camera against his chest and raised his hand. "I suggest," he said when Fritz acknowledged him, "that we drop in on Gregor and shower him with blessings."

Fritz laughed. "You know that just might work. I must confess I don't feel very benevolent toward Gregor, but suppose Herbert leads off that way and then each of us steps forward and speaks his mind. He may just change his tune."

Knecht Rupert snorted. "Fat chance."

"Hold on, Rupert," said Gustav, hugging a pillow as he sat cross-legged on the bed. "We won't know until we try. I think that's better than shouting him down in public. He would never listen to us then. There's nothing like putting someone on the defensive to close off debate."

Johann shook his head. "There should be no debate about this," he said. "Gregor has turned us into pariahs. For what? For picking each other's noses. Fritz is right. It's pleasurable and it's good. It draws us closer. Why, you might as well debate the morality of sharing a smile or a laugh, or patting one another on the back!"

"We ought to string the bastard up," said flaxen-haired Franz with a gimlet eye, "him and his complicit brothers. That would put a stop to this."

Fritz was appalled at the suggestion, and said so with great if respectful force. That launched a spirited discussion about prejudice and tolerance and whether such a thing as *righteous* intolerance could exist, and if so, how one could possibly be sure, with any certainty, that one's own intolerance was righteous.

But in the end, Herbert's plan prevailed.

Before leaving, he convinced them to pose, arm in arm, by the foot of the bed so he could snap a few photos. Then they doused the fire, straightened the bedclothes, and made their way through the woods toward the stables.

***

Gregor sat brooding at his desk. A large green-glass lantern of the ancient design cast its glare everywhere, upon straw and stall, upon slumbering reindeer and his brothers' made-up cots. For fat Josef and Engelbert now slept in the elves' dormitory, so as to be ever vigilant over Santa's weak-willed helpers.

Resident spies gave Gregor the edge. Their absence also allowed him to pick his own nose in peace. Which he now did, half-conscious of his actions but fully attuned to the pleasures they delivered. Did he feel the hypocrite? No. For he was Gregor, brave condemner of the practice. And who better to condemn, on what better foundation built, than he who, wracked by the pangs of temptation, on occasion yielded to them. In among the pleasures, he felt a terrible guilt, a guilt whose spice made the practice all the more enticing.

Lately his mind had been preoccupied with the half-dozen helpers who had confessed to sharing snot with one another. Knocking Fritz off his high horse fit in well with his plans, but they all partook of that rebellious streak. He had shamed them to such an extent that...well, he hoped it had squelched the practice entirely, but perhaps the very act of shaming had sparked curiosity in everyone else. Perhaps the slippery slope of deviance had already claimed new victims, smarter ones whom it would be nearly impossible to ferret out. If only there were some foolproof method of detection, fingerprints left on nostrils, trace elements one could plant among clumps of mucus and geiger-counter in a night-sprung scan of slumbering elves.

Gregor shuddered. What possible attraction could so repulsive an act hold? Taking up his lantern, he strode among the reindeer, their antlers bramble-high, Lucifer's pulsing on and off in REM sleep, Donner and Blitzen dozing flank to flank. The opaque sheen his lantern cast upon the windows made him feel cozy and protected. He held the light up. There lay Comet and Cupid, their nose leather glistening black and smooth.

"Comet," he whispered. "Cupid."

They stirred, raised their great heads, and blinked in wonder.

"Don't rouse the others." He settled on a hay bale before them. "No need to get up," he said, waving them back down. "I have a favor to ask. Now watch. You see this? It looks vile, doesn't it? But it's really quite tasty, to my tongue at least. And perhaps to yours. Would you sample it, oh, just a little? That's right, that's my good boys." Their tongues were warm and rough on his fingertip, which he restocked so that each reindeer received his gift in equal measure. They seemed to like it, not shying away in the least.

"And now," he managed to gasp, "do you think I might return the favor?" Again, they did not say him nay, nor did they resist his bold probe, an index finger exploring the leathery tunnel of Cupid's right nostril; the other, Comet's left. Their mucus was grainy and gritty as he rolled it betwixt thumb and forefinger. His heart pounded. The stuff revolted him, even as it captured his fancy. Dare he sample it? Having gone so far, why not? Yet his fingers refused to rise to his lips. Don't be ridiculous, he thought. I'll try it once. If it's wretched, I'll spit it out. A bit of rum will kill the taste.

He shut his eyes, took a deep breath, and inserted his fingertips into his mouth. Far from grossing him out, the taste delighted him. "Again?" he pleaded. To which the reindeer obliged with sharp snorts that brought their offerings to the very portals of their nostrils. Gregor's bolder second attempt was wicked and delicious, his mind delirious with malfeasance.

I ought to stop, he thought. This is madness, a moral lapse unworthy of me. But he could not stop, not until he had had his fill. At length, Gregor gave over, outraged at his sinfulness and vowing to redouble his condemnation of this practice on the morrow. Moreover, he would yank one of his brothers, Josef, yes, fat Josef, from dormitory duty and reinstall him yonder in his rightful bed.

He would not risk further exposure to temptation. Why, what if he were seen at this? He suddenly had misgivings about the windows. He shuttered the lantern. When his eyes adjusted, he breathed a sigh of relief to see no one peering in, nor anyone moving across the blue moonlight of the commons.

Fritz and the others, rounding the stables from the back, could barely contain their glee at the sight that greeted them. Johann saw it first, slapping a guffaw-muffling hand over his mouth and waving his companions forward.

Quickly they hurried Herbert to the fore, gesticulating wildly at his camera until he caught on and shuttered picture after picture. It was all they could do, not to jostle him nor obscure his line of sight. They crowded his shoulders, nearly crawling on top of him to get the best view of their compromised tormentor.

Fortunately, Fritz noticed Gregor's sudden look of panic and shoved them below the windowsill just before the lantern went dark. There they stayed, hushed, hunched over, bunched together, until Fritz signaled them to creep around the side of the stables and tiptoe back to the dormitory.

Resuming their nightshirts and tucking themselves in, they took a long time getting to sleep, giggling amongst themselves but not so loud as to wake Josef and Engelbert or anyone dozing nearby.

"We'll bide our time," said Fritz, pondering whether payback was a worthy elfin impulse, but having a feeling that in this case it was. "The ideal moment is bound to present itself."

As indeed it did.

30.
DISASTER LOOMS

THE WEEK LEADING UP TO HIS special holiday, the Easter Bunny flew into a tizzy of last-minute preparation, his brain abuzz with frenzies of bliss. As for Santa's recent visit and the horrendous memories they revived, they had been utterly forgotten; for so had he been reinvented eight years prior, God knowing he would otherwise be useless, come Easter.

The hens, used to his pre-holiday hyperactivity, paid him little heed. Steady and reliable industry was their watchword. Nor was it in their nature to speed up a process calibrated to produce exactly the number of eggs he would need by Easter Eve.

The remaining processes were likewise engineered to a tee, the cutting of shreds of fake grass, the continual clatter of jelly beans down distant chutes, the orderly sweep along conveyor belts of yellow marshmallow chicks with perfect black eye-dots, chocolate poured into and painstakingly removed from bunny molds by well-oiled machine arms—everything assembled into baskets and kept as fresh as the day of their assembly in cool, dark, well-nigh limitless caverns.

But the Easter Bunny was one excitable creature. And excited he grew. A few more days would usher in his moment in the sun, or to be more precise, in moonlight as the world slept. He vaguely recalled a time when he had resented and envied Santa Claus for being associated with Christ's birth while he, the Easter Bunny, had been saddled with the Savior's suffering and death. That vague recall had surely to be a delusion.

For Easter celebrated rebirth, new beginnings fresh-wrapped, all sufferings past, forgiven, and forgotten. What though the day had been adapted from pagan fertility rites? As far as he was concerned, this day was a day equal in generosity to Christmas. Equal? Nay, Easter *surpassed* Christmas in that wise. Not that he was competing, mind. He shook his head so emphatically that his ear tips snapped like fresh sheets on a clothesline. But this day, to which mortals would wake joyous and spring-fresh, celebrated the generous earth opening its fecundity out of the frozen months of winter, seeds germinating in riot and sprout, fresh buds tremulous and green wherever the eye chanced to light. On this day, people were kinder to one another. They wore pastel, the women and girls. As for the men and boys, though their ridiculous façade of ba-rumph and macho zombie-ism slipped but a fraction, yet it slipped indeed. And behind it could be glimpsed the randy zest of gentle goats, not the grasping of satyrs but the full bloom of vigor and vitality. Tamed, to be sure, by Mother Church. Such goatishness could not frisk too boldly in the sun, oh no indeed. For where would commerce be, where war, where the gladiatorial thirst for blood, both virtual and real, if all decorum were tossed aside and an unfettered celebration of rutting life were to sweep the globe?

For an instant, the Easter Bunny's heart leapt. Then *he* leapt, high in his burrow so that his ears brushed the earthen dome. Deftly landing, he scurried about the exercise area, burning energy at once renewed. In tip-top shape. That's what he'd have to be three nights from now. Through the air he would fly, tumbling silently into homes frozen in magic time and pulling out just the right Easter basket for Joey or Jane, setting it down, straightening the red ribbon about its wicker handle, then dashing off through wall or window toward his next destination.

With joy he chittered, scurrying so fast that his feet rose up along and pounded the cylindrical walls, which grew warm and then hot from the repeated friction of his passing. In the distance, he heard and delighted in the white-noise click and clatter, the hum and buzz, the clip and rustle, the rump-roll of ovoid wonders in all their glory down innumerable chutes.

Readiness was all.

And the Easter Bunny, Christ love him, was raring to go.

Two days later, as brilliant sunlight burnished the edge of Good Friday's gathering dawn, Santa Claus summoned the entire community to their favorite forest grove. Fritz had looked up in surprise from his workbench, a moo-box in his right hand, a plush empty-bellied Guernsey in his left. There before them all stood Santa and Wendy, looking more radiant than ever.

"If I may have your attention," said Santa, not raising his voice one iota, but cutting straight through the stitching and hammering and sanding and packaging, so that all activity at once ceased. "Leave off your industry for awhile, lads. We have something to celebrate, and we shall do so this glorious morning in the Chapel. Our special Christmas Eve deliveries are nearing fruition. To mark this moment, Wendy will project scenes from humankind's altered future."

Fritz had nearly forgotten that miraculous night, so deep into the delights of toy manufacture had he immersed himself. Now, called to mind, its memory brightened him. Setting the cow and the moo-box aside, he slid off his stool and shared a moment of speculation with Beckmesser, the bushy-browed elf who tinkered beside him at the workbench.

Gregor and his brothers had taken to sitting in shifts, off to one side, observing. When Santa had asked what they were doing, Gregor replied with a shrug, "Quality control," an answer Santa had accepted without further probing. Now Fritz saw Gregor leap from his stool and draw Santa aside. Nearby, master weaver Ludwig canted his head. When Santa nodded assent, Gregor bowed perfunctorily and went his way.

Fritz made his way swiftly to the master weaver. "Ludwig," he said, "what's up with Gregor?"

Ludwig started, mulled, and squinted. "Why, old Buttinski Bushy-Brow there wanted the chance to address our gathering first, a matter of great urgency, he said, and Santa agreed to it. Some fool harangue, I imagine. Up to no good. Ranting in front of Santa and his family. First time he's done *that*, eh? Us weaver folk, we call it Gregor's warped woof. Behave, he tells us. By which he means cower before my whip, set me on a pedestal, and bow so low you breathe dust bunnies. Well, my lad, maybe our purblind master elf will finally figure out what's up and put Gregor in his place. End this infernal nonsense so Gregor and fat Josef and Engelbert can devote full time to tending the reindeer, as they're meant to, and not getting high and mighty with the rest of us."

Fritz waited until Ludwig paused for breath, then thanked him and slipped away. He spied Herbert wrapping things up at his workbench and revealed his idea even as he hatched it. "It's our golden opportunity. We couldn't have planned it better."

"Your eyes are so bright, Fritz. I like that. May they always glisten so. But I wonder if Gregor's will dim."

"Dear Herbert, always considerate of others. Usually I am too. But Gregor has brought this on. I've given it lots of thought, and if we do this in the spirit of fun and not with vengeance in our hearts, I'm convinced it's the right path."

"May God be with us then," said Herbert.

Quickly, they enlisted Gustav and Knecht Rupert to help haul equipment on sleds, snowshoeing along a shortcut as the winding train of helpers made its predictable way to the Chapel.

The first elves to arrive did not question their presence there, and soon the Chapel filled, and Santa and his family stood before the gathered multitudes.

Santa had no idea what bee might be frantically buzzing beneath Gregor's bonnet. Whatever bit of gristle had stuck in his craw, to hear him harrumph about it would doubtless provide a few light moments to set the mood for the main event. Gregor's feints at meanness tickled Santa's funny bone. Call it a peculiar flirtation with crossing less than acceptable lines of decorum. Whenever it was, it made for good theater and had never, to his knowledge, harmed a soul.

"Friends, colleagues," he began, "before Wendy and I launch our celebration, Gregor has asked to say a few words. Now, now, none of that hissing and booing, lads. It isn't elflike. I'm sure whatever the master of the stable has to say is of great import, and we will all benefit from hearing him out. Gregor, lad, you have the floor."

Gregor marched boldly out of the crowd, nodded to Santa, took his place at the lectern, and cast a cold eye upon his brethren. "I stand here today," said he, "because it's high time a certain jolly old elf understood the depths of deviance and degeneracy which have befallen our number and led directly to our shoddy work of late. Good master Santa, you have told us we have it in us to solve our own problems. Until a few days ago, I concurred in that judgment."

Wherever was this leading? Santa wondered. Tone often told the tale long before words. This felt like a different Gregor, for whom there *were* no lines that couldn't be crossed. This was no feint at meanness, but the thing itself, and alarm bells sounded in his head.

He was on the point of taking the stablemaster aside for private conference, when he noticed Gustav and Knecht Rupert shimmying up two young oaks and dropping a pale-yellow bedsheet between them, pulling the corners tight so that only their heads and their bloodless knuckles could be seen above the horizontal stretch of fabric.

"Over yonder are two of the malefactors I was about to name,

Santa, up to no good. They hope to divert us with some nonsense, but they shall not stop me from exposing their perversity to all and sundry. These two, and the other four, Fritz, Herbert, Franz, and Johann, have been caught or confessed to the vile practice of...of—"

Bold upon the bed sheet, from a suddenly switched-on projector, were thrown images of Gregor and Comet and Cupid, images in quick succession which left no doubt what they were doing. Swells of disbelief and then laughter rippled through the crowd. Gregor turned absolutely white, his jaw moving but his lips lax and incapable of forming words. His eyes grew wide and his neck took on a pronounced blush. The crowd's nervous titters turned to giggles, then to guffaws and belly laughs. It was all Santa could do to suppress his own jolly outbursts, though he was, at the same time, appalled at the breakdown in civility he was witnessing.

This smacked of payback. Gregor had pushed the elves, had beaten them over the head with some utterly harmless little habit—nosepicking it appeared, something Santa himself occasionally indulged in—and now the stablemaster had been exposed as a hypocrite.

This had to be stopped. But before Santa could take his first step forward, Gregor found his voice. "I'll see you all in hell for this," he shouted. "You have no call to humiliate a fellow elf thus. I declare this community stone-cold dead, its bonds of fealty shattered." With these words, his exasperation broke and he fled the proceedings, snow kicking up at his heels as he dashed between the trees and fell and righted himself, a diminishing figure in green, his cap's jingle bell ringing sharp and high as it jounced upon his head.

A few elves jeered after him, but mostly, and all at once, they fell silent. Knecht Rupert and Gustav let the sheet drop and climbed down from the trees, caps in hand, acting sheepish and ashamed.

Wendy gave Santa a look of anguish.

"No need to doff your caps, lads," said Santa, stepping forward. "I sense you were driven to extremes. I sense as well that Gregor had it coming."

"He did, Santa," said Fritz, "though I regret it went so far."

Santa nodded. "Your behavior, as his, I find very odd indeed. Later, you will unfold the tale to me, I will meet with Gregor on my own and smooth things over, after which I will apply myself heart and soul to fixing what I hadn't known was broken. Meanwhile, I want you and Herbert to pursue Gregor. Find him, ask his forgiveness, entreat him to a peace. Bless him, Herbert. And give him my assurance—the assurance of all here assembled—that he shall not for more than one brief hour be outcast from this community, but be welcomed warmly into its fold and brought most gently to see the error of his ways."

"We will, Santa," said Fritz, and he and Herbert headed off along the erratic snow trail blazed by Gregor's hasty departure. Other elves clustered about Engelbert and Josef to comfort them.

For a moment, all was gloom about Santa's heart. But he shook it off, determined that the celebration would proceed as planned.

As Wendy listened to Santa's fresh recounting to his helpers of their recent extraordinary Christmas Eve and his introduction of her, she vowed to make Gregor and Josef and Engelbert a special dessert, chocolate mousse perhaps or crème brûlée, delivered with the kindest words of which she was capable. Gregor had always frightened her a little. But now she had seen, as had they all, the confused little boy beneath the bully, and she felt the need to comfort him in some way.

Applause broke out, more vigorous than was strictly warranted. Good. They weren't about to bear Gregor a grudge. Wendy expected no less. "Thank you," she said, raising her hands to quiet them. "Santa, of course, made all those millions of insertions. My role was merely to hold the divine egg-seed; Santa's, to shape and place its clone just so in their hearts, knowing them with a quick intimacy, flaws and all, so that the implant precisely met their needs. Applause, please, for the good Saint Nicholas."

Again the crowd thundered their approval.

Santa laughed and blushed and waved it away.

"All right, then," said Wendy. "The egg-seeds have taken a dog's age to germinate, have they not? But our patience is about to be rewarded. Easter morning, when our visitants wake, we shall taste the first fruits of our labor. But this day, Good Friday, their growth is sufficiently advanced to allow us to glimpse the future."

Then Wendy touched that place inside her, unvisited for months, where her powers of projection dwelt.

"Jamie Stratton first. Recall, he was fated to throw himself into oncoming traffic. Let's see what he'll be doing instead on that day at that precise moment."

But nothing came up, nothing at all.

"Hmm, just a minute, I'll find him."

Nothing the year before, nor the year before that.

"This is ridiculous, I...no, Daddy, I'm okay. Let's start with Easter and scan from there, shall we?"

There lay Jamie in his bed two mornings from now, blinking sleep away, a look of sheer terror spreading its pall over his face. Wendy leaped ahead, random glimpses into his life projected large before the assembly. Snippets of sneers and harsh words flew all about, and four days into this bleak world, Jamie was ambushed by young toughs from school and bludgeoned to death. Wendy was in shock. What was this world he had awakened to? She opened the floodgates to it. There, projected before them, was an inferno of chaos and hatred, of men and women who condemned others upon the instant and meted out death as easily as a look of scorn. Strange fruit sprouted on tree limbs and lampposts. Beneath a barrage of fear, imagination was curtailed and joyously anarchic creativity clamped down upon. But paranoia ran wild and with good reason. Projections of inner uncertainty flew out to cloak strangers, leading swiftly to degrees of inhospitality which did not stop at beatings or ostracism but went straight to murder and mass graves. Life became cheap; or rather, the judgment of a stern god, stern beyond the worst human imaginings, led to its utter devaluation before an overriding myth of eternal life in heaven or in hell. But hell was unacceptable, and to earn heaven meant to be this false god's deputy and dispatch those even *suspected* of being unable to control their ungodly desires. Beasts these sinners had become, and beasts were meant for slaughter and sacrifice.

Wendy swooned. When she came to, she found herself cradled in Santa's arms. The projections had ceased. Rachel, wearing a fretful look, had her palm pressed against Wendy's forehead. "Stay back, all of you," said Santa, but Wendy took comfort in their closeness.

"I'm all right," she assured Anya, who knelt beside her and said, "There, there, child." But she had misplaced the soothing grandma face that went with those words.

And Wendy was suddenly not all right at all. Sobs bubbled out of her. It felt as if she had lost her footing on a tightrope over a vast canyon and was falling to her death.

Then Santa leaped to his feet and shouted into the heavens with a desperate cry. "Michael! If ever we needed you, we need you now, and at once!"

***

One moment, the archangel has been one with the plenum divinum, his mercurial mind shifting from bliss to bliss, as in a lucid dream where instantly fulfilled whims convey the dreamer from one perfection to another. The next, a Clausean shout rang in his ears and he found himself hurtling, before he realized he had willed it, downward toward a snowy clearing at the North Pole.

This incessant summoning was growing a bit tiresome, as far as he was concerned. But a vow could not be gainsaid.

The whole community had gathered about a stricken Wendy. Beside her stood Santa, eyes upraised, demanding his presence. At the abrupt splash of heavenly light emanating from him, the elves, Santa's family, even flickers perched in the treetops and snow hares and foxes lightfooting it through the underbrush, stared upward in wonder.

"Trouble, Santa?"

"You bet there's trouble," said the red-suited fellow. "Take a look at the implants. Look at Easter morning, and beyond."

Puzzled at Santa's distress, Michael turned to examine the world, scrutinizing with angelic precision the about-to-sprout potential that waited in millions of hearts, the mayhem shortly to be unleashed, and the orientation—dear God, the orientation—of the egg-seeds. He was stunned. "They're upended. Every one of them."

It was Santa's fault. But how could that be? Michael's instructions had been exact and Santa had been nothing if not meticulous in carrying them out.

"I placed them precisely as you said I should."

"I'm sure you did. But how...?"

At that moment, Michael noticed Gronk at the edge of the gathering and two thoughts clashed like shiny brass cymbals in his mind. The first of them comprehended all, Gronk listening unobserved, the Tooth Fairy slipping in and doing irreparable harm. But the second he found far more disturbing. When he had conceived of the egg-seed, he had created an ovoid polarity, a big end and a small end, a right and a wrong orientation, the possibility—and now the inevitability—of a horrendous foul up. Why had he done that? Why?

"The point is," said Santa, "the clock is ticking. Humankind, it would appear, is doomed. What are you going to do about it?"

There must be no further discussion in front of the imp. That much was clear. Spines of heat bit into the base of Michael's brain. Fixing this would require nothing less than a miracle. Somewhere in there, he would be punished. How could he not be? I'll throw myself on his mercy, he thought. Kowtow. Grovel. Accept demotion to plain old limp-winged angel.

Whatever course Michael chose, it had to be swift.

"Come," he said. And out of the multitude, he plucked Santa and Wendy. Below them, ever dwindling, stood rapt in marvel Santa's helpers, his wives, and the invisible imp, as Michael folded his wings about the stricken pair and sped heavenward.

31.

A PLEA TO THE
SOUL OF CREATION

ONE MOMENT, WENDY HAD BEEN overcome with the horror of what she and Santa had unwittingly unleashed, the terror that, in less than forty-eight hours, would engulf the planet. The next, she and her father found themselves tucked beneath the quintessence of softness, shooting through the stratosphere straight toward the Empyrean. She felt toasty warm and perfectly safe, breathing free without a care and giggling at the wondrous expanses through which they passed.

I ought to feel shame, thought Wendy. Catastrophe would shortly strike the mortal world, all because she and Santa had underestimated the forces arrayed against them and the need to continually verify their results. Instead, she felt giddy and blessed and forgiven in advance, not simply by God but by the whole of suffering humanity, by her stepfather, and most importantly by herself. She had to assume, from Santa's laughter and his boyish glee, that his burden of guilt had been likewise lifted.

"Will you two kindly shut up?" came Michael's gentle suggestion. "I'm trying to think."

That set them off all over again. Each angelic syllable blessed them in myriad ways, despite the urgency in Michael's voice.

"Fine, fine, laugh away," he said. "I'll just close my ears to every last chortle and guffaw, and focus more intently."

So permitted, Santa pealed forth with great rolling gales of laughter, and Wendy set loose high-pitched squeals of her own. If this was what the journey to heaven was like, she regretted her immortality. For the acceptance, the perfection, the beauty that greeted her senses at every turn kept increasing. When the limit seemed to have been reached, they quantum'd higher. How could she love Santa more than she already did? And yet she did, over and over and over.

"Isn't it wondrous?"

"Oh my word yes it is," replied Santa. "Look there, and there."

Everywhere about them rose up marvels, stars and comets and galaxies and great clusters of celestial phenomena. Then began clouds, not the earthly kind, no. For these clouds were made of condensed bliss, and on each one perched and plucked an angel with a harp and an O'd mouth from which issued forth the purest ode to joy. Each was unique, each perfect, berobed in simple finery yet unclothed and revealed without guile or guise.

They grew more numerous and ever closer together until, if it had been a human gathering, Wendy would have worried about colliding with one of them. But this was like passing through a thousand-voiced Bach fugue, always room for one more melodic thread, with nary a sense of excess. At last, they rose into a space intimate yet infinite, and there at its center sat enthroned, oh mercy, it was the Father, just as he had appeared in the Chapel to marry Santa and Mommy and Anya, but he looked ever so much more at home here. To his right stood his Son, and Wendy thought with a giggle, I've died and gone to heaven. And she was half right.

When God looked up from his conversation to make eye contact with her, absolute calm and wonder claimed her, all comprehensible emotion utterly transcended.

God's first thought when he saw Michael flying so swiftly toward him was, Again the bumbler. Whatever was he about, bringing two of the earthbound immortals to heaven? And not simply to heaven, but here, where all that ever was, or shall be, is masterminded?

Then he observed the creatures beneath the archangel's wing and admired his handiwork. Even in their perceived imperfections, they were perfect, the child he had resurrected into immortality and the master toymaker who had once been king of the satyrs.

"Michael has a good excuse," said the Son.

"Which I'm sure," said the Father, "we're about to hear. From the beginning I knew we would, and from the beginning you knew I knew. But never mind all that. I only wish he weren't about to grovel and gush so."

But grovel and gush he did. "O most Holy," said he, having left his charges free to stare and gape and marvel in each other's arms, "I have majorly messed up this time. Giddy with the success of saving one small boy, I tried to universalize, all on my own. I thought that this effort too would achieve success, that once that success was realized, you would cast your great orbs upon it with delight and be proud of me. But, oh forgive me, Lord, forgive me and please, please make it right, you see what a mess I've made, what woes are shortly to be unleashed among mortals because of my botched efforts at reform." He was on his knees, and now his halo'd head fell before the Master's feet in abject humility.

God made a great show. He pretended to be startled and upset at what he observed on earth. Yet though he railed mightily, he cushioned the effect on those observing him, especially the newcomers, lest they be stricken unto death. "You did what?" thundered he. "And without my permission? O perverse and o'erstepping angel, I ought to strip you of your wings, I ought to fling from your head that halo and banish you to the outskirts of heaven with nary a hope of glimpsing me more, yea not from afar. You dared, without even grudging assent, to challenge—nay dismantle—a fundamental perversity of this my most wondrous creation, to whit, the temptation which besets mortals, in even the smallest matter, to pretend godlike judgment over their fellows. Do you not suppose there is a balance to all this, and a rather delicate one at that?"

"Father, don't be upset," said the Son.

"How can I not be? Observe the corruption in their souls. How could I ever have created them with the potential to go so wrong? And now, capping all, the festering pustule introduced into so many of them last December is about to burst open and overwhelm the planet! I blame not you, Santa. Nor you, Wendy. But Michael? Oh, thou art in a heap of trouble. Well dost thou cower, well doth thy bones quake before the Lord thy God."

"Please make it right," said Michael. "Undo it, I beg you."

"Ah yes, with a sweep of my all-powerful hand, I am to reverse it, am I? I'm to kiss the owie and make it better. Well, I'm going to make you sweat. In fact, I'm going to turn to other matters. There's far too much to oversee in the running of this vast universe to spare one more thought to the impending ruin of the human race. I have all the time in the world. I can always begin again, if need be. But that would be a lousy way for their story to end, I suppose. This calls for delegation. Son, I delegate you, if you're so inclined."

"Of course, Father. I accept."

God admired his boy's doe-eyes. He, once Dionysus, now Christ, infinite in compassion, good cop to his father's bad—he would devise means to achieve a satisfactory resolution. Another feather in his cap, a new cause for renown, something to make his mother proud. "Find a way," he commanded. "Take these two immortals and find a way."

"So I shall."

"As for you, Michael mischievous, stay here and grovel some more. It's good for the soul, this contrition, even in archangels; and I like lording it over you."

In the distance, he watched his Son confer with Santa and Wendy. And though his attention was, as usual, everywhere, not scattered but razor-sharp upon every infinitesimal nook and cranny of creation, he also focused entirely on the abject penitent, enjoying the elaborate rollout of his own towering wrath and Michael's torment most majestic.

The journey to heaven had been exhilarating. But now, as Santa witnessed God's condemnation of the archangel, sobriety and terror held sway in his heart. If the Father refused to undo the terrible perversion his deliveries had suffered, he would remain forever the bringer of ruin to all humankind.

But when the Son accepted the task of addressing the issue, it eased his upset, though doubts arose. Wouldn't the Son be too soft for this task? He was gentle, loving, and kind, a shepherd to his sheep. Weren't the Father's bluster and thunder needed to reverse the Tooth Fairy's misdeeds? Nonviolence was all well and good, but fixing so great a problem would surely require some healing counter-violence. How could parables, the spouting of pious and unworkable beatitudes, the doffing of dusty sandals and the ceremonial washing of feet, be enough?

"Take heart," Santa told Wendy, but his words lacked conviction.

Then the Son came to them. And his look also said, Take heart. And Santa's spirits brightened at the presence of this being who had sacrificed everything for humankind.

Wendy gasped in wonder beside him.

"Santa," said he, "let us take counsel with one another. Wendy, dear heart, abide awhile as I walk aside with this worthy saint. Be comforted and know that thou art blessed."

"Um, okay," she managed.

At once Santa and the Son stood apart, facing one another in what felt like a meeting of equals. Even so, to stand before the greatest of all sacrificers exposed Santa's generosity as but a pale copy of what he observed.

"We have a crisis," came the Son's assured voice.

"We do. And I—"

"Have done with apology. Michael meant well, though he made the egg-seed reversible. Interesting, that. You and Wendy did the proper and generous thing, a grand gesture blocked by the Tooth Fairy's desire for revenge. Your failure to observe the progress of seed and sprout was entirely innocent. No blame. If I wanted to blame anyone, there would be plenty of mortals upon which to cast it."

Santa nodded. "I have seen into their hearts. So many buried children beneath the greed and envy and self-righteousness. We thought to tweak one small area of prejudice, yet it sobered me— beyond what I revealed to Wendy—to witness close-up such a dark inheritance of folly and ignorance."

The Son's gentle grasp enclosed Santa's hands. Those pure eyes gazed into his, glistening with tears and love. Santa grew aware that the Son, though to all appearances muscled and solid, was, so near the anniversary of his crucifixion, flush with liquidity.

"You bleed," said Santa, observing his palms, the spear wound at his ribs, blood streaking his feet.

"I do. The passion leaps in me. Tears flow easily. On Easter Day, they turn to tears of joy. But this year, they shall not do so, unless we can devise a plan."

A plan? Santa stood helpless. "If I revisit them," he said, "and turn the egg-seed, they will die."

"Yes."

"It's too late."

"It is."

"Why?" asked Santa. "Why must there be such wickedness in them? And so much of it in your name?"

"Invented deities always excuse cruelty. I descended. My message was clear. But the bickering and misinterpretations began before I left. To this day, they continue and intensify. Splinter factions, many of them, have gone astray. They roundly condemn the speck of sawdust in their brother's eye and miss the forest in their own. I love them all, even so." Those eyes opened Santa to the soul, all of his secrets exposed and caressed and cared for, even the Pan part that so shamed him. Before him stood complete acceptance in the form of a man. And Santa could peer deep into this man's heart, intimate now with his infinite love. "Saint Nicholas, kind heart, I love you."

"As I, dear Lord, love you." He thrilled to say it, frenzies of joy pinwheeling inside him. He felt like a naked babe caressed by an adoring mother and swaddled in woolen warmth.

They gazed into one another's eyes and wept.

Still, no plan came.

But Santa soon became aware of a sound, deafening in its clamor yet whispered and faint. He knew, though he could not tell how, that it was the sound of Christ's flesh wailing, in all its suffering, back to its origins, back to the Divine Mother. Though she was nowhere to be seen, Santa felt her presence deep inside her child's loving gaze. Come inside me, he heard, but the Savior's lips had not moved.

"Yes," said Santa, falling into those inviting eyes.

Then they were standing before her, a majestic woman seated, in robes of sheer evanescence, the transparent raiment that covered and discovered all of creation, every curve perfection, the nipples of her breasts moist with milk, that same milk that had nurtured the Christ child centuries before in Bethlehem.

As the Son interceded with his mother for the sake of mortal men and women, her eyes moved from him to Santa and back again. Though she knew all, though from her womb all creation had sprung and back into her womb would all creation, at the end of time, return, she listened with perfect patience.

"My child," she said when he had finished, "this short span of days celebrates humankind's redemption. Through your triumph over death, hope is ever reborn in the hearts of the living. But more than mere hope. An assurance that, as surely as spring revives the dormant earth, spreading wildfires of vitality across the globe, so too can the embers of compassion and fellow feeling be sparked into life in humankind, even when those embers seem cold and lifeless."

Though the naked perfection of the Divine Mother's body graced the eyes, her robes, opaque yet transparent, were the blue of carnations, her hood falling in folds along her temples. How grand, thought the Son, her having come to earth to conceive him and give him birth, to sustain him with her milk in babyhood, to nurture him as he grew. She had grounded him. By her presence and example had she taught him the wisdom of the flesh and the righteousness of rejecting every authority but the still small voice within.

"Such," she said, "is Easter. And so shall it continue. What

219

Adrasteia intends as a day of slaughter and hatred shall be transformed into a new birth of compassion."

The Son's heart leaped in him.

Beside him, Santa's spirits were similarly revived.

"You would ask how," she continued. "It is ever so with wonder. After exuberant joy comes the question. But before I demonstrate how, we lack two of our number. Wendy, of course. And another recruit who, though quite busy at the moment, is critical to our success."

The Son followed her gaze earthward, her eyebeams carving out a vast inviting highway that stretched down into a certain burrow where immortal hens incessantly lay their eggs and ever-lubricated machines hum, buzz, and clatter in celebration of her child's triumph over death.

32.
TWO IMMORTALS
GRANDLY TASKED

THE ROUTE THE EASTER BUNNY WAS preparing to travel flared vividly in his mind, right down to his precise manner of entry and exit, the precise number of bunny heartbeats allotted to each house *in toto* and in each house-quadrant traversed, and the precise gestures of paw and whisker. For he was nothing if not a perfectionist, an over-planner, a rehearser-into-the-ground of his Easter Eve scenario. This was, for him, not a simple matter of travel and delivery; it was a work of art, a living sculpture, a dance. Every prior trip—all of them stored in instantly recallable detail in his memory banks—had had its thematic shape, informed by geography, economic status, age, or by the degree of wisdom or creativity attached to each recipient. This year's trip he had decided would be alphabetical, by last name, then first and middle, breaking ties with pet names and hair color, and he had just launched into the P's on his seventh mental run-through.

In the midst of envisioning the living room of Pankin, Alexis George, he had been abruptly sucked upward, passing through the earth and sky into the stratosphere and beyond, stunned in wonderment and a little bit panicked at the steady grip of...what? Then up into the Empyrean he rose, shooting past the Father and an archangel bowed low before him. Hadn't the Father visited his burrow a few years earlier? Of course. To praise his work, as he recalled, though there had been another reason that, for the life of him, he could not recall.

No wait, hadn't Santa said something about something being taken from him? As he flew, he glanced between his legs. Can't quite grasp to what he had been referring. The memory's going, it appears, as concerns visits. Ah well, no matter.

Abruptly the Father was left behind and there before him loomed an amazing sight indeed: the Divine Mother and next to her the Son, Santa, and little Wendy. He dropped into place beside them, the force that propelled him making graceful his landing.

Some sort of shame began to rise in him. Odd, very odd. But at the Divine Mother's gesture, it fell away.

"Everyone's here," she said with a lilt. "Good."

"I'm not sure I can...with all due respect...there's so much preparation yet to be...my God, you're so amazingly...beautiful!" He was babbling and his heart went pitty-pitty-thump, astounded as he was to be here, yet anxious about his looming task.

"Be calm, bunny," she said, and at once he was.

"We have a crisis," confided Santa, to which Wendy nodded.

"Crisis? Dear me. But what's that got to do—?"

"Simply everything." The Divine Mother was smiling. She wasn't saying that he had *caused* a crisis, not at all, but that by him might it be attacked and resolved, by him might the crisis be...well, de-crisised.

"In the course of your deliveries tomorrow night," she said, "I ask that you adhere precisely to Santa's itinerary last Christmas. He and Wendy will accompany you. Inside many millions of fallen mortals, Santa placed a wondrous engine, a prejudice-remover, to restore them to reason and godliness in the matter of sexual orientation. Alas, the creature known as the Tooth Fairy perverted their magnanimous gesture into unreason and devilishness. But your special delivery will trump her efforts."

"My special...but aren't we talking about a whole heap of houses here? In addition to my regular stops?" The jitters seized him anew. Yet he also felt a burgeoning excitement. And a hope that this would, what, somehow *redeem* him, though for what he needed redemption he could not say.

She nodded. "You can do it. As Santa and Wendy discovered, magic time is sufficiently expandable to accommodate vast amounts of travel in one night; not easily, mind, but with no wasted effort, no lingering, and with the purest motives driving you."

"This special delivery. Of what does it consist?"

Her face beamed compassion. "As light floods through a pane of glass but breaks it not, so my Son, whom you see here, flooded through me, flesh of my flesh yet not born in the ways of men. With this milk, which each year at this season so freely weeps from these nipples for all humankind, I fed and nourished him. Observe this flesh and this milk, so easily transmuted in a good cause."

The Easter Bunny's eyes widened. For he gazed into her womb and witnessed, miracle of miracles, the plucking and week-long fermentation of cocoa beans, browned and dried in the sun, roasted to separate the shells from the nibs, which nibs were milled, pressed, and pulverized, the whole conched for many days, turned and turned again with the sweet additive of the Divine Mother's milk, then poured into a mold, cooled, and extracted, until there before them, in the tenth part of a breath, the Divine Mother held, balanced upon her fingertips, a three-foot-tall milk chocolate egg, suggestions of lace drapings at its top and bottom.

"For each mortal incubating an egg-seed shall I produce one of these, fashioned to his or her culture's taste in chocolate and to his or her precise spiritual needs, to halt and reverse the damage done by the Tooth Fairy. These I shall convey into the Universal Womb from which all new-created things come." So saying, she slipped the egg into a vertical opening beside her, which reminded the Easter Bunny in shape, color, and texture of an immense sun-dried tomato. "And out of your knapsack"—a thing of silk and velvet materialized on the Easter Bunny's back, its strap slung bandoleer-style across his chest—"shall it emerge when you summon it."

Which he now did, gesturing behind his shoulder where the divine pouch had grown heavy. The egg she had produced leaped parenthetically betwixt his paws, its aroma rich with generosity, chocolate, and the milk of human kindness. He savored its divine bouquet. Never had he tasted—for his nostrils were as sensitive as a mortal's tongue—such chocolate, more medicine than confection.

"You are to set the egg beside each sleeper, then proceed to the next."

Wendy tugged Santa's sleeve and whispered in his ear.

"If I may," said he, "what of the Tooth Fairy? What's to stop her from destroying them before they can work their wonder?"

The Easter Bunny's ears drooped. "There you go," he lamented. "She'll find out. She'll pulverize them. Sleepers will wake bereft, our prodigious night of deliveries all for naught."

"Fear not," said the Divine Mother. "Adrasteia and her brood will be repelled by these eggs, unable to remove or adulterate them, unable to approach them at all, so overpowering is the aura of heavenly goodness that surrounds them. But I have presumed too much."

The egg vanished from his paws and at once he grieved its loss.

"What is your reply?" she asked. "Will you do it? Will you accept my charge?"

The Easter Bunny began to sweat. Everyone was staring at him. The Son, Wendy, Santa, the Divine Mother. Indeed, the Father himself must right now be turning his way, as also that groveling archangel and everybody in heaven. It was up to him. But agreeing to this would upset his plans, his perfectly devised alphabetical scheme of delivery. To say nothing of the sheer magnitude of the task. Somehow he would have to coordinate his Easter basket delivery with the delivery of these divine eggs. The complexity staggered him. How could both tasks possibly be accomplished without flaw? He would miss someone. He was bound to disappoint. These eggs were clearly more important than the baskets, yet both were critical. He would be exhausted, particularly near the end. Exhaustion led to mistakes, to houses overlooked. And what if he delivered the wrong...but no, the eggs would pop out one at a time, their perfect match to each visitant's need a thing the Divine Mother would see to. He was the bird whose wing brushes one grain of dirt from a great mountain, coming back again and again for eons until the mountain flattens to a plain—and all of it had to be achieved in one night.

"I have made you capable," she said, a voice of reassurance amidst his internal blather and negativity.

And again he grew calm, resolute, and quite insane. He had to be insane to...to throw all planning to the wind, trusting instinct to weave his meticulous way through a long and complex maze of visits.

"I'll do it," he said. "And I'll succeed, not missing one house, one sleeper, one precious egg delivery, nor any of my scheduled basket deliveries either."

"Thank you," said the Divine Mother. Wendy clapped her hands, Santa beamed, and the Son nodded. "Bless you." And he felt blessed by all creation, having arrived at a critical choice point and chosen correctly.

"If I may be permitted," said the Easter Bunny, trilling with joy irrepressible. Without waiting for permission, he leaped and chittered and raced all about heaven, circling again and again to the delighted foursome, pounding past clouds and angels and God on his throne, laying claim to all he surveyed and knowing that his task was the most important task he would ever perform and that he would triumph in the end, saving humankind from disaster, exhausted perhaps and lying spent and panting on his burrow floor, but elated in that exhaustion, memories of an extraordinary night burned forever into his brain.

***

Gronk cowered before the Tooth Fairy, his misshapen body pelted by raindrops as big as dimes. His brothers hung back among the dunes, wary of getting too close.

Wimps, she thought.

"They were whisked to heaven?" It was beyond belief.

"Yes, by the archangel Michael. I tried to follow, but they went too fast. And when I reached heaven, I ricocheted off the Empyrean's underfloor. I looked for a way in, but couldn't find one. Don't hit me, Mommy, I did my best."

Rage boiled in her veins. She scooped up clumps of moist sand, heavy and gray as her soul, and flung them into the sea, the surface of which they pocked and pitted between random patterings of rain. Into the sky she sped, so swift that her necklace gave a sharp Venetian-blind slap against her chest.

"Foul trickster," she shouted into the heavens, "you dare snatch away my triumph? Well, I shall topple you, I swear it. Headlong into Hades shall you be hurled. Your throne I will claim for my own and my sons will sprout wings and pluck discord from misshapen harps forever. From mortals, choking on the bile of misery, shall I pluck the tasty-boned. Their young I'll devour, pelting anguished moms and dads with money in trade. Wasting and spending shall they seek to evade sorrow, making war, worshiping false gods, burning the meek in sacrifice to them—all in vain. Torment shall rain upon their heads all the days of their lives."

She shot down among her brood. Slashes of rain sliced across their faces and their frog eyes blinked. "Your mother's a fool, boys. Zeus has an ever-replenished quiver of thunderbolts. What have I got? A nasty streak and insufficient courage or cleverness in carrying out my transgressions. This requires thought. Be gone. Let me brood."

At her shout, they scattered, Chuff ever at the hindmost.

"You too, you spy of nothing!"

Gronk turned tail and loped away.

On the sand she squatted, staring out to sea, not blinking though high winds assailed her and rain scoured her face.

Zeus hadn't carried Pan and his bitch-brat to heaven on a whim. Miracles were brewing: creation loosed, if but for a moment, from its bonds. That meant chaos had been invited in. And chaos, so invited, brought opportunity.

225

But what was afoot? Where lay her advantage?

She railed against blindness, tearing her hair and shaking her fists heavenward. She had planned to topple humans; now that plan had been dashed.

Then a thought struck her and she calmed. No matter what plans the Almighty was hatching in heaven, she could still make Pan bleed. She would hit him where it hurt.

Wendy.

Though a child in appearance, Pan's stepdaughter was no longer a child inside. Void then the injunction Zeus had laid upon her to harm no brats, that day when he had thirteen times blasted her innards with the brood-seed of her imps. True, he had commanded her to leave Pan and his family in peace. But what was life if one did not test the limits? Test them? She would defy them. Better to suffer payback than slink away in mewl and flinch.

Yes, Wendy.

A kidnap. A torment. It had been a joy, not so long ago, to rip out her teeth and snack on them, to traumatize her in the graveyard by summoning her dead daddy's corpse and taking her pleasure with it. Now the child was immortal, those memories erased. But Wendy was still feeling her wings, according to Gronk, not yet fully understanding the immense powers immortality bestowed.

She would succumb to torment. And through her would Pan suffer as well. Perhaps Pan would himself turn against Zeus.

He might, she thought, if the trauma suffered by his stepchild was sufficiently terrible.

"There's one thing more," said the Son.

In a transition as smooth as silk, Santa found himself walking beside the Son in a garden, taken into his confidence. The air was redolent with rose and hollyhock and hyacinth.

One thing more.

Santa had gathered as much during the recruitment of the Easter Bunny. His own part had to involve more than simply ferrying the furry creature about.

"The inverted egg-seeds cannot remain in the hearts of those you visit. You need to remove them."

"Fair enough," said Santa. "No sooner suggested than agreed to."

The Son smiled, and Santa chilled at what lay beneath that smile.

226

"Removal so late in the cycle of growth, when so many roots have thrust so deep, can cause unbearable pain, pain unto death. Only if the one who removes the egg-seed bears the brunt of that pain will the mortal live."

Santa halted beside a fruiting pear tree. "I have touched their hearts and seen how unrelentingly vile they are in ways beyond number. From childlike purity have so many devolved into monsters. Gropers for power, hard-hearted consumers, idle spendthrifts of their precious time alive, the envious, the lustful, lackhands and lunkheads—the list has no end. Were I to assume their pain in removing the egg-seeds, I would not have *begun* to heal all the diseased parts of them. Better they die in the extraction."

"You don't mean that," replied the Son, condemning him not in the least. "My Father, infinitely wise yet inscrutable in his ways, has granted this one alteration in his creation's plan, but only through you can it be achieved."

"I seated the egg-seeds with the best intent. The Tooth Fairy about-faced them. Why shouldn't she be ordered to remove them and suffer the pain you speak of?"

"Would you have it so?"

Santa hesitated. If forced, she would seek means to do worse. No, the Tooth Fairy should come nowhere near the sleepers. Besides, he felt like a shirker. There was a reason he had been chosen to walk with the greatest of all sacrificial lambs in this garden.

"Thy will be done," he said finally.

"My will is that *thy* will be done. That is, that you willingly embrace this task, not provoked by feelings of obligation or guilt but out of love for these once innocent creatures. Observe."

Santa gazed upon the earth, taking in the seething masses and focusing on each of them, seeking the uncorrupted infant at the heart of every mortal.

"Observe the children," said the Son. "They live in them still, buried in the barren earth of despoiled community. If you make this sacrifice, it will be as the planting of a fresh bed of flowers, an invitation to these children to rise from dormancy."

Santa fell in love with the buried boys and girls, their eyelids closed, their lips parted, their tiny noses no longer breathing.

"Mortal grown-ups can choose redemption at any time, if they will only give the child free rein. Eating the Divine Mother's chocolate egg opens one small way to do that. And a goodly number will apply that lesson in other areas of their lives. You alone can give them that chance."

Santa returned his gaze to the loving god who had given up his life to save all humankind, and who continued to bear the unbearable burden of their sins. "I'll do it," he said.

"Be blessed in that choice. And know that I am with you always. Take heart. This will not be easy. Often you'll wish you had refused this task. But be assured, release awaits you on the other side."

"Release?"

"When it is finished, you will understand."

The Son's remarks had turned cryptic, but their conversation was at an end. And now Santa stood where he had before, between Wendy and the Easter Bunny, as if there had been no walk in the garden at all.

"Go thou," said the Divine Mother, "and heaven go with you."

As the Easter Bunny sank through the clouds and picked up speed, Wendy shouted after him, "We'll come for you."

She took Santa's hand then and they drifted earthward without regret or depression. Their visit had, after all, reached its natural conclusion, there was much to do, and they were determined to do it correctly.

"We can save them, Daddy," she said.

"I know we can," said Santa. "I know it, dear."

33.
RACING AGAINST THE DAWN LINE

WHEN TWO SLEIGHS LANDED in the clearing before his burrow, the Easter Bunny was surprised, though he knew Wendy had her own sleigh. "We'll make better time," said Santa. "A lighter load for the team."

"Oh, I see," he said, tumbling in beside Santa.

Santa glared. "Lighter than that. You will fly beside me, on your own steam. And never," he added significantly, "are you to drop back and converse with Wendy. In fact, you are not to converse with *me,* unless I initiate it or it's germane to the task at hand."

"Ah," said the Easter Bunny. If he thought about it, he could have read much into Santa's words. He decided not to think about it. Tonight would be long enough without erratic detours into valleys of fret and fidget.

Santa turned about, the heavy reins creaking in his hands. "All set, Wendy?"

"Yep," she said.

"Off we go, then!" A whipsmack, and their sleighs rose into the air, the Easter Bunny easily paralleling Santa's maneuvers. So swift they flew, in one breath they had landed on their first lawn. In the time it took Santa and Wendy to reach the first sleeper, the Easter Bunny dashed through the house, pulling baskets out of the air, placing them just so, and dotting the back lawn with concealed Easter eggs. He met them in the bedroom, where the pouch slung upon his back took on weight for the first time that night. He gestured toward his shoulder and a chocolate egg leapt between his paws. Before him, Saint Nicholas removed with a grunt some terrible excrescence from the sleeping mortal's chest, a thing of blood and tendrils, which crumbled to dust and blew away in his hands.

"Leave the egg and let's go."

The look on Santa's face shocked him.

229

"Are you okay, Daddy?"

"Yes, dear." But the Easter Bunny, placing the chocolate egg on the sleeper's nightstand, wasn't so sure.

Quickly they established a routine, flying and landing, dashing through the house for his annual deliveries—and into neighboring homes where no implants had been left—then to bedside, where Santa did his best to absorb the pain as he grimaced and extracted and the vile dust fell through his fingers, after which the Easter Bunny set beside each dozing extractee the Divine Mother's redemptive gift.

Never did it become monotonous, though tens of thousands of homes went by in a normal-time's heartbeat and their routine never deviated; they couldn't spare the time to pause or ponder or trade idle remarks. The Easter Bunny imagined a sorrow-filled world, vast looming mountain ranges of gloom everywhere, each delivery of a heavenly egg replacing a tiny smear of gloom with a brilliant dab of lemon. Their way was long and tortuous, but when they were done, the world would be bathed in the purest light, an entire race of beings transformed.

His one worry, though he dared not voice it, was for Santa. The tormented elf moved more and more as though he amassed worlds of pain. And he began, almost imperceptibly, to slow.

Every so often, Wendy voiced her concern. "Are you okay, Daddy?" she would repeat, doing her best not to sound alarmed.

"Yes, sweetheart," he would answer, the soul of patience and dissembling, minimizing the seriousness of what was happening to him. But though sunrise lay far off, the Easter Bunny knew they were racing against time and that it was a race they could not afford to lose.

On, on, on they went, through a world of darkness, leaving tiny spicules of light by each bedside, next to huddled homophobic homeless men and women, alongside hospital beds, and marriage beds in honeymoon suites, and deathbeds. He neither stinted nor scrimped on his regular deliveries; even so, this grand odyssey had the spirit of Easter writ large upon its face, the dark sorrows of the Savior's sacrifice, from which would emerge a rebirth of hope, of generosity, and an embrace of the astounding variety of the Father's creation.

At first, the *impression* of Santa's slowing and not the fact came to the Easter Bunny. Then the fact. But he saw the worthy saint fight back, driving himself and his reindeer even harder. If but one sleeper woke to a prejudice unleavened with the least modicum of good will, the world might be utterly lost. For as Santa had commented in heaven, one determined miscreant can change the course of history.

Another image sustained him.

He fancied he was delivering one gargantuan Easter basket to the entire world. If you could step back and view all the divine eggs they were leaving, you would see in minute detail the woven basket, the towering chocolate bunny, surrounding him a generosity of jelly beans, peeping marshmallow chicks, and brightly wrapped ovoid confections, everything cushioned in green cut shreds of plastic grass. And on the morrow, a slumberous and reinvigorated World Soul would wake and blink and scarce credit its eyes, delighting in heaven's miraculous gift and striding into a new day, the burden of one sad sin lifted from its shoulders.

Holding off the night even as they sped through it, on the trio flew, the Easter Bunny soaring along their redemptive path with mingled hope and anxiety.

Santa's first instinct was to recoil from the task, to perform it mechanically, shutting off all feeling. If he deadened himself to the extraction and the lances of pain, becoming nothing but a red-suited, black-booted automaton, he could, he thought, maintain the stamina to survive the night's work.

Very quickly he learned that that was folly. More intimate than during the implantation must he now become with these sleepers, lest he extract imperfectly. He could not afford to overlook any abortive matter nor feel inattentively the agony attached to the removal. He had to stay focused on the pain.

One hundred homes in, as he grasped the gangrenous implant in seventy-six-year-old Benjamin Norton's chest, deftly wrenching it free of its moorings and drawing it forth to pulse and die and turn to dust and then to a pestilent vapor in his palms, two significant shifts occurred in him.

The first was the realization that the suffering he had taken on was not going to diminish or dissipate in any way, that all of it would persist as the night progressed, piled on top of what had come before.

The second was the beginning of resentment, the first small wedge that signaled Pan's return. Why couldn't the Easter Bunny assume *his* share of pain? Why not Wendy, who could have monitored the implants as easily as he? Why not the mortals themselves? Why, instead of merely the spiritual emptiness attendant upon extraction, did they not suffer even the slightest discomfort? Something, anything, to take the edge off his one hundred percent suffering on their behalf!

Anger, resentment, and shame grew in Santa's breast. And these feelings too were part of the torment he took on, which wasn't simply the physical pain that went with the extraction, but the pent-up evil the sleepers had been poised to unleash upon waking, and on top of that, all of his feelings about them and Wendy and the Easter Bunny, about having to perform this task instead of staying home, comfy with his pipe and slippers, imagining the Easter joy being spread by that other great deliverer of goodies.

Take for instance, the Baptist minister Calvin Jurgens and his wife Betty, good souls as far as humankind's compromised notions of goodness went. Their bedroom in Ashland, Ohio smelled of pressed flowers and pinched-off dreams. As Wendy stood by to give moral support, and the Easter Bunny hopped about placing chocolate eggs on their nightstands, Santa bent first to Calvin. The minister's egg-seed pulsed with ill will. Its root tips wormed their way into a dream in which Calvin rehearsed remarks that would replace his prepared sermon. Santa was privy to it all, the pretense at non-interpretation of the Holy Bible, the selective dismissal, adoption, and distortive magnification of key passages, the equating of homosexual practice with lying and cheating, with murder and adultery and stealing and fornication. He heard too the words that would explode from this wretched pack of lies, that would incite the congregation, themselves turned in the night, to kill gays in God's name, giving teeth to the Levitical injunction to put to death men who slept with men, and extending it to embrace lesbians, bisexuals, and the transgendered. Santa absorbed the whole bundle of judgmentalism masked in piety, which was but a fraction of the vileness in Calvin's inverted egg-seed. Extracting the implant would not *begin* to address the waywardness of this man's heart. What's the use, Santa thought, and cursed himself for thinking it. Why should I taste the bitterness of this wretched fellow's prejudices, the nastiness beneath his transparent veil of goodness? Why should *he* not suffer a little for his misguided choices?

Then Santa caught himself.

He recognized what he was about—the demeaning, the demonizing, the intolerance—and rejected it. The whole swirl of emotions tapped directly into Pan, not lending him power but making

Santa aware that he lurked just below the surface. He began to question how far his generosity went. How shallow was Santa, how unendingly deep Pan? But that fear too was surely an illusion. He was all generosity, and by God he would prove it by continuing to take the weight of suffering upon his shoulders, house by house, sinner by sinner.

Still, the strain grew as the night progressed.

Then there was Wendy.

Sometimes, as they swooped toward a home, she would project its inhabitants' coming nastiness. And when they flew away, she would project what had replaced it, to lift Santa spirits and to keep their task from seeming an endless, undifferentiated round.

But what also developed, because Wendy had not so long ago been mortal, was an aversion to the sight of her.

Surely this would pass, he thought. If it did not, the night's effort wasn't worth the candle. He was glad that they had taken their own sleighs and that he led the way through the night sky. More and more, he avoided eye contact with her. When she asked if he was all right, there was a barely perceptible pause before he marshaled his generosity and said, "Yes, dear."

She was a good girl. Even at nine, and mortal, she had been very good indeed. But given the depths of wickedness he had plumbed this night, even in the young, he had to wonder what unworthiness lurked in *her* heart. Or in her mother's. He already knew what lurked in his own.

Had his nice list grown so much longer than his naughty list merely because he hadn't looked deep enough into mortal hearts? After tonight, could *any* boy or girl be counted nice?

Nonsense. There were countless homes he hadn't visited, neither for insertion nor extraction, because not a trace of homophobia dwelt there. Ah but what of their other failings?

He wanted to laugh. He wanted to cry.

The qualities that moored him to his role as Santa Claus felt as if they were becoming unmoored.

No! Cling to generosity and all else would return. Did it hurt to give? Then he would increase his giving. Was the pain crushing? He would pile it on. Was there far more to forgive in mortals than he had ever guessed? Why then, he would forgive and keep on forgiving.

He knew he was slowing.

He pushed harder.

Fortunately, the Easter Bunny avoided conversation and kept his distance, tending to the placing of the Divine Mother's eggs with a subtle smugness that grated only a little.

Santa had no idea if he would survive the night. But he was determined to go on, right to the last house. Like a roused bull, he lowered his great head and charged with a will into the unspeakable darkness ahead.

34.

HEADING HOME, HEAVY LADEN

FINE. HE WASN'T WELCOME at the North Pole.

Santa had snubbed him. He had provided reasons in his visit to the burrow, though memory refused to divulge them. The Easter Bunny wore a sheen of shame and accepted that his sins, whatever they were, were irreversible and unforgivable, no matter how contrite he carried himself, no matter how changed he was.

But one's emotional field is ever rich and loamy.

As he flew home in the pre-dawn hour for a well-deserved rest, the Easter Bunny flared with pride. Umpteen million chocolate eggs from the Divine Mother's womb had he held and marveled at, sniffing them and caressing them and setting them beside as many homophobic mortals. Each such egg, unique in its perfection, had thrilled him. To hold such goodness between his paws, to leave a heavenly confection where each hungering soul would find it upon waking—what a privilege it had been to be the Divine Mother's go-between.

Dare he say it? Why not? No one else was about, as he trailed a gaping wake of night air behind him. It had been a privilege as well to be in the presence of Santa's suffering. For hide it as Santa might, he hadn't been able to hide it at all. The robustious elf had grown dark and depleted, in physique and spirit, as he carried out his charge. His eyebrows bristled in all directions, his boots lost all sheen and buff, his suit had been soiled with the dust of dissolving nastiness. His chubby face grew gaunt and lined. His walk lost its bounce.

To watch it occur had been magnificent and terrifying.

He, the Easter Bunny, would not collapse in exhaustion when he reached home, despite tonight's extra duties. The divine fires within were banked too high for that. He would dash about his burrow, trumpet his triumph to the hens, kiss every square inch of his abode, leap to the ceiling, dash again everywhichwhere, and return and regale anew his puzzled-eyed, rump-egged layers.

Santa? Only the Father knew what the pain would do to him. If indeed it dissipated, it might not do so soon enough. By the time the Easter Bunny had veered off with a farewell wave, Santa was swimming in aches, his face scandalous with hurt.

Speeding along, the Easter Bunny stroked the strap across his chest, feeling at his back the featherweight pouch. This sacred womb he would enshrine in his quarters, his first sight upon waking, his last before closing his eyes. He prayed for Santa's survival and recovery, worrying what the world would be like if that recovery was slow in coming or Santa's survival thrown into doubt.

But his heart was filled with too much joy to entertain these worries long. No more would he quiver in dread, having done what he had done this night. He had gulped down panic, embraced an impossible challenge, and seen it through. He had changed his itinerary, been nimble in his planning, and not missed a single house (he stopped, did a mental scan, and assured himself that this was so). If the archangel showed up to thank him, fine. If not, fine. The doing had been all.

Ahead, a familiar forest rose into view. The Easter Bunny put on a last burst of speed, scurrying along the treetops toward home and an exuberant, if solitary, celebration.

Wendy followed her stepfather's sleigh through the gathering dawnlight, eager to entrust his care to Anya and Mommy. It was all she could do to stay back, as he had asked. Were they to travel side by side, her words might comfort him; instead she trailed after and fretted.

"What can I do?" she asked Galatea. "He's so frail, every move so full of pain."

Santa gave a half-hearted wave into the air and they were free of magic time, the halted flurries of snow now like a tunnel of white fury through which their sleighs passed. The bright lime beacon that beamed from Galatea's nose lit Wendy's way, and up ahead, Lucifer's antlers pushed against the encircling storm with a blinding white light. Santa's reindeer, taking their homecoming cue from the resumption of normal time, pounded the sky with renewed fury.

An idea occurred to Wendy.

At once, she scanned Jamie Stratton's future and projected signal moments, majestic in size and sound, upon the surrounding walls of snow off to their left. Here walked Jamie and his future mate Tom, holding hands with the complete assurance heterosexuals take for granted, while passersby took no special notice. There sat a younger Jamie attending Mel White's Truth and Reconciliation Conference, at which Jerry Falwell and Pat Robertson and Fred Phelps gave speeches of contrition and were forgiven, Phelps emerging at long last from the deep closet he had so long hunkered down inside. They were afforded too a glimpse of Jamie in old age as he knelt at Tom's grave, weeping for the rich life they had shared.

When the storm eased, Wendy let her projections vanish. Santa, with great effort, glanced back over one shoulder. His lips formed a thank you, though he had no wind to put behind his words. He turned again to face forward, starting to raise his whip hand, then thinking better of it.

In the distance, Wendy saw the lush green inside the temperate bubble that protected their community.

Almost home, and none too soon.

Zeus had declared the North Pole off-limits, the occasional lost elf-tooth unreachable since that injunction. Dead ahead, she spied Pan's brat and, a quarter mile on, the satyr turned elf, fresh from undoing the Tooth Fairy's mischief. No bedroom they visited had she been successful in entering, even those of budding homophobes with teeth under their pillows, so repulsive was the stench of sanctity that surrounded the chocolate eggs the Easter Bunny left.

From a distance she observed Pan falter in his sleigh. His suit was streaked with grime. His shoulders slumped. He was clearly weak and distracted; the girl, a healthy ways back from him, ripe for the plucking. This would be easy.

As soon as the lead sleigh pierced the bubble, the Tooth Fairy sped beneath the other, its runners coated with back-shooting arcs of ice. The hooves of the white-furred doe soundlessly pounded the sky. A soft keening whistle slipped along the sleigh's underbelly, and the Tooth Fairy, matching its speed, made ready to snatch the child. Not too soon, not too late.

They were fast approaching the bubble. When the green glow of the reindeer's nose touched and then passed through that barrier, the Tooth Fairy came up on the right and swooped in, grabbing the startled girl around the middle, tearing the reins from her hands, and plucking her off the seat so that the sleigh passed beneath them.

"What...?" began Wendy. But the Tooth Fairy clamped a hand

237

over her mouth lest she call out and Pan, far distant, hear her, turn about, and try to save her. The empty sleigh, drawn by a heedless Galatea, hurtled onward toward the North Pole.

35.

SANTA CLAUS CRUSHED

THE PROPORTIONS WERE all wrong.

As Lucifer's glowing antlers led Santa's thundering reindeer homeward, they seemed—these undying beasts that pulled him through the sky—monstrous in size, shape, and smell. The ground below was too white, sick and pulsing like flocculent pustules. The buildings glared red, blue, and green. And what caricatures of his helpers swarmed from the workshop, each looming large in his too-much-ness as the sleigh drew nearer. There sprinted Fritz, his limbs stretching like taffy, his garish hair matted and crushed beneath his cap.

All of them moved like taffy. Had they lost their bones?

Santa's vision blurred, then focused and blurred again. The reins felt like lead weights in his hands, which lay helpless in his lap. The reindeer knew the way, but surely he ought to guide them. He owed it to himself to make a grand entrance one last time. Summoning every ounce of will power, he raised his arms and tugged the reins this way and that, banking wildly, then correcting too far in the opposite direction. As he spiraled downward, exaggerated panic filled the faces below. Too wide, more like a palsied series of ellipses, his descent. The left runner hit first, oddly angled, almost tipping him out before it righted itself. Then the other runner rumped down hard, as the reindeer's hooves thundered upon the snow-packed ground.

Every jar of the sleigh punished him further. Even the glide's smoothness roused nausea in him. Though the sleigh came to a halt, it felt as if it continued, spinning and turning. Then the flesh of his helpers flowed in. They looked like little human beings, little sinning men in green—and their resemblance to mortals repulsed him, even as he knew their kind intent.

His elves' hands swept in to help him down. When they set him on his feet, he staggered in their arms and their green-clad flesh collapsed into a cushion to lie upon, he in a soiled suit that stank of sin and misery.

His wives came in then, sweet-smelling and agonized. Anya asked something and Rachel touched him, so precious and repulsive were they both. "I'm dying," he said, the words shapeless in his ears. Who was he? What part of him spoke? "We did well. I ask one thing. Forgive the Easter Bunny. The simple creature saved the world tonight. He's not what he used to be. He..."

Then Rachel, panic in her eyes, said she would, though he didn't believe her and he knew she didn't believe herself.

Anya glanced here and there into the sky. Then she knelt again beside him. She asked him a question that made no sense. She repeated it, and the concern behind her repetition brought it into focus.

"Right behind me," he managed. "I needed solitude. She can't be long."

Then he heard the jingle of Galatea's bells, distant at first, then louder, and commotion overhead as her sleigh came spiraling in. Wendy would tell them. She would relate their triumph. He could go now. He could leave his injuries behind.

He began to slip away.

But Rachel shook him. Fresh panic stood in her face. New dread took hold of him as she began to make sense, but Santa had no strength left to feel anxious.

An empty sleigh. His daughter missing. Foul play. The Tooth Fairy. These were the words that formed in his mind. His last thought before he died was, I have a child to rescue, the most precious little girl in the world. "I must save her," he managed.

Then all structure fell away. His vision went and his hearing, the pain leaving his swiftly failing body.

Rachel feared the worst. The Tooth Fairy had perpetrated the mischief Santa and Wendy had undone tonight. There could be no doubt who was behind Wendy's disappearance.

Forced to postpone her sorrow over Santa's death, she dashed through a cluster of elves, kicking up snow. Wendy's sleigh stood idle, Galatea's nose gradually dimming.

"Galatea," said Rachel. The doe's intelligent eyes widened at her panic. "Wendy's missing. I know you've had a long night. But we've got to find her. *You* must find her." She snatched Wendy's fur-lined gloves from the seat and held them to Galatea's nose. "Got that?" The reindeer gave a whinny and a nod. "Good girl." She leaped in and grabbed the reins. "Let's go," she said, smacking them sharply against Galatea's flank. Up they rose, the angle steep, their speed blistering.

Then Rachel was seized with fear of the Tooth Fairy, who had once devoured her whole. But greater than that fear was her need to protect her daughter. The last time Wendy had fallen into the Tooth Fairy's clutches, she had been hurt in mind and body. So severe had that hurt been that God had removed the memory of that attack when he granted her immortality.

The thought of her baby...

No! Suppressing the dreadful images, she spurred Galatea on with a slap of the reins and a sharp command. Back through the protective bubble into the snowstorm they raced.

Santa's shade drifted downward, all urgency gone, all pain and earthly care. So this was death. But how could he, an immortal, die? He carried with him a semblance of body, his clothing purified, fresh smelling, and intact.

Wendy was in trouble.

He had to save her.

His calm was a thing to marvel at. Here he was, casually drifting toward the underworld. Tonight, he and Wendy had helped the Easter Bunny save millions of souls. But alas he could not save her. That task, if salvation was to be her fate, must fall to another.

Through the earth he went, pockets of shale and oil not stopping him, the heat of molten rock not searing him in the least. Then a vast deep opened before him, the air dank and murky. He skirted the great palace of Nyx, piercing the three layers of night and the brass wall beyond them, until he reached the outer rim of Tartarus, where he stared into the depths of the underworld. As he drifted down along its cone, shades suffering eternal torment passed by in unhurried succession.

Fancy that, he thought. All of the human failings he had been forced to touch on Easter Eve now appeared anew. First came the minor transgressors—the mewling, the envious, the regretful—shades lost in replaying the past or agonizing over future woes. Then more serious sins paraded before him, ill will and ill acts to bring others down so that the perpetrator might fancy himself rising. Backbiting envy gave way to the literal biting of backs; knives flashed from pockets and were plunged home. Blood flowed, wounds closed, blood flowed again. Further down, rising swiftly past him, were the worst of all, leaders in realms corporate, religious, and political who out of ignorance or design betrayed the trust of their followers, leading them along paths to ruin that assured power for themselves but tarnished human nature entire.

Familiar ground to Santa, who had so recently become intimate with so many fallen hearts. It surprised him to see two kinds of shades. Some were fully dead. But others were the tormentable parts of those yet walking the earth. Indeed, every soul he had visited that night was represented among that number.

As he drifted lower, Santa felt the increased presence of Hades, the hidden god who pervaded all.

Below lay a darkling plain, the underworld's endless center of gloom, treeless, arid, the air as still as death. Here his boots touched down at last upon soft gray moss. Toward him sped a being, indistinct at first, then face to face. It galloped at blinding speed on goat hooves, a horned leering beast tautly muscled and matted with thick dark hair.

"I take," declaimed Pan. "You give. Now that you've tasted their hidden desires, it's clear, is it not, that mortals belong to me?"

"Much of their goodness lies dormant," said Santa. "Yet it still composes the bedrock." He marveled how confined he sounded beneath the wide sky.

Pan mocked him. "You like to believe the little shits are born pure, that previously fallen grown-ups warp their good little brains into mouthing piety while they pick pockets and snatch at power. Nope. They're *born* bad. As for you, before you were Santa, you were me."

"I am the soul of generosity," he protested. "The Father put you down in me, though you live submerged."

"Then why am I here with the other suppressed shades? Tell you what. Let's wrestle for your precious brats." He reached forth and seized Santa's shoulder and arm, his grip tight and taloned. "Two out of three falls. Do they belong to you, or me?"

Sudden rage seized him. He thought he had left all rage behind. But he was not about to abandon the children, or the adults either. As wicked as they were, they were not beyond redemption. He matched the goat god's stance, feeling strength fill him for the coming struggle. They began to circle one another. "You're on."

242

At his words, the shades of those Santa had visited drifted down to cluster about, their mouths narrow as straws, their eyes bereft of all but curiosity.

"Watch out now, I'm a tricky little devil," said Pan.

A goat leg shot between Santa's ankles, tripped him up, and took him down.

36.

WRESTLING IN THE
PIT OF HELL

THE ELVES STOOD DUMBSTRUCK, UNSURE WHAT to do. Then, though no one took charge, they began to find purpose. Gregor and his brothers unharnessed the reindeer and walked them to the stables for a rubdown, food, and much-needed rest. The sleigh remained where it had landed. Across the driver's seat and spilling along its sides, master weaver Ludwig draped a rich brocade, upon which they laid Santa's body.

Those who had placed him there stepped back, and everyone stared in shock at the fallen saint. Herbert cleared his throat. "Dear God," he said, "comfort us in our sorrow." But his voice broke and he hung his head and cried and was promptly smothered in hugs.

The rocking horse contingent had wandered off into the woods. Now the tubby little fellows returned, their arms piled high with snow crocus, which they distributed to as many elves as they could. Others, taking the hint, dashed into the woods and returned with more. When everyone had a flower, Knecht Rupert offered his to Anya, who solemnly approached her husband's corpse, kissed him on the cheek, and folded his hands about the snow crocus. Then began a great procession of mourners, touching their leader in disbelief, murmuring thanks in his ear, or gazing in disbelief upon his ruddy cheeks and the lips that would speak no more.

Blooms of yellow and purple piled up, filling the sleigh and covering him, top to toe, until only his face and ears, his generous white beard, and the red, mounded peak of his belly could be seen.

Though the queue that wrapped around for repeat visits was at first silent, whispers began to circulate. What's to become of us? Who will lead us? Who will make deliveries? Beneath those questions were ones as yet unspoken. How could an immortal die? Would he decay? And if he stayed dead, would they *all* begin to die? They might simply vanish one by one. Or topple from their stools as they tinkered with a doll or a toy truck.

Eventually, every last farewell had been spoken and the ritual came to its natural end. Then Anya stood before the sleigh and its precious cargo. "When Rachel and Wendy return and have had their mourning," she said, "we will hold a memorial service in the Chapel and bury Saint Nicholas near the skating pond, where his gravesite will watch over us in perpetuity. Tonight, he and Wendy saved humankind from disaster. So overbearing was the suffering he took on, that even immortality could not save him. Let us mourn. But let us rejoice that we have lived to witness so selfless an act. All of his gift giving was prelude to this, the ultimate gift of himself entire."

She would have said more, but faltered and left off. Several onlookers helped her through the crowd to the cottage porch. She stood at the doorway, beseeching them to let her know as soon as they sighted Galatea. When they assured her they would, she nodded and went inside. Then they joined the others in milling and moping about, consoling one another at a very dark time indeed.

Surrounded by shades, Santa and Pan fought grip for grip and fall for fall. Theirs was a wrestling match without rules. They raked one another's flesh, opened wounds, tore out hair by the roots, tattered garments. And the garments untattered, the hair resprouted, the wounds closed, and the flesh healed all in an instant. They grunted and swore, the rage high in Santa, the concentration maddeningly cool in Pan. Nowhere did they bump against a shade, though near them the squinty-eyed onlookers loomed. When one wrestler threw his foe, the shades parted like mist, then drifted in again when the thrown one returned to the fray.

Santa couldn't shake thoughts of Wendy. His new strength trumped resignation and gave him hope. If he triumphed—but it must be soon—he sensed he could somehow use what he learned to rescue her. In this rescue might also be found a way back from death.

Pan pretended to falter, then dove at Santa and lifted him up, pinwheeled him about with dizzying speed, and flung him far into the gray air. Santa sprawled supine, staring for an instant at the stars high above before Pan fell heavy on him and pressed hard against his shoulders. The stars, it was unmistakable, had begun to lose all luster.

The match went on, neither combatant able to pin the other. Santa failed to see how this might ever end. They would wrestle interminably, and Wendy would die. He had to win. The will to do so charged his sinews with new reserves of energy, reserves maddeningly countered by the savagery of Pan's attacks. His throat constricted by Pan's chokehold, Santa managed to gasp out, "Michael!"

"Ah," said Pan, "you'd call upon Hermes, who parades as an angel of the Lord. Well, let him come. He'll not help you, but fall himself into a trap."

Santa thought to withdraw his summons. But already it had sped heavenward as swift as thought. Pan gripped Santa's shiny black belt and whirled him about, spinning on the axis of his twirling hooves like a muscled Scotsman about to release a chained hammer and gouge a deep furrow in distant ground.

Michael was chomping at the bit. "Can't I go?" he said. "I've got to go. *Please* let me go."

Ever since Santa's shade had begun its descent to the underworld, the fever had run high in him. He had pleaded to accompany the jolly old elf there, passing through gravel and ore with him, guiding him along the outskirts of Tartarus, plunging downward with him past the circles of the dead, leaving him there to be ferried by Charon across the Acheron and the Styx. Before the Great Transformation, that had been his job. Psychopompus they had called him when he played that role, he who guides the dead to Tartarus.

But God had refused. "Let the good Saint Nicholas find his own way to hell," he had said. Now, however, Santa had called to the archangel from the depths of the underworld. Even so, given the outcome of Michael's recent meddling and his current engagement in continual kowtow, he held back, waiting for the nod of the Divine Head.

"What do you think?" asked the Father.

The Son replied, "What do you *think* I think?"

The Father humphed. "Michael, you rank incompetent—though I detect a touch of the trickster in you, more than the bumbler you pretend to be—because your usurpation of the divine prerogative got Saint Nicholas into this mess, go thou and do what thou canst to extricate him, drawing on all of thy strength and godly glory. And may my blessings go with thee."

"Amen," said the Son.

God raised his hand in benediction, but Michael had already

zoomed away, speeding through the Empyrean and earth's atmosphere, smacking meteor-swift against the crust and penetrating it as if it were an insubstantial custard, passing then through the threefold layers of night and the wall of brass, hurtling down-down-down until he arrived at Santa and Pan locked in their death struggle.

A trick of the light tormented his eyes. At first he mistook it for his reflection in the hazy air. But no, there flew in to challenge him a figure wearing only golden winged sandals and a great round hat, carrying a herald's staff with white ribbons, intelligent and guileful his gaze. "Not so fast," said the figure. "I'll stand side-by-side with my son to fight you."

No cakewalk this, then.

The speaker was Hermes, his shadow side. This god had he once been, the majestic schemer, a self he had agreed to abandon for the exalted position he now enjoyed in heaven. Busy had he been in the old days with his mercurial flittings about, stealing the cattle of Apollo by wrapping oak bark about their hooves so that they left no tracks, inventing the lyre and winning Apollo's forgiveness at the touch of plectrum to string, inventing the shepherd's pipe from reeds, learning to divine the future in a basin of submerged pebbles. He had been a devious little fellow then, though archangel had proven a most worthy alternative, and his regrets had been carefully masked, from himself especially, for ages.

"Strike him, father," shouted Pan to Hermes.

Michael started to say, "Let us forswear all violence."

But Hermes swung his staff, which made a loud thunk against the archangel's skull and sent him tumbling. Pain. How long had it been? No matter. Michael lay sprawled on the cold gray moss, robes entangled, limbs askew, the shades scattering before him like so many dead leaves. He rose up and shook himself.

"Sir," he protested, "I am an angel of the Lord."

But Hermes bulleted toward him and butted him ("Oof!") in the gut, so that his air was expelled and he struggled under the renewed assault of this wily and loose-limbed pagan god, his Hermetic staff abandoned for the nonce.

Time to set sanctity aside, thought Michael, grasping fierce Hermes by the arms and throwing him off. "You'll not best *me*," he said, flying at his opponent, who sidestepped and sent him tumbling, wings over halo.

247

***

Though for a spell, the archangel had the worst of it in battle, Santa took strength from the zeal with which he wrestled. Not that he had much time to observe the new combatants before Pan again dove in to attack him. They grew slippery from the exertion, though Pan had the advantage; Santa's suit gave his opponent purchase, while Pan's goatish sweat made him nearly ungraspable. So Santa, hurled away, took a huge breath and blasted his adversary with a gale-force wind, evaporating the moisture from his skin and making it easier to seize him, slam him down, and nearly pin him.

But as he worked toward that end and as millions of shades choked the air about them, he grew frantic with worry. He must triumph soon or it would be up with his stepdaughter. Violence was foreign to her, immortality still fresh, and he wasn't sure she understood what vast reserves she had to draw on; nor was he sure what would happen to her, did she not draw upon them. Michael, who had descended to give aid, was caught up in a struggle with his own elusive foe. Oddly enough, the archangel had taken on some of Hermes' characteristics in self-defense.

Had Michael lost his dignity? Not in the least. He had tossed it aside with a vengeance!

Still, he and Hermes appeared equally matched, as did Santa and Pan, no end to the struggle in sight. And each time Santa or Michael tried to turn things verbal instead of physical, their enemies charged them anew.

Pan loomed large, his hands groping everywhere at once. His goat breath blasted hot and fetid against Santa's face. His hooves hammered bone-crushing blows and tore great rents in Santa's suit, though the damage was quickly undone.

Absurd. He was Sisyphus, doomed to roll a boulder uphill, watch it thunder down, and roll it up again. Dear God, he prayed (though he had scant room in his thoughts for prayers), help us. Keep Wendy safe until I come.

More shades swept in, above as well as around them now, darkening the air with stares of torment and the hungry-straw pinholes of their mouths.

Pan barked defiance and leaped in, hooves first, to crush Santa's chest and hold off its healing, breaking his ribs and fighting against their reformation, failing and breaking them again.

***

"Faster, girl," coaxed Rachel, pleading with Galatea as gently as she could. "You can find her, I know you can."

The young doe galloped soundlessly through the air, guided by the green glow of her nose, her legs pistoning in a milk-white blur. Rachel marveled at Galatea's boundless energy, despite her visit to countless homes just hours before. When they were done, whether Wendy survived or not...but Rachel put that thought right out of her head.

She turned her mind to Santa...and again rejected what arose in her. There wasn't time to indulge in an iota of grief or worry. Later. All of that could wait.

Galatea gave a short whinny, almost a snort. Through great gray clouds they passed. And there ahead, swiftly growing in her sight, was an island. It seemed little more than a gash on the dull steel surface of the sea, torn by some gruff god and left, open and oozing, for eons. Trees stippled the slopes that rose from its beaches. And on one of those beaches, Rachel made out figures, tiny dots that soon took on definition.

37.

THE SECOND HARROWING OF HELL

HIE WE NOW TO HEAVEN, THERE TO FIND the Father steaming and the Son calming him as best he can. Everywhere, angels go about their business, used to the Ancient Almighty's irascibility. He grumbles. He thunders. He broods. At rare moments, he sits on his throne in relative calm, though the beginnings of a scowl are never far from his lips. Being the presumed creator of a failed creation isn't a hell of a lot of fun, not on earth nor in heaven neither.

But now God's wrath is raised to fever pitch. And every angel, archangel, and elevated soul pauses in his or her eternal routine to take notice. "Stay calm, Father. Michael's doing his best. He'll figure it out eventually."

The Father broke in. "Look at him. You call *that* an archangel? I've never seen anything so absurd. Where's dignity? Where's decorum? More important, where in the name of me is wisdom? Utterly ridiculous, the way he and Saint Nicholas are carrying on."

"Trust me, Father, it's easy to judge in heaven. But when you're in the thick of things—and while earth is bad enough, Tartarus is worse—the right hand often battles the left, forgetful of their common bond. Such battles pretty much define the human predicament."

"But these aren't humans. They're bloody immortals!"

"True." The Son paused. "But they, like we, are created in the image of humankind. And though you, and I, and the Divine Mother have somehow managed to escape imperfection, the other immortals have not."

This raised a ruckus in the Father. "Imperfection? There is no imperfection anywhere in my creation. From me came all beings, each fitting precisely into my inscrutable plan—don't you dare ask me, I'll not reveal it, not even to you—"

"Yes, Father. Forgive me, I meant no criticism."

God huffed. "You'd better not have. Oh Christ, look at the silly buffoons. A couple of bumbling dunderheads. You know what I want you to do."

"Go a-harrowing?"

"Yes, yet again. Set our beloved bozos right. Knock them upside the head if you have to. And while you're there, pick out a few score worthy shades—the dead ones, of course—clean them up, bring them here, and make them angels. I begin to grow a tiny bit deaf, and the angel choirs could use some beefing up. Have Raphael give them harp lessons, Uriel fit them with robes, and Gabriel instruct them in the proper way to worship me."

"It shall be done."

The Father looked at him askance. "Of course it shall. Don't waste words. Just do it. Why do you choke the time with superfluous chatter?"

But the Son had already pulled away, jumping the continuum past the layers of night, hovering then before the brass gates of Tartarus, which unlocked and swung free. Down he descended, spreading glory upon each tormented soul making its hopeless meander along the underworld's narrowing slopes. Beneath him, then beside him, wrestled the mighty combatants. At his coming, the shades parted.

"Hold," said he. But before he could say more, a figure sprang out of his bosom fully formed and ready to fight. A young man was he, with much of the feminine about him, but wild, powerful, and impossibly gentle. His physique refused to settle. A barefaced youth, a bearded man, a lion, a horse, a serpent, a bull—he was all of these together and each in turn.

And the Son laughed. For he recalled with perfect clarity his previous incarnation—emerging from Demeter's womb; being dismembered, roasted, and devoured by the Titans, all but his heart; how Zeus, with the juice squeezed from that heart, had impregnated the mortal Semele; how she overstepped and was incinerated by the revelation of Zeus's glory; his rescue by the same Hermes who now fought Michael; his implantation in the thigh of Zeus; and his descent into the underworld to rescue Semele and bring her to Mount Olympus where she was made immortal. Oh, how he had reveled then in the wild variety and loin-zest of nature herself; in the drunken orgies and fertility rites that went into mortals' worship of him; in partaking, sometimes not symbolically, in the flesh and blood of sacrificial beasts.

But the battle stance of Dionysus, because they were comfortably one, was naught but pretense, and the Son said, "Come into my embrace."

"With pleasure," spoke the ecstatic one.

He stepped forward and the Son gripped the mad god's manflesh and drew him in, skin to skin, absorbing and combining, their wrestling far more an act of love than one of conflict or violence. He subsumed him, embracing in pure reenactment the totality of this aspect of himself, regretting that they could not share power, but putting the pagan god gently under nonetheless.

Should he say anything to the four combatants, who had stopped to witness the battle that was no battle? Yes, a few things. But not the exhortation he had planned. "Hermes, you rescued me from the flames at my rebirth. To Olympus you brought this Pan, a monstrous babe who made us laugh so hard, I gave him the name he bears. All of you, all *two* of you, may heaven's blessings be upon you."

And he went out from them, passing swiftly to Elysium to gather the worthy souls the Father had requested of him.

As the incoming sleigh made its descent toward the island, the Tooth Fairy watched her brood kick up a counterclockwise circle of sand below it. They gaped skyward, all but moping Chuff, at the bitch-brat's mom, blinking, drooling, beckoning her with their three-fingered hands as they ran. The brat herself sat bound and gagged, her eyes big with terror and dawning hope at seeing her mother come in behind her swift-paced reindeer.

So tight was the cluster of imps on the sleigh's path that it struck one and then another, canting sharply as it landed. A frantic Rachel gripped its sides to keep from tumbling out. As soon as she skidded to a halt, the imps piled in upon her.

"Get off," she screamed, grabbing and tossing them away like so much refuse. But there was always one more coming on, and the poor dear made no headway.

"Give her room to breathe," commanded the Tooth Fairy. Fear flared in her imps' faces. They bumbled off the sleigh at once, backing away and glaring at the child's would-be rescuer.

Then the woman saw her daughter. "Let her go," she said, leaping from the sleigh and racing toward her.

"Hold her at bay, boys." Her offspring blocked the way.

"Please, Wendy has done nothing to you."

"True," the Tooth Fairy said, hands on hips, her feet planted like an inverted Y, her nipples ice-tight, her sex bold and open. "Through your enemies' loved ones shall you strike them. Or him, in my case. I had hoped to lure the goat god turned goody-goody for a tumble full of blood and fire. Until he shows, you'll do."

Something unreadable rose in the woman's face. "You've already triumphed," she said. "Santa has...perished."

That caught her short. "I don't believe you."

"It's so. Reversing your attack on humankind and absorbing the pain of extraction proved too much for him. He lies in state on the commons, mourned by his friends and family."

The Tooth Fairy turned her head sharply north, peering into the distance. "It's as she says, boys. His heart beats no more. The king of the satyrs is dead." Her smile vanished. "But dead immortals have a habit of resurrecting. No, I'm afraid this triumph, sweet as it is, will turn bitter before long. Meanwhile, I've got *you*. You went down smooth as hot chocolate the last time we tussled, your crushed skull between my teeth a prelude to gustatory delight. You're itching to reclaim your uppity girl and I'm itching to stop you." She hunched into a defensive stance, her nails ready to rend. "Boys, surround us. But keep your distance. I've got lots of pain to inflict and I don't want you getting in the way."

"Don't worry, Wendy," Rachel called out. "Mommy will save you."

"Naughty Mommy," said the Tooth Fairy. "You would steal away our guest? Well do your worst, tasty cakes. It'll be a pleasure to strike and flay and tear you limb from limb."

The bitch glared back. Not convincing. She entertained doubts, and that put her one-down. The Tooth Fairy waited. At last Rachel gave a roar and rushed her.

38.

FREE FROM THE
JAWS OF HELL

AN INSTANT after the Son melded with Dionysus and vanished from their midst, Pan leaped upon Santa, tumbling him down onto the plains of Tartarus, choking him, his grin wide and cruel above Santa's face. His head sprang forward and he bit into Santa's nose, the pain sharp, Santa's cheeks wet with blood.

His first instinct was to resist. But keeping the Savior's example before him, he yielded, clear in his mind that he was fighting only himself. With every blow, the rage and animosity had risen high in them both, matched like mirror images. And now, unlike an opposing adversary might act, he discovered that remaining in a state of peace drained his foe of hostility in equal measure.

Santa had endured far worse pain than his shade-body now suffered. Don't resist, he told himself. Surrender to him, observe him, love him as your hidden self, and forgive yourself for being not quite the saint legend proclaims.

In giving no energy to resistance, Santa saw clearly the impulse at the heart of Pan, the hoarder, the grasper, the one who uses others to exalt himself. He was able to suspend judgment of that impulse, to own it, which brought it at once into subservience to his nobler side. Far better admit than deny. His compassion grew greater for the sin-sick mortals he had touched that night. In every case, the one thing they had in common besides their bigotry was a denial of their shameful selves, which grew more powerful and perverse lurking in the shadows.

Though the goat god's musky sweat overwhelmed him, Santa gripped his hairy flanks, suffered the rutting thrust of his thighs, observed without judgment the ravenous glint in his eyes, and affirmed, "This too am I." Selfishness melded with generosity. The satyr's bone and blood mingled with his, the lips in rough kiss coming down and in, mouth to mouth, skull to skull, chest to chest, hip to hip, until they became one and the saint took easy command.

"Father," he murmured as he watched the titanic struggle between the archangel and Hermes and felt the bond between the latter and himself.

Then, remembering Wendy, he glanced out into the world and found his trussed-up stepdaughter and Rachel locked in combat with the Tooth Fairy, her imps everywhere goading and jabbing. Up he sprang with renewed strength and sped from the pit, piercing the gates of brass and three-layered night. Should he make for the North Pole? No time. And restoration into the body was hardly guaranteed. Besides, he sensed he had more power as a shade to defend his loved ones.

So to the island he beelined, through bedrock and crushed layers of geologic time, parting it in his urgency as though it were insubstantial air and he the pure impulse to rescue the imperiled, come what may.

Michael tried to flee, now that Santa had gone and his mission was accomplished. But Hermes grabbed the hem of his robes and yanked him back into battle.

"Wait," said Michael, wincing, "you and I are one."

"The hell we are," said Hermes.

His robes were always in the way as they fought, his wings highly uncomfortable to land on when Hermes threw him. As they wrestled, he tried to fix upon an idea, but his thoughts were as mercurial as the attacks coming in at him.

"A truce," he said.

"No truce."

Michael kneed Hermes in the gut, then flipped him and flew upon him, nearly brushing against the shades that crowded around. I'll surrender my mind, he thought. I'll meet his quicksilver instincts with my own.

And so it was.

The fight became a dance, energy shifting this way and that as the combatants huffed, tugged, closed, and clipped. In the midst of this thought-free effort, Michael honored every movement as his own. And the two became one, an archangel in appearance, but inside, with an equal voice now, the god Hermes. The Father had it right, he thought. I wasn't just a bumbler. I was wilier than that, for having tricked myself so long.

255

Pausing above the onlookers, he raised his hands in benediction. "To the extent possible, be blessed, o ye shades. Go thy ways. Our fight is finished. Both won. Both lost."

The shades stretched forth their bony arms in supplication, one great moan of despair sighing from millions of throats.

"Sorry. I'm not authorized to—"

Realizing that no words would suffice to ease their suffering, he rose from their midst, speeding swift as thought toward heaven. But halfway there, a new call came.

Jeepers, what now? Relief gave way to exasperation, fully felt in a most unheavenly way. But what the hell, he had accepted his trickster side and all that went with it.

Earthward he sped once more, regretting that he had put himself at the Easter Bunny's beck and call.

39.

WENDY AND RACHEL
IN TROUBLE

THE EASTER BUNNY HAD BEEN too het up to sleep.

Jazzed by memories of the Divine Mother and the night just passed, he had stroked the velvet strap of the heavenly pouch hanging on the wall. Now he slipped it over his head, so that it rested like a blessing against his back. The thrill of miracle and privilege once more filled his breast. About the burrow he zoomed, bursting with energy.

Sleep no longer possible, he decided to engage in some innocent voyeurism at the bedroom windows of several non-homophobic couples who had roused one another in the waning hours of night to try a bit of babymaking. There he gawked and gaped, obliging them by giving his nose a twitch at just the right moment for one lucky spermatozoa to be welcomed into a waiting ovum.

On his third such visit, as he observed Anna and Lorenzo Calderon in Taos, New Mexico, the Easter Bunny let two wonderings distract him. He wondered how Santa, whom he had last seen in excruciating pain, was faring. And he wondered why the archangel had not dropped in to give him the heavenly praise he deserved. Perhaps he was being chastised, though he couldn't imagine for what. Or perhaps his actions this night had so exalted him, that even the top halo-heads stood in awe of him.

Well, he would help out. Two birds, one stone. He had been given permission to summon Michael whenever he wished. And so he did, standing outside the Calderons' bedroom window, as Lorenzo took a slow hand to his wife's sex and she nibbled on his earlobe.

Beside him hovered the archangel, as invisible and inaudible to the mortal couple as he himself was. "You summoned me?"

The Easter Bunny knew how shamelessly he preened and strutted in manner and voice. Yet how could one so heroic keep from preening and strutting? "I was wondering," he said, "how Saint Nicholas is doing. At our parting, he seemed on his last legs."

"You're concerned."

"I am."

"I expect he'll soon be fine. He died and descended into the underworld. Now, now, there's no cause for alarm. On the plains of Tartarus, he wrestled with Pan. I flew in from heaven to help but was soon caught up in my own struggle with Hermes. Then the Son came down to show us the way. Santa embraced Pan as his alter ego and sped off to be resurrected at the North Pole. I did something similar with Hermes and was flying heavenward when you summoned me."

Panic gave way to relief. He nodded, he tut-tutted, he widened his eyes in wonder. "Do tell."

"Yes."

Still no praise. Maybe Michael needed a goad. "Santa and I and the little girl did pretty well tonight, I thought."

"You did indeed." Michael's eyes strayed to the couple in the bedroom. "Oh my."

"Ah, thanks. My mind had wandered." His nose twitched. "It'll be a daughter. They'll call her Maria."

"Well, if that's all," said the angel, "I..."

"What's wrong?"

Michael scanned the earth. "Santa's body is still dead. The elves have covered him with flower petals and are making speeches. And his shade is headed for the Tooth Fairy's island, where Rachel and Wendy are in trouble!"

Wendy sat terrified on the beach, her limbs bound, her whimpers muffled by a gag so tight it made the back of her head throb. As much as she wanted to look away from Mommy's battle with the Tooth Fairy, she found it impossible. They clawed at one another, yanked out hair, scored breasts that bled and healed and bled again. Whenever the fight went in Mommy's favor, the Tooth Fairy's disgusting imps surged in to poke and pinch her until their mother recovered and renewed her attack.

One of them held back, his leers unconvincing. "Come on, Chuff," cried the others, cuffing and goading him to act meaner. He was definitely the nicest one. Wendy had seen it from the first. But not nice enough to turn against his brothers and rescue them. Still she was amazed at hints of kindness in him, given his family's nastiness.

"Well, well," said the Tooth Fairy, "look who's joined us."

Mired in fear, what Wendy saw next brought forth an abrupt surge of hope. "Oh!" she said, which came out "Mm!" For the shade of Santa Claus, his body transparent and the red and black of his suit muted to pinks and grays, had burst up through a sand dune and now surveyed the scene. Wendy thrilled to see him floating in the air, his eyes kind yet powerful. But wasn't he dead? She glanced north and saw his body lying in state on the commons. Yet here he was as well.

He blew her a kiss. Then his finger flicked the tiniest bit and the gag disintegrated and her bonds fell away.

Wendy tried her mouth. Her arms and legs were stiff from long confinement. Before she could rise, the Tooth Fairy rushed in and bowled her over, her face blotting out the sky.

"Leave her alone," Mommy shouted, but not before that awful fairy opened her jaws and slammed down, finding Wendy's front teeth and biting deep into her gums to wrench them free.

Then her attacker was flung back, caught in Santa's distant gesture. Wendy's teeth sprouted anew in instantly healed gum tissue. The pain lifted. "You're immortal," said Santa, his words a gentle whisper in her ear, though he hovered at the spot he had first appeared. "You have far more power than you imagine. Imagine anew."

That simple assurance burst Wendy's internal bonds, so that she threw off her timidity and found that same strength that allowed her mother to sustain bodily injury, secure in the knowledge that swift regeneration would repair all damage. No longer did stiffness hobble her limbs. Being hurt still terrified her, but it was as if she were in a dream and knew she was dreaming and that nothing could ever really hurt her, not permanently. Meanwhile, every wound would remind her that she fought on the side of good. She leaped up and dove into the fray, the imps stunned at her boldness.

Then they too piled in, Santa's shade as well, and all was a chaos of violence and shouting, of attacking and being attacked, until Wendy could barely see the sky for all the blood and all the bodies colliding and tearing at one another.

"Trouble? What sort of—?"

The Easter Bunny followed Michael's gaze. There before him arose the hellish shoreline of his nightmares. Erased memories flooded into his mind. Santa had shown him this past shame, but once more he had forgotten. How he had flown to the Tooth Fairy's island to snitch on Santa Claus, telling her of Santa's preference for the mortal woman Rachel, the very woman whose flesh she now scored. And how the Tooth Fairy had ravished him, turning the sand red until he agreed to be her henchman, to spy on Santa and help her harm his loved ones, even Wendy's kitten Snowball.

"Dear me," he said, placing a paw, its leather chilly with fright, against one cheek as he watched the pitched battle. "You've got to help them."

"I can't. The Father's got me on a tight leash. No more interventions unless he expressly commands it." The Easter Bunny was shocked to see Michael's confidence flag. Then a peculiar look, the bold look of the trickster, stole across the archangel's face. "You, of course, are under no such constraint."

"Goodness gracious, what could *I* do?" Inside, Anna and Lorenzo Calderon had settled back into sleep.

Panic seized him. "The Tooth Fairy will be apoplectic. Fighting's simply not my style. For all my stature, at heart I'm just a sweet little bunny rabbit, more fit for kootchy-koo than clash and clobber. I could never strike anyone. Though I suppose, if push came to shove, I could shoulder the imps away from Wendy and her mom and...well I guess Santa's shade doesn't *need* defending, though even with his powers, naughty appears to be triumphing ever so slightly over nice."

"They could use reinforcements. There, you see? The jolly old elf's calling me again. You go instead. I'm forbidden."

"But how could I possibly help? I mean, other than chittering nervously, clearing my throat, and saying, 'Unhand that woman, you vile creature,' I don't see what—"

But as he spoke, he observed his right paw idly stroking the plush velvet strap at his chest, and an idea came full-blown into his head. The chocolate eggs from this pouch were anathema to the Tooth Fairy and her imps. Why not simply—?

"You're on to something, I see."

"I am. But there's no time to explain. I've got to go. All due haste, you know. Your help? It's been...helpful. Oh, most. Have a safe journey heavenward. Give my regards to the blissful folk and to the harp strummers. Wish me luck. I'm off. Oh wait, what if this no longer works?" He gestured behind him and at once a huge chocolate egg appeared between his paws. "Good. This one belongs to you, o angelic friend. Take, eat, indulge. All right, this time I'm really off."

With that, the Easter Bunny shot past Michael, hurtling in a beeline toward the island of his onetime lover and dominatrix.

Santa knew the frustration of the disembodied. Though he was distinctly visible and audible to all and felt as much proprioceptive presence as in life, down to breathing, sweating, and the occasional urge to belch or fart, blows passed harmless through him. A slow-learning imp who dove at him ended in a sprawling heap on the sand. But that went both ways; he found himself incapable of laying hands on any of the attackers.

Moreover, though his finger flicks were powerful indeed and he could mold them minutely to his designs, the Tooth Fairy and her imps adapted quickly to them, coming back almost as soon as they were flung off. And he was unable to deliver his gestures as fast as the fight demanded. They needed time to recharge. But with fourteen assailants who, no matter how far inland or how high into the sky he threw them, surged swiftly back into the fray, he could but diminish slightly the attacks on Rachel and Wendy.

They fought valiantly. Wendy especially showed a ferocity he would not have thought she possessed. But then she *was* fighting to defend her mother, as her mother defended her in return.

At one point, he said, "Michael, we need you."

But no archangel appeared.

I'm a shade, he thought. I guess he's under no obligation. Oh, but he came at my summons on the plains of Tartarus. Maybe he's still fighting there. Maybe he lost.

That thought sobered him.

Whatever the reason, Santa couldn't afford to be distracted from defending his loved ones. He hovered just above the fray, a dim shade in dismal air, gesturing to repel the worst attacks, his eyes darting between daughter and wife.

"That's it, Wendy," he shouted, "toss the bastard off."

But inside, Santa harbored doubts. Fourteen against three was horrendous odds, especially when the imps, all but a half-hearted one with a prognathous jaw and the look of a halfwit, attacked with such vicious glee, and Rachel and Wendy (and, dare he admit it, himself) were good-hearted souls fierce in defending those they loved but not quite as fierce as their adversaries. The scales had begun to tip in favor of the bad folks. He knew from recent experience that there was a limit to his immortal strength. And no archangel, no reinforcements of any kind, had come.

But as he teetered on the edge of despair, through the sky came careening what seemed at first a bit of fluff. Then that fluff grew bulk. It sprouted paws and hind legs, a furry head and tall pointy ears pressed flat against its skull from the swiftness of its flight, and two righteous red eyes ablaze with the fires of helpfulness and goodwill. One who had acted shamefully now acted nobly, carrying on his philanthropic activities earlier that evening.

The Easter Bunny paused beside Santa.

"Where's the rest of you?" he said with a wink, but stayed not for an answer. Ahead he flew, not into the melee but above it. He gestured to his pack and a large chocolate egg sprang into his grasp, expertly bobbled and balanced, though his pace never slackened.

Chuff knew there'd be hell to pay once this fight was over.

He had always been the odd imp out. But not until this moment had he called it quits on wicked deeds. His brothers and his mother kicked and cuffed him out of his inaction. At first, he kept up the façade, zooming in to brush past the girl or her mother, then darting away. But in the thick skull that encased his brain, there dawned a glimmer of decency, though he could not name the alien feeling.

It came down to role models. Though he felt a perverse loyalty to his wretched family, he sensed nobility in these creatures from the North Pole and revulsion at the riot and rot surrounding them. Santa's shade had more integrity, more kindness, in its little finger than any of Chuff's family.

So when the Easter Bunny showed up, Chuff stood slack-jawed in awe. And when the first imp-high egg thumped into the sand, big end down, he forgot to breathe. His brothers skidded to a halt, their faces wrinkled in distaste and panic. Then they scampered away from the egg. A dozen more swiftly followed, making an all but complete circle around the woman, her daughter, and the sleigh the woman had arrived in. Into the last gap in the circle, the largest egg of all made a resounding thunk, with all the finality of a portcullis rumbling down for good.

The aroma of milk chocolate filled the air. But these eggs were more than mere confection. They threatened annihilation, or rather a leap from one's familiar self to a self unknown—death, and the promise (who could say how valid?) of rebirth.

One egg in particular called to Chuff. Each imp fixed upon an egg, repelled by it even as he drooled for it. Inside the protective circle, the woman and her daughter hobbled together toward the sleigh. Santa's shade swooped in to encourage them.

"Don't let them escape," shouted the Tooth Fairy, unable to penetrate the force field the ring of eggs had created. "Bastard!" she shouted at the Easter Bunny, a look of smugness plastered across his puss, "take those things away."

She flew at him, gripped his floppy ears, and wrenched them off at the roots. They fluttered like dead flounders to the sand. But a new pair at once sprouted from the sockets. He darted from her grasp, ducking and dodging and weaving until she gave up the chase and turned her attention below.

Now or never, thought Chuff, making his decision.

"Out of my way," he yelled, strong-arming his brothers aside and surging toward his egg. In the blink of an eye, he devoured every last morsel, down to the sculpted lace decorations, taking a heady whiff of the divine air inside the shell. His vile acts and urges passed before him, acknowledged and forgiven, and he was utterly transformed.

But his quick communion had opened a breach in the circle.

"Hold your noses, boys," shouted the Tooth Fairy, "stop them!"

He was determined to stand his ground. Behind him, Santa's shade urged his loved ones along. But they were only halfway to the sleigh. When his brothers surged in, Chuff kicked, clawed, and battered them for all he was worth. His mother swooped down to strike him, but he fought back for the first time in his life and it felt grand.

He glanced over his shoulder. Mother and daughter had gained the sleigh, Rachel desperately groping for the elusive reins and yelling to the white doe to take off. My one chance, thought Chuff, abandoning his post at last. He sprinted toward the sleigh, his brothers nipping at his heels. He put on a burst of speed, but the sleigh was moving too fast. He leaped and missed. Then he glimpsed Santa's finger-flick and felt an extra push that tumbled him over the trailing lip into the back seat. The sleigh bucked and bobbled as his brothers made a grab for its runners, their fists closing on air as the sleigh swiftly rose out of reach.

The shouts that skirled up past Chuff's ears fell away in the distance. Wendy's face flared in panic at the sight of him, but she looked deep into him and chose to smile instead. Rachel took even less time to accept him. "Hold on, you two," she said, "we're not out of the woods yet."

But, miracle of miracles, no one pursued them.

Santa's heart leaped at the turn of events. Up flew Rachel and Wendy and the imp who had helped them escape. The remaining twelve, disheartened, were not as quick on the uptake as before. The handful that tried to fly after the sleigh he finger-flicked away with ease.

Some forgot his permeability and turned their attacks on him, darting through him and knocking one another senseless. Others went after the Easter Bunny. But he, a seasoned flyer indeed, shot out of sight, pursued in vain by a small band of stragglers.

The Tooth Fairy rose into a rage, barking incomprehensible orders at her remaining sons, half of whom cast barbs of ill will ineffectually about, while the rest stared hypnotically at their designated egg.

I ought to be getting back into my body, thought Santa. Then a pang of anxiety lanced through him. Would he be able to resurrect? Or would he arrive and be naught but corpse and shade immiscible, the joys of corporeal existence—the feasting, the hugs, the pipe, the bed— forever denied him? There was but one way to find out. With luck, he would commingle spirit with flesh and revive in time for sunrise.

He dove into the sand and beelined toward the North Pole, solid rock yielding to his desire to reach home as quickly as he could manage.

40.
SOUR GRAPES, SORROWS O'ERTURNED

NEVER HAD SUCH RAGE consumed the Tooth Fairy.

For the longest time, she could not bring herself to touch down. She scored her breasts until they bled, tore out clumps of hair rooted in bloody divots of scalp, and shook her fists at the heavens, shouting her defiance of Zeus, the Fates, and scores of others who fell into the hopper of her invective. They were all to blame, every last immortal arrayed against her.

"Blustering thunderer!" she railed. "You think you've won this round. But I have more tricks in store. What they are I cannot say, but they will be terrible—and I'll start with these eggs." Glaring earthward, she dive-bombed them, anticipating the impact, the delicate shells smashed into shards, and the shock rippling through the heavenly host at her affront to the Divine Mother. But as she neared them, so repellent was their stench that she glanced off just before impact.

"Boys," she screamed at her bewildered imps. The loss of her last-born was a bitter pill. She would miss kicking the little shit around. "Hear me well. You are to fetch me the skulls of bad little boys and girls, as many as you can carry. When you chase them down, squeeze the rich red nectar of fear from their bodies. Hold it in your mouths—don't dare swallow a single drop—for my delectation when you return. Now go."

They hesitated, consumed with hunger for their eggs.

Through them then like a fury she raced, seizing each of her bastards and pinwheeling him into the sky, Gronk first, the others swiftly following. And out into the world of mortals they spread, seeking mischievous tykes who roamed the streets, tearing into them, chasing them into alleyways or across moonlit parking lots, snapping their leg bones, sucking up the marrow, imbibing their cries of pain, wrenching off their heads, peeling back the flesh, and tucking the still-warm skulls under their arms, then hunting down the next little miscreant.

Cheeks bulging, arms a-topple with precarious pyramids of fresh skulls, they sped back to the island, where their mother continued to swirl above the circle of eggs in whirlwinds of fury. She babbled incoherently, out of her mind with rage at her deflected revenge.

In a mad parody of communion, the Tooth Fairy gagged down whole skulls like horse pills, one imp's armload after another. With a savage kiss, she drank terror from their mouths, its taste blistering her throat with bile. Once an imp was deskulled, she discarded him and reached for the next, eager to quench her unquenchable thirst. And when she had bolted Gronk's offerings and quaffed from his lips a long slow chaser of fear, she tossed him aside as well and positioned herself precisely above the circle of eggs.

Through her digestive tract slithered her dreadful meal, turned to currency in her colon, bone to gold, soft first, then solidifying into serrated disks. Out from her fundament flew a great clatter of coins, raining down in flurries upon the eggs. Each bore the face of a screaming child, panic on one side, pain on the other, flipping end over end. Heavy suckers they were. If an incisor might convert to a quarter, each skull became a hundred-dollar gold piece.

She expected her monetary payload to pock and pelt the eggs into oblivion. Instead, as each coin reached its target, the stamped urchin's face relaxed, the child's spirit emerged and evaporated upward into bliss, and the smooth-faced coin melted, coating with gold leaf one small part of the shell, until all thirteen eggs had been gilded thick, not one patch of chocolate showing.

Dismay lay heavy upon her sons' faces. Those who tried to rush in before the gold hardened proved too late. A few broke their teeth in their attempt to batten on the inaccessible food. They skittered away, holding their jaws and wailing. Others sat stunned, bewildered, and disoriented.

Down flew the Tooth Fairy, her anger spent. "Scan this beach," she said. "Commit it to memory. Never are you to return here again, on pain of death. Our island is vast, many its miles of shoreline. One day, I will figure out how to shatter these abominations to kingdom come. On that day, we will reclaim this place. Until then, get you gone!"

Before their mother's command, they scattered.

The Tooth Fairy gave a last look around and went to brood in her mountain cave. Her frenzied dance of defiance, she knew, had sprung from utter impotence. Thwarted from unleashing chaos on the world of mortals, she had let it out here.

Her time was not yet, but it would come.

She would send Gronk out to spy again in a few hours, not this second. There were times to act and times to simmer in the juices of hatred. And she knew one from the other.

After the elves had helped Anya to her cottage, they stood in the commons looking dazed and confused. They had said their farewells to Santa, whose body remained in the sleigh, covered with snow crocuses. Gregor and his brothers had long ago led the reindeer to their stalls, rubbed them down, fed them, and drawn thick drapes over the windows to prevent the coming brilliance of sunlight on snow from disturbing their rest. They were concerned about Wendy and Rachel, of course. But they were too numbed by Santa's death to share that concern with one another.

It was odd. Though they avoided looking at their master's corpse, each elf felt connected to it, each knew precisely where it was behind his back. How could they go on? No groomed successor waited to assume the mantle of leadership at the North Pole. Immortals weren't supposed to die. And if no one delivered toys, what was the point in making them?

Gregor stood, arms folded, observing his aimless brethren. He had been tricked out of his sanctimony, humiliated to the depths, and briefly ostracized. Then they had taken him back, showering him with all the kindness and generosity in their natures. Well and good. He had deserved what he got. Indeed, he had deserved far more. But that didn't mean he had to put up with their endless moping and pining.

"I have something to say," he said. Heads turned. His gimlet eye narrowed. "Gather 'round, I don't intend to shout. But I'm going to speak, loud and long, about the greatest saint that ever lived. And what he meant, what he means, to me. He was a grand chubby old fellow, generous through and through, who liked you just as you were. Now I'm not the easiest joe to get along with. Everyone here knows that. But he got along with me. He got along with all of us. He was our father, our brother, our friend—one on one and right on your level, looking you smack-dab in the eye so that you felt, well, 'put together' and squared off from top to toe. Damn fine soul, that fellow yonder. We'll not see his like again."

Gregor shared dozens of moments in his many centuries with the good Saint Nicholas. And when he had finished, Knecht Rupert stood up and spoke his piece, followed by Fritz, and Sigmund, and Karl, each elf stepping into the speaking place as if he'd been told when his turn was, brightening the blue-gray commons with anecdote, remembrance, and thanks, filling every eye with tears, constricting every throat, and warming every heart.

Finally, Herbert stood upon the well-worn patch of snow. Doffing his cap, he held it before him in both hands, his flaxen hair sweeping across his forehead, mustard yellow in the murky light of pre-dawn. "Dear brothers," he began, "fortunate are we for having known Santa Claus, fortunate in having worked for him. And fortunate are we in his death. That sounds strange, I know, and not one of us stands here but would give up his life to have him back.

"I look out over a familiar sea of faces. And beyond that sea, beneath a soft quilt of crocus petals, sleeps peacefully the blessed saint who has shaped and guided us from the beginning, from that time when the Father brought us into being out of...well, I suppose it was out of nothing, though we have often wondered, have we not, in late night discussions bunk to bunk, whether we had past lives, glimpsed on occasion in dream, lives different from those we now lead.

"Much praise could I heap upon this good elf.

"But I want to focus on the events which have brought us to this moment. For when I say we are blessed in Santa's death, I mean that he gave his life for the most noble of causes, first to spare the life of a child, and then to remove one sorry blight from all human souls, taking on the pains they would have suffered in that removal.

"Santa died that others might live.

"Yet even at the end, with the crushing weight of so much misery upon him, his last words were not of himself, but focused still on being generous toward others. 'I must save her,' he said. So those near him report. I must save Wendy. Has there ever been in the history of the world so selfless a soul as this our Santa Claus? You will mention the Son, and indeed that is the only comparison worthy of our master, whose actions this night must surely elevate him higher in heaven, into a sainthood above all other saints. We have witnessed his sacrifice. Even the pain of having lost him, as terrible as it feels, celebrates our connection to him. It touches us to the heart. For great joy and sorrow are of a piece. They bless us and make our lives holy and good. This our role model, our beacon of goodness, has gone from us. But our connection to him will never—"

Those listening saw something odd cross Herbert's features. His mouth opened and closed. His eyes, which had roved amongst them as he spoke, were now stuck at a point beyond them. Over their heads. In the general direction of—

Gasps escaped those who had already turned. Then everyone looked back. And lo, they beheld Saint Nicholas, suit spotless, sitting up, his thighs and hips buried in flower petals, but the rest of him rising red, white, and rosy-cheeked from them, they having fallen to either side of the sleigh, random blobs of color twirling gently to the snow or winking purple and yellow from his beard.

Then the first light of that Easter dawn struck his face, which split asunder with a laugh as deep and jolly as any that had ever issued from him. "Don't stop, Herbert," he said. "Go on, go on. I rather *like* what I'm hearing."

Joy flared then in every elfin heart from the dormant embers of their sorrow. Up into a roar of thanksgiving rose their shouts. They rushed the sleigh, lifted Santa to their shoulders, and tossed about the laughing saint who had returned to life behind their backs. Over and over and 'round and 'round did they pass him. Somewhere in the midst of their raucous commotion, Anya emerged from the cottage. A breakaway crew swept her up into the maelstrom, clapping her hands and kissing her hubby and laughing and crying beyond measure as she found him and lost him and found him once more in the continual swirl above his helpers' heads.

As soon as they were out of danger, her mom handed Wendy the reins. Then she got to ride beside Chuff, as he had shyly introduced himself, while Mommy sat in back.

At first she had a hard time looking at the imp, he was so god-awful ugly. But the more he spoke—surprisingly modest was he in his speech—the more she warmed to him.

"I'm sure your mother," she said, "has a little bit of good in her somewhere, like maybe way deep down inside."

Chuff shook his head sadly. "None. She hurt Chuff. The others hurt Chuff. She egged them on. She drove us to do bad things. Real bad things."

"Oh." Wendy, at a loss for a response, slapped the reins lightly against Galatea's flank. "I hope my daddy's okay."

"The dead guy?"

"He was pretty spry for a shade, I thought. Maybe there's hope."

The bubble about the North Pole rose before them and they slipped through it like the point of a needle through muslin.

"Ooh," said Chuff. "That felt good."

"It's our sanctuary," said Wendy. "The Father's hand rests upon it. I don't know how you'll be received. But I'll bet it's a vast improvement over what you're used to."

Rachel piped up from the back seat. "Chuff will be given a royal welcome. Everyone's likely to be a little subdued, though, at first."

"Oh yeah. My dad. But I'll bet his shade pops up. Maybe it'll even somehow get together with his—"

"Sweetheart, let's not get our..."

But the buildings and the commons and the skating pond, shiny as mica, came suddenly into view. And a swirl of green shapes resolved itself into ant-sized elves, handing around a cherry-red figure, very much alive, over their heads, and the gaily clad Anya as well. "It's Daddy! He's okay!"

Oh my, did Wendy's spirits brighten then.

Rachel gripped Wendy's shoulder. "Look at him down there," she said through tears of joy.

"Isn't this neat?" asked Wendy, aware how silly she sounded but not caring a whit.

"Uh huh," agreed Chuff, grasping the curled scroll of the sleigh before him.

Everyone was now grasshopper-sized below. They had spotted the sleigh and were waving wildly and tossing their belled caps into the air, though Wendy was still too high up to hear the jingle of those bells, and their rowdy shouts thinned to faint huzzahs.

But Galatea spiraled in and Wendy gave the reins to Chuff so she could reach back and hug her mom. "Just hold them, is all," she instructed him. "You can do it."

He was uncertain at first. Then he gripped them proudly, and the ugliest smile, with a center of pure goodness, beamed from him. He giggled like a little boy about to pee his pants with excitement, and his eyes grew wide.

Down they spiraled. As they runnered to a stop beside Santa's sleigh, the elves began to stream toward them. Then they noticed Chuff and came to a halt.

"Everybody," said Wendy proudly, "this is Chuff."

"Lads," said Santa, sensing his helpers' uncertainty, "I'd like you to meet a very brave imp indeed, the last born and least mean of the Tooth Fairy's brood, who defied his mother, ate of the divine egg—the first on earth to do so—and surrendered to his better angels. Let us welcome this goodhearted fellow to the North Pole."

And Santa stepped forward (how it thrilled Wendy to see him alive!), lifted Chuff from the sleigh, and embraced him like a returning son.

The commons exploded in cheers.

Then he gathered Wendy to him and she buried her head in his belly, his fresh-baked-bread generosity filling her with contentment. Rachel left the sleigh and joined their embrace, and radiant Anya came forward too, tears smudging her glasses.

"My dear friends," said Santa, "what a glorious Easter morn has burst upon us. All humankind has waked to goodness. And one utterly lost has been found. Accept Chuff as your own. Fashion him a suit to cover his nakedness. Give him the best bed in your quarters, and the best bench in the workshop. Tonight we shall feast in his honor. From this moment, he is one of us. Gregor, be so good as to lead Galatea to her well-deserved rest. I'll catch up my family on my adventures, and they shall do the same. Then will we witness the changing of the world of mortal men, the highlights of which Wendy will share with you at tonight's feast. For I have no doubt, after our yeoman efforts, that change it will."

Then Wendy walked between her mother and her stepdad, Anya on Santa's far side, toward the cottage, in the radiance of a new day's dawn.

271

41.
REBIRTH, CONFESSION, REDEMPTION

DIVINE MUSE, MORE DIVINE than the Christian God could ever hope to be, grant me now the artistry to depict in vivid tones and textures the great day of awakening on this bounteous earth. In every nation, in every nook, sin-sick sleepers, saved by the hand of Santa from simmering hatred, poked their sleepy heads out of a haze of dreams into wakefulness. Words cannot adequately paint that critical moment, multiplied umpteen millionfold across the globe, when those mortals awoke, and ate of the divine egg, and were in some small but magnificent way redeemed. But with your help, good muse, I shall try, I shall try.

Picture then the slumberers. Divide them into two camps. Those who had slumbered unvisited, whose hearts had not been touched by Saint Nick because they were free of homophobia; they slept the sleep of the righteous, though they were by no means sin-free in other regards. And those from whose hearts the up-ended egg had been extracted, whose nostrils were filled with the redemptive aroma of chocolate made from the Divine Mother's milk, waiting at arm's reach. It is to them that our story must turn.

Initially, they woke to emptiness and sorrow. For their hearts had been touched by the immortal saint, whose coming death they felt in their bones. Thoughts of suicide occurred to them then, for a world lacking Santa Claus is hardly worth the candle. But the chocolate egg's allure and the strong sense that death was losing its hold over him quickly dispersed such thoughts. So attuned was each egg to its mortal, that its aroma, perfectly engaged in magnificent molecular intercourse with the mortal's olfactory nerves, made it seem as though the eating and the comforting had already begun.

But oh, the first taste. When lips kissed chocolate, when teeth broke with a twin snick the shiny brown surface, when the heavenly air trapped inside escaped to delight the nose, and the taste buds rioted in exultation—then did they realize how famished they had been for so many years. Before them, in their hands and in their mouths, lay a confectionery opportunity, a means to unburden themselves of a terrible vice which many had thought a virtue. Carla Shengold of Boise, Idaho, a clinical psychologist, understood as she bit into her egg, how hard it was to overcome prejudice, to turn one's back on it and never entertain it again. As she chewed, she knew herself blessed by miraculous chance, and wished for a houseful of such eggs to obliterate each of her failings.

At the first swallow, renewed love for humankind filled these awakened ones. In particular, generosity of spirit toward those of a non-heterosexual bent bloomed in them, an acceptance and an embrace. Marveling at the abundant variety of God's creation, and the diverse nature of adult love, they saw through faux-religious demagogues— and these same demagogues acknowledged their longstanding delusions and wept with relief to let them go. They observed as well, with utter clarity, their own sexuality, recognizing that none of them, when it came right down to it, was one hundred percent heterosexual. Each felt some measure of attraction toward his or her own gender, and many were surprised and delighted—though, but an hour before, they would have been mortified—at the intensity of that attraction.

But I have not yet revealed the miraculous synchronicity that surrounded that first bite. For every one of these eggs was tasted worldwide at the precise instant that Santa Claus opened his eyes to the first light of dawn and inhaled his first post-resurrection breath. For generosity of spirit is all one, in mortal and immortal alike. And the childlike acceptance and embrace of human beings different from oneself keeps Santa Claus alive in our hearts.

Thus did they eat, savoring the aroma and the taste, filling their bellies, and satisfying with this divine food their hunger after righteousness. And when they had taken the last bite, something even more astounding took place.

Now, the Father had accepted the archangel's overreaching— which from the beginning had of course been part of his master plan— and saw that it was good. But the exposure and healing of so much ill will in mortals skyrocketed him to heights of rancor, impatience, and guilt over his sorry creation. So unlimitedly divine the potential, so damnably devilish the reality.

He therefore chose this moment, at the final taste of heavenly chocolate, to clone himself as umpteen million burning bushes and give them the tongue-lashing of their lives.

Now some say the Father elected to manifest as a voice from the flames because an unmediated glimpse of the Almighty drives mortals insane. Balderdash. In fact, it was because God at the height of his wrath cannot keep Zeus from showing, the chiton, the hairy chest, that swarthy Mediterranean cast to his skin.

Better then to be a voice.

Which voice, into ears made receptive by reborn generosity, poured these words: "O ye sinners, made less sinful by one thin hair this Easter morning, damnable have ye been and damnable remain. You would pretend to know my thoughts, conforming your phantasm of me to your absurd prejudices.

"Not simply in this, your now-abandoned ignorance about sexual orientation, but in ways even I find it hard to keep up with, you cling to foolish religions, fighting and dying and hating and preening and judging and praying, holding up this or that book as sacred scripture, but freely interpreting it into a tangled mishmash, even as you deny doing so. Now hear me. No book is more sacred than any other. No idea is worth the taking of a mortal life; nor the shedding of one drop of human blood; nor the easy sneer of judgment, behind which sneer you have the temerity to presume God stands foursquare.

"Take the Bible, much touted and much abused. Verses torn from context were once used to justify slavery. When that folly fell into disfavor, the Bible was tortured into justifying the prohibition of interracial marriage. And until this moment, the same prejudiced bunch, conveniently forgetting this history of ever-shifting interpretation, has condemned loving same-gender relationships. And all in my name. Better burn this Bible than blaspheme against the Godhead thus. Thou shalt have no other gods before me. No idols. None. A book held up as my unchanging word is an idol, and if thou wouldst be wise, thou shalt have none of it. Regard it as it is: a compendium of stories, some wondrous, some horrendous in their import. Its authors? Storytellers. Only to such mortals is it given to *pretend* to know my mind. And the best of these know they're only pretending, and that playful pretending is the highest form of truth there is.

"But to take one's pretense as gospel? To believe it utterly, condemning any other variant of belief as ungodly? By heaven, that is spiritual pride at its worst, and I ought to slaughter the whole pack of you this instant!

"You feel blessed, even as I berate you. You marvel at the burning bush, which is real, yet consumes not the combustible stuff of your dwelling place. And you feel dismay at my anger, even though not one of you will remember this visit. But hear me, while I have your ear, and hear me well.

"For this your sin of homophobia, of perversely judging adults who love one another as my Son long ago instructed this infuriating race of creatures to do, you were all headed straight for the hell you were so quick to condemn others to but thought you had escaped. Well, I have some bad news. Many of you are *still* headed there if you don't take steps to reform the *rest* of your sin-sick lives—which, alas, you will not do despite a direct plea from Almighty God himself.

"Thank Santa Claus and his friends for removing at least *one* sorry blot from your soul. But habit, the Great Deadener, shall sap your resolve for more universal change, and back into the Great Bog o' Shit shall you, by the weakness of your dronish will, slip."

So towering was the Father's fury, which towered still higher at the shame of beholding his botched creation close up, that he grew apoplectic. Fearing he would destroy them all in a fit of pique and regret having done so ever after, he swept away the millions of burning bushes and regained heaven. There upon his throne he brooded, his Son silent at his right hand, while he lost himself in thought.

And as he had foretold—for the Father knows all—the mortals at once forgot his visit and gloried in the aftertaste of the chocolate, as well as the change in them, which felt like the putting on of a new soul, or more precisely, the washing clean of the old. In abeyance, for the nonce, were their other failings. Instead they gloried in this new-struck gem at the heart of their being and rose to greet the day.

Santa witnessed the great transformation sitting before the fireplace with his family in the comfort of their cottage. Wendy projected soul after soul without a tinct of homophobia on that now spotless place in their hearts. As he watched, the backward laws of Iran, Cuba, and Saudi Arabia were stricken from the books and the crust of homophobic prejudice everywhere on earth was softened and dissolved by right reason.

Santa delighted in how complex, compassionate, and grown-up his stepdaughter was. Why hadn't he noticed it before? Perhaps it was clear now because he had fully accepted his failings. He could relax and open to Wendy entirely, knowing that she too no longer expected him to be forever a saint.

Santa could hardly believe how good he felt. Wonder filled him to observe this or that mortal. How different were his past glimpses of them, their damaged hearts as he deracinated the egg-seeds, and now the redeemed, blessed, chocolate-coated goodness that greeted him at every turn. Laughing to the point of tears, he was seized with the desire to grab his toes like a giggling infant.

Then he thought, Why not?

Sitting on the carpet, he kicked off his slippers, reached over his fat belly, and grabbed his big toes in their bright red wool socks, flexing them so that they slipped inside his fists. He giggled uncontrollably and took delight in that lack of control. Wendy clapped her hands and laughed, as did Anya and Rachel, to see her stepfather so happy.

After they had exchanged hugs and toasted one another with hot cider, Santa begged for the solitude of his workshop office. The elves busy at their benches cheered him anew when he strode through the door. He obliged with a short speech on the order of all's-right-with-the-world-and-I'm-in-tiptop-shape-too. Then he vanished into his office and closed the door, lighting his great lantern and savoring the silence.

He had been reborn, quite literally.

It was good to acknowledge and embrace the Pan in him.

He had regrets, yes, but no guilt for his behavior eight years before and earlier. He would confess to his little girl and beg her forgiveness. That was the right thing to do.

He strode to the Coke dispenser, lifted the lid, and guided the neck of a clattering bottle along its metal tracks and out. The opener affixed to the side crimped the cap and snapped it off. Santa observed the familiar mist drift at the bottle's mouth, like smoke lingering at the wanton O of a smoker's lips.

Then he paused. Staring through the dark glass at the teeming bubbles that urged the bottle's uplift, he peered past the fleeting pleasure promised by the cola's tang.

And what he saw appalled him.

There were no proteins, vitamins, or minerals in this drink. Instead he saw phosphorus, which could deplete mortal bones of calcium; acids that etched tooth enamel, encouraged cavities, and might well lead to inflammation of the stomach and the duodenal lining. Then there were the caffeine and sugars, which provoked a tachycardial upbeat in the heart rate. And a dark brown dye (E-150, wasn't it?) that went hand-in-hand with vitamin B-6 deficiency, hyperactivity, and depressed levels of blood glucose. The whole poison-laden concoction could cause insomnia, headaches, gastric ulcers, anxiety, and obesity. Far worse, week after week, its steady assault on bone calcium led to fractures in teenaged girls and osteoporosis in older women.

None of these ill effects redounded to him, of course. But that made his habit worse. Ever since Haddon Sundblom had spent decades depicting him in glossy magazine ads, a Coke bottle cradled in his hand, his image had nudged generations of boys and girls toward the frequent consumption of soft drinks.

Well, thought Santa, if millions of mortals can find it in their hearts to abandon the habit of homophobia once and for all, then jolly old Saint Nick, gone to hell, re-integrated, and reborn, can swear off the self-destructive swill he now holds in his hand.

And so he did.

He poured the contents of the bottle down the sink drain at his workbench. Then, calling in his favorite elf, he gestured toward the dispenser. "Do me something pressing, Fritz."

"Anything you like."

"Pour every bottle down the drain. Recycle the empties; here, take this one too. Then, if you would be so kind, you and some of your more muscular co-workers are to unplug this dispenser, cart it to some far-off place in the woods, and bury it six feet deep."

Fritz goggled. "Six feet?"

"Deep enough so it's out of sight forever."

"Yes, sir."

Within minutes, an obliging host of elves had emptied the thing (all that clattering as bottle after bottle traveled along the tracks and was lifted free), yanked the plug from the wall, taped the cord to the side, and struggled the dispenser onto a flatbed dolly equipped with skis that could be lowered when they were outside. Knecht Rupert stayed behind to sweep and mop the floor upon which it had sat for more than sixty years.

Santa pictured Fritz and the others sledding the dispenser into the woods. No doubt he would see the tracks and know in which direction they had headed. But he felt no temptation to go after it and retrieve it, and he knew that that temptation would never plague him again. There were the children to consider, their health, both as youngsters and as grown-ups. Until quite recently, he had ignored grown-ups, giving little thought to boys and girls on the cusp of adulthood.

Now he took a longer view.

Milk and cookies. They weren't the greatest food either. Maybe a nibble at each house. Moderation was key. He would slim down, pay attention to diet, exercise more. The subliminal message would get through quickly enough to the world of mortals. And even if it helped only a little, forever swearing off Coca-Cola would remove a harmful association and upgrade his status as a role model. No ill will did Santa harbor toward those in the soft drink industry, nor toward anyone at all. He was simply withdrawing his image from the promotion of a product detrimental to human health.

The empty spot in his office? More space. Less clutter. A place for a cushion, somewhere he could sit and meditate on his good fortune, his integrated spirit, and how best to increase the world's store of generosity.

Why wait?

Summoning master weaver Ludwig, he described what he wanted, a firm wide cushion covered in plush burgundy fabric, simple yet of the finest quality, dignified but not showy. From this cushion would arise plans of the utmost benevolence. Foregoing all expectation, he would invite those plans and they would come. Ludwig nodded at Santa's instructions, clouds of confusion obscuring his features as usual. But Santa knew he would return with just the right item, as he always did, as everyone of them always did.

So it was within the hour. And Santa shut the door and sat and stilled his mind. Two images came up.

The first was of Wendy at the Chapel, as he bared his past and begged her forgiveness. That he would see to this very day.

The second was of the Easter Bunny standing at bedsides the night before, an aura of calm emanating from him and, from Santa, a complete lack of envy and loathing. One could despise the Easter Bunny's past misdeeds yet not judge the transformed creature himself.

And life for the nonce was utter bliss.

42.

MAKING SPIRITS BRIGHT

THE SON WAITED PATIENTLY BESIDE the throne (for what time had he to lose in eternity?) until the Father emerged from the depths of his brooding, turned his magnificent head, and said, "I created them with the best of intentions. Perfect I claimed this, my creation, to be. For perverse and foolish choices are as much a part of perfection as correct and wise ones."

"You did. It is. They are."

"On the other hand," said the Father dolefully, "it may be time to reengage. Yes, yes, I know. I work my will, whose ways cannot be fathomed, through human agency. But hands-off simply isn't working. Do you agree? Of course you agree. You're an agreeable sort."

If the Son had been capable of feeling insulted, he would have felt so now. No matter. Suppressed bemusement sufficed.

"There are blemishes," admitted God. "They bear removing. Corrections are in order. Oh, perhaps not as dramatic as what occurred last night. By dribs and drabs. A sweeping gesture now and then, perhaps. Michael, incline thine ear." At the hummed 'M' of his name the angel appeared, supple to the whims of the Almighty.

"It is mine to listen and obey."

"Enough of that rot. I have a job for you." And the Father set Michael the task of annunciating before Santa and Wendy one more time, setting forth new responsibilities. The details did not surprise the Son, though Michael brightened and flitted off toward earth.

"I suppose," said the Father, "I'd better clear this with the *true* fount of creation."

The Son watched him step down from his throne and draw near the Divine Mother. As he approached, the muscled thighs of Zeus emerged, a leather chiton, wild dark hair and a beard of swirls and ringlets, his great fists gripping thunderbolts. That regression evoked a counter-response from the Divine Mother, whose pristine virginity fell away,

279

as did her blue robes. Out emerged the six mothers of Dionysus—the moon goddess Semele, Demeter, Io, Dione, Persephone, Lethe—and seventh, Eurynome, queen of all creation.

Shrugging out of his chiton, Zeus plunged his godhood deep into the six, but deepest of all into Eurynome. And from the seven impregnated bellies emerged one slinking creature of shame, the newborn embodiment of the Father's guilt for a flawed creation.

To his throne he returned, his offspring slumping behind. The Son remained at God's right hand, even as the younger son crawled abashedly onto his father's lap. He spoke a few shy words in his ear, to which the divine head nodded.

"He needn't whisper," said the Son.

The hairless thing again whispered.

"In due time," said the Father, his voice not as commanding as it had been. He patted the pinched shoulders of his newborn child. "That's a lad."

Well, thought the Son. Thy will be done.

In spying at the North Pole that Easter Day, Gronk resisted the urge to blow his cover and pummel his turncoat brother.

Not his task, he had been told. Spend the day and report back.

So Gronk bumbled about, checking in on Gregor the grump, gawking at the obscene perfection of the elves' handiwork, green too with envy at the solicitude of Santa's family toward one another, the older wife, the younger wife, the girl who was grown-up inside and who had fought bravely on the island. He hovered nearby when Santa swore off Coke forever and had the dispenser removed. He watched Snowball and Nightwind pounce on balls of red yarn in Wendy's bedroom.

And he kept within earshot of Santa and Wendy on their afternoon walk. Deep in the woods, just as they were preparing to turn back, the sunlight suddenly muted itself, the air bloomed with the scent of rose petals, and Wendy gasped, "Look." Before them, above the snow, appeared the archangel Michael in all his glory.

"Well, hello again," said Santa.

"Blessed art thou among immortals, and twice blessed for having saved humankind from itself."

Wendy clapped her hands. "I'm so pleased you dropped by."

"Ah, but I'm not here to reminisce. Nor," said Michael, raising a

280

finger toward Santa, "need we discuss what transpired on the plains of Tartarus. For I bring glad tidings of a different sort."

Observing Santa and Wendy's pleased looks, Gronk felt fit to gag. Nasty suited him better. Nasty was down to earth, more attention-grabbing. Nasty had more meat on its bones, somehow, than nice. There was nothing like crushing the skull of a misbehaving child to make one feel alive.

"Glad tidings?" said Santa. "From the Father, I presume."

"His lips to my ear, and mine to yours: From this day forward, on Thanksgiving Eve shall you and Wendy visit three mortal households of your choosing, expressly to persuade them away from ill will and bad behavior toward godly thought and act. Though your success be not guaranteed, Thanksgiving morning shall brim, worldwide, with renewed respect for all people, a hint of it in every waking soul, accompanied by delightful aromas straight from heaven to remind humanity of its origins in the divine and its potential to act divinely. Alas, that reminder will fade, and inhumane behavior will once more be championed by the straying masses."

Santa bowed his head. "You honor us beyond telling. Gladly do we accept your charge. Do we not, Wendy?"

Wendy took his hand. "We do! You sound different, Michael. Not just formal—which you are, and that's okay, that's great—but more in harmony with yourself, if that makes any sense."

"It does." There was an enigmatic glint in his eye.

"Can you stay? Can we offer you some tea, or something?"

But the archangel begged off. And Gronk let the sanctimony of his final words glide past his ears. Mommy wasn't going to like this. At the angel's concluding gestures, Gronk flew off, heading for Mommy's island and the inevitable beating she would give him when he delivered the bad news. But beatings were never lethal and they bonded him to her. All in all, she was a swell role model, and being firstborn carried, after all, great responsibility. A torn ligament, a broken rib, even the temporary jellying-out of his eyes was small price to pay for that position.

Michael, winging heavenward, grew righteous with pride. Melding with the repressed Hermes and giving that side of him equal weight had lifted much guilt from his shoulders. All of his bumblings—failing to prevent Santa and the Tooth Fairy from crossing paths three decades before, an earlier incident that had resulted in the birth of the Orgasm Fairy, and his more recent creation and dissemination of the ill-fated egg-seeds—he realized now that they hadn't been bumblings at all.

They had been intended.

Which really wasn't such a bad thing.

For one thing, it relieved boredom. It stirred the pot, kept it simmering: no cooling, no coagulating, no settling of ingredients which tasted better well-mixed. Real life bubbled and blistered and burnt the tongue sometimes.

Besides, it was all part of God's plan. Oh, he pretended to be miffed. And Michael as always would pretend anguish the next time God called him on the carpet. But they would both understand, behind the berating, that it was a game, that each had his role to play and the obligation to play it to the hilt.

Spotting the floor of the Empyrean above, Michael laughed out loud. How wonderful it was to be an archangel. And how wonderful to fully embrace the trickster god within.

I believe I'll keep this job, thought he. Good benefits, steady employment, constant surprises, and delightful bouts of bumbling and upset, swiftly followed by equilibrium regained.

And upward into ever holier realms did he speed.

42.

EMBRACING WHAT IS AND WHAT COULD BE

LONG BEFORE MICHAEL'S APPEARANCE, Wendy knew Santa had something on his mind. On their outbound trek, as fresh snow draped soft curves over every angle and edge, turning the landscape into a wonderland, he had been quieter than usual. Their boots crunched and squeaked as always, but they paused less often for conversation. And when they did, its content, though pleasant, never strayed far from the trivial and safe.

At age nine, she would have worried his silence signaled his displeasure with her, a girl whose mortal origins meant she would never measure up; at seventeen, she was far more assured. Whatever was on his mind he would reveal in his own good time.

When Michael showed up, she turned giggly and girlish. Through him had she and Santa made a dent in mankind's nastiness. He seemed almost like family. It was strange to hear him deliver such a formal message. But she noticed the impish gleam in his eye and understood he was playing his proper role.

When he vanished, she and Santa sat on twin boulders, sharing a childish excitement for their new task, mixed with grown-up sobriety about the responsibility it entailed. Still, that unrevealed something lurked behind many of Santa's glances toward her and inside each pause in their exchange.

"No, Wendy," he insisted, "I think *you* should be the one to plan our agenda next Thanksgiving. You retain a child's sense of fair play. That, coupled with your ability to project futures and your superb choice of Jamie's worst tormentors last year, suggest that you, if you'd be so kind, ought to decide which homes we visit."

"Goody," said Wendy. "I accept."

"Wonderful." Then he paused, huffed out a sigh, and shook his head. "My darling girl, now that your mind is more grown-up than childlike and we have been newly blessed, it's high time I revealed what happened at the end of your mortal stay up here, not so long ago."

"Only if you want to," she said, seeing how stricken he was.

"I need to. And I want to. Tell me what you remember of that time."

Wendy scrunched up her face. "You came home from your Christmas deliveries. Mommy and I had been sad because our year here was up and we had to leave. Then somehow Anya fell in love with Mommy after all, and we were suddenly going to stay and be very happy. There was a big celebration on Christmas Day. Then I went to sleep, but in the middle of the night, I tiptoed past Fritz, who was snoring in a chair in my bedroom. I went potty and wiggled my loose tooth out. Let's see. I rinsed my mouth a few times, feeling very proud to be a big girl, slid the tooth under my pillow, and fell back asleep. Next thing I knew, I woke up and there were all these jingle bells on me, which fell with a clatter to the floor, only I wasn't in my bedroom, I was by the picture window, and everyone was really happy and they said I had been dead, but now I was not only alive again but immortal too. Somewhere in there, I lost nearly two months."

Santa nodded. "Let me tell you what happened to you during that time."

"'kay," she said, trying to be as nonchalant as possible.

Then did Santa unfold the horrors that had been expunged from her memory: the Tooth Fairy's horrendous extraction of her teeth; that same fairy's devouring of her mother and minting of her as a large gold coin; Wendy's being kidnapped and her bone-chilling flight to her father's burial plot, where the Tooth Fairy revived the corpse of Frank McGinnis and forced Wendy to watch her couple with him; Santa's fight with the monstrous fairy in the graveyard and his rescue of Wendy in exchange for a week's dalliance with his lead reindeer; his rescue then of Snowball from the rapine clutches of the Easter Bunny ("Oh, he was a heartless beast back then, nothing like he is now."); her descent into catatonia, being fed and bathed and dressed, looking at no one, saying nothing; Santa's creation of a love doll that looked just like Rachel; Anya's repulsion at same; and finally Santa's burial of the doll beside his hut in the woods, witnessed and misunderstood by Wendy herself in concealment, after which she had relapsed into catatonia and frozen to death, found too late the next morning by a frantic dragnet of elves.

All of this, Santa revealed with the most heartrending mien and the greatest anguish she had ever witnessed. But not one iota of love or respect left her for a single moment, despite her amazement at what he told her. Indeed, she was greatly relieved to hear his confession. Santa had descended from his perch of perfection to admit imperfection. This together with Michael's bumblings had erased her silly notion that immortals were pure and spotless and that she, when set against them, would always be found wanting.

"I had been Pan, the goat god, king of the satyrs, a fact I had forgotten. But now I freely admit it. I am Pan, as well as Santa. His urges triumphed because I tried to suppress him. Now I embrace him in all of his waywardness and without reserve, though I, not he, hold and ever shall hold the reins."

Santa's eyes were moist, his manner fretful.

She put an arm around his shoulder. "Father, I love you. You're the soul of generosity. You could never be less than that, not to me."

This made him weep the harder. But for joy. She felt the guilt and fear lift from him. "I've wanted to be a great father to you. But I've always known I was holding this thing back."

"And now," she said, "you've stopped holding back. You've shared it with me. And it's all right. You are a great father."

"I've wondered how to parent you, especially now that your mind is pretty much grown-up."

Wendy laughed. "You do it by loving me, silly, by trusting that you'll do and say the right thing, by trusting me to accept you as you are, to ask for guidance when I need it, and to follow my own instincts otherwise."

"And you're okay with...with your situation?"

She shrugged. "We're all dealt our lot in life. I'll never know what it means to be an adult in an adult's body. Never marry. Never bear a child. It can't be helped. Meanwhile, I'm immortal, I live in the most wonderful community on earth, I get to please children, and now I get to guide grown-ups toward a better life. I have the sweetest mommies and the very dearest daddy there could be, one whose generosity led him to take on the pain of the world, even unto death, in order to *save* the world. I'd say it doesn't get any better than that!"

Releasing a great sigh, Santa crushed her tearfully to him in a rolling, rollicking embrace. "Oh Wendy, I love you so."

"It's mutual, pardner!"

Thus they wiled away the hours appreciating each other and their lives, good and bad alike, until the waning light told them it was time to leave the boulders and head home.

The Tooth Fairy stoically digested Gronk's report as he grunted it out before her throne of bones. She did not cuff him or kick him or fly into a rage. Instead, she commanded him to assemble his ragtag band of brothers by the blasted cedar at the island's northern extremity.

There they gathered, cowering before her. Planting her feet in the sand and her hands on her hips, she trained her hard eyes on them. "Miserable wretches, rapine whelps of Zeus," she said, "it's clear that your father has decided not to punish us for inverting umpteen million egg-seeds. In the end we failed. But the big blowhard in the sky has stayed his hand. Glowering coward. For all his bluster, there appear to be limits to his power, and we are testing them.

"The eldest among you, the least doltish in this festering lot of blockheads, informs me that Pan and his insufferable brat will be meddling in a handful of mortal lives each Thanksgiving, by order of that same Father God. Know this: We shall not only do all we can to stop them; we will corrupt the very mortals they would make pure."

"Mommy."

Who dared interrupt? Ah yes. Frash, youngest after Chuff and the latest butt of her offspring's torment.

"Won't Zeus hurt us if we do that?"

The imps jeered and threw catcalls and then clumps of wet sand at their brother, who fisted his face in rage but dared not look at them straight on.

The Tooth Fairy laughed. "Is that the best you can do? You would pummel him, but for your fear of me. Well, you're right to fear me. But you're wrong not to pummel Frash. Do it. Do it now. Pummel the little bastard. Beat him to a pulp!"

Tooth and claw, they sailed into him. With eye gouges and torn limbs did they vex him, whose agony gave her great delight. When they were spent and Frash lay asprawl on the sand, groaning in misery, the Tooth Fairy berated him. "You would whimper? Rather curse Chuff for abandoning us and shifting your brothers' taunts to you. Never interrupt me. Stifle those moans. Stifle them, or my worthier sons will give you cause for more.

"Now boys, it's true we lost this battle. But we shall not lose the next one, and we shall not lose the war. From what Gronk tells me, Hermes, playacting the angel, has been reined in. Next November, the power imbalance will be less pronounced. Moreover, the big blowhard has overstepped. He has altered hitherto unalterable laws, and his creation will crumble because of it. Guilt gnaws at him. In our next skirmish, he'll prove a weaker adversary. As for Pan, our guile and determination will trump the fat satyr's feigned goodness, and we will drag his straying mortals deeper into the muck and mire of their sins. See if we don't.

"As for homophobia, that's the *least* of humanity's inexhaustible store of failings. Let it go. We don't need it. The mortal masses provide plenty of fodder for mischief. And we shall feast upon that fodder like flies upon the droppings of a centaur.

"Dwell upon mischief. Ponder and scheme how you might mete out torment to grown-up mortals. That's your task for spring, summer, and early fall. Now be gone. The sight of you sickens me. For the space of three heartbeats, I'm going to close my eyes. Anyone still cowering on the sand when I open them shall pay dearly for his disobedience."

Then she lowered her eyelids, heard them scurrying, felt clumps of sand kick in panic against her ankles. Silence. She opened her eyes to behold a beach devoid of impish ugliness.

Near the cedar she squatted, gazing toward Pan's northern abode and lifting her palms to the gray-clouded heavens. Though slaps of rain battered her face, not once did she blink against the pelting, but brooded deeply on revenge.

The Easter Bunny had watched with quiet satisfaction the waking of select mortals on Easter morning, how they had eaten the divine egg and been transformed. He had also thrown his gaze northward to witness Santa Claus's resurrection and Chuff's acceptance into the community of elves. Ah well, he thought, that's nice for the ugly little fellow. It can't be helped, my being banished from the North Pole. I did some pretty terrible things, some horrendously horrible unforgivable things, though I can't for the life of me recall what they were. Whatever the regrettable deeds, I shall not soon stop browbeating myself for them.

Imagine, then, his surprise when Santa's lead reindeer, antlers aglow, made a graceful swoop-down, landing right in front of him in the clearing before his burrow. He wore a saddle, and tucked securely into the right saddlebag, one corner peeking out, was a large green envelope. Inside the envelope the Easter Bunny found a simple card, serenity pictured upon it, a snow scene, a hut with candles in the windows, white wisps of smoke lazily skirling up from its chimney top. Inside, in a graceful looping hand, it said: "I would like to see you. Lucifer knows the way. The Easter baskets are missed. Rachel."

The summons threw him into a tizzy. How could he possibly face this woman, sensing the horrendous wrong he had done her? And why ever had she requested a visit from him? Was it out of obligation, for the recent good he had done? He neither wanted nor deserved that. It was in his transformed nature to act thus, to assist Santa with his Easter task, to do his part in saving Jamie Stratton's life, and to help Wendy and Rachel escape from the Tooth Fairy's island. Whatever had provoked this invitation, he must go, if only to endure the shame. Snubbing Rachel was unthinkable. She must have thought long and hard before sending this card. He felt obliged, at the very least, to show up, if only to accept and humbly acknowledge whatever shame she might cover him with. If she summoned him a thousand times to berate and humiliate and heap scorn upon him, it would be as a pinch of dirt removed from the Everest of his disgrace.

"All right, Lucifer," he said with a sigh. "Forgive my weight." Wriggling a furry foot into one stirrup, he swung onto the reindeer's back, gripped the saddle horn, and tightened his legs about Lucifer's flanks. Then up they rose. Despite centuries of flying on his own, the abrupt lift tickled him. It was a different thing entirely, zooming into the sky upon Lucifer's back, watching the forest collapse into green bristle below, the earth passing beneath them, sea and land and cities and farms and streams as thin as hairline cracks, then the arctic wastes, brilliant and blinding in the sun, and finally the North Pole, temperate inside its bubble though snow sprawled soft and fluffy everywhere he looked.

When they passed over the commons, a few figures looked up and pointed, including Wendy, who broke into a run but was soon left behind by the skating pond. Lucifer knew the way. That's what Rachel's card had said. So the Easter Bunny contented himself with skimming along treetops dusted with snow, delighting in the stately march of spruce and pine and fir, and anticipating with dread his impending meeting with Santa's once-mortal wife.

Straight ahead, a brilliant patch of orange-yellow winked into view, the color of egg yolk before it pales into the over-boiled hue of sulfur. A tent. The sort a pasha might raise to hold court, spacious with pole supports, its taut ropes angled to metal stakes pounded deep into the ground. In front of this tent they landed, Lucifer stamping and snorting as his rider dismounted. At once, he flew off. High up, the treetops stirred into a sigh, then grew still.

The Easter Bunny hopped to the entrance. The tent flaps were held aside by rope and grommet.

"Ah, there you are," said a voice from within. "Wipe your feet and come inside."

He gulped and dutifully obeyed. Two sets of snow boots stood at one edge of a throw rug, on which he wiped his feet. Then he ventured into the tent proper, moving in small tentative hops across an Oriental rug that felt as if it had been spread over plastic sheeting to keep it free of moisture. Rachel McGinnis sat in a plush armchair, cherrywood at the arm ends and down below. Off to the left, knitting, sat Santa's first wife, doing what she could to keep her glower from being too obvious. A bodyguard, he thought. To be expected.

He stopped a respectful distance from Rachel.

"First," she said, "thank you for coming. This isn't easy for me, and it can't be easy for you."

"No, ma'am."

"You have demonstrated, in rather dramatic ways, how very much changed and chastened you are. I need not enumerate them. What most impresses me is that the Divine Mother chose you as her emissary, when she could just as easily have entrusted her miraculous pouch to Wendy or Santa. And then you were chosen once more by heavenly forces to rescue me and my daughter from the Tooth Fairy's island, for which I thank you with all my heart. So..."

She paused. He saw her blink away tears. But he felt paralyzed to do or say anything. She wasn't in physical distress. Anya shifted in her chair as if to speak. But Rachel waved away her help, smiled, stopped smiling, and went on: "So if you wish, you may once more leave Easter baskets here every spring on your long night's journey."

He kept his eyes averted. "That would be an honor."

"Come and go, as you did before the bad times. Leave them beside our beds if you think it best. I cannot quite offer my forgiveness—"

"Nor do I expect it."

"The scar will always be there. But I will no longer allow our past to dampen the joys of Easter for this community of worthy souls.

289

And I want to state, right here and now, that I *do* forgive you, even as I cannot *ever* forgive you—I know that makes no sense at all, and yet it does—"

"Perfect sense."

"Yes. And now you may go."

Her words abruptly broke off, as though a rope had paid out and slipped from her grasp. He longed to see the expression on her face. But he simply nodded, said, "As you wish. Thank you," and hopped back through the makeshift vestibule into the snowy patch in front of the tent. Colors seemed sharper now, scents more redolent, textures as vivid as if his paws were touching them.

No Lucifer.

His own steam, then.

As he was about to lift off and head home, flashes of hollyberry red shone through the trees in a rustle and burst of exuberance. "It's you!" exclaimed Wendy, kicking up snow as she came on. "I thought so. I followed Mommy's and Anya's boot prints."

"Yes, I—"

She rushed into an enthusiastic hug, which he awkwardly returned. Then she stepped back. "I just had to tell you. I peeked in on Jamie Stratton and his family, just to see how they were doing? Well, they're fine. They're astounded at how the world has changed, as well they might be. But what I wanted to say was that Jamie told them he wanted a little sister and they said they would see what they could do about that but not to get his hopes up because getting pregnant wasn't always easy."

"Unless a certain—"

"Exactly! I knew about your magic nose thing, and I was hoping that maybe you could, you know...."

"Well I don't see why I couldn't." His spirits brightened considerably. "I'll drop in on them as soon as all the stars, urges, and hormones are properly aligned. No more than two or three months, at the outside."

"Great! So what's this tent all about, and stuff?"

"Oh well, your mother wanted to thank me for...well I'll let her tell you yourself. But the upshot is that I'll be leaving Easter baskets at the North Pole again."

"That's super!"

"Dear me, I've got to be off. You take care now, sweet pea."

"You too. And don't forget the Strattons."

"I won't." He gratefully accepted her parting hug, then waved a paw, flew up, and shot away southward, much relieved his visit hadn't been as dreadful as he had feared.

Easter baskets? Next year, Wendy and the others would receive the finest ones he, his hens, and his machines were able to produce!

Rachel heard Wendy's voice piping animatedly outside. Then into the tent she burst, kicked off her shiny red boots, and ran across the carpet onto Rachel's lap.

"Well, aren't you the enthusiastic one?"

"I sure am. Hi, Anya. So what's with the Easter Bunny's visit? And this tent? Neat! Oh, Mom, I told him about Jamie Stratton, just like I wanted to. And he said he would *do* it. He's going to make his nose twitch at just the right moment to bless Jamie's mom and dad with a little girl."

Rachel loved her childish enthusiasm. "Well, dear, he did so many good deeds for us and Santa, I thought I'd thank him in a special way. He appreciated it, I think."

"Yeah, but why not in the commons in front of everybody? Give him a medal and a kiss, or something?"

"Um," said Rachel. "Oh, he's the modest sort. Shy and self-effacing to a fault. I didn't want to make him uncomfortable. Public adulation sometimes does that, even to the worthiest soul."

Wendy said, "Great," and told her how much she had missed having candy at Easter, even though the day meant so much more than that, in terms of Christ and salvation and stuff. But Rachel only half heard her, her mind teemed with such conflicting emotions. She felt as if she had been caught in a secret, which indeed she had, telling white lies—something she hated doing—and that any moment now, her daughter was going to turn all solemn and say, "Mom, level with me," and the whole sorry rape would come out, right there in the soft sad orange glow of the tent; and Wendy, in that knowledge, would be unalterably changed. Nevermore would girlish glee irrepressibly erupt from her, as now it did.

But Wendy never went there.

Instead she looked about and laughed and said, "We really have it great, Mom, don't we?"

Rachel, relieved, smiled. "Yes, we do."

"It's super, being immortal. And I don't care—though of course I regret it, heavens, who wouldn't?—that I'll never have a grown-up body nor any kids of my own. But what I do have are perfect health, the companionship of elves in abundance, the wonder of the workshop, and Santa reading me bedtime stories. He's the greatest reader. I can see and hear all the characters as if they were standing right in front of me. And now, Santa and I get to change some mortals' lives, or do our best anyway. That's so amazingly cool!"

Rachel agreed that it was, thinking about the withering violence inflicted on them by the Tooth Fairy and her imps, but she wasn't about to bring that up. "We are indeed blessed," she said. "Never aging, never dying, never getting sick—there's much to be said for immortality. I'd say you can't get much closer to heaven on earth."

"Yep, and I'll tell you something else. If that terrible fairy tries anything again, I know now I can fight her right back. Not that I like fighting. I don't. But I'll protect myself and my loved ones, you can count on it."

"I doubt she'll bother us again."

"Why is she so mean, Mommy?"

Rachel demurred. "That's a long story, sweetie. Another time, perhaps."

"Okay." Wendy was so fired up with happiness, she hugged and kissed Rachel, then raced over to Anya and leaped into her lap, causing her to drop a stitch. But Anya just tilted her head back and laughed in that old-lady way she had, hugged her stepdaughter in return, and said, "You dear sweet girl."

Then Rachel announced it was time they headed home, so the elves could strike the tent and life resume its normal routine.

And so they did.

44.

SANTA AMONG THE ELVES

SINCE HIS RESURRECTION, Santa had been learning to embrace himself in all his contradictory dimensions. He felt relief that Wendy had accepted his confession with such good grace. His fear of her rejection had proven groundless. All he needed was to be open, moment by moment, trusting in her nonjudgmental response.

No longer did he avoid observing grown-up mortals. As always, he kept lists of naughty and nice children. But now he began a few new ones—considered compilations of naughty and nice adults, primarily to help Wendy decide which households to visit on Thanksgiving Eve.

Some grown-ups were very nice indeed, a seasoning and maturation of the good children they had been. Others hadn't been so nice as kids, but had reformed by some means or other and struggled daily to embrace virtue. But many of them were very naughty indeed (he was forced to invent sublists for nasty, psychopathic, and beyond the pale), a far larger group and one that made Santa Claus very unhappy indeed. So much potential for goodness wasted; so many lives frittered away; so much love never expressed, indeed never felt, for the fear or low self-esteem that concealed it.

Santa sighed. He and Wendy had much work to do. And with only three households to visit each year, they would have to choose wisely for maximum impact on the human race. Michael hadn't said it would be easy. But Santa relished the challenge. He would be sure to adjust Wendy's expectations before they began. Then they would barrel in, full force, spiritual guns blazing.

A week after Easter, Santa called the elves into his office one by one. Wrapping their conversation in magic time, he told them he had changed and felt the need to reacquaint himself with his helpers. He also wanted to assess the community's health after the recent brouhaha over Gregor's misguided condemnation of nosepicking.

Chuff he summoned early in the game, so as to assure the imp that

293

he was a highly prized addition to the community. Because he excelled at heavy lifting, Chuff had become a free-roving assistant to any elves who dealt with outsized, bulky, or otherwise heavy and unwieldy toys: ping-pong tables, swing sets, tree houses, and the like. Santa had heard many of his helpers remark how cheery and helpful the imp was, and how undyingly grateful to have escaped his torment on the Tooth Fairy's island. Indeed it was all Santa could do, when came Chuff's turn, to keep him from kissing his boots.

"No, no, Chuff," he laughed, "that isn't necessary. Sit there, lad, and tell me how things are going."

He gave the imp an extra hour, delighting in what he had to say and how he said it. "Chuff's little friends are so good to him," said Chuff. "His skull fills more every day with smarts and barrels of joy. Might be the air, I betcha."

"Any regrets?"

At first, Chuff shook his head. Then he managed through tears, "I miss my mommy. I wish I could make her and my brothers as happy as I am." At Santa's invitation, he pillowed his ungainly head on Santa's belly, his tears as wet and slobbery as the dewlap drool of a purebred boxer.

"There, there," said Santa.

At last the imp composed himself and regained the stool.

"Chuff, I hate to bring this up. But I've recently learned to accept, and so diminish, the power of my naughty side. We've both undergone a transformation recently, though yours was the more extreme. I know your former self was very nasty to bad little boys and girls, even to the point of ending their lives. But eating the Divine Mother's chocolate egg has utterly changed you. Of that I have no doubt. Still, I wonder how you feel about your past deeds."

There was a knowing look in the imp's eye. Santa was pleased to see it there. Better a well-rounded helper than one acquainted only with his own veneer. "They were very bad. But Chuff has waked from the bad dream. I was the best of my mommy's sons, but that's no help. The pain I put on rotten kids I carry inside me, here." He thumped his chest. "They cry. I see them and my new eyes cry too, though their pain cannot be cried away. Then I turn to my present joys and hug them tight. I could never turn my back on those. Not when I feel your heart and my elf sibs' hearts go thump like mine."

"Good, Chuff," said Santa. "Carry on then, and know that everyone here loves you without reserve."

Chuff left all aglow.

Santa made a point to bring in Gregor early too. To the gruff fellow, who huffed and grunted his way onto the tall wooden stool opposite, Santa said, "Let's get to the point, Gregor. I don't ask you to stop being judgmental. As well ask the sun to douse its fire. Being judgmental gives you your charm. But I do ask that you refrain from amplifying your prejudices, and that you do nothing to prevent consenting elves from expressing their love and affection in whatever way they choose. And that goes for you too."

"Disgusting," muttered Gregor.

"I could barely hear that. Good. Now try it without moving your lips."

Gregor scowled.

"Perfect! Well, I believe we're done."

Santa was pleased to see that his elves bore no ill will toward Gregor and his brothers. Indeed, Josef and Engelbert had decided to continue bedding down in the dorm. Though Gregor huffed that that was perfectly fine with him, his loneliness was palpable. Santa prudently left that tender subject alone.

Into weeks of magic time the queue of helpers stretched. Santa saved his favorite elf for last. Red-haired, gap-toothed Fritz took to the stool with gusto, a broad grin carved into his face.

"Why so happy?" asked Santa, basking in Fritz's joy.

"Life is grand. Our once-compromised craftsmanship is as precise as before. You're alive again, and more astounding than ever. For the past eight years, something's been distracting you. I could feel it. But since your brush with death, you seem, I don't know, more complete, more yourself, than you've been in a long time."

"Very observant, Fritz. Someday, you and I will speak of that, how things have shifted for me in the best possible way. But today, I'm taking a sounding of each of you to confirm that no sour notes, no strident chords, are being struck just out of earshot."

"None that I'm aware of, Santa," said Fritz thoughtfully.

"Good. As for Gregor, he well deserved what all of you have had of him—a good-natured ribbing. I wanted to make sure that the ribbing has stopped. You nod. That's good. For our recent fall-off in toy manufacture, instead of blaming his own browbeating, Gregor scapegoated the nosepickers among us. He has, in his own gruff way, repented. He mustn't be scapegoated in return, not even years in the future, through festering resentment."

Fritz waved it away. "I truly believe we have put that behind us. Gregor's Gregor. He got a little bit out of hand. But now he's back to being a simple grump, and everyone accepts and loves him for that." He leaned forward conspiratorially. "By the way, sir. Congratulations on your promotion."

"My promotion?"

"You know. The thing with you and Wendy and the night before Thanksgivings to come. I think that's grand."

Santa laughed uproariously. "It will do us good, me and Wendy. May it do humankind some good as well."

"Amen to that."

"Oh and one more thing. I shamed you and your bunkmates at the replicas last November. Please accept my apologies. I've spoken to Max and Karlheinz already."

"Apology unnecessary, but gratefully accepted!"

"Wonderful," said Santa. He placed his hands on his favorite's shoulders, then gathered him into a warm embrace. "Had I a son, Fritz, I could wish for no better son than you."

"And you, a father, to me."

Arm in arm, they walked out into the workshop. With the lift of his hand, Santa halted the workbench racket and clatter. "Lads, a wondrous consult all. It draws us closer. I'm proud to work side-by-side with each one of you and pleased to observe the restored integrity of your toymaking. Industry in a worthy cause does a body good. And what cause more worthy than bringing a smile to the lips of a child? Happy little boys and girls, given the proper mix of responsibility and pride in their endeavors, become happy grown-ups. But you know that, and I'll keep you no longer from your nimble-fingered handiwork. Carry on!"

And so they did, but not before they rose and cheered and clapped so vociferously that Santa jollied up a shake-belly of laughter, coyly curled his snow-white mustaches, and winked in genial conspiracy. At length, he waved away their applause and regained his office, closing the door to mute the joyful noise outside. When it died down, he gave a contented sigh and sat at his desk with an exceedingly warm glow in his heart.

***

Shortly before dusk, Gregor brushed Galatea down, the burnished sunlight splashing odd-angled slats and rhomboids on the stable walls. His brothers, though their spying had ended with Gregor's humiliation in the Chapel, had retired to the dorm, where they had elected to keep their beds.

"Just as well," he said to the doe. "It lets me give full voice to my thoughts when they're not by, my expendable brothers, the lack of whose company I could give half a withered sugarplum about. Not that I mind audiences. They amplify my grumpiness. But there's plenty to be grumpy about *without* amplification, even in this demi-paradise. I'll tell you something, Galatea. They're too happy, this lot. Is there not one burr up their scrawny little butts? Make toys, adulate Santa Claus, take Christmas Day off every year to indulge in skating and snowball fights. Bah! There's no depth to them."

Galatea's nose cast its limelight everywhere. If she had been a cat, she would have purred. "Take my railings. I admit I may have overstepped, even veered into hypocrisy, I confess it. But they came alive then, those I tormented and lorded it over, more alive than I've seen them in ages. Chastise me as they might, it takes *conflict* to bring out the high and low terrain in every creature's soul. And I gave it to them in spades. Nosepicking is wrong, no two ways about it. I don't give a good goddamn that I too indulge in the filthy habit from time to time. Had it no allure, it wouldn't deserve the name of sin.

"But I'll bide my time, little doe. Keep you eye on that imp, that Chuff fellow. There's a heap of bone-dry tinder lying about that one's heart. He'll flare up one day. And there are plenty of leaks waiting to be sprung in this community's supposedly tight-caulked hull. Santa admitted there are many things in our past that we've forgotten. Well, I mean to probe into those things. Not content with ignorance shall Gregor live out his days." Damned if he would!

"I'll let you in on a little secret, Galatea. This ferret-eyed old grouch believes in inertia. Elasticity has its limits. Stretch a rubber band and it eventually snaps back. Consider the mortals whose image the archangel showed us, whose altered hearts led to the egg-seed. Impressed was I, and impressed I remain. I was sure that Santa and Wendy would find it impossible to pull humankind free of the muck of their antediluvian prejudices. And they proved me wrong. Ah, but time

297

works deterioration, even upon what seems an irreversible success. Here's another secret, my white-furred doe, just between you and me. A near blasphemy. I don't even put much store in the Divine Mother's chocolate eggs. Mortals are far too nasty to embrace goodness in one area of behavior but resist their natural impulse toward wickedness in every other arena they enter. I doubt this change will hold. And when things revert, look out for the wrath of the Almighty. He's taken a huge gamble up there. Muck with creation, and it'll bite you on your divine posterior every time. That's Gregor's credo.

"But no one listens to me. They hear what they want to hear. They laugh me off. Well, Gregor will have the last laugh, see if he doesn't. By hook or by crook, Gregor will whip his elfin brethren into shape, relieve Santa of his burden of command, and restore our memories of times past. You can bet your glowing nose on that!"

Galatea whinnied a soft protest.

"Am I bearing down too hard? I'll lighten my stroke."

And on Gregor babbled as daylight waned, scowling and muttering, brooding upon Chuff and how malleable he might prove. There was depth there, and nastiness not all that far from the surface.

Chuff.

Much might be made of him.

Just before bedtime, Wendy sat on Santa's lap in the living room by the cozy narrative glow of a floor lamp. From a great old book of tales bound in cracked leather and redolent of ancient times, he read stories about werewolves, and mutilation, and dark woods filled with creepy ghosts, but always eventual redemption and turnabout, the bad folks punished, the good rewarded. His belly provided a soft cushion. His low baritone boomed out terror, and fear, and the assurance, at long last, of a happy ending.

Then they went hand in hand to her bedroom. Secure about her he tucked the covers, the oil lamp by her bedside casting great bird-wing shadows everywhere.

"I love you, Daddy," she said.

"I love you too, Wendy. More than words can say."

She patted his hand where it rested on the coverlets and looked concerned. "Do you think, in the grand scheme of things, we'll really make much of a difference?" She tried to keep disappointment out of her voice, but she was determined to be realistic about their new task and three was such a small number of households to visit.

"It's good you're not letting hope run away with you. It helps keep me in check too. On the other hand, to hit a far target—"

"One must aim one's arrow high."

"Forty-five degrees, to be exact. You and I, young lady, should aim high. Take me, for instance. Let's see if I can walk the talk. I feel such depths of generosity toward my beloved boys and girls. Year after year, I have dedicated my life to abundant giving. Well, I vow right here and now, on my honor, to extend that generosity to grown-ups too. Go back far enough and all of them have a worthy child buried in their souls. It's our task to revive and strengthen and put that child in charge of their lives. Many manage to keep it alive themselves, to nurture it, to be generous toward themselves and others. They're the ones who honor the spirit of Christ, of Buddha, of all divine avatars. Good grown-ups abound. But alas, there are far fewer among the rich and powerful, who climb ladders, adopt warped credos, lie, cheat, and steal, scratch, claw, and scrabble for advantage, rattle sabers, appeal to baser instincts, monger war, the list goes on and on. It would be easy to grow cynical and lose ourselves in despair. But you and I are going to focus on their worthiest ideals and how those ideals might be strengthened and encouraged in the mortals we visit. Those few, we will pick with care."

"Indeed we will," said Wendy, beaming.

"Consider Nelson Mandela. Now there's an extraordinary fellow. Were it not for him, South Africa would have devolved into factionalism and mass murder. Instead, despite the years stolen from him in prison, he preached peace. Preach it? He practiced it."

"But let me not babble on endlessly into the night. We both need our rest. Next Thanksgiving, with luck, we'll set a few mortals on the path to goodness. We must be patient. Change the right man or woman and it makes all the difference. But whether they stick to that path and change the world will be up to them."

"I can't wait," she said.

"Sleep tight, darling Wendy. I'll let my two yum-bunnies know you're ready for your goodnight hug."

"G'night, Daddy," she said, her eyelids heavy. Snowball and Nightwind padded in then (from the catch on the carpet, they clearly needed their claws trimmed) and leaped upon the bed, circling nests into her comforter and flopping down to either side of her.

It had been a full day. But she vowed to stay awake long enough to feel the warmth of Mommy's kiss and Anya's granny-lips on her cheek.

It was a struggle, yet she managed it. Just barely. But by the time they rose from her bed and reached the door, Wendy had utterly and blissfully entered the land of dreams.

45.

A SMALL SIGNIFICANT SHIFT

FROM THAT DAY FORWARD, Santa looked in on the human race to gauge its progress. In that one small area of interaction, they had of course enjoyed instant improvement. Day by day, its effects rippled throughout the world, although spillover into other attitudes and behaviors was hard to discern.

One day in June on their walk to the Chapel, Wendy said, "It's frustrating, I agree, to watch them one day at a time. That's why I prefer to project their futures."

"Of course," said Santa, feeling foolish. "Project them for me, would you, please? I'm particularly interested in the ones we dropped in on to save Jamie Stratton."

Wendy laughed. "Sure thing!"

Perched on a large boulder, Santa watched Wendy paint the arctic air with vignettes. Before granting his request, she showed him in quick succession some of the worst homophobes who had been chocolate-egged into reason and goodwill. Not only did they behave better, but they looked more youthful, wrinkle lines relaxed away, acceptance far more frequent in their demeanor, judgmentalism in general diminished. At his urging, Wendy brought up Meg Weddle, whose turned nature made her nearly unrecognizable, so completely had she let go of her unnecessary defenses.

After Meg came Matt Beluzzo. Santa watched him try at first to remain with his gang of unsavory friends. But they, alas, clueless in a new key, had refocused and intensified their hatred onto women. So Matt left the gang, and six years later, was going steady with Terry Samuelson. As he matured, he eased out of his manic need to appear manly and macho. His features softened. Indeed, Santa had witnessed, worldwide, a subtle softening of men's features.

"Here's Ty Taylor," said Wendy. And there was Ty indeed, in a private huddle with high mucky-mucks, speaking the word of God

301

from the pulpit of a progressive church and pounding podiums on the lecture circuit. A fully recovered and repentant fundamentalist, he called himself, roundly condemning the wrongheaded views of literalist sects on abortion and capital punishment and goose-stepping jingoism, even as he bore not the least animosity toward those who held such views. "The follies done in the Father's name," tut-tutted Santa. "Some Thanksgiving, we ought to tackle head-on the evils of wayward religion."

Wendy brought up more of Ty's triumphs, as his hair grayed and he became more righteous in his pursuit of truth. Somewhere along the way, he picked up a wife, the pert Mimsie Bannerman, an exquisite complement and a compassionate communicator in her own right. "Oh, I remember Mimsie," said Santa with boyish delight. "When she was five, she asked one of my surrogates for, received, and took much delight in a Betsy-Wetsy doll. A darling girl. A fascinating woman!"

"Now for the Strattons."

At once, good old Walter and Kathy lived and loved before them. They were far happier these days, with less to prove, less to agonize over. There they sat, their sons between them, in a more compassionate church. They encouraged, Walter even more than Kathy, Jamie's violin playing. "They're also far more encouraging of each other. Walter was never much of a hiker, but Kathy loved it. Now they hike frequently. In fact, that's what they're doing at this very moment."

"Show me," said Santa. And there before them, along the trail to Bierstadt Lake in Rocky Mountain National Park, hiked Jamie's mom and dad. Then they ventured off-trail to enjoy a snack of almonds, dried apricots, egg-salad sandwiches, and one another.

"Wow, look who's with them."

Santa looked and saw the Easter Bunny standing beside a tree not twenty feet from the Strattons, who, concealed from other hikers, were growing decidedly amorous. Rachel had told Santa of their meeting in the tent and her forgiveness of him. "Hmm, I wonder—"

"I know *exactly* why he's there. He and I discussed it." Wendy wiped the scene away. "But modesty forbids."

Santa boomed out a laugh. "All's right with the world, then."

"For the moment. This little corner of it, anyway."

"Perhaps," said Santa with a sigh, "that's as much as one can expect."

Then they headed home. As he followed Wendy through the winter wonderland, Santa gave silent thanks for the life he had been granted and the beautiful beings he shared it with. Anya. Rachel. Wendy. The elves. The reindeer. Chuff. Every last one of them beautiful beyond beautiful.

"What are you chuckling about back there?"

"Oh, nothing," said Santa. And he chuckled again, sending up gales of laughter to dance among the treetops.

Whenever the Easter Bunny watched mortals make love, he found them utterly enthralling. Every coupling came about differently and progressed at its own pace—clothing tossed or ripped away or gently removed, the touch tentative or abrupt or soft and sure, words halting or beguiling or shocking or sweet—and every coupling sounded, in a transposed key, the truth of the relationship entire. He had observed acts that gave every sign of hearts and flowers; but at the core, they were without joy or love, and both parties knew it. Conversely, just the night before, he had watched and enfertilized a taciturn pair, not a word spoken between them, not a smile exchanged; yet their love had been profound and all encompassing. What were their names? Ah yes, Reiner and Matilde von Huene, living in the heart of Rottenburg ob der Tauber.

Now, on a bright sunny Colorado afternoon, there had come into his ken Walter and Kathy Stratton. He had last seen them, in person no less, on Thanksgiving Eve. A crisis point. They had been traumatized in dream by the Tooth Fairy and her bastard imps. He and Wendy and Santa had reconnected them to their childhood impulses, and they made the correct choice vis-à-vis their son Jamie. Which in turn had led to the disaster of the egg-seeds and the triumph—joy, oh radiant joy—of the Divine Mother's chocolate eggs, each of which had passed between these very paws. He held them up, admiring their blessed leather.

Marvelous.

Now here lay the Strattons on a large crinkly blue poncho Kathy had stowed in her backpack. Walter, having enticed her out of her hiking clothes, shrugged off his own. "Shall we have a girl?" he asked.

"Okay, let's," she said. "Oh, but what if it's a boy?"

"Jamie will adjust. And we'll try again later."

"Nope, this one's the last. Then comes your vasectomy."

"Ouch. Well then, we'd better do this right."

Kathy laughed. "It feels pretty right to me." She gave a sigh. "You know how we're always fretting about infertility? Well, suddenly I'm not worried about that at all. How strange."

"We're blessed by the gods. Mmm, do that again."

"This?"

"Yep."

"I think we *must* be blessed."

And the Easter Bunny watched as Walter moved upon his wife and ventured inside her. Sheer beauty, this joining of the flesh. He, of course, had none to join. God had seen to that. All he could do was give the kiddies a moment of pure spring bliss each year, baskets and egg hunts. And a teensy bit of that bliss rubbed off on their parents.

But this was no time, he mused, to let himself be distracted by his past misdeeds, whatever they were, and his correction at the hands of the Great Deity in the Sky. No. His attention must be fixed fully upon the entwined couple, upon the movement of their organs, the sacs, the ducts, the fluids, the projectile surge of ejaculate, the motility and stamina of scads of spermatozoa, the womb's moist receptivity, and the egg's tremulous surface.

Then came the twitch of his nose, giving just the right zygote-English to the triumphant swimmer who would, ovum-conjoined, lead nine months hence to little Jamie's longed-for sister. What would they call her? He hadn't a clue.

Oh my, to what throes mortals abandoned themselves at the point of orgasm; or in Kathy's case, faked orgasm. But her joy was genuine enough, and her love for Walter. What a privilege it was to view this thigh-to-thigh, skin-to-skin activity. If there was incontrovertible proof of God's existence, the sight of mortal copulation was surely it. Perhaps if humankind ever gave up its joyless lust for power and its fascination with violence and death, it would turn to marveling at the spectacle of lovemaking.

An idle thought.

Men especially were too much enamored of playing king-of-the-hill ever to give up their fists and bombs. Not, at least, as the world was presently constituted.

But he had seen a subtle shift in the Father's creation. Indeed he had been its agent, and knew how beguiling such changes felt.

One good shift deserved another.

And another.

Who knew what lay in store for this odd race of beings?

Maybe the Father would make other tweaks to the space-time continuum. And maybe the Divine Mother would remember a certain bunny's role in this first one, and he would get to reprise it. Wouldn't that be grand?

Pointless musings. Pointless, yes, but grand. Still, he was more than content with what was. Santa's younger wife had forgiven him, if tentatively, in the warm glow of a great tent. What precisely she had forgiven, he could not for the life of him remember. But it felt grand nonetheless, and once-faded colors had retained their new intensity. Best of all, he had permission to leave Easter baskets for everyone at the North Pole again, and Wendy would receive the most opulent one of all.

He sighed happily. Then he blinked, blew a good-luck kiss to the impregnated woman and her hubby, and leaped skyward, heading home.

That night, as Santa Claus tucked her in and Snowball and Nightwind nestled against her, Wendy felt a shift in her outlook. Though her voice and body remained those of a child, she suddenly felt very grown-up and grave. "Daddy?"

"Yes, dear."

"You mentioned shooting our arrow high."

"I did."

"Well, just look at these people." Not wanting to upset her two mommies, she draped her bedroom in magic time and filled it with the sights and sounds of human beings doing the most horrendous things to one another. Rapes and murders offended their sight. Harsh words barked from dark corners, the moans of the suffering assaulted their ears, and the thunderous destruction of bombs and missiles shook them to the bone.

Then she swept the horrors away, her room regaining its wondrous calm, and rushed into Santa's arms. "I'm sorry," she said, sobbing with him. "But I had to remind you. Because we need to do far more than visit three households next fall. I mean, we can and we should choose those three wisely. But whatever our theme, we've got to aim for the kind of massive transformation we were allowed to bring about a few months ago. We've got to push Michael on this. We've got to fall on our knees before God and the Divine Mother and implore them to extend our charter. We really must aim our arrow high. Because you know why?"

Santa's face was white with shock. "Why?"

"If we don't, I'm afraid in a few years there won't *be* a human race."

Santa tried to speak but could not. She could tell he was struggling, but this time compassion for fallen mortals shone in his eyes and he did not flinch. "Wendy," he said at last, "you continue to astound me. The little girl is gone, or rather she sits enthroned in the heart of an adult. And I joy in, and am in awe of, the young woman I see before me. So tell me, my wise fair one." Wendy laughed at that, and Santa smiled. "What is the greatest failing of humankind? What does having seen what we've seen tell you about that?"

Wendy grew still. She took her stepfather's hand and furrowed her brow. "I think," she said, "no, I *know* what their worst failing is. They forget what their kindergarten teachers taught them. They give lip service to great spiritual leaders, but fail to heed the import of their words. They band together in groups and champion crude systems of belief and act, systems that pretend to be kind and loving, but are not. This or that set of constraints, they insist, are for their own good. They come unmediated from God. Sacrifice an eye to see as we see. And though you suffer on earth, you'll have your reward in heaven. Perhaps the original impetus of these groups is fresh and creative and free. But over the years, they fall into corruption, luring the next generation in. So they lead little boys and girls astray, in the name of keeping them from falling into savagery. Where is Christ in this? Where is the Buddha? Where Gandhi, and Martin Luther King, and that Nelson Mandela person you mentioned?"

"Where indeed?" said Santa. Then he peered at her with untold depths of love and a look of utter despair. "But Wendy dear, how can we hope to address all of that?"

"I don't know," said she. "Not yet. But we're going to do it. And we're going to make a real difference. This is no misguided hope on my part. This is resolve. Because we mustn't fail. Our generosity must stretch even farther than it did last Easter. I know we can do it. I'll settle for nothing less. We wise fair ones have guts, and if I've learned one thing growing up under your tutelage, it's that we can do anything we apply our hearts and minds to. Anything. I'm not about to take my immortality lightly. Yes, we ought to follow the promptings of our wise child, but it's time we both grew up, took the bull by the horns, wrestled him to the ground, and kept him pinned until he cries uncle and turns into a lamb."

Santa was stunned. "I never knew you had...no, that's not true. I *always* knew you had this in you. Good for you." He gave her hands a squeeze. "Goodnight, sweetheart. Tomorrow, the world begins anew. When one is immortal, there's no such thing as taking on too much responsibility. The ball's in your court, dear. Let's do the right thing!"

Wendy embraced him. "I love you, Daddy."

"And I you, dear one."

"Send Mommy and Anya in, okay?"

"You won't saddle them with this?"

She laughed. "Not yet. But soon."

"Soon it is."

Then Santa winked, blew her a kiss, and left the room. Wendy lay back, glowing with resolve. "We're going to do it," she told Snowball, raising a dynamo of a purr with her stroking. "See if we don't."

In the fullness of time, Wendy told her moms and started planning for the fall. What she and Santa (and yes in the end the Easter Bunny joined them too) did the following Thanksgiving was astounding indeed. But what their great deeds were, how they achieved them, and their long-term ramifications shall be left for another tale and another time.

Let us focus briefly, instead, on the Christmas Eve that came after.

Santa Claus made his usual rounds, visiting slumbering households, leaving gifts and good cheer, taking bites of cookie and sips of milk, feeding all but the last bit of carrot to his reindeer, and tingeing the air with hints of evergreen and magic that tickled good little boys and girls in the belly and provoked in them great giggles of wonder.

Wendy visited her hundred children, taking each one on a wondrous sleigh ride to wherever they pleased; granting them glimpses of their futures and firing just a bit higher the gentle obsessions that lead to great things; and finally tucking them in and, just before vanishing into magic time, giving them a kiss on the forehead which wiped away the memory of their frolic but left a tingle that remained with them forever after, even unto their deathbeds.

But by prearrangement, Wendy added a hundred-and-first visit that night, a little boy she and Santa dropped in on after the toy shelves at the North Pole were depleted and Santa's pack lay spent against his back.

Through the door of Jamie Stratton's bedroom they passed. Jamie had turned nine since the previous Christmas and now teetered on the edge of unbelief in Santa Claus. But when he opened his eyes to the wondrous beings before him and his nostrils filled with the rich scent of pine needles and hot apple cider and cinnamon, he instantly recalled Wendy's visit the year before, and his spirits soared at the sight of an utterly convincing and all-embracing Santa.

I'm home, thought Jamie.

By which he meant far more than simply being in this house in the bosom of a loving family, though he meant that too. His new sister—ultrasound had confirmed her gender—would arrive by the last week of February, or early March, tops. His mother and father had changed from loving to *ferociously* loving parents. The new church seemed to have enlivened them overnight and removed some great fear; of what, he had no idea. All of that was wondrous indeed. But here stood Saint Nicholas and his daughter. There could be no mistaking them. For a good long time, Jamie's mouth refused to close; his eyes, to return to normal size.

He got to toss back the covers and meet Santa's reindeer and feed them carrots. Powerful beasts they were but extremely gentle, smelling like farm animals, yes, but with a special bouquet full of nobility and grandeur and nature at her most magnanimous. Into the night sky they carried the trio, passing over Paris and Mount Rushmore and the Grand Canyon, along palm-swept Tahitian shores, across vast arctic wastes which were not wastes at all but filled with wonders of their own, sweeping past tall minarets and opulent Russian palaces, circling the moonlit castle of mad King Ludwig of Bavaria, gliding by the Sphinx and the pyramids and every notable landmark Jamie could summon out of his geography book. Best of all, they made special trips to the workshops of violin makers and saw and got to gently handle and play instruments from the workshops of master craftsmen like Guarneri and Stradivari, Vuillaume and Fagnola and Guadagnini.

When the trip was over and they whisked Jamie back to his bedroom, they told him he could keep his memories of this night, if he swore never to reveal them to a soul.

"Wow, that's neat," he said. "But how come I get to keep the memories? I thought you said everybody always forgets."

"You set us on a very special path last year, Jamie," said Santa, "didn't he, Wendy?"

"Uh huh."

"What path?"

Santa laughed with great gusto, and Jamie felt as if he had been answered, even though no words had been spoken. For Santa's laugh was replete with generosity, the mysteries and wonders of childhood, and the wisdom of grown-ups who root their lives in innocence.

"But before we go...."

Santa reached deep into his sack and pulled out, by a wrenched fistful of jerkin, a blond-haired elf with a camera dangling from his neck. "This is Herbert," he said, setting his wide-eyed helper on the carpet. "Herbert, Jamie."

"Pleased to meet you," said Jamie, shaking the elf's hand. Sugarplums danced in Jamie's head at the sight of the creature, such strong yet delicate hands, such creativity in his eyes.

Herbert snapped picture after picture of the three of them, and Wendy took a bunch of Herbert and Jamie, arm in arm, the elf beaming, the boy stunned at his good fortune. They left a few photos with Jamie but took the rest with them. And even though, the morning after, the photos in Jamie's possession were blank, he kept them, cherished, in a shoebox for the rest of his life, touching them, sensing their magic, and gazing at them in a vain attempt to call the images forth. But his memories of that visit remained sharp even unto the far reaches of old age, when other memories had faded, taken on fuzzy edges, or vanished altogether.

Just before they left, Santa said, "What a glorious finish to a glorious Christmas Eve visiting you has been, Jamie. I feel so full of joy and exuberance, and, well,...Herbert?"

"Yes, Santa." The elf snapped to, one stray strand of hair not quite combed into place.

"Herbert is the finest blesser the world has known, Jamie. Grace us, won't you, with your best effort."

"Of course," said Herbert. He drew himself up to his rather diminutive height, cap in hand, and beamed with joy. "Jamie Stratton, special child, be thou blessed forevermore. Bless you, Santa. Bless you, Wendy. Let our every breath give thanks for the lives we lead. And may all mortals be blessed, even those who curse and fret and fear and bluster, may even they be blessed, and changed in the wink of an eye. For mortal life is too brief to founder in woeful quagmires of negativity. All souls have the power to alter the world in startling ways. May they prosper in that endeavor, and may heaven not only descend on occasion to touch earth but expand downward to dwell among the creatures that live upon it. So be it, dear Santa, dear Wendy, dear Jamie, and may God grant it so."

"Cool," said Jamie, and Santa said, "Amen."

Herbert waved farewell and climbed back into the sack. Then Santa and Wendy hugged Jamie one last time and were gone.

But Herbert's last words lingered long in his ear, a phrase that took on, for him, musical urgency, and which became the *cantus firmus* for his violin playing ever after, in those early years, at the conservatory, and finally on the concert stage and in the recording studio.

"God grant it so," the elf had said.

And grant it God did.

ABOUT THE AUTHOR

Robert Devereaux made his professional debut in Pulphouse Magazine in the late 1980's, attended the 1990 Clarion West Writers Workshop, and soon placed stories in such major venues as Crank!, Weird Tales, and Dennis Etchison's anthology MetaHorror. Two of his stories made the final ballot for the Bram Stoker and World Fantasy Awards.

His novels include Slaughterhouse High, A Flight of Storks and Angels, Deadweight, Walking Wounded, Caliban, Santa Steps Out, and Santa Claus Conquers the Homophobes. Also not to be missed is his new short story collection with Deadite Press, Baby's First Book of Seriously Fucked-Up Shit.

Robert has a well-deserved reputation as an author who pushes every envelope, though he would claim, with a stage actor's assurance, that as long as one's writing illuminates characters in all their kinks, quirks, kindnesses, and extremes, the imagination must be free to explore nasty places as well as nice, or what's the point?

Robert lives in sunny northern Colorado with the delightful Victoria, making up stuff that tickles his fancy and, he hopes, those of his readers.

You can find him online at Facebook or at
www.robertdevereaux.com.

deadite press

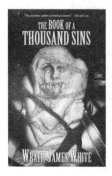

"The Book of a Thousand Sins" Wrath James White - Welcome to a world of Zombie nymphomaniacs, psychopathic deities, voodoo surgery, and murderous priests. Where mutilation sex clubs are in vogue and torture machines are sex toys. No one makes it out alive – not even God himself.

"If Wrath James White doesn't make you cringe, you must be riding in the wrong end of a hearse."
-Jack Ketchum

"Highways to Hell" Bryan Smith - The road to hell is paved with angels and demons. Brain worms and dead prostitutes. Serial killers and frustrated writers. Zombies and Rock 'n Roll. And once you start down this path, there is no going back. Collecting thirteen tales of shock and terror from Bryan Smith, Highways to Hell is a non-stop road-trip of cruelty, pain, and death. Grab a seat, Smith has such sights to show you.

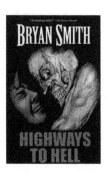

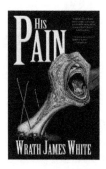

"His Pain" Wrath James White - Life is pain . . . . . . or at least it is for Jason. Born with a rare central nervous disorder, every sensation is pain. Every sound, scent, texture, flavor, even every breath, brings nothing but mind-numbing pain. Until the arrival of Yogi Arjunda of the Temple of Physical Enlightenment. He claims to be able to help Jason, to be able to give him a life of more than agony. But the treatment leaves Jason changed and he wants to share what he learned. He wants to share his pain . . . A novella of pain, pleasure, and transcendental splatter.

"Bullet Through Your Face" Edward Lee - No writer is more extreme, perverted, or gross than Edward Lee. His world is one of psychopathic redneck rapists, sex addicted demons, and semen stealing aliens. Brace yourself, the king of splatterspunk is guaranteed to shock, offend, and make you laugh until you vomit.
"Lee pulls no punches."
    - Fangoria

"Whargoul" Dave Brockie - It is a beast born in bullets and shrapnel, feeding off of pain, misery, and hard drugs. Cursed to wander the Earth without the hope of death, it is reborn again and again to spread the gospel of hate, abuse, and genocide. But what if it's not the only monster out there? What if there's something worse? From Dave Brockie, the twisted genius behind GWAR, comes a novel about the darkest days of the twentieth century.

"Super Fetus" Adam Pepper - Try to abort this fetus and he'll kick your ass!

"The story of a self-aware fetus whose morally bankrupt mother is desperately trying to abort him. This darkly humorous novella will surely appall and upset a sizable percentage of people who read it . . . In-your-face, allegorical social commentary."
- BarnesandNoble.com

"Slaughterhouse High" Robert Devereaux - It's prom night in the Demented States of America. A place where schools are built with secret passageways, rebellious teens get zippers installed in their mouths and genitals, and once a year one couple is slaughtered and the bits of their bodies are kept as souvenirs. But something's gone terribly wrong when the secret killer starts claiming a far higher body count than usual . . .
"A major talent!" - Poppy Z. Brite

"Baby's First Book of Seriously Fucked-Up Shit" Robert Devereaux - From an orgy between God, Satan, Adam and Eve to beauty pageants for fetuses. From a giant human-absorbing tongue to a place where God is in the eyes of the psychopathic. This is a party at the furthest limits of human decency and cruelty. Robert Devereaux is your host but watch out, he's spiked the punch with drugs, sex, and dismemberment. Deadite Press is proud to present nine stories of the strange, the gross, and the just plain fucked up.

THE VERY BEST IN CULT HORROR

CPSIA information can be obtained
at www.ICGtesting.com
Printed in the USA
BVHW061444011218
534527BV00001B/51/P